l

A Phoebe Harkness Novel

James Fahy

For Laura

Table of Contents

1

I fell out of bed in my efforts to reach the phone. Not the most graceful thing I've ever done, I admit, but in my defence it was pitch black in the room, and when the phone rings at 3.30am, the body reacts automatically. At that godless hour, it's only ever one of two things. Somebody's dead, or somebody's drunk.

Unfortunately for me it was the former.

"Dr Harkness?" a hesitant, almost apologetic, male voice stuttered down the phone line as I fought my way out of the disorientation of being rudely awoken. Griff, my assistant. I made a kind of gurgling half growl in reply as I picked myself up off the floor and clambered back onto the bed, phone in hand. I had meant for the growl to convey the irritation and obscenity of being rudely awoken in the middle of the night, but in truth my tongue was asleep in my mouth and, in my dramatic tumble from the tangle of bedcovers, I had managed to inhale my own hair.

"Griff?" I managed, trying again and sounding slightly more human. What the hell was my lab assistant calling me for at home? He had never called me before. No one ever called me. I squinted, bleary-eyed, at the glowing red numerals of the alarm clock on the bedside table. "Griff, it's stupid o clock. What do you want?"

"I know … erm … sorry," he said, sounding it. "Trevelyan needs you in the lab, now."

Great. Vyvienne Trevelyan, my supervisor. A woman utterly devoid of charm, compassion or social skills, and the person karma had seen fit to have direct power and authority over me. My boss is the only woman I've ever met who I'm fairly certain has molecular acid for blood. She quite possibly showers in liquid nitrogen and considers it too warm. Most tellingly, however, she has far too many 'V's and 'Y's in her name. It sounds like a bag of razor blades falling down a flight of stairs. That's never trustworthy.

"Trevelyan can wait until morning like normal people," I muttered, pressing the heel of my free hand against my eyes wearily. "So can you. Why are you even at the lab?"

"I'm not, Doc," Griff replied. "I'm outside your place freezing my arse off. Figured you'd need a ride in."

This woke me up slightly. Griff, while talented and hardworking, clocked in and out of the lab strictly on business hours. He wasn't paid enough to care out of hours –unlike yours truly, who still wasn't paid enough to care – but due to my position, I'm apparently on twenty-four hour call.

"Trevelyan called you in too?" I asked. This was unlikely. I don't think I'd ever seen my boss speak to any of my small team except myself, and that was only grudgingly when she had to. Lesser grunts and drones were usually beneath her contempt. People like Griff, however easy on the eye he might be, were of no interest to ambitious women like her. They didn't offer any advancement, therefore why bother even learning their names?

"She had to call me, she doesn't have your home number," Griff explained. "No one at the lab does. You know what you're like about that. I've only got it 'cause you legally have to have a work contact in case you contaminate yourself and need collecting. But yeah, we're all going in. I'm on strict orders to get your backside out of bed and get you there now. I've never heard her sound so angry." He took a weary breath down the phone line. "It's bad news."

All going in? That would be me, Griff, our sweet-natured graduate dogsbody, Lucy, and Trevelyan herself. In the middle of the night? This was unprecedented bad news.

"Tell me." I braced myself.

"It's Angelina," he said, his disembodied voice oddly intimate in my ear in the still-darkened room. "We just lost her ... She's ... she's dead, Doc."

I was already up and hunting around the floor for socks. My face felt unconscionably hot and numb.

"How?" I demanded, curt in my attempt to remain businesslike and detached.

"She ... she ... exploded." Griff sounded hopelessly apologetic.

I paused in the darkness, phone clutched in one hand, a pair of thick woolly socks in the other, and sat down heavily on the creaking bed in my pants and vest.

"Bollocks," I replied.

2

I'm not a very good morning person. Especially not a good three in the morning person. So the drive from my modest flat, which is roughly the size of a postage stamp and located over a late night cyber-cafe, over to the lab on the other side of Oxford in Griff's beat up blue Kia Picanto was filled mainly with a grumpy and uncomfortable silence. I tried desperately to wake myself up, and he tried heroically not to mention the fact that I hadn't taken any time to fix my hair. It was mercilessly restrained under a rather festive wool cap like pale candyfloss. I usually try at least to appear like a professional, well-turned-out bloodwork paratoxicologist when I'm at work, even if I don't feel it, but lack of sleep and the news of Angelina's death had soured my mood even further. I don't usually socialise with my work colleagues, or anyone for that matter. I took heart in the fact that it was early November, so at least my hat was seasonal, if not sombre.

The dark and deserted New Oxford streets slid by as we drove, gloomy and ice cold, wet cobbles and venerable grey stone lit at intervals by dim sodium vapour streetlamps. There was no one at large at this ungodly hour, not in this district of town anyway, and the world looked like a shadowy and frosty stage set – unreal and empty. The ancient buildings reared around us. The only signs of our brave new world having any impact in the last few hundred years were the searchlights which nestled like alien tripods in the roof-scapes and the occasional DataStream screen affixed to the side of a building – great television screens which daily brought the message of our noble leaders to the people in the streets. At this hour of the night they were uniformly blank, emblazoned only with a scrolling message repeating like a screensaver, the motto of our people: *ex umbra in lucem*. The Kia's headlights cut two yellowish beams ahead of us through a thin fog laced with ice crystals. The car rattled around like a bean can on the rough roads. I considered it an old wreck, but my lab assistant was very proud and called it 'vintage'. There were only a hundred or so left in all Britannia, he had told me once. Griff, God bless his cotton socks, had at least had the foresight to bring coffee to appease me somewhat for dragging me out of bed in the early hours, and I hugged the piping hot Styrofoam cup with my gloved hands like a lifeboat as we juddered towards the campus.

Griff was sweet and thoughtful by nature, and probably deserves someone more patient and pleasant as a boss. If I worked for me, I certainly wouldn't bring me coffee, or if I did it would be decaf. I don't know why he bothered making the effort half the time. He wasn't uneasy on the eye either, in a hopeless, eternal student kind of way. Square-jawed and always carelessly unshaven, his hair was a mop of knotty dark curls and his large eyes a pale caramel behind glasses that just managed to land on the cool side of the nerd spectrum. He always gave the impression he had just stumbled out of bed, late for a lecture somewhere. It was an odd combination of clumsy geek and public schoolboy yumminess. Quite the contradiction. You never knew whether you would prefer to jump his bones or tuck his shirt in properly and give him a hot meal. I'm not much of a cougar for younger men, so he was thankfully quite safe with me. Our relationship was strictly professional. He did what I told him to do, and he did all my maths for me.

Not all scientists are good at maths, incidentally. Don't tell anyone though; it's a closely guarded secret in the scientific community. It helps to have reliable flunkies.

"Thanks for the coffee," I muttered as we chugged along, my breath making a cloud in front of me. Griff's salary did not, evidently, stretch to car heating, vintage or otherwise "So do we know what's happened? Between you and me, I'm not sure I want to be going in there blind if Trevelyan is going to be spitting acid."

I saw Griff shrug from the corner of my eye, hunched over the steering wheel in that comical way of all tall men in small cars. "I only know as much as you do, Doc," he said. "Just that Angelina's dead, and there's an issue, and that you better get there yesterday and clean up the mess." He risked tearing his eyes off the road to glance over at me sympathetically. "Trevelyan's words. I don't know if she meant the potential political mess or … you know … the actual mess." He made a squelch noise with his cheek, which was in fairly poor taste. I chose to put it down to nerves.

I glowered and sunk deeper into the passenger seat, disappearing into the folds of my winter coat until I was just a pair of eyes frowning out between collar and woolly hat. When precisely it became part of my job description to deal with death by spontaneous explosion, I don't recall.

3

Blue Lab One, the place where dreams are made (bearing in mind not all dreams are pleasant) is the glamorous headquarters of the Para-Toxicology-and-Applied-Genetic-Research-and-Development team, of which I am but one humble cog. There is no good acronym. Trust me, I've tried PTAGRD. It sounds like some kind of Dwarven swear word or a raven coughing into a spittoon. The facility lies in, or rather beneath, part of the hallowed and ancient New Oxford University Campus. I had only left the lab a few hours earlier, after a seventeen hour stint working on the latest refinements of the para-vaccine, Epsilon strain. It had been a long day, I had been tired. I had been looking forward to at least eight hours sleep.

It was beyond grim to be back at work so soon.

Griff parked the Kia expertly in the quad car park, gravel crunching deafeningly beneath the tyres in the silent night, and we made our way briskly through the misty campus – dreaming spires, vaulted arches and ancient towers stark and dark around us. The place looks like Hogwarts writ large, at least until you get to the BL1 entrance.

Griff scanned us through the automatic doors with his security pass. From the outside, facing across the campus green towards the distant river, they look like ancient oak, banded with curly black iron hinges. From within however, they are a foot thick and reinforced steel. They open with a vacuumed whoosh and hissed closed behind us like an airlock.

Blue Lab One within is nothing like Hogwarts. A long wide corridor of plain white tiles, looking more like a tube station, and unflatteringly lit with harsh strip lighting leads to a circular atrium, surrounded by several elevators and a semicircular reception desk. There is nothing magical, ancient or whimsical here. The place is as modern and bright as a space station, all glass surfaces and brushed steel.

"Hey Mattie." I nodded to the night security sitting behind a row of thirty or so CCTV monitors. Mattie nodded back in greeting as he got to his feet. Mid forties and heavyset, he looked like every night security person I have ever seen anywhere.

"Doctor Harkness, Doctor Grace," he said amiably, one hand on his hip where his gun sat in its holster. Our security at Blue Lab are all heavily armed. I find it reassuring rather than intimidating, considering what we deal with here. "You two working late tonight?"

"Not by choice," I replied, crossing to the desk and offering my right hand which he took unceremoniously in his.

To an outsider this might look like an odd gesture, oddly genteel, as though he were about to bend and kiss the back of my hand like some kind of Southern gentleman. But it was merely routine and not nearly as romantic.

Mattie took a small hollow cylinder of pale brushed metal from his pocket and slid it over my finger. He pressed a tiny button beneath the tube and I felt the familiar prick of the needle inside the tube jab my flesh, so quick and deft it barely hurt. There was slight pressure as a vacuum formed around my finger tip, and then a cool spray as antiseptic was released. I withdrew my finger as he released my hand, shaking my hand at the wrist to dry it off.

Mattie turned and slid the hollow tube, now containing a sample of my blood, into a receptacle on the desk. A second later a tiny green light pinged on one of the many monitors.

"You're all good," Mattie told me. He turned to Griff, withdrawing an identical tube to repeat the procedure.

"Good to know I'm still human," I managed to half smile. "Even if I don't feel that way right now."

While Griff was getting his DNA scanned for abnormalities, or 'signing in' as we called it, I crossed the lobby and swiped my clearance pass to call the elevator. There are seven elevators radiating off the circular lobby. They all only go down from here. Blue Lab is subterranean. Makes sense really. The college campus is above, and we burrow under it, our various departments spread out around a central hub like spokes on an underground wheel.

I heard Griff hiss under his breath as the cylinder took his blood – he's such a baby about needles – then the familiar reassuring ping which told us that he hadn't been replaced by a Genetic Other during the night. I often wondered what would happen if the light ever pinged red one day. I didn't think it had ever happened. Sure, we'd had 'visitors' before, but only with lots of red tape and chaperoning. And they never got lower than level one.

Mattie told us both to have a nice night, which I found increasingly unlikely, and we stepped into the elevator, the doors closing swiftly and silently as we began our descent. Griff sucked his finger absently, which I avoided doing every day as the antiseptic tasted foul. He was a wuss. A pretty one, but still, I rolled my eyes. Not everyone at Blue Lab seems as impervious to Griff's innocent charms and winning calculus skills as me though. He seemed to be rather popular with the girls up in applied sciences on level B-10. Poor thing. Those women can be intense. They don't get out much. Sending Griff up there to beg, steal or borrow data supplies was like throwing a kitten in a shark tank. It could only be worse if I went up myself half an hour earlier and sloshed a bucket of chum in there to get the bloodlust going.

The floor indicators on the lift display panel told us we were descending rapidly, although the elevator was so smooth we couldn't feel a thing. At level B-14 we slid gently to a halt and were ejected into Blue Lab.

You don't get in here easily. The DNA testing in the lobby is routine, it merely tests to see if you are human. Down here on level 14 I was faced with the usual iris scanner, fingerprint reader and security pass combination before the doors finally gave me access. Griff and I eventually strode into the corridor beyond.

It's an odd sight, this entrance corridor. As long as a city street, it is narrow and covered entirely with bright blue ultraviolet strip lighting. It's like walking through a nightmarishly long sunbed, turning your lab coat hi-glow blue instead of white. It makes my hair look bright and ghostly instead of blond, and tints the whites of your eyes and your teeth, oddly. It's the reason Blue Lab is called Blue Lab, and its purpose is functional not decorative. The Pale cannot stand sunlight. They suffer from extreme Xeroderma Pigmentosum. It's an autosomal recessive genetic disorder of DNA repair in which the ability to heal damage caused by ultraviolet light is deficient. Some humans have suffered from it in rare cases, but the Pale, as a species, have a fatal level of reaction. Sunlight burns them to a crisp.

We don't use the word 'vampire' down here. Pedantic, I know, but them's the rules. It's not considered a valid scientific classification. I would argue that 'the Pale' sounds like an emo band from way back when, but I wasn't on the political committee who decides such things. I'm just a lowly drone from B-14. Besides, nobody gets my references anyway. I'm a geek for pre-apocalypse culture. I practically lap up anything pre-wars. Music, movies, shows they used to have for entertainment, way before our DataStream. It gets me a look of polite but blank looks. The Pale and vampires are different creatures anyway. They're both Genetic Others. Neither of them human. But we shouldn't lump every GO together. They're as different as, well, not chalk and cheese perhaps. Maybe Brie and Emmental.

If one of the Pale ever did manage to infiltrate BL1, get past the DNA scan, bypass elevator security, fool a palm and iris scan, and make it to the corridor, they would be in flames before they made it halfway along and would arrive at the other end as a charred microwave meal.

The doors at the far end led into the lab proper where Lucy, our 19 year old medical intern, was waiting for us with my supervisor, Trevelyan. Lucy looked monumentally relieved to see us. The poor girl had no doubt been getting the sharp end of Vyvienne's tongue while they waited for us to show. Lucy was a kind and gentle soul, and didn't deserve that. No one did. I nodded a hello as I shrugged out of my jacket and grabbed a lab coat. "Where is she?" I asked, not bothering with further pleasantries.

Trevelyan, standing with her arms folded, glared at Griff and me murderously. She was a large, heavy-set woman, expensively dressed in what she would no doubt consider a power-suit. She looked like the kind of no-nonsense woman who would have been head girl and captain of her school's hockey team, and who wouldn't have thought twice about breaking both your legs with the stick if occasion arose.

"Your experiment?" she snorted humourlessly. "She's everywhere. That's the issue, Harkness."

"Poor Angelina," Lucy murmured, looking genuinely downcast.

I followed them to the glass-walled cubicle which served as a holding pen, or less frequently, as a mortuary. The usually pristine and clear white tabletop was a bloodbath. I have a strong stomach, but even I was momentarily taken aback. It looked for all the world as though someone had filled a large water balloon with chunky tomato sauce and lobbed it joyfully into the space. Spatters arced across the walls and soiled the floor. The work surfaces were smeared and painted gloopy red. In the centre of the chaos stood a wire cage, roughly twice the size of a shoebox. It was twisted out of shape and convulsed, like some kind of grotesque modern art.

"Good God," I muttered, surveying the carnage. I grabbed a spatula from a nearby tray and gingerly picked through what could only be described as the remaining chunks of Angelina littering the blood-sodden desk. "When did this happen?"

"About an hour ago," Lucy said from behind me. Unlike Trevelyan, old iron stomach, and Griff, whose duties included far more stomach-churning things than this, she hadn't entered the gory cubicle, but stood at the threshold in her plastic covered lab shoes as though afraid to enter. She was hugging herself and looked a little wild-eyed, clear signs of trauma – though whether from witnessing this scene or having to talk to my supervisor on her own for the last half an hour, it was impossible to tell. "I was finishing up the data reports from the Epsilon we ran yesterday afternoon, and then … bang!" Her eyes were wide. "It was so loud, like when a baked potato explodes in a microwave, you know? I screamed."

My spatula had found something solid in the goop. I held it up. It looked like a forkful of over-tomato-sauced pot noodle. Griff leaned over to peer past my shoulder.

"What are we going to tell Brad?" he whispered. "He's going to be heartbroken. They've been a couple since they got here."

The object on my spatula was a tiny severed bloody paw. I sighed. "I told you and I told Lucy," I said patiently. "If we name the lab rats, we only end up getting attached to them."

4

I left Griff and Lucy the glamorous job of mopping up the gore while Trevelyan all but picked me up by my ear and dragged me to the other end of the lab like a bad-tempered PE teacher.

"What the hell is going on, Harkness?" she demanded to know in a stage whisper hiss that I knew full well my team would be listening to. "Cabal is going live with these results tomorrow, and we have test subjects exploding all over the fucking place? Jesus!"

I leaned backwards out of her coffee breath. "Servant Trevelyan, Epsilon has tested stable at every level for the last four months," I began, trying to sound reassuring. "This is clearly an anomaly, but I'm really not going to have an answer for you until I get a chance to run some samples. I'm not sure what else you want me to say."

Trevelyan's nostrils flared. "Stable?" she repeated. "Stable? You think your vaccine is stable? In case you're confused about what has happened here tonight, Doctor, you have just painted the walls of this room red with your miracle cure. How is that in any way stable? And I think exploding bodies and organs are more than a bloody 'anomaly'!"

I held up my hands in frustration. "Epsilon is not a cure. It's not even a vaccine, it's … or rather it will be, when we figure it out … a retardant. An inhibitor. The idea is to control the genetic branching, not reverse it. There's no bioscience in the world that can turn a monkey into a fish, and you're not going to turn the Pale back into people either…" Sometimes my supervisor's shaky grasp on what my research actually entailed terrified me.

Trevelyan pinched the bridge of her nose. "Harkness, I don't care if it's a cure, an inhibitor, or magical snake oil. What I care about is that Cabal have ploughed a huge budget into your pet side project here at Blue Lab, and so far, the only decent results we have are Gamma strain, which seems to paralyse the fuckers temporarily, and Epsilon, which was supposed to have significant results in time for tomorrow's meeting."

"Gamma was abandoned," I argued. "It didn't work. It's not a very effective inhibitor if it causes prolonged spasms followed by bouts of catatonic immobility. My work here is supposed to stop further mutation and enable some level of reintegration into society. I don't appreciate the fact that you seem to think that weaponising its negative side effects is a good plan."

I pushed away from the table and crossed to my databank, logging onto my files with a swipe of my hand across the screen. God bless whichever tech-wizards fitted out the computer systems at Blue Lab – I think they may previously have worked on Star Trek. At home I have trouble operating the TV timed-recorder, but here in the lab I can totally Captain Janeway my way through the day.

Then I noticed Trevelyan was following me. Pursuing might be a more accurate term.

"And Epsilon?" she pressed.

"Well, clearly not as stable as we'd hoped," I admitted grudgingly, flicking a glance over her shoulder to where Griff was on his knees with a blood-soaked mini mop. "If I can't get it to level out, I'm sure you can pass it off to the military as another bio-weapon gem. I can see the marketing now: 'We can't help or aid the afflicted, but we can blow them to pieces. All thanks to Blue Lab'." I flicked through my electronic file notes from the previous day's testing. Graphs and figures flew across the screen in rapid succession. There must be something in here to explain such a reaction.

"Maybe if you give me a week … I need to run further tests, bloodwork on what remains of Angelina, find out what caused the exothermic combustion."

"You don't have a week," my boss told me, looming over the screen. "The presentation is tomorrow. I am going to have to go into a hall filled not only with the Cabal representatives but also face the press and the public. I need something to tell them."

My eyes flicked up from my screen. Tomorrow's meeting was public? Well, this was news. "Why are Cabal going public already?" I asked. "We don't have any definitive results yet."

"They trust we do," Trevelyan growled. She gave me a significant look from beneath her beetling brow. Her arse was on the line, it said. Which implied that my own was dangling precariously over the edge.

"Then they are going to be disappointed," I said, mustering my best sympathetic face. "I mean, we can be honest and tell them research is ongoing, that we are making progress…"

"Explosive progress," Griff's voice called out from across the lab, safely hidden as he was behind the cubicle of gore. I hated him slightly for a moment.

"Cabal don't want to see a report card for Blue Lab saying that we are all doing well in class and playing well with others, Harkness," Trevelyan snapped. "They want updates, they want successful animal tests. They want positive and measurable results. And the public want to know that Cabal is looking after them, and making the world a safer place."

Making the world a safer place? Please. I work for a government bio-chemistry unit, not Disney. My job is not PR. Cabal have their own spin-doctors for that. My urge to say this out loud was only just drowned out by my urge not to get fired and starve homeless on the streets.

Instead I hit a button on my touch screen, causing my DataStream report for the last 48 hours to print out swiftly and silently elsewhere at the other end of the office. Star Trek-inspired techno-wizards can do a lot of impressive things with lab computers, but no power on earth can ever put a printer conveniently near the workstation you are actually sat at. "I can give you what we've got so far. I can look into this … incident … and have the results on your desk by nine."

"By seven." Trevelyan turned and stormed out of the lab. "I want real results and hard data, because if I don't have anything to take to them tomorrow night at this review, then your little vaccine project will have every penny of funding cut. Do you understand that, Harkness? It's not my decision. They will close you down." She clomped out of the vacuum doors with a resounding swoosh.

"It's not a vaccine," I muttered under my breath through gritted teeth.

Griff and Lucy both appeared after Trevelyan had gone, their heads poking out of the blood-spattered cubicle like nervous meerkats emerging tentatively in the calm after a thunderstorm.

"She was pissed off," Griff said observantly.

"Would she really shut us down?" Lucy asked, looking worried.

"Ignore her," I said rebelliously. "She's annoyed because she has to go before the board tomorrow and she is going to be humiliated if all she can say is that we've figured out new and exciting ways to stun and kill rats. She doesn't give a damn about the actual work we do here, she only cares if it reflects well on her in Cabal meetings."

"I guess rats exploding don't reflect well on anyone," Griff said, peeling off his plastic apron, which was so red with gore it made him look like a modern day Jack the Ripper. "I think your boss believes advances in science are made by shouting loudly enough at scientists to make advances happen. Was she ever in the military?"

I smirked despite my mood. "Not as far as I know. Powerful family though. She's a bureaucrat, not a scientist. She does make sure the money gets thrown our way though, so we need her to keep loving us as much as she does."

Lucy, being an actual angel from heaven rather than a squeamish intern, had made coffee and brought me a steaming cup. "Is it true what she said about the aborted strains of the inhibitor?" she asked, concerned. "Gamma I mean. Do they really have plans to make that into a weapon against the Pale?"

I shook my head. "Only in her Rambo fantasies. Gamma isn't stable enough to be weaponised, even if you could get that through the ethics committee. And besides, it's my formula, and I wouldn't release it anyway. Blue Lab isn't military." I took a sip of my coffee, picking up my printouts. Eighty nine pages of them. Oh happy, happy day. "Forget about Gamma anyway, that was a dead end. We need to go over everything and figure out where Epsilon is going wrong. And we need to do it by seven. Trevelyan needs to be able to tell the board some good news."

Griff looked at his watch. "That's three hours from now."

Fuck, I thought genteelly to myself. "I'll throw in a lot of extra-sciencey words in my report. They'll lap it up," I said briskly. "Maybe a pie chart. Board members love pie charts."

"Griff, I'm going to need your brain on these." I handed him a sheaf of papers. "Run the numbers again, see what we missed, cross it with the DNA bank for subjects T1 to T11. All the rats, even Jennifer."

He groaned, but quietly. I looked up to Lucy, who stared back at me wide-eyed and expectant.

"We will be needing a lot more coffee," I told her.

5

It was close to midday when I stumbled back into my tiny flat on the other side of town. I had thrown together everything we could find on Epsilon, and had managed to find a reason behind the extreme reaction suffered by subject T10, otherwise known as Angelina, which handily could only be coherently expressed in pure maths. My boss couldn't argue with that, and neither could the board members. The report had been on Trevelyan's desk by 7.30. Oddly, she hadn't been in her office. Her assistant, a dangerously-efficient woman called Melanie, whose pristine and immaculate appearance always managed to make me feel a slovenly helpless mess despite the fact that she was briskly pleasant, informed me that she hadn't been in all day. I was slightly pissed by this, as I had been bracing myself in the elevator all the way up for the screaming and spittle. I'd planned and practised all of my rebuttals.

Now I discover that she must have gone straight home after leaving us in the lab, probably to go back to bed, leaving us all to sweat through the wee hours of the morning getting together a report which she wasn't even here to look at, and didn't actually need until the meeting this evening.

I'd left the report with the immaculately coiffed Melanie, trying my best not to hate the fact that she looked well-rested and stylishly turned out, unlike myself who hadn't had time to brush my teeth before being dragged out of bed at three am. I resisted the urge to suggest she file it up Trevelyan's arse, and politely complimented her brooch instead. She tried to compliment me in return, but the only adornments I was wearing were my swipe pass, on which I look like a washed out Russian figure skater turned crack whore (my own interpretation), and a biro in my hair.

Back home, after a mercifully long shower, and reassuring myself that, while I may not be a twenty year old PA with a tiny, gravity-defying arse and elfin smile, I at least have a double doctorate and a PHD, I had collapsed back into bed. The plan being to sleep the rest of the day away. With any luck I could sleep through the entire review tonight. Thank God I didn't have to be there – that was Trevelyan's problem. Griff and

Lucy had been given the rest of the day off too. We would work on Epsilon tomorrow. Right now, I was freshly washed, smelling of mango soap, and drifting into blessed salacious daytime sleep. I had no plans to wake up again unless there was another exploding rat drama.

As things turned out, what happened was worse.

6

Good news in my life always seems to come by phone.

"Dr Harkness? It's Melanie Potts again. Sorry to disturb your evening, but I've been instructed by the board to advise you that due to Director Trevelyan's unwarranted absence, you are to give the Blue Lab report this evening at the college."

Great. This is what I get for being the head of the bloodwork department. Just so we're clear, even having 'happy birthday' sung to me by work colleagues makes me want to disappear into a hole in the ground, so this was hardly my idea of a calm and relaxing evening. I'm not a fan of the public eye. I mentally made notes to find inventive ways to make my boss suffer when she resurfaced from wherever the hell she had dropped off the map.

A couple of hours later, I stood in the wings of the oak panelled and venerable lecture theatre of the Pepys Library, waiting to go and face roughly a hundred expectant faces with a report which I had invented only hours earlier and which was mainly theoretical supposition. I should have just brought a rat and made it explode. Show and tell is always more entertaining.

"Why am I here again?" I asked Lucy, who was darting around in what I had mentally dubbed 'backstage', carrying my notes and reports. "I mean, I know why I'm here, that's not a philosophical question; what I mean is, why specifically me?"

"Well, I guess until Director Trevelyan turns up, you're the authority, Doc," Lucy said. "Do you want me to get you a drink of water before you go on?" She looked genuinely worried for me, or possibly for herself. I was representing the entire department after all, whether I wanted to or not. I shook my head. "No, thanks. Vodka might have swayed me, for courage, but water, I will just need to pee halfway through."

"You'll do fine." Lucy straightened my papers in my hand. "You look great, Doc. Very chic." She smiled at me encouragingly. I thought for a moment she might punch me in the arm like a football coach.

We were in the Second Court at Magdalene College, in the lecture hall situated in the large lower ground floor of the Pepys. It was 7.30pm and I was about to deliver the Blue Lab findings and development to an audience of Cabal board members, fellow scientists, academics, the press and the public. Trevelyan had never gone AWOL before. I wondered if she were punishing me for being smart-mouthed earlier. I never did know when to know my place.

I had tried to look a little more professional that I had appeared this morning. I was wearing my most serious pantsuit in pale charcoal, and had swept my hair up into a sleek style I saw on some late night NBC show and now refer to as my 'ice queen lady lawyer hair'. I looked every inch the professional and well turned out scientist, right down to the frameless glasses.

"Let's just get this over with, and we can make the voodoo doll of Trevelyan when I get back," I said.

I waited for my cue, being introduced by some professor of the college whose name had been told to me but which I had now completely forgotten. He was explaining Director Trevelyan's sad absence this evening due to ill health, but reassuring the crowd that to present the findings he was honoured, truly honoured, to have the illustrious paratoxicologist currently spearheading the Blue Lab's R&D program, Doctor Fiona Harkness.

I entered to applause, shook his hand on stage and took my place behind the podium, staring out at the lecture hall. It was packed. Tiers of seats like an amphitheatre rose around me on three sides. I had no idea who was who in the sea of faces which stared expectantly back up at me. I could tell where the press were, as they stood at the back of the lecture hall, up near the doors. TV had been given limited access, I saw. Channel Seven and the official Cabal network. I waited for the applause to die down, which it did very quickly, and leaned into the microphone.

"Phoebe," I said quietly. It echoed and bellowed around the room, followed by a harpy like screech of feedback, which had several people wincing, including me.

Some invisible sound engineer made an adjustment somewhere, and I tried again.

"Sorry about that. It's Phoebe, that's all, not Fiona. Phoebe Harkness," I clarified. Someone coughed in the audience. I shuffled my papers on the podium slightly.

"Thank you all for coming. Please bear with me as due to the ... um ... ill health of the good Servant Trevelyan, tonight's report is coming straight from the horse's mouth, as it were. It isn't often that us lab rats have the chance to get out and face to face with our funding bodies, our academic peers and of course the public, so I will try to attempt to keep things as brief and as clear as possible for you all. No complicated and impenetrable paratoxicology terminology, I promise."

There was a polite murmur of laughter at this, especially from the press at the back, which gave me a slight confidence boost.

I'd planned to begin with a little background on the Pepys Building itself. As I've said, I'm a history geek for anything pre-wars. I had a whole anecdote about Samuel Pepys and the Bibliotheca Pepysiana, but it withered under the expectant stares of the audience.

I skipped ahead in my notes. "We're here in the Pepys," I began. "A building which like so many others started off in a different city and ended up here, salvaged by New Oxford, saved from the wars. It's a fitting place for our subject really, as included in the design of this great and accomplished place was the eminent architect and polymath Robert Hooke, whom I'm sure all of you, and indeed anyone connected with science, has heard of."

Some nods. Good, I wasn't the only person with an interest in humanity's back-story then. Most folk in our brave new world only knew as much as the last hours DataStream told them.

"Robert Hooke was known for many things," I continued, "... but he was perhaps best known for coining the idea of a biological cell. He discovered this back in 1665. Of course, discovery, while impressive, is not everything. The cell theory itself was developed from Hooke's initial discovery much later in 1839 by Schleiden and Schwann, and it's a remarkably simple theory."

I pushed my glasses up the bridge of my nose and cleared my throat. "Cell theory states that all organisms are composed of one or more cells; that all cells come from pre-existing cells; that vital functions of an organism occur within cells, and that all cells contain the hereditary information necessary for regulating cell functions and for transmitting information to the next generation of cells. This we know. This we have known since the nineteen hundreds. It's impressive, and it's elegant in its simplicity, but it's not what brings us here tonight.

"What we also know," I continued, "... is that the more complex the organism, the more impressive and complicated the cell count. The cell is the basic structural and functional unit of all known living organisms. It is the smallest unit of life that is classified as a living thing – except of course a virus, which consists only from DNA and RNA covered by protein and lipids, so for the sake of expediency, we will skip viruses. The cell is often called the building block of life. Organisms can be classified as unicellular which means they basically consist of a single cell, bacteria for example, or else multicellular, which pretty much covered all plants and animals. Human beings contain about ten trillion cells. Just to put this in perspective for the work we are doing at Blue Lab, samples we have been able to take from the Pale indicate that their average cell count is roughly fifteen trillion."

This got murmurs from certain parts of the audience. "I understand the immediate question is going to be, does this mean the Pale more evolved than us? More advanced? Are they perhaps the next stage of evolution? The simple answer is no ... and yes."

I seemed to have their attention. I wondered if there were any Church representatives in the audience. They were often rather vocal when it came to any public discussion of the Genetic Others.

"The Pale are certainly more complex structurally than we are, as are almost all of the Genetic Others we are working to understand," I continued. "But to fully understand the Pale, perhaps it would be useful to remember why they exist in the first place. Where they came from. They did not evolve from humans. They were made, engineered, by humans. We created the Pale genetically, as a weapon. We manipulated their cells, we tampered with their DNA, their RNA, and we grew them, in layman's terms, the first generation at any rate, in tubes. This is public knowledge. This is our history."

The room was uncomfortable now. Hundreds of eyes trained on me. We all knew our history. Mankind's legacy, how we created our own worst enemy by playing God.

I pressed on against the sea of silence. "And just as those who first used nuclear weapons back in the twentieth century had no idea they would be dealing with the radiation and the fallout for a great deal of time to come, so too those who came before us here today could not have known that their decision to create this breed of other would have far reaching implications for our own society."

"Dr Harkness?"

The voice came from a woman in the third row. She was expensively middle aged, with a severe black bob of hair and wearing a plum-coloured suit, a choker of black jet like a net around her throat, and a mildly bemused expression.

"Veronica Cloves. I have a question from the board of Cabal," she said crisply, lowering a gloved hand. "Forgive my seeming impudence, I am aware that this presentation has been somewhat thrust upon you at the last moment due to the Servant being indisposed, but usually the purpose of this meeting is to present the current research and development findings of your area." She toyed with her choker with a polite smile that did not remotely reach her eyes. "It would seem that, though entertaining, Dr Harkness, you are presenting a history lecture."

I knew her face of course, everyone did. Cabal may be our overlords and government, but they ensure they keep a very open and public face. No accusations of secrecy, no cloak and dagger nonsense. Cloves was their favourite figurehead. The PR queen. The people loved her like a celebrity.

"I thought that it would be useful to put our findings in context," I explained. "Especially for the benefit of the wider public present here."

"I understand your motivation, Dr Harkness," the member of Cabal replied, again in a soft and polite voice which somehow managed to carry throughout the hall. "However, I think it fair to assume that we are aware of our history and of the issues surrounding the Pale and the Genetic Others, and the threats posed by them. Perhaps it would be more scientific for you to stick to the relevant facts at hand?"

As usual with the all-powerful Cabal, it was an instruction presented as a suggestion. Veronica Cloves' make up was too pale, her skin just ever so slightly too tight on her face. But she smiled like the nation's sweetheart.

Usually, I would have been cowed merely by being under the scrutiny of someone so much higher in the food chain that Trevelyan. Maybe it was the lack of sleep that made me argumentative, but her words riled me.

"I feel I should make a distinction on your comment regarding the Pale and the Genetic Others, before I continue in any fashion," I said. "You cannot simply lump them all together as a 'threat'."

I made quotation marks in the air ... God help me. "The Pale are creatures we created. They carry the condition we seek to cure. The bloodlust, the inherent violent tendencies, the danger they pose to society – they are all our doing. The others, the group we have deemed to class together as Genetic Others, are not of our making."

Veronica Cloves' expression had frozen in a tight smile. Her eyes were murderous. "We are here to discuss the Pale, Dr Harkness. Not the current issues with ... other things."

"But it is exactly the mentality you just exhibited which is counter-productive to the work we are trying to achieve," I replied, trying not to sound exasperated. I addressed the room at large, part of my mind half-expecting Cabal to take me out right there and then with a well-placed sniper.

"When the wars came, and we created the Pale, we lost control of them. We had literally created a monster, and it turned on us. A new war began which humanity almost lost, let's not forget that. Almost a third of our population was lost in the thirty years which followed. Our society was very nearly not here at all. It was only then, when our total dominion over the world was no longer so certain, that the Genetic Others came forward. When they came into the light, as it were, and for the most part, they came to our aid."

"Can you elaborate, Doctor?" came a question from one of the press officers at the rear of the hall. "You're talking about the vampires, right?"

A ripple of noise rolled through the crowd. I raised my hands. "This is the distinction I am trying to make clear," I said. "We do not call them vampires. But ... yes, all of the ... others, who had always lived hidden within our human society came forward. Many types of Genetic Other, not just the ones the media have called vampires, types of being we had no idea we had been sharing our planet with, they all made themselves known – to combat a common enemy, an enemy we had created, the Pale." I looked back to Veronica Cloves, who was still staring at me tight lipped. I think if she could have stood up and shot me dead right there and then, she wouldn't have hesitated. I had a giddy mental image of her standing and pulling a silver pistol from a stocking garter. "These Genetic Others, the 'vampires' if you will, and the ones who call themselves the Tribals, the Bonewalkers, and who knows how many others, they helped humanity repel the genetic horror of the Pale, murderous creatures we had brought upon ourselves. Their world was in danger as well as ours. They couldn't stay in the shadows anymore, not with the Pandora's Box we had opened. And afterwards? When we had won, in a fashion ... when we were rebuilding our cities and countries, what were left of them, putting the shreds of our civilisation back together? Well, let's be honest, after the war, well, the cat was pretty much out of the bag. We share our world with all these creatures now, and we cannot make the generalisation that they are all a danger, as the Pale are, when the groups could not be more distinct."

"This is mostly off topic," Cloves said. "We are here to discuss the impact of your research. Not the questionable rights of various subhuman groups."

"Subhuman?" another voice called out in the crowd. I inwardly winced. The social and societal rights of the Genetic Others was a hot topic at the moment. They lived among us, in our cities, in our communities. They held jobs, they had their own neighbourhoods, their own districts, but we knew so little about them. To many, they were fascinating; to others, they were monsters to be feared. The current debate in the media was whether Genetic Others should have the right to vote or to hold public office. It was hotly contested. Most people seemed to forget that without the help of these peoples, the Pale would have overwhelmed the world during the war. We would have been killed by our own creations if these creatures, once myths and legends, had not come to our aid.

"I'm sure there are many who would argue with the term 'subhuman', Servant Cloves of the Cabal."

The voice was coming from the other side of the lecture theatre. A man. People craned their necks to see who was challenging the great and powerful Cabal. He was tall and pale, dressed in a simply cut black suit, the shirt beneath crisply white. His dark hair was shaggy and long, falling carelessly over his ears. His skin was only a few shades richer than his shirt, a pale ivory.

"Dr Harkness," the man called, sounding confident and a little amused. "Tell me, do you see my people as a threat, or as a scientific curiosity?" His voice practically purred across the lecture theatre, as though it had been rolled in honey. It was loud enough to carry, to ensure that all present heard the question, but somehow crafted to seem like a soft whisper in my ear at the same time.

I stared for a few moments, utterly lost for words. He was one of them. I'd never seen one close up. New Oxford has a few districts, like most towns, for Genetic Others. They're not officially ghettoised, but they keep to their own areas, and we keep to ours, for the most part. They had a killer nightlife – no pun intended – but I'd never really strayed into it.

I had my own reasons for that.

"You're a..." I faltered.

"Genetic Other?" He grinned at me, entertained by my surprise; his smile was wide and white. "You can use the word 'Vampire' if you wish. Your people seem most fond of it. It does not offend."

The crowd became louder and more agitated. Some of the people sitting close to the man practically climbed out of their seats in barely controlled panic, trying to get away from him. Others seemed to clamour to get a better view, as though he was a movie star. One of his kind in the midst of the Campus was very rare. One of his kind in the same room as several members of Cabal was absolutely unheard of.

Veronica Cloves was on her feet in the rows of chairs so quickly I swear to God she had viper in her DNA. I wondered vaguely if she had biomodifications. It wouldn't surprise me. "This is a private function by invitation only," she said coldly. "Not a three ring circus. Official Cabal business is being discussed this evening. The only people ... *or otherwise* ... who should be in attendance are those by invitation. This is certainly no place for..."

"... for an undead bloodsucking vampire?" the man asked, cocking his head to one side, still looking faintly amused as his eyes flicked over to the woman on the other side of the lecture hall. "Perhaps not, Servant Cloves. But part of your audience here tonight are members of the public, chosen as per rote as with each of the presentations to ensure a representation of the vox populis. I am one of those. I applied for a seat, and was selected with my fellow guests."

I could see Veronica Cloves' jaw work for a moment, and knew that what she wanted to say was that the section of the public was meant to mean the human population, but of course she couldn't say this. There was no box on the attendance forms to tick to indicate your species. There had never been any need for one. None of the Genetic Others had ever yet shown even the slightest interest in our affairs. They moved amongst us, lived amongst us now even, but they kept apart, like gypsy travellers in a foreign land. I found myself wondering why there was suddenly a change in that. What on earth was one of his kind doing here?

His eyes flicked dismissively away from Veronica Cloves and back to me. Even across this distance, they pinned me to the spot, a soft grey and piercing pair. I noted absently amidst my confusion that he was astonishingly beautiful. Not handsome, that word was too heavy handed, too gung ho American and plain. He didn't look feminine in any way, despite the flowing dark hair – his jaw was too strong for that. But his features on the whole made him look like a Rossetti painting. I wondered how old he was. Some of them were hundreds of years.

"You haven't answered my question, Doctor," he smiled,

"Your question?" I heard myself say.

"Whether you see my kind, vampires, as a scientific curiosity or a threat."

"I…" I faltered. "GO studies … that is, my area of expertise, is not … sociological," I managed. "I work with blood. I've not had enough exposure to Genetic Others to form an opinion one way or another."

This seemed to amuse him further. "By a happy coincidence I work with blood also," he said, which got a nervous laugh from some of the media presence, who were lapping him up, capturing every moment of this on camera. He shook his head in mock disappointment. "But that is a shame, for you not to have been, as you say, exposed … to us."

I felt myself flush. In my periphery, Cloves hovered. I dared not look over to see if she was glaring at me or the otherworldly creature stood in the audience. I don't think I could have moved my head if I tried; his eyes held me trapped like a pinned insect. The part of my brain that never stopped being an analytical science geek, even when faced with supernatural creatures, wondered absently if it was some low level hypnosis. Were the GOs telepathic to some degree? I had never heard as much, not confirmed anyway.

"If you are to venture an opinion on a subject," he purred, "... surely you have to know it first, to get under its skin? And please do call us vampires; it's not a dirty word."

His tone suggested, with little room for misinterpretation, that it *could* be, if the situation dictated.

A scoff from Veronica Cloves seemed to disagree most strongly. "Your name please, Mr...?" she demanded.

He didn't even glance over at her. His eyes still trained on me, as though we were the only people in the auditorium. "I am Allesandro," he told me.

What was he doing here? Except possibly trying to get me fired and my career completely destroyed?

As this thought passed through my head, something unreal happened. I could see his lips moving, addressing Cloves, but his words and the rest of the noise in the lecture hall, were utterly drowned out. It was suddenly as though I was watching a silent movie. His voice appeared simultaneously, right by my ear. As though he were standing right behind me on the stage, close enough to touch, whispering in my ear. "Allesandro," he repeated. "It's an old name from the old country, the Italian form of the Latin Alexandrius, in fact – it means defender of mankind. Fitting, no? Given what you were just saying to these fine people, about how we selflessly came to your aid in the wars."

His voice was intimate, warm and utterly inside my head. I stared down from the stage, frozen to the spot, watching him engage in some kind of back and forth argument with the member of Cabal.

"To answer your questions," his voice murmured inside my mind, sounding faintly amused, "... yes, we do have telepathic capabilities to some degree, amongst others. As you have no doubt figured out by now. You seem as smart as you are striking, Dr Harkness. Also yes, I do agree that the hideous woman you see me speaking to has had expensive work done to lift her face, and no, she did not pay enough for it. And ridiculous as she may appear, she is very, very dangerous. As for what I am doing here, I am here to warn you."

"Warn me?" I whispered my lips barely moving, my voice low enough to not carry to the microphone. I felt like a rabbit caught in headlights. A

33

bead of sweat rolled between my shoulder blades and down my spine beneath my suit jacket, like a traced fingertip.

"Do not confuse the words warn and threaten, Doctor," the vampire whispered. "I mean you no harm ... But terrible things are coming. And we vampires will need someone on your side of things if they are to be prevented."

"What things?" I asked, certain now that I wasn't even whispering, but equally sure that he could hear my words, even inside my own head, if I allowed it.

Down in the rows of seats, his eyes flicked from Veronica Cloves' to mine briefly.

"You will need someone on our side of things too. You will see. I came here to find someone useful, from within your organisation." He sounded pleased with himself. "To tell the truth, I am glad it is you, not that other woman, Trevelyan. You are far more ... interesting."

"What things are coming?" I asked again. Something brushed against me. For a moment I was certain he was standing right beside me, and that his arm had slid around my side, his fingertips brushing my hip. I jerked around instinctively, but there was no one on the stage with me of course. He was right where he had been all along, in the rows of seats, keeping the audience and the media entertained with whatever he was saying to Cloves.

My sudden movement seemed to capture everyone's attention, and all eyes flicked onto me. *Great*, I thought wincingly. I just had a little seizure on stage by myself ... smooth. My ears seemed to pop, and suddenly I could hear the room again. Allesandro's voice was no longer in my ear but back in the audience, where his body, I think, had remained.

"... If the Cabal representative insists, however, I will of course bow to the wishes of the masses and remove myself from the hall. I came here through curiosity only," he was saying, in a friendly and amiable way. "Much like the other, more human members of the public, I presume."

Veronica Cloves smiled her tight media-friendly smile. "I think given that this is indeed primarily a meeting to discuss scientific results for the outcome of human led research for a human cause, it may well be appropriate for you to leave, Mr. Alexander."

"Allesandro," he corrected her gently. "No 'x'. I understand." He turned to the stage. "Dr Harkness, my apologies if I have in any way disturbed your presentation. My people may well, as you so rightly put, have been a help to mankind, but as we cannot yet vote or truly class ourselves at citizens, perhaps my curiosity into human affairs should be elsewhere." He grinned, much for the sake of the media presence, and put his hand over his heart contritely. "I confess I have an unquenchable thirst for all things scientific."

He bowed courteously, his hair tumbling forward, and just like that, he left. Leaving his row and walking without a backward glance the length of the auditorium, banging out of the double doors. At least half of the media crew followed him.

The room erupted into chatter and gossip. Veronica Cloves, her face a thinly disguised mask of white fury, shot me a look of death, and began calling for order.

7

"Holy fucking shitting crap!"

Such were the first words uttered to me by Lucy when I eventually appeared backstage, released from the presentation. The girl was practically jumping up and down on the balls of her feet.

"Did that really happen?" she squealed. "He was one of them, wasn't he? I mean really? You got hit on by a GO?"

I grabbed her by the elbow as I unpinned my thankfully deactivated microphone and practically dragged her down the corridor, wanting nothing more than to get the hell out of the building before Veronica Cloves, or any one of the press or audience members, could find me.

"Can we just go? Please?" I almost begged. "Yes, it was a vampire, I mean, a GO, and no, he wasn't bloody hitting on me. Jesus, could that have gone worse? In any way, shape or form? Vampires aside, I was just forced to report that in our ongoing quest to find a vaccine serum to reverse the effects of the Pale infection, our greatest success of the quarter has been to make a rat explode."

Lucy was optimistic as always as we made our way through the college. "I don't think Trevelyan could have done any better, Doc," she assured me. "I mean, who knew one of them was going to turn up and cause a big scene. God, I was only listening from backstage, but the way he and that lady from Cabal were going at each other, GO rights here, legislation there, it was like the most polite and politically correct boxing match I'd ever seen. Talk about a bad atmosphere! I love her on the talk shows, she's so sweet."

I hadn't heard a word of this exchange of course, but I could hardly tell Lucy that the reason for this was that I had a vampire whispering sweet nothings in my ear at the time and groping my...

At the memory, my hand went to my hip as I walked. To the pocket of my suit jacket. My fingers closed around something. A square of card. He must have slipped it into my pocket.

I tried not to process how he could have done that. How he could have been in two places at once, having two different conversations. I was just realising how little we knew about the Genetic Others, really. What else were they capable of?

I kept my hand clutched firmly around the card as we left the building and erupted into the blessedly icy night air of the car park. For some reason, I didn't want to inspect it while Lucy was around. She didn't notice anyway.

"God, he was lush though." She was smirking as we walked to my car. "That voice too, I love an accent. You can see why people think the GOs are charming."

"Not all of them," I said blankly. "Don't even get me started on the unsolved murder statistics in this city in the last ten years. The DataStream might insist on telling us everything's happy and shiny, but talk to the police sometime." I fumbled in my bag for my car keys while Lucy rearranged the folders she was carrying, hopping slightly from one foot to another in the cold.

She gave me a wary look. "Do you think Cabal are going to cut our funding?" she asked tentatively, referring to my not-so-amazing report on our complete lack of viable lab results.

Inwardly I did a kind of half hysterical laugh. Cut our funding? I'd be amazed if they didn't shut us down completely. Frankly, I was half expecting to be summoned for questioning by the Cabal council themselves first thing in the morning to investigate any questionable relationships I might have with the Genetic Other society. I didn't say this, of course. For the same reason I wasn't sharing the card in my pocket with Lucy. I felt stupidly protective of her and Griff. They were my team.

"Of course not," I lied. "Trevelyan will spin it. It's the one thing she's good at. When she gets back on the radar from wherever the hell she's got to. We'll be fine. Look I need to get home, it's been a hell of a day, can we pick over the bones of the battlefield in the morning?" I pleaded.

Lucy agreed and retreated with good grace to her own car. I sat in mine, the heaters on full blast, slowly dissolving a porthole in the frost on the windscreen, and plucked the card from my pocket.

It was a business card. Plain white stock, very expensive thick card. On one side was simply a telephone number, printed, and beside it, a handwritten scrawl: 'when you need me – A'.

I flipped the card over. The reverse showed a stylised raven, wings spread, looking like a Rorschach ink-blot. The script below was a single word, '*Sanctum*', in spiky, gothic script.

I'd heard of the place – a nightclub, members only. In the GO district. I'd never been there. Didn't plan to either.

'Terrible things are coming'. Allesandro's voice in my head again, but not telepathy this time, only memory. I slipped the card back into my pocket.

Starting the car, I reflected on my exceedingly unusual day. None of this would have been my problem if Vyvienne Trevelyan had just shown up and done her God damn job. I was going to find a way to make her suffer for this, I promised myself.

As it turned out, someone beat me to it.

8

Driving home in the snow, I wondered how much of the night's events would actually air on the DataStream. As I later discovered, very little.

Cabal had taken power for a reason in our brave new world. Building order out of the chaotic and tremendous shit-storm of a war we had created for ourselves had not been easy. Despite what most people might individually think about freedom and liberty, people en masse want order. They want to know someone is in charge of things and making the cogs of our world turn. Most people had been glad that someone, anyone, was taking charge, forming some manner of government after the years of confusion and terror. Thirty years later, and we were all now finding out what happened when you gave all your human rights to a group of people who insisted their agenda was to ensure you remained human enough to have rights.

People don't like upset. Cabal make sure that doesn't happen, for the most part. Content citizens are easier to manage I guess.

DataStream screens on the sides of dark buildings were already showing the evening's roundup as I drove the dark streets. All the usual stories concerning rolling brown-outs across New Oxford and the need for all citizens to do their part, pull together, blah blah blah. After the usual power crisis story there was a segment concerning the crop circles again. Seriously, who makes these things? Certainly not humans; we don't live in the countryside anymore. That's Pale territory. We stay behind our nice safe, high, thick, heavily-guarded perimeter walls.

New Oxford was cruel in wintertime; there had been ice on the inside of my apartment windows all week. By the time I got home, curled up in bed hugging a fluffy hot water bottle, the DataStream had already finished, the segment on the Blue Lab R&D aired and gone.

My phone rang almost as soon as I turned off the DataStream, slightly disappointed to have missed the segment. I flicked on the bedside lamp, which sputtered at half wattage for a moment, before deciding to come on full beam after all. It was Lucy on the line.

"That didn't go as bad as I thought!" She sounded monumentally relieved.

"Lucy, how did you get my number?" I asked.

"Oh, sorry, I'm at … I'm with Griff," she said awkwardly. "We thought you might need checking up on, bit of a team high five that we didn't get crucified on screen tonight, you know?"

With Griff, eh? My eyebrows crawled up my forehead, and I was glad Lucy couldn't see the expression. Well, this was news to me. See what happens when you absorb yourself in your work so much? You become the cranky, work-obsessed spinster while everyone around you gets coffee and long walks on the beach. Maybe I was reading too much into things, though. They could be just hanging out. People did that right? Other people I mean. Not me obviously. My closest acquaintances were lab rats.

"I didn't catch it," I admitted. "Did the camera add ten pounds? I hear that happens."

"Oh, there was a fault with the equipment at the lecture theatre apparently," Lucy revealed. "Something to do with all the brown-outs. They didn't show any footage from the lecture, just the anchorwoman, that Poppy Merriweather with the red hair, interviewing Veronica Cloves."

Of course, I thought.

"She was very complementary about Blue Lab," Lucy said. "Talked us up big style. She's so lovely!"

Orwell had been almost, but not quite right. Total world domination hadn't been achieved through a fascist boot stamping on the face of mankind forever. It had been achieved through glossy, impenetrable and perfect PR.

"I take it there was no mention of a vampire being there?" I asked.

"No, I dunno … maybe they didn't have time on the segment." She seemed to sense my mood. "I would have thought you'd be happy you weren't on screen?" Lucy asked. "I know you didn't want to take Trevelyan's spot anyway."

"I don't really care how much screen time 'Doctor Fiona' got," I muttered. "I just wonder at the famous transparency of Cabal."

"Don't be silly," Lucy insisted. "They can't help the power crisis. If anything it shows it affects them too, not just us lowly citizens. I know the only light that's been bothering to work at my place all night has been the one in the fridge for some reason." Good old Lucy. She did insist on seeing the bright side of everything. "I'm just super-happy they made us sound good!"

"They made *themselves* sound good, Lucy," I sighed with a wan smile. "We're still going to get it in the neck from Trevelyan tomorrow."

"If she even shows up," Lucy pointed out.

As it happens, our absent supervisor did show up in the lab. Just not quite the way we'd expected.

9

I should have guessed there was something wrong as soon as I stepped into the atrium at Blue Lab the next day.

It was a crisp sunny morning. Bitterly cold, the kind of cold which gets inside your hat and gloves and lies there like dry ice under your clothing. The sun was bright, dazzling off the snow and making the quad at the college look like something from an old sentimental biscuit tin, the ancient buildings dark spikes against a shocking, cloud-free sky the colour of spearmint toothpaste. I had actually quite enjoyed the walk to work, crunching through the park and across the campus in my boots, but as soon as I was through the heavy vacuum-sealed doors and inside the unrelentingly modern interior, the atmosphere was somehow even chillier.

Miranda, our day receptionist, was sitting at the check in desk, Mattie having clocked off for the night. She was a handsome, heavyset woman with a tumbling mass of dark curls, and always looked like she should be clucking around a bride at a giddy Greek wedding, but this morning, as I made my way into the circular atrium with its elevator lined walls, her demeanour was stiff and her face looked concerned.

The reason for her discomfort was immediately apparent. Three men were standing by the desk, dark suits, close cropped hair, ramrod straight posture. Anonymous faces set in varying degrees of granite. Everything about them screamed secret service, or at least ex-military. The only thing missing were those twiddly little earpieces you always saw them wearing on TV. I didn't know any of them, but I recognised them for what they were immediately. Here at the lab, we called them ghosts. They were basically Cabal security. Henchmen and bodyguards to the highest of the high, and lo and behold, as I squelched my way toward the desk, acutely aware I was leaving puddles of melting snow on the pristine floor as I advanced, I saw the fourth figure, previously screened by the ghosts. An older man, late fifties, solidly built, with short silvery hair, and a face which looked as though it had given up smiling long before the wars. I knew the face from TV. This was Leon Harrison. Servant Leon Harrison.

"Dr Harkness," Miranda said, her voice rather strained as she tried to appear breezy as always. "I was just about to try and call you. These … gentlemen are—"

"Here to see you," Servant Harrison cut in, silencing our secretary effectively. His voice was severe. "We need a moment of your time. I am—"

"I know who you are," I said, tugging my gloves off as I reached the desk for Miranda to DNA-check me in. She stared at my hand as though she didn't have a clue what she was supposed to do. These guys had her really spooked. But, I suppose that's the effect Ghosts have.

"You're Servant Harrison of the Cabal High Council," I said, peering at Harrison and his silent goons. "I didn't realise we warranted level two scrutiny here in the trenches, but still, I don't think there's a employee here who doesn't know *your* face, sir."

To explain Harrison's position in the food chain, he was basically a lion to Veronica Cloves' hyena. The Cabal member who had all but roasted me at the lecture last night was a dangerously powerful woman in her own right, but she wouldn't dare approach the half-eaten zebra until Harrison had filled his belly, licked his bloody muzzle and wandered off to sleep in the savannah. He looked rather unprepossessing, even in his crisp suit, but he was practically royalty. The fact that he was here at Blue Lab was worrying in the extreme.

"And indeed *I* know *yours*, Dr Harkness," he replied. "You are correct, I would not usually pay a personal visit to R&D, but this is a somewhat sensitive issue…" This was even more worrying. I had no idea why I would be on the radar of someone like him. I work with rats. It's not a glittering career. I try to stay off the map as much as possible.

He gestured towards one of the elevators as Miranda removed the tube from my finger and busied herself checking that I was still human as usual.

"I really must insist you come with us at once," he said.

I turned to Miranda. "Are my team in yet?" I asked. She shook her head mutely. I had never seen her so quiet, but then the three hulking ghosts were practically oozing silent government menace from every pore. "Then will you let them know I'll be down as soon as I've …

assisted ... Servant Harrison with..." I glanced at him, "... whatever it is I'm needed for?"

He gave no indication that he had any intention of discussing anything here in the lobby. I had half-hoped he might at least give me a sketchy idea as to why I was about to be frogmarched into an elevator by Cabal nobility, knowing that Miranda, who was not the embodiment of discretion, would be sure to tell Griff and Lucy everything as soon as they arrived. I felt like I was trying to leave a message for my own protection, like in an old movie ... *if my lawyer doesn't hear from me in half an hour...* but he wasn't biting.

"Of course, Doctor. I'll let them know you have business upstairs," Miranda said helpfully.

Upstairs is figurative at Blue Lab, of course. Of the many subterranean levels, those with the tightest security are the lowest. Our high up's work deep down in the burrow, which we affectionately refer to as 'the pit'. But we still call it 'upstairs' officially. It makes us feel more like we work for the good guys rather than on various levels of Dante's Inferno.

"Shall we?" Harrison said, somewhat impatiently, and he guided me to one of the many elevators, one of his Ghosts having already summoning it like an MI5 bellboy.

Some people are just naturally guilty by nature. You know the kind, driving along and a police car passes and suddenly they're all nervous and sweaty-palmed as though they expect to be pulled over for some hideous crime or other. The face of authority is enough to make some people sweat even if they're innocent. Miranda, practically jittering in the presence of Cabal members and their entourage, was clearly a prime example, but in her defence they were quite intimidating.

I'm not one of those people, however. I don't like being pushed around, or 'escorted', by less than friendly Ghost agents, and I wasn't particularly cowed by Servant Harrison and his 'stern-headteacher' act. I was more irritated. But I'm also not entirely stupid, and sometimes even I know well enough when to keep my mouth shut. At least until I have some clue as to what's going on. Not all the time ... but sometimes.

So I got in the elevator with the old man and his dark-suited muscle like a well-behaved and meek lab drone, and rode down further than I'd ever been before, feeling like Alice being frogmarched down the rabbit hole.

"Can I ask what this is about?" I queried, as the floors whooshed by. We were already ten levels lower than my own lab and still descending. My ears had popped. "My supervisor usually deals with anything outside of the lab, you see. I'm more the mad scientist type." I tried a smile. It wasn't returned, and in the withering atmosphere it kind of died on my face.

Servant Harrison did not reply immediately. Indeed, for a moment, I thought he wasn't going to at all.

"I am aware of this, Doctor Harkness. Indeed, as will soon become clear, I have good reason not to be going through the usual channels of Ms Trevelyan."

My inner ten year old sniggered at this, but I was too spooked to find it really funny.

The elevator, after what seemed an eternity, finally stopped and ejected us into a long low corridor, which was nicely appointed in expensive, if bland, corporate tastes. Charcoal walls, soft but dull carpet underfoot, recessed soft lighting. We marched to a kind of sub-reception, where a desk jockey, a young Asian man I had never even seen before, barely glanced at Servant Harrison's clearance before directing us onward. There were lush and healthy pot plants in the little lobby down here and elegant grey seating. I was pretty sure the plants were real. We didn't even get decent coffee in my lab. How the other half lived. I was impressed.

The corridor beyond the reception hub led to various offices, some glass-walled and all nicely appointed. There were no labs or heavy machinery down here, as far as I could see. I figured this was where the paper gets pushed. The expensive paper I mean, not the filing which even Trevelyan and her svelte assistant have to deal with like the rest of us mere mortals.

Harrison led me into one such anonymous office, through some silent instruction leaving his cheerless buddies outside in the corridor. Standing guard? That was reassuring.

There were two people already waiting for us inside, seated behind an outrageously big desk of some very dark and highly polished wood that I immediately ached to mar with a fingerprint. One of the people I didn't know, a forty-something man, rather overweight, but the tailoring of his suit was expensive enough that it hid it well. His skin was a pallid greyish colour, his face rather slack and bored looking. I was guessing he didn't get out much. The other person present, to my mute horror, was Servant Veronica Cloves herself.

"Dr Harkness, have a seat," she said, as Servant Harrison closed the door behind us. She was wearing a pale grey business suit, rather more muted than the jungle flower plum ensemble from the previous evening, but the glittering black choker was still present around her throat. What wasn't present was the sweet-natured and earnest expression she had worn during her DataStream interview. He face today was severe and cool. No media-pleasing masks for a private audience, it seemed.

Fighting the urge to flee the office, I sat down slowly in the large chair on the near side of the desk. The leather creaked alarmingly.

"Would someone mind telling me what I'm doing here?" I asked, as politely as I could. I felt like I was going to be court marshalled, or possibly sacrificed. What worried me most is that, of the three powerful people in the tastefully lit room, under whose scrutiny I now sat in my big hot winter coat, I only knew two of them. The overweight, sickly-looking guy hadn't even spoken or looked up from the glass monitor he was currently streaming. He acted as though we were not even there, like he was tuned out on standby or something. I'm quite good at vibing a hierarchy, and if Harrison and Cloves were here, I was guessing they lined into this unknown quantity. It was quite possible I was in the presence of a Level One. A minister. They don't do public PR, and I couldn't help wondering why one would want to speak with me over exploding rats.

Of course, it was bound to be nothing to do with the rats. It would be to do with the GO from last night, Allesandro. Nothing puts you under the microscope like a run in with the vampire population.

"Dr Harkness," Harrison said, still at the door. "It is imperative that you understand that you are here under Cabal security clearance, and as such, you will not repeat, reveal or discuss anything said in this office beyond these four walls. Is that clear?"

"What am I not repeating?" I asked, aware that I was being irritating on purpose. I was too hot in my coat and the pristine tabletop was bugging me. I could see the numerous chins of Mr Maybe Minister reflected on its surface.

"When did you last speak with Vyvienne Trevelyan?" Cloves asked me curtly.

I stared at her confused. "Trevelyan? The night before last. Well, technically, yesterday morning, around 3am. Why?"

"You are required to answer questions at this juncture, Doctor, not ask them," Cloves replied dismissively. "And this was in the lab? BL4, yes? Toxicology."

I nodded. "She called us all into the lab in the middle of the night," I explained. "There was something of an incident with the Epsilon strain which … she felt needed our attention." I was really hoping they were not going to pry on that. I had been very careful to keep the R&D findings vague in the presentation the night before. I didn't want to have to baldly admit that one of our rats blew up and we had to come and mop it up.

"We're aware of the exotherm; we've read the report you filed with Trevelyan yesterday," Harrison said impatiently. "This was the last time you saw your supervisor? In the lab? You did not hand her your report later that morning?"

"No," I said, thoroughly confused. "She wasn't in her office when I went to drop it off. I left it with her assistant. I think she'd gone home by then." I looked from Cloves to Harrison. "Is that what this is about? Is she still missing?"

They both bristled at this. I wasn't sure what I'd said wrong. "Look," I said. "I haven't seen her since. I had to do the R&D presentation because she didn't show up. Even her assistant couldn't get hold of her."

If Trevelyan was still missing, that was indeed strange, but it was much stranger that two – no, three (don't forget fat silent man) – bigwig Cabal Servants would give a damn. She was only a department supervisor, after all. It was like the Pope worrying personally about the ill health of a church organist in Surrey.

"Dr Harkness…" Cloves drummed her fingers on the desk. "What level of interaction have you had with the GOs who call themselves vampires?"

Aha. So this *was* about the guy in the lecture hall last night. But what connection could he possibly have with Trevelyan?

"What *level*?" I almost laughed, but guessed from their expressions it wouldn't be wise at all to do so. "No level. Level zero. I hadn't even *seen* a GO in person before last night. I've studied them genetically, of course, along with the others, the Pale, the Tribals, even Bonewalkers, but I don't even go to their part of the city to be totally honest."

My three inquisitors exchanged silent glances. "Are you aware of your supervisor being … mixed up … in any GO business?" Harrison asked me, choosing his words carefully.

This seemed the most outlandish statement so far. "My supervisor isn't really the caring-sharing type, sir," I said, quite truthfully. "We don't really talk much about any interests outside of work. In fact, I'd be surprised to hear she had any interests at all outside of her job spec, but I'm fairly certain she would be the last person to be on friendly terms with an GO. From what I gather she's very much a … humans … person."

I didn't want to say flat out that Trevelyan hated GOs and considered them all dangerous freaks, which was what I had always assumed from her demeanour. Cabal themselves are fiercely Human First, but they have political red tape to dance around, and would never openly admit dislike of the GOs. I was swimming in very murky waters here.

Completely forgetting I had been instructed not to ask questions, I asked. "You don't think Trevelyan has gone AWOL with a secret vampire lover, do you?" It was a joke. I make poor jokes in serious situations. It's a bad survival instinct. I'm the sort of person who gets nervous giggles at funerals.

"Vyvienne Trevelyan is not missing."

The large man had spoken for the first time. His voice was like gravel, his words a little slurred. I wondered if maybe he'd suffered a stroke in the past. He sounded like the godfather. "She was … until this morning. She's next door now."

I was now deeply confused. "Then why on earth are you talking to me? Why not just ask her yourself?"

Harrison crossed the room and opened an adjoining door, which evidently led into the next suite. "Please come through, Dr Harkness, and you will see that your suggestion is quite impossible."

With no small amount of trepidation, I followed Harrison into the adjacent room. Cloves followed at my heels. Nameless godfather guy stayed where he was behind his desk with his chubby fingers laced together in front of him – either too important to join in whatever version of show and tell was happening here, or else simply too damn lazy to get up.

The room beyond was not another office. It was brushed stainless steel, steel sinks, tiled floor with drains inset. One whole wall had a plethora of small rectangular doors, like oversized gym lockers. Interesting. This level may not have any labs, but it did, apparently, have a morgue.

"What the hell?" I asked.

Harrison crossed to a locker and opened the door at chest height. My blood ran suddenly cold, and I was convinced the sliding drawer was about to reveal the corpse of my supervisor, exiting the wall on a smooth gurney like a pizza out of a stone bake oven.

There was indeed a gurney rattling noisily from the drawer, but to my surprise, there was no body on it, no sheet. Wisps of cool dry ice curled out from the dark opening, suggesting that this was refrigerated storage of the highest order, but all that was on the shining metal slab was an incongruous and opaque Tupperware box, as though someone had a very morbid place to keep their lunch.

"I must remind you, Dr Harkness, of the security level clearance you have been temporarily granted, and the implications once more of revealing to the outside world what is discussed down here today," Servant Harrison said in a calm and measured voice as he donned a pair of bright blue surgical gloves.

The implication, as far as I could gather, was that I would end up in one of the freezers here.

He prized the lid from the medical grade Tupperware box, and beckoned for me to approach, which I reluctantly did, not sure what to expect.

"This morning, we received an anonymous package by mail," he explained. "Within the package, there was a DataStream message clip, and these items. We find this worrying."

I peered into the box as the last of the dry ice dissipated. I'm not sure what I had braced myself for, but it certainly wasn't what I saw. A cluster of small white pellets, jumbled together like mints. It took me a moment to recognise what I was peering at.

"Teeth?" I glanced up. Harrison regarded me steadily, his expression unreadable. Cloves stood behind me, uncomfortably close, her arms folded.

"Thirty two teeth to be precise," she said coldly. "It's all we have found of her … so far."

Her? I blinked and stared back into the suddenly macabre box. "These are…" I faltered.

"They belong to your supervisor," Harrison said bluntly. "We have dental records, and much more, of every employee of Blue Lab. At 6am this morning, just before sunrise, someone delivered the entire contents of Vyvienne Trevelyan mouth to us, neatly packaged, if rather … crudely extracted. I imagine the experience was not a pleasant one for her."

My hand covered my mouth involuntarily. I felt sick. "Oh my God. What … what the hell?" My boss was never going to win my nomination for hero of the month, but I wouldn't wish dental torture even on her. "Who did this? Why?"

"We were hoping *you* would be able to assist us with these questions, Dr Harkness," Veronica Cloves said close to my ear, making me jump. "Someone has kidnapped, tortured and mutilated a member of Blue Lab One, and has now sent a rather enigmatic ransom note along with some of her body parts to us. Needless to say … this does not sit well with Cabal."

I turned to face her, as much to not have to look at the box full of teeth as to confront the woman. "This is unbelievable," I managed. "Good God, poor Trevelyan. Jesus."

I'm articulate in a crisis, I know.

I shook my head, trying to clear it. The teeth glittered up at me obscenely. "But … I don't understand why … I mean, I'm a blood doctor, I didn't exactly swap Christmas cards with my boss, we hardly got on like a house on fire. I don't know how you'd think I could shed any light on something like this?"

"Partly because we believe this crime was committed by a GO," Harrison said behind me. "And they seem to have suddenly taken an interest in you." I didn't like that comment one little bit. It sounded like a trap, or an accusation. Or both.

"But primarily…" Cloves said, her voice like an icy razor, reaching into her suit jacket and withdrawing a DataStream clip, a kind of slim

USB, which she brandished like evidence in front of me, "… because the message which came with the teeth, the message sent by who or whatever has taken and tortured our staff member … is addressed to *you.*"

10

When I was a little girl, I wanted to be a vet. Well, originally I wanted to be a ballerina, then there was a fire-fighter phase I went through, but it turns out I was neither coordinated nor inflammable, so time and again I returned to my main theme of vet. I pictured myself wandering around healing sick animals, the occasional bit of horse dentistry, birthing a cow, splinting the legs of cats. I was an animal lover, you see.

Of course, things don't ever work out quite as we plan them. Fate and fortune led me down a very different and more specialised path. My father was a scientist once, before the wars, long before I was born. He was a medic later on. Trying to save the dying human population. I kind of followed in his footsteps after he died. I still, some would say, work with animals, if you could regard the genetically engineered rabid killing machines we call the Pale as such, but I would point out that it's hardly the same thing trying to undo the Faustian meddling of the last generation. It's a long way from caring for sick puppies. The only interaction with actual animals of the small and fluffy variety I get these days is with rats, and I tend to kill them – not always entirely by accident.

My point is that we never really know, no matter how sure we are of ourselves and our place in the world when we set out, exactly where it is we are going to end up. For example, even after accepting my fate as a lab drone, I had never expected to now be sitting in a subterranean office complex with three extremely important government Servants, corralled on all sides and wedged into a high backed and expertly leather-worked office chair, watching a DataStream clip which appeared to implicate me not only in extreme fraternisation with Genetic Others, but also with kidnappers and torturers. It was not what I would call comfortable viewing.

The visual on the clip, which Cloves had inserted into Fat Godfather's monitor, was grainy and shaky. Handheld footage. Too old-fashioned to be any kind of cranial implant, which is what a lot of the news crews were using these days. It was hard to make out much other than a featureless, grey room, I was guessing a basement or storage locker. The walls were old blocks of stone, damp-looking. Like a crypt. The only thing on screen was my supervisor, tied to a run of the mill four-legged chair with generous amounts of duct tape. Her clothes were those I had last seen her in, though crumpled and dirty. Dusty looking, as though she had been dragged along the floor, the coat of her blazer torn. Her hair was in disarray, falling forward over her face, and her mouth was obscured behind yet more silver duct tape. She was missing a shoe. For some reason this detail stuck with me, a distressing sight. I had never considered my boss as a vulnerable person. She would have survived a direct nuclear hit, but the sight of her stockinged foot, bent at an odd angle to the chair leg, made her seem like a small child.

She was clearly out of it, either drugged or beaten senseless. It was hard to see. The light was so poor and the camera kept jiggling, like one of those annoying found footage horror movies which always give me headaches.

It lingered on her a moment or two, blurring and refocusing, and then a voice, so low and guttural it was almost a growl, echoed from the monitor's speakers.

"Familiar sight, eh?" the voice spat. There was a burst of static, interference. "Used to seeing test subjects? Makes for an interesting science project. You humans are so fond of those." The voice sounded furious, lip-biting, blood-spitting angry. "Well, it's your turn now! How many killed? How many for the sins of mankind? This is only the beginning! I promise you."

The picture was lost for a second. More static, a high squeal, and then it was back. A hand had entered the frame. "You think you are untouchable! Cabal, the new order. You think you own the world! But we remember what was done! And there will be payment, an eye for an eye..." The hand raised up in front of the camera; it was gloved and gripping a pair of large and unpleasant pliers. "And a tooth for a tooth! Five sinners, five will pay!"

The camera became too shaky to make much out, the cameraman was shuffling toward the chair, towards Trevelyan, pliers held aloft. She was beginning to stir, groggily. The cameraman chuckled, a noise that chilled me, in the midst of all the anger and the shouting, a bubbling wet chuckle which sounded utterly unhinged. "Five will pay, and the sun will rise!" it spat. "Harkness, Harkness, poor poor Vyvienne needs your help … the sun *will* rise!"

The screen went to full static-hissing snow.

I sat frozen. Servant Leon Harrison turned the monitor off and silence descended.

All three Cabal members were looking at me closely. Cloves and Harrison with calculating looks. The minister, or whatever he was, gazing at me emptily through heavy lidded eyes. I stared at the blank screen, mute with horror. That thing doing the talking, the kidnapper, whoever, whatever it was, so angry, so utterly bat-shit crazy and dangerous, had just sang my own name out of the screen at me.

"Now perhaps you understand why we are hoping for your cooperation, Dr Harkness," Veronica Cloves said. She sounded roughly two minutes away from fetching thumbscrews and starting her own fun home video interrogation.

"I don't know what to say." I looked up at them, still feeling nauseous. My forehead had broken out in a sickly sheen of sweat, I was deeply hoping they would recognise it as revulsion and not interpret it as guilt. "I don't know … I don't know why it said my name."

The person who had made the DataStream clip, was almost certainly a *he*, but I couldn't help thinking of it as an 'it'. I'd never heard a voice like that. Almost animal.

"Voice pattern analysis suggests that the speaker, and, if we can assume, the kidnapper, is a Genetic Other," Servant Harrison said. "Specifically of the type who deem themselves 'vampires'. You met with a vampire only last night, the same night your supervisor went missing, and only hours before this DataStream was made and her teeth were returned to us here."

After the initial shock, I was slowly regaining my equilibrium. "And what?" I asked. "Are you suggesting that this is a personal issue? Revenge on me for something, because I've had a few bad break ups, believe me, but none of my exs have been quite so gibberingly psychotic, and as far as I remember, they all had pulses."

"We're not suggesting that you were involved with the abduction, Dr Harkness," Harrison countered.

"Really? Because that's pretty much what it sounds like! Okay, yes, I met a vampire last night, but to put things in perspective, so did everyone else in that damn auditorium. The only reason he was speaking to me is because Trevelyan hadn't shown up herself. If anything, it's more likely it was her he wanted to speak with in the first place. She was certainly the speaker on the bill when he applied for his ticket."

I mentally counted to five (I couldn't make it all the way to ten) but it still managed to give me time to stop my voice becoming increasingly shrill. "And if you think I have some kind of involvement with the Genetic Others further than my work here at the lab, and that this is some kind of a warning to me or a punishment, trust me, any GO who knew me even slightly would know that if they wanted to get to me, taking Trevelyan out of all the people I know is a pretty unlikely call."

This sounded mean, even to my own ears. I had only meant that if someone was sending me a personal message and wanted me to suffer, why wouldn't they hurt Griff or Lucy? Someone I actually cared about on a day to day basis. Trevelyan was basically my archnemesis under usual circumstances.

"There is no doubt that the kidnapper is addressing you specifically, Dr Harkness," Cloves pointed out helpfully. "Whoever has done this knows Trevelyan's team. Knows you work here, and fully intended you to receive and view this ... clip."

"I wish I could tell you why," I said, with absolute honesty. "I genuinely do."

"You are certain..." Harrison said, "... that there is nothing you can think of. Nothing your supervisor shared with you, said to you, which could shed any light on these events?"

I was getting restless now. "I already told you, we were not best buddies. Vyvienne and I didn't exactly braid each other's hair. If she was talking to me, it was mainly to shout." I had the feeling that these three were looking for a fall guy. That somehow they wanted to incriminate me, have me take the blame for these terrible events. My temper made me bolder than usual.

"Look, if you're going to arrest me, just do it," I said. "Because I honestly have no idea what's going on here. I don't know the first thing about my supervisor, I don't know who the scary movie maker is, or why he's so obsessed with the sun coming up. But if the police are going to be involved here, call them already, and maybe I can go and answer their questions in a nice cell downtown." I was painfully aware that 'downtown' was an Americanism, but I was feeling understandably dramatic, given the circumstances.

The godfather spoke, looking directly at me for the first time since he had directed me into the morgue. He had the dead eyes of a fish. It made my skin crawl.

"You misunderstand, Dr Harkness," he rumbled slowly. "You are not being arrested; you are Cabal's only link to the world of the GOs. You're our only agent who has any interaction with those we study outside of chemical testing." He leaned forward across the desk toward me, his movements laborious. "Your encounter last night with the one who calls himself Allesandro. It may be essential to us. I mean for you to exploit it."

I opened my mouth to reply, or protest, but he held up a stubby finger patiently.

"You are not being arrested or accused, Dr Harkness," he said, and his small eyes glinted. "You are being promoted."

"And if I don't want the promotion?" I asked.

"Trevelyan's influence was largely the only thing keeping funding flowing into Blue Lab, Doctor Harkness," Servant Harrison said lightly behind me. "If she is not found, well, let's just say it would be likely that certain areas of interest would need to be cut."

"These are tough economic times," Cloves agreed. "Your life's work? The careers of your young team, those you care so much for, as you say." She folded her arms. "Trevelyan threw a lot of weight at the Cabal Board to continue in her field. It would be a terrible shame for everything to fall apart without her."

I'd never been threatened with a promotion before. Hold a gun to my head and you might get a stubborn smart-arse remark. Threaten to take away my research, disband my team? That's different. A doctor without access to Blue Lab, without resources? I'd be selling snake oil in two weeks. No hope for my research, no future for my team.

The dead-eyed godfather smiled. "Congratulations, Dr Harkness. I'm sure you'll be a most useful asset to us."

I did the only thing I could. Mustering what dignity I had, I stood, chin up, and smeared my palm the full length of the desk.

11

Lucy and Griff were both waiting for me in Blue Lab 4 which, after escaping the hideously oppressive depths of 'upstairs', felt like a breath of fresh air and a home away from home.

They both stared at me in quizzical silence as I entered my own territory, finally shedding my winter coat and sliding into my lab whites. Both of them had faces like expectant puppies. Clearly the fact that I was two hours later than usual for work, and undoubtedly with only Miranda's sketchy report of the scene in reception to go on, meant that they were waiting for me to spill the beans.

Problem was, I was on strict orders not to. Level One security clearance meant that I knew what I did. It also meant that no one else did, and part of the job role I had just been very unwillingly ushered into was to ensure it stayed that way.

"Morning," Griff said eventually, when I was evidently not going to explain my tardiness.

"Morning," I replied, as normally as possible. "Look guys, Trevelyan … isn't coming in again."

Lucy clapped her hands with glee at this news. "Yay! At least this means she hasn't given the order to pull the plug on our funding yet. I told you things hadn't gone as bad as you thought last night." She paused mid-clap. "So did she turn up eventually then? I'm guessing too many margaritas and now a sick day."

"No idea," I lied, trying to keep it brief. "She's not here, though, so as far as I'm concerned it's business as usual. You guys keep working on Epsilon. I want all the data we worked up for the presentation running parallel with the overnight strains, match what we know against whatever new data have come in during the few precious hours we weren't actually here last night."

"I hear there was some excitement at reception this morning?" Griff probed, bringing me a coffee from the warming pot, which I took gratefully as I slid into my station and ran my hand across the screen, firing up the systems.

"Yup," I said as breezily as I could manage. "Just some Cabal admin, that's all." He didn't move away. "Our noble leader normally deals with this, but as she isn't here, looks like I have to shake all the hands and kiss all the babies' heads."

Griff frowned at me. God, I am a terrible liar.

"That's all?" he said. "Huh. We thought the men in black had taken you away to put a chip in your brain or something, Doc."

I had a folder in my hand as I sat at my desk, and I slid it straight into my drawer, making sure neither of my team saw it. I was going to have to look through it ASAP, but I was doing everything in my power to keep Griff and Lucy out of this whole mess. The less they knew the better, as far as I was concerned.

"Nothing out of the ordinary," I said, amazed that I could even manage to say that, considering what I had just seen. As far as ordinary went, I was about as far out of it as I ever wanted to be.

"What did you mean when you said 'you guys'?" Lucy asked suddenly, looking confused as she perched on the edge of Griff's desk.

"What?" I asked distracted. I was staring at my screen, scrolling quickly through folders and sub-files.

"Just now, you said you wanted us guys to work the Epsilon data, me and Griff," she elaborated. "So … what are *you* going to do then?"

I had just found the files I wanted on my system. I tried to keep the look of surprise off my face. With a gesture or two on screen I created a further subfolder, then I dumped them into a DataStream clip and unplugged it, pocketing the stick.

"I have to go out," I said simply.

"Out?" said Griff perplexed. "But … you just got in." I was acutely aware how unusual this was. I never go out. I even begrudge fire alarm tests. If I had my way, I would sleep in the lab. I had considered in the past if some kind of hammock could be arranged. It certainly would have saved me on rent.

I chugged my lukewarm coffee and retrieved the paper file I had just hidden in my drawer, pocketing it along with the DataStream stick.

"I know," I said. "Sorry, just in and out today, needed to pick up some stuff. You two will be fine here, you both know what you're doing, just … run the parallels okay? Admin stuff, while Trevelyan is off, that's all."

I had already shut down my system and was headed back for the door, completely forgetting my winter coat.

"Dr Harkness?" Griff called after me, sounding genuinely concerned. He caught up to me at the inner lab doors, my coat in his hand. I took it gratefully. "You *sure* everything's okay?"

I waved a hand flippantly over my shoulder as I entered the long ultraviolet corridor.

"Nothing I can't handle. Don't worry," I said.

Later on when things got bad, that claim would come back to bite me right on my arse.

12

I managed to escape the Blue Lab complex without encountering anyone else. Even Miranda on reception was otherwise engaged dealing with a huddle of scrawny-looking techs from level six who were checking in for the day. This was a distraction for which I was ridiculously grateful. I was able to sneak out without the hundred or so questions she would doubtless have had for me. I headed for the main exit, feeling like a fugitive escaping a maximum security prison, certain with every treacherous step I took towards the main doors that at any moment, someone was going to call me back, demanding to know what on earth was going on. No one did.

The sight of Veronica Cloves waiting for me outside in the university quad, huddled behind the wheel of her demure acid yellow twin turbo Ferrari made my stomach flip. Of all people to get in a car with, I would not have chosen this woman. I would rather have climbed in a car with Oliver Reed after a serious night on the booze. To be fair, she didn't look too happy about the pairing either as I slid into the passenger seat, shooting me a cool sideways glance. Neither of us were particularly pleased with the setup.

"You got the files?" she asked curtly, putting the car into reverse and executing an exciting handbrake turn in the crunching gravel and slush. A couple of nearby students actually had to leap out of the way.

"I did, but I don't know what you expect to find on them. As far as I could see, they're encrypted anyway."

Cloves put the car in gear and shot us out of the campus parking lot with a squeal of tyres and a shower of pebbles. I wondered at this woman. Purple suits, a bright yellow car and the driving style of a demon – she was hardly low key. Perhaps all the media attention, all those chat shows and talking head panels had gotten to her over the years. Veronica Cloves, force of nature.

"That won't be a problem," she sneered with a shake of her sleek black bob, clearly flabbergasted by my naivety. "We have people for that." She urged the Ferrari past the Mathematical Institute, along Kebel Road and out onto St Giles, blending us with the main off campus traffic of the city with only a smattering of panicked horns.

*

The last hour had been a worrying one for me. Down below in Interrogation Boardroom, after we had all watched the DataStream video again just for kicks, Mr Godfather, whose name I still hadn't been given, explained that the reason I'd been brought in was not only because I was referred to directly in the ransom note (or threat, or whatever the hell it was) but also because Cabal, for all their influence and power, had overlooked one rather important thing in their quest to control our brave new world. They had forged no bonds whatsoever with the societies of the GOs. There were no vampire informants, no avenue to which Cabal could turn for information. The government that was dedicated to keeping its human population as human as possible, the government that poured almost endless funds into enterprises such as Blue Lab, defending our humanity, had not a single person placed inside the alternate society.

Humans mixed with the GOs of course; the GO rights movement lobbied on their behalf, and then there were the fans who haunted every vampire hotspot, hoping to spot an immortal. But not one such person was Cabal. I personally considered this a particularly idiotic oversight.

This, however, was apparently where I came in. With hooded eyes, the large nameless man explained that Cabal wanted me to make contact with the vampires, to act as a kind of unofficial ambassador, make links, dig around. Find out if anyone on their side of things might know what the hell was going on. And all of this because I had happened to catch the eye of the tousled-haired undead at the R&D presentation.

The one time I get flirted with, it gets me drafted into the secret service.

"I'm not sure what you expect *me* to find out," I protested. "I'm a paratoxicoligist, not a private eye, and besides – and I'm sure this is more of a concern to *me* that it is to *you* – but if there really is a crazy vampire torturer running around the streets of New Oxford, there's a good chance I could end up getting kidnapped and tortured myself." These were two of my least favourite recreational activities, for the record.

The Cabal member had been utterly unconcerned. "You will not be working alone, of course," he told me in his gravelly murmur. "Servant

61

Cloves here will be at your disposal. She is, I assure you, more than just a reassuring face on the screens of our city's inhabitants. She is also a most competent agent."

From the look of shock and horror on Cloves' face, this arrangement had clearly been news to her. She looked thoroughly appalled at the thought of working with me. It was clear testament to how much she was outranked by the nameless man, however, that she hadn't argued. She simply opened and closed her mouth a few times, and then folded her arms and shot me a look of pure and undisguised hatred. Seriously, as if this was *my* idea of a good time.

The nameless man had slid a manila file across the desk towards me, advising that it was all the intelligence they had been able to gather on 'your mysterious Allesandro'. I wondered briefly at what point precisely he had become *my* Allesandro.

"Where do we start?" Cloves had demanded, sounding very put out.

Servant Harrison stepped in. "As you may know, Dr Harkness, Vivienne Trevelyan, as well as being the area supervisor for your own division in BL4, was also over several other … more *sensitive* departments."

I hadn't known actually. Colour me out-of-the-loop.

"Our findings from an internal search this morning show that approximately fifteen minutes after your last conversation with her, she wiped her own internal hard drive here in the system. We don't know why; we are working on retrieving the information. However, we *have* found the ghost of a trail which suggests that immediately before she wiped her entire work board clear, she remotely downloaded several files onto your personal workstation."

I was surprised. *Mine*? Why on earth would she do that? And why hadn't I noticed?

"We have been unable to retrieve these from your system this morning," Servant Harrison sounded slightly embarrassed. "You have a rather … impressive set of personal firewalls set up, Dr Harkness. It does *not* suggest a trusting nature."

Good thing really, I thought, considering people had been trying to hack my system to hell while I was strolling to work.

"We could break through *eventually* of course," he assured me. "But as time is something of an issue here, it will be far easier for you to simply log on, find these files, and extract them. We want to know what's on them."

*

And so now here I was, driving away from the lab in Veronica Cloves' funhouse-coloured Batmobile, with a DataStream stick of encrypted information my boss had hidden in my computer, and a worryingly slim file of intel on a vampire I barely knew. This was an odd Tuesday morning, all told.

"Nice ride," I commented. "Not very subtle for a secret agent though."

"Cabal doesn't have secret agents," Cloves snapped. "It's important the population know that we have nothing to hide. Why do you think I spend so much time on the DataStream? People fear a shadowy, faceless government. Give it a friendly face, mine to be exact, and everyone's happy. As far as New Oxford is concerned, Veronica Cloves is a sweet-natured and reassuring voice in the darkness. Cabal cares deeply about its people. That's the message. I'm as visible as I can be."

"You were pretty visible in that purple suit at the lecture," I nodded.

"Where are we headed, Harkness?" Cloves glowered at me, not rising to my comment. Clearly she was still fuming that she and I were apparently Cabal's version of Cagney and Lacey. Not that she would know who that was if I pointed it out. No one watches the classics except me.

I needed more of a plan than I had currently formed. Ideally, I wanted to hole up in a Starbucks somewhere and read through the file on the vampire, but not with Cloves at my side. I didn't like the woman, and certainly didn't want her breathing down my neck all day. Part of me was still distracted by the fact that Cabal even *had* files on the vampire. Did they have similar files on every known and named GO? Did they have them on humans too? I pictured a vast warehouse filled with filing cabinets somewhere deep underground, and a dusty folder with my own name, containing everything from old diary pages to my hard-earned primary school swimming certificates.

"Look, if you seriously want me to do this, we're going to have to do it my way," I said, sounding far more resolute than I felt. "You want me to schmooze vampires on behalf of Cabal, and you want me to do it under the radar. Well, I don't think rocking up to the district with a high ranking and very public Cabal figurehead next to me is perhaps the most subtle way to do it."

Cloves glanced at me sidelong. "I'm *hardly* thrilled about this arrangement myself," she said. "But it sounds awfully as though you are desperate to ditch me."

I bit my tongue. I would have called an exorcist if I thought it could get rid of her. "I just think we can save time if we divide our labours," I said. "You work on decrypting the mystery files my boss thoughtfully dumped in my computer. Trust me, I would be absolutely no help at all with all that superspy stuff, anyway. I can't even do Sudoku."

"And you?"

"You can drop me at my place, Bartholomew Road, down in Iffley, east of the river. I have to read up on my vampire homework if I'm going to make contact with this guy from the presentation tonight."

"Tonight?" Cloves snapped. "Time is rather of the essence, Dr Harkness. We need to move on this as quickly as possible."

I sighed. This woman's attitude was grating on me already. "I might not have had much interaction with the GOs, Servant Cloves, but I am fairly certain of only one fact, and that is that they are definitely night owls. There's not much to do with them while the sun is up. Unless you want to play giant Jenga with a lot of coffins."

Cloves snorted down her nose most attractively and hung a left, heading the car into my neighbourhood. She had probably never even been to such a poor district before. From the look on her face, she didn't have much interest in slumming.

"So what is your plan for this evening then?"

My mind went to the small business card which was now in my apartment, sitting on my bedside table. Sanctum, the vampire club.

I raised my eyebrows, surprising myself with my own suggestion. "I'm going clubbing."

13

Cloves had dumped me unceremoniously outside my tiny flat, giving the street and the coffee shop-cum-cyber café a disdainful once over as she did so.

"You actually live here?" she asked, unable to keep scorn entirely out of her voice, if she was even trying to. "Above a café?"

"Such is the glamorous life of a Blue Lab toxicologist," I replied unapologetically as I finally got out of the car. "Maybe you can suggest a pay rise in my next review."

Cloves' face did not crack. "Listen to me, Harkness," she growled. "I want you to check in with me tonight, as soon as you've done whatever it is you plan on doing. You're on my payroll now. Don't do anything stupid."

For a moment I thought she was concerned for my safety, but then realised her own ass was on the line as my babysitter. Cloves seemed to be a woman used to getting results, and definitely used to being obeyed by her Cabal underlings.

"And there I thought it was *you* who were at *my* disposal," I said lightly. "I'll call you from the club if I need a ride." I slammed the door before she could reply, and she peeled away with a squeal of furious tyres.

*

Later, I sat nestled in the battered old armchair in my lounge, a cup of much needed hot chocolate in my lap. I have few pleasures in life, but imported cocoa, hard to come by in our day and age, is one of my guilty luxuries. I took a deep breath and flipped open the manila file.

There was a photograph attached to the inside cover with a paperclip. A covert-looking shot of Allesandro, evidently taken at the R&D presentation the night before. I studied the photo. He was certainly a striking figure. I studied it some more, for the sake of thoroughness. People tend to avoid outright detailed inspection of others when actually face-to-face. It's a bit rude and tends to make one look like a nutter. Thankfully though, technology has saved the voyeuristic day, and now you can stalk whomever you like with relative impunity. With this in mind, I flicked through to see if there were any other photos. Nada. It didn't give me enormous faith in the spying potential of Cabal if the only photograph they had of this GO was from the same function where I had met him. I had been expecting years' worth of impressive surveillance. A full dossier on his every movement. No such luck. It was evident with every passing moment that I would be flying blind.

Subject 142531
Designation GO anima-mortis.
Colloq: Vampire
Age: undetermined
Origin: undetermined. (Suggested Italian/Caecilian/Hispanic origin?–
tbc)
Known associates:
Subject 476421
Subject 343465
Subject 763541
Subject 244356
Subject 432126
Subject 145552
Current loc: New Oxford, Saint Giles, Neo-Vampire-District
Other known/suspected Pre-wars loc: Geneva/London/Florence
The genetic other known as Allesandro (no known surname) currently resident and working under the GO Registration Act 2017 in New Oxford, west of the reclaimed Cambridge Campus site. Believed to be employed under subject 145552 in the GO entertainment industry. Currently resident at sanctum /e&c. No known undesirable activity. No criminal record post wars. Identifying marks, none.

There was nothing else.

I flipped the page, just to check the back sheet was indeed blank. It was.

Seriously? This was intel? About as useful as a thumbnail sketch. For a start, I had no idea who the other 'subjects' were. I assumed this meant there were other manila folders somewhere in Cabal's archives, but without access to them these numbers it was all meaningless to me. Other GOs perhaps?

They knew where he worked, of course. Every GO residing in New Oxford and every one of the other free towns was required to register and be on record, but this was hardly rocket science. The man had given me his business card, for God's sake; he clearly wasn't in hiding.

No rap sheet. He seemed to have stayed off the law's radar. Undesirable activity, as far as vampires were concerned, was human attack. It didn't happen often, but when it did, the GOs generally dealt with it internally, swiftly and sternly. It was bad PR for both sides, considering they were picketing for equal rights. A rogue human attack could set things back years, and the great and good of the GO cause had little patience for any of their own kind who were unable to keep their fangs behind their lips.

No tattoos either. This didn't shed any light on anything either, although I admit part of me was oddly disappointed with the news.

Don't judge me. I never said I was Snow White.

I flipped the useless file closed irritably and finished my hot chocolate in as angry a manner as is possible when slurping hot molten goodness. I burned the roof of my mouth, which only made my mood worse.

Truth be told, I was shook up. Scared and well out of my depth. It wasn't just the fact of what had happened to my supervisor, which was horrific in itself, or the fact that my bosses were trying to hush the whole thing up. It wasn't even that I had been press-ganged into this unwanted new 'promotion' of unofficial Blue Lab Snoop. It was that I was having to lie by omission to my team. It was that I was well and truly out of my – admittedly narrow – comfort zone. Perhaps most of all, it was that despite Cabal's seeming faith in me to be a team player, the very private conversation I had held with the vampire Allesandro at the lecture put me in a very difficult position.

He had told me bad things were coming. That *they* would need someone on *our* side of things. I had apparently been hand-picked by the other side as well.

Gosh, I was popular all of a sudden. Go me!

I hadn't revealed the details of this exchange to Harrison, Cloves or their senior, of course. I did retain some small sense of self-preservation, after all, but what did this make me? An unwitting vampire conspirator?

Some kind of double agent, a go-between for two very suspicious and unfriendly teams. I wasn't sure quite what I had done to get myself dragged into this odd mess, but I was feeling very sulky about it.

I had been twirling the business card Allesandro had slipped into my pocket, flipping it over and over in my fingers while I stared out of the window from my perch on the old armchair, furious with the world at large. Now I stared at it.

The telephone number, and the handwritten message, in frankly very un-gothic biro: '*When you need me – A*'

Sighing, I dialled the number.

It was still daylight hours, so the young female voice which answered was undoubtedly human. I had assumed, and she confirmed, that the number on the card was the number for the vampire club.

The nocturnal GOs often had human staff to do their day work for them. Sanctum was a vampire club, run by them for the burgeoning human tourist trade, but it had human staff for such mundane day-to-day tasks as table bookings, taking deliveries, all those pesky things which had to be done under the sunshine (such as it ever was in Britannia).

The woman on the phone sounded breathless and sultry. Professionally so. In my opinion, she was trying a little too hard, but I reasoned it had taken her a while to answer the phone when I'd called, so for all I knew she was out of shape and had to run up a flight of stairs to answer. Probably corsets were involved. I decided not to judge.

I enquired after Allesandro and was told he was 'resting', which was euphemism for the strange paralysis which affects all vampires from sunup to sundown. It's more than just a heavy slumber. They are literally dead to the world and no good to anyone, unless you needed a door propped open.

I asked the breathy staff member to pass on a message that I would be calling in the club this evening. When she asked to take a name for the message, I hesitated. I wasn't sure if Allesandro had approached me representing the wider GO community, or if his … interest, if that was the word, was of an individual nature. In the end I told her to just tell him the doctor called to make an appointment and hung up before she could question me further.

The thought of my actually attending a vampire club filled me with quiet, toe-curling discomfort. I didn't even like *human* clubs. The vampire district which had sprung up around St Giles was notorious. The human clientele who went there were generally either very gothic, in it for the glamour-by-association, or hopeless vamp-worshippers, rather sad and desperate people half-hoping to be chosen to be bitten and feverishly seeking eternal life and beauty.

This never happened by the way. Period. Vampires are not flighty when it comes to turning humans. If they were, there would be a hell of a lot more of them. The very fact that they were so notoriously picky proved that there was at least some form of common sense at work in the GO community. If you face spending the rest of eternity in someone's company, it's unlikely you are going to choose a drunken nightclub patron with an Anne Rice obsession and a penchant for morose internet poetry. That would get old fast, even if the individual didn't.

Even if the vampire lovers went home without their dreams of eternal life coming true, they still had a good time. The vampires had no problem entertaining said people, as long as they were happy to buy drinks and part with their money. Business was business.

Still, I didn't fit into the usual clientele by *any* stretch of the definition. I didn't even think I had anything suitably dark and moody to wear. A quick inspection of my rather capsule wardrobe confirmed this. I had work clothes, sweats for jogging, pjs, and some rather older work clothes which had been relegated to 'weekend wear'. As I may have intimated already, I don't have time for much of a social life. Astonishingly, I found I was clear out of blood red corsets, leather pants and PVC stiletto boots.

I had a moment's shining hope when I thought I had found a suitable off the shoulder black top, but my euphoria was quickly crushed when I pulled it off the hanger and discovered it was a long relegated-to-the-closet number which actually had a line of stylised Hello Kitty silhouettes along the waist.

What the hell I had been thinking when I bought that, I will never know. I wasn't cute enough to pull off the Hello Kitty look. Neither were most people I saw wearing Hello Kitty to be honest.

There was nothing else for it. Going completely against every natural fibre of my being, I admitted I needed help. After pacing my flat a few times, listening to the hubbub of the cafe below drift up through my floorboards, I dialled the only person I could think of who might be able to solve my pending crisis.

Lucy answered on the second ring. It was past six by now, and she couldn't have been long back home from the lab.

"Doc!" She sounded surprised to hear from me. I had never called her before, so I wasn't offended by this. "Everything okay? We missed you today. Weird day all round, huh?"

"Yeah, sorry about that, I had to go over some files for the big bosses in Trevelyan's absence," I said apologetically, which was only half a lie so I didn't feel too bad. "Listen, Lucy, this is kind of a random question, I know, but are you doing anything tonight?"

Her silence was rather suspicious for a moment. God, was I really so unsociable that she was reeling from even my phone call? Mental note, spend more time with people before you completely morph into crazy cat lady.

"Do you need me back in the lab?" she asked warily.

"No, no … nothing like that," I winced awkwardly, pacing my bedroom avoiding balled up socks and discarded piles of resolutely non-gothic clothing, with my phone clutched to my ear. Was I really such a slave-driver? I decided just to spit it out. "This is going to sound odd, Lucy, but I'm going vampire hunting tonight … and I desperately need a wingman … oh, and to borrow some clothes."

14

"This is a truly *terrible* idea," I said as Lucy and I stepped out of the taxi on the corner of St Giles. It was almost midnight, traditionally the time that most of the GO clubs opened their doors. We were only a short walk from Cornmarket Street, the University and St John's College, but we were well out of normal human territory here. The wide four lane sweep of St Giles was thronged with thrill-seekers – the brave, the brassy and the bold, all out to have a good time in the vampire district of New Oxford. On a Tuesday. Didn't these people have work in the morning?

"Don't worry, Doc, you look totally awesome," Lucy said in her usual bubbly, slightly over-excited way, as she paid the driver and followed me onto the street. Across from us, beyond the shiny snow-wet cobbles glowing phosphorently in the amber streetlamps, stood a rather unassuming pub called The Eagle and Child. As Oxford pubs go, it wasn't a bad pedigree. It had been the watering hole of several of our previous society's dreamers. C S Lewis used to wet his whistle here with Tolkien back in the day. They had called themselves 'the Inklings', meeting up to drink and weave strange tales and new and wonderful worlds out of the ether. I wondered briefly what those two legends of literature would have thought of the place in its present form, considering the pub was now nothing more than the antechamber to the large, subterranean vampire club known as Sanctum. Times change, I guess.

Despite Lucy's reassurances, I did not, in my opinion, look fine. Lucy had come over roughly half an hour after my phone call, having almost bitten my hand off at the offer of a night on the tiles. She'd been bearing a selection of outfits which made me immediately reassess my estimation of her. It just goes to show, what people appear to be in the daytime isn't necessarily who they are at night. Lucy in the lab had always seemed to me a meek wallflower. Not tonight.

She looked gothically stunning herself, in that effortlessly unselfconscious way achievable only by svelte nineteen year olds without a single inch of body fat. She looked like an upper-class Goth on her way to undead Ascot. Classier than your average Helsing, the affectionate term we use for desperate folk hunting vampire attention.

I, on the other hand, had rejected roughly six or seven proposed outfits, each of which had, to my mind at least, made me look like either a hooker, a drug addict, or at worst, a schoolteacher trying to be risqué on a hen night. I had settled eventually on a simple pair of black leather trousers, which at least covered my legs, albeit in a significantly snugger manner than I was used to, and a simple and slightly sheer white vest top. Lucy had tried to convince me to wear some costume jewellery, a large ornate crucifix. "The vamp guys go *wild* for this stuff," she had assured me giddily, but I had drawn the line at looking like Madonna in her 80s phase.

I don't normally bother with much makeup unless it's a wedding or a funeral, but to avoid looking like a seven year old playing dress-up, I had allowed Lucy to smear my eyelids in a soft reddish sweep, lined with red eyeliner. She assured me it made me look seductively gothic. I thought it looked as though I'd been crying, as if there's any difference. My hair was loose and fell down my back in a smooth pale curtain, offering at least a small bit of warmth against the freezing night air.

At least there was one part of me I was happy with. I have good hair. I'm allowed to be vain about that. As a natural golden-head in a world of bottle-bleachers, my hair is frickin' awesome.

"I still can't believe you invited me here!" Lucy was all but squealing, as we made our way up to the doorway of the venerable old pub, her heels clattering on the pavement like Bambi's hooves. There was already a queue forming outside the entrance, a red velvet rope strung between brass poles barring the dark open vestibule. "I mean, I've worked for you for what? Two *years* nearly, and we've *never* had a girly night. I didn't think you were even *into* the GO scene. You sure kept that quiet!"

I'd pretty much called Lucy out of desperation and lack of options. I didn't say this, of course – it would have rather ruined her mood. Happily it seemed I had struck oil at my first swing. Ditzy, innocent-looking, butter-wouldn't-melt-in-her-mouth lab gopher Lucy was apparently a closet fangirl. A Helsing of the highest, most rabid order.

"Same here," I admitted. "You actually come to these places a lot then? I wouldn't have guessed."

"Oh, totally!" she nodded enthusiastically, like an excited bunny. "God, who wouldn't want to be around them, right? There's nowhere better; trust me, I've done the whole circuit. Yellowmoon over under the Bear, The Crimson Parlour, all awesome, but *this* is like the lottery win! I've only ever been to Sanctum once, though, on an open night, it's practically *impossible* to get on the guest list, it's so exclusive! How on earth did you manage it?"

I shrugged in what I hoped was a mysterious way. This certainly explained why Lucy had been quite so excited when Allesandro had turned up at the lecture hall. She had that slightly crazed look in her eyes you normally only saw in the feverish eyes of a boyband concert-goer. It was practically hypnotic.

"Okay, fine, don't tell then," she teased, grabbing my arm companionably. "You are *such* a dark horse though, Doc! I was *so* shocked when you said you had tickets for Sanctum. I never would have put *you* here in a million years!"

Me either, I thought, as we approached the front of the line. Frankly, I was just glad I wasn't here with Veronica Cloves. I tried to imagine an evening of cocktails and dancing with that woman, and failed utterly. I actually shivered. The only social event I could imagine going to with Servant Cloves would be a funeral.

The doorman at the Eagle and Child was large, a solid slab of extremely white muscle wrapped in a very tight black vest and pants. Easily six-six, with shoulders like an ox. He looked like a bond villain henchman to me. Emphasis on 'hench'.

"Name?" he rumbled at me, looking us both over with careless eyes, as though he was choosing lunch. He wasn't a vampire, just another wannabe. But he was trying damn hard, and Lucy at least seemed to be impressed with the effort.

I smiled my sweetest smile. "Phoebe Harkness. Allesandro's expecting me."

He glanced down at his clipboard, scanning names. "The Doc ... right?" He smirked after a moment. It seemed my phone message had been passed along after all. He glanced at Lucy and then back to me, his eyes glinting in the street-lights "And ... a plus one?"

"A friend," I confirmed. Lucy still had me by the elbow. I could feel the heat of her arm in the cold night. I could practically sense her pouting seductively and being pert beside me without even having to look. I tried a charming smile too.

The doorman chuckled. "Whatever. Allesandro doesn't get off until two, but you girls enjoy yourself in there. Plenty of vamps to go around." He lifted the hook and cord, and stepped aside to let us enter. "Welcome to the Bird and Baby, have fun at Sanctum."

I brushed past him, entering the dark interior of the former pub, feeling as though I might as well be stepping through Lewis' wardrobe into Narnia after all.

"Maybe I should book myself an appointment with the Doc too?" he called after us, eying our rears. "Think I might be coming down with something myself."

"Sorry," I smiled back. "It's a *very* private practice." I was getting the hang of this.

Inside, the ground floor was still a pub, old fashioned, wooden beams, slate floors, basically a long corridor. The only vampire cliché addition was the red velvet upholstery on the seats and benches, and the heavy ornate drapes which completely covered the windows. We fought our way through a crowd of spiked dog collars, silk and leather, and made our way to the bar, where I had decided to order something with large amounts of vodka before we headed downstairs into the club proper. Turns out the underground vampire scene was literally underground.

Most vamp clubs in our city lay beneath existing pubs and bars. It was almost as though they wanted to ease you into their strange world slowly, through a reassuringly familiar airlock. Considering the alternative would be to descend straight from street level into what was basically a dark hole in the ground filled with carnivores higher up the food chain than yourself, this was understandable. But even if it was clever marketing, it still reminded me of those plants which lured insects in with sweet smelling and promising nectar, only to find themselves trapped and unable to leave, consumed in a leisurely fashion. Yes, I'm aware I am a party mood killer.

Lucy ordered a bloody Mary, rather predictably. The barman was human as well, a tall Asian man with creamy skin and very long bone-straight hair which, for all its silken finery, must have taken him a good hour with the GHDs every evening.

"So," I said to Lucy, as we sipped our drinks and made our way through to pub to the back stairs. I could already feel the thrum and pound of the music below through my feet. "Griff doesn't, you know, *mind* you coming out to these GO clubs. Hanging out with the vamps?"

Lucy looked genuinely confused. "Griff?" she said. "Griff-from-work Griff? What's it got to do with him where I go?"

"I ... sorry, I thought you guys were kind of an item?" I faltered.

Lucy stared at me over her drink. Her Kohl-smudged eyes comically wide. "Me and Griff?!" She burst into laughter. "Oh my God, no! Seriously? Why on earth would you think that?"

I cringed and sipped my woo-woo. "It's just that when you called the other night, you guys were together, I suppose I just assumed..."

"Nooooooo!" Lucy said, still deeply amused. Her hand fluttered to her chest. "We're just friends, Doc. We hang out sometimes. Especially with the citywide brown-outs. If my power's off he lets me move food to his fridge. That's about the extent of it." She grinned. "Oh my God, I can't believe you thought ... I mean he's a sweet guy, but ... no way." She tittered as we reached the back of the ancient pub. "That's so funny. He's way too normal for me. I like my guys with more ... bite." She looked at me in what I imagine she hoped was a dangerous way.

I inwardly rolled my eyes. Which is not to say I rolled them into my head. That would have been both gross and disturbing. I mean that I *mentally* rolled my eyes ... figuratively. My *actual* eyes looked back at Lucy in what I hoped was an approving manner.

"Besides, Griff is married to his work. I think the only thing he truly loves is his crappy little car. Come on, let's get downstairs."

I followed her down into the belly of the beast, downing my drink in one and already wishing I had another.

15

Stepping beneath the Olde-Worlde charm of the Eagle and Child pub into the club below was a startling juxtaposition. The stairs emptied us into the vaulted roof-space of what looked like a large sunken cathedral. It was a riot of carved stonework, high arched ceilings and stained glass windows lit in riotous funhouse colours. The whole thing was fabricated, of course, but it looked authentic, as though we had stumbled into some ancient long-buried church. The windows, being underground, didn't really look out on anything other than coloured lights making them blaze from behind. The fluted stone columns which littered the massive hall were probably only resin. It was like a film set, but a pretty impressive one, I had to admit.

The entirety of Sanctum was rigged throughout with industrial scaffolding. Galleys and balconies ran the perimeter of the fake church. There were bars, tables and barstools on each of these levels, and spiral staircases in overwrought ironwork linking the levels and leading down.

At the lowest floor, a large bar ran the length of the far wall, where the altar would have been were this a real church. The centre of the space was the vast dance-floor, which was currently crammed with gyrating bodies. Flashing and sweeping lights poured down on the whole setup from a suspended rig in the ceiling. From my high vantage point I saw that there was a raised dais where the preacher's pulpit would be, currently occupied by a very complicated and extravagant DJ booth. *Nice touch*, I thought. Preach the music.

Along each of the walls were large, multi-screen displays showing looped footage from classic black and white vampire b-movies and other kitsch horror classics.

The music, deafening and industrial, thrummed everywhere in the writhing darkness. I could feel it vibrating in my ribcage as we descended to the first level balcony and peered over at the vast sea of dancers below.

"Nice place!" I bellowed at Lucy, who didn't hear me. She was already scanning the crowds below excitedly. She tugged at my arm, almost

76

making me drop my empty cocktail over the balcony, where it would almost certainly have ruined some clubber's evening. I followed where she was pointing. She had found a vampire.

Bizarrely, in the strobing darkness and confusion of the club, it was easy to pick out the Genetic Others. I spotted at least five straight away, and it wasn't as though I'd had much practise. The DJ for one who was a heavily muscled Hispanic-looking chap. He was making the most of his well chiselled guns in a sleeveless mesh top. His arms were covered in full sleeve tattoos, his shaved head covered by an enormous pair of earphones and his eyes hidden behind outlandishly large sunglasses. He looked like Calvin Harris on steroids, but even at a casual glance he clearly wasn't human. It wasn't just the whiter-than-white skin, there were plenty of pale human people here too. It was more the way he moved. Faster than a normal person, oddly more fluid, and, goofy as it sounds, there was some kind of almost magnetic field about him. It's hard to explain really, but vampires seem slightly more *in focus* than regular folk. I don't know if it's part of their genetic makeup or just undead charisma, but they stand out like there's an invisible spotlight on them, parting them from any crowd.

There was another vampire sitting on a barstool down at the far end of the club. This one was female, twenty-something in appearance, though that didn't really mean much; she could have been older than my grandmother. Nothing helps a flawless complexion like immortality.

She was dressed in a rather dominatrix-themed blood-red jumpsuit, her long white-blonde hair in neat dreadlocks down her back, lips red on a white face. She was smoking a cigarette in a long Audrey Hepburn style holder. Even without the strange sense of 'presence', it was obvious she was a GO just by noticing the gaggle of adoring humans gathered around her, all vying for her attention like puppies looking to get their ears scratched.

The others moved through the crowd, working the room, their job seemingly to be seen and to interact with the lowly humans who had come to bask in their reflected charms. I picked them out one by one. Vampires, here and there, amongst the humans. They seemed like basking sharks moving through a shoal of helpless fish to me. All white smiles and languid grace, and like sharks, all just one small blooddrop away from turning into a feeding frenzy.

What I *didn't* see, however, despite my roving eye was the vampire I was actually looking for. Allesandro, he of the wavy hair and sharp suit, was nowhere to be seen.

"I'm going down to the bar," I yelled to Lucy, who seemed perfectly happy to ditch me immediately with a thumbs up, melting effortlessly into the crowds, off hunting her own Great White, I suppose.

Wingmanless, I made my way down and around the edges of the dance-floor. Skirting and weaving through frenzied dancers, half-clothed bodies swaying and bobbing under the thunder of the aggressive music like a mass mating ritual around me.

Did I mention I hate clubs? It always seems a little, well, desperate to me. All the bumping and grinding, the sweaty bodies, the low lights.

Maybe I just needed to loosen up. I'm a crap dancer, that's the issue, really. I'd love to love clubs, but when the music starts, I have all the natural rhythm of a set of castanets being dropped down the stairs.

This was probably a lot more fun with a few drinks behind you. I really quite liked the idea of just getting drunk and going with it. Problem was, I just wasn't entirely comfortable cutting loose when I knew there was a psychotic, pliers-wielding maniac on the loose in my town, a GO who apparently knew my name and could very well be somewhere here right now.

I was almost at the long bar, having fought my way across the dance-floor and was now weaving through the tables and steps where bodies lay causally, like the fallen in battle, sipping bottled water, and gaining their second wind before they attacked the music again, when someone grabbed my wrist from behind.

I whirled, expecting to have to fend off some drunken clubber who had decided to try and drag me to the dance floor for a dry hump, but whatever expletives were forming died in my mouth. It was Allesandro.

He looked different from when I had last seen him. Same perfect cheekbones and wavy hair, same direct and personal eyes, only he wasn't dressed like a Gucci catwalk model anymore. He was in dark trousers and a black biker jacket over a white t-shirt. It made him look younger, although my initial impression was that I was staring at a creature trying to camouflage itself as a human and almost – but not quite – managing it. What was this look anyway? The vampire Fonz? He might be old enough to actually remember who that was. Maybe I had some common ground with the vampires after all. Only they and I seemed to remember the old world.

The main difference, however, was that my vampire was *not* looking at me with a knowing seductive mirth in his eyes, as he had back in the lecture hall. In fact, here in the strobing lights of Sanctum he looked shocked and pretty damn close to panic.

"What the hell are you doing here?" he said. His grip tight around my wrist as he looked around urgently.

"It's good to see you again too," I replied, not thrilled with this less than warm welcome. Part of me was even a little hurt. But the rest of me was mostly annoyed. *"You* invited me here remember? What's the matter with you?"

I tried to shake my arm free of his grip, and was faintly alarmed when I found that I couldn't. He hadn't even seemed to notice I had struggled. Mental note, Phoebe. Vampires are strong.

"No, Doctor Harkness," he practically hissed. "I told you to *call me,* not to *come here!*" He was still looking around, as if expecting a piano to fall on the two of us or something.

"I *did* call you!" I snapped. "I left a message. I thought you wanted me to come! Why in the world would you leave a business card with someone for a nightclub if you didn't want them to come to the bloody place!?"

"You called me? When?" His eyes flicked back to mine. They were cobalt blue, like Clint Eastwood's in the old westerns. The whites were very white indeed.

"A few hours ago, this afternoon," I said. "I left a message with someone at the club."

He closed his eyes and seemed to be mentally counting to three. "You called in the daytime?" he said, raising his eyebrows. "You may not be aware of the fact, Doctor, but I'm a late riser. I didn't get any message from you. You really shouldn't be here." He looked exasperated with me. "Who the hell calls a vampire in the *daytime?*"

"Who the hell calls a vampire, *period?*" I countered.

Now I was pissed. But before I could speak, his hand slid from my wrist to my hand, lacing his long white fingers in mine he led me into the crowd, making me feel ridiculously like a prom date. "Don't cause a scene," he suggested. His voice had become very low, but through some magical vampire acoustics, somehow it was managing to carry clearly to my ear over the throbbing bass of the music. I guessed this was a similar trick to how he had whispered in my ear at the lecture.

"I'm not angry, please don't misunderstand," he said. " It's just that it's … not safe for you here. Just come … dance with me."

"What?" I practically dug my heels into the floor, but to my alarm he just pulled me onwards as though I hadn't stopped at all. My heels squeaked along the floor comically.

He pulled us into the crowd and gathered me close to him, his arms sliding around my waist. I held my hands up, ready to push him away, but under his jacket he was as immovable as stone. His chest felt cool through the t-shirt, as though he were lightly refrigerated. Not the most pertinent observation of the evening so far, I'm aware, but I admit, despite my confusion and anger I didn't find the sensation entirely unpleasant.

"Have you lost your mind?" I shouted at him, trying to make myself heard over the din of the music. "I didn't come here to dance with you!" He pulled me closer and practically buried his face in my neck.

"Look," he whispered in my ear. "People are watching us. People are *always* watching here. Dance with me, Doctor. If we have a conversation in the middle of the club bellowing at each other, we're both going to get in a lot of trouble. You need to act normal."

"Nothing about this is *normal*," I said. His hair was slightly brushing my lips. This was a tad more intimate than I had planned on getting with any vampire this evening.

"Trust me, you have no idea," he said. "Your people come here to dance with my kind. To be with us, so just … be with me, okay?"

I shivered despite myself as he purred in my ear. I made a mental note to check when I got back to the lab whether there was any record of vampires releasing pheromones.

"That is the worst pick up line I ever heard," I managed. He was ridiculously close to me. I could smell his hair, soap and something dark and oddly smoky, but not entirely unpleasant. He moved me around the dance floor. "Dance with me like your life depends on it … please."

I felt him grin suddenly, against my neck, clearly amused by my protests even through his strange panic. He was an unusual one, that was for certain. His lips brushed close to my ear.

"It's not just *your* life I'm concerned about, Doctor; my own is on the line here too now." His hands were on my ribcage. They were large, making me feel like a child.

Okay. I desperately needed to regain the upper ground here. I slid my hands around his shoulders, convincing myself it was done reluctantly and entirely in the name of keeping up appearances for any watchful eyes, and allowed him to lead me in an ambient sway. The music had changed to something slower and trance-like, which was probably a good thing. I don't think we could have held a clandestine conversation whilst moshing frantically.

"I gave you my number to call *me*, not to come here in person," he said. His voice held nothing more than rueful remonstration. "You are surprisingly unpredictable. Why did you come. Curiosity?"

"Why not?" I said, as he turned me slowly round, his fingers playing in my hair at the nape of my neck. I was dimly aware of eyes on us. Mainly other jealous clubbers, die-hard Helsings wishing they were the one dancing with the undead, impatiently waiting their turn. So this was what the vampires did. They danced with the poor needy humans, made them feel special for a while.

"My boss," he said simply. "That's why not. I would have come to *you*. You being here, tonight, it's *very* bad timing. It's better if everyone thinks you're just another Helsing out looking for a ride."

"A *ride*?" I frowned at him, trying to ignore the strange presence radiating off him like a fever. "What exactly is it you GOs do here? You just work the room, dancing with the adoring humans who worship you? Seems a bit ... cheap to me." Allesandro was beginning to seem an awful lot like a gigolo in my eyes, which was a shame, as he really was quite striking in an otherworldly way. I realised on some level I'd been hoping for something more interesting. To my chagrin, he looked momentarily wounded at my comment, but before I could even really register that I might have said the wrong thing, his face hardened into something like cold amusement.

"You're clearly not used to our scene, Doctor," he said softly. "We vampires give you people what you want. Or what you think you want anyway. What's wrong with that?"

Our impromptu dance shifted, and he twirled me away from him, then drew me back so I was leaning against him but facing away, his arms encircling me from behind.

"And what is it you think we want?" I asked. The lights flickered and strobed above us, red and white in the darkness.

"Mostly to dance, sometimes to be … tasted," he whispered. He must have felt my body stiffen, and not in a good way. "Don't be prudish. It's on everyone's mind here, trust me…" he said. "One little bite, just to see if it's as good as they say it is. You humans are a very curious species." He leaned in to whisper in my ear. "You would be surprised how many come back for more once they have a taste for it."

I disentangled myself from him, turning to face him again. I couldn't think of anything I wanted less in the world than to be bitten in the neck. "That's *not* what I want," I said. "Plus … eww!" I added for good measure.

He smirked. His eyes were still occasionally darting around the room, more subtly than before though. He was looking for someone, still nervous, still a little jumpy, even hidden here in the crowd. I wondered how long he had worked at the club, how long he had carefully honed his seductive-undead persona. And how much of it was just complete crap.

"And what it is, then, that you want?" he asked, sliding close to me again. I put my arms around his waist, trying to keep up the pretence of the perfectly-normal-for-a-vampire-nightclub dance. I mentally screamed at myself: *dear God, woman, don't grab his ass*!

"What do *I* want?" I said out loud. "Information. What the hell is going on? Who *are* you? Why do you want to speak to me? Everything you said to me the other night … things have *happened* since then. Really bad things." I narrowed my eyes, trying to read his reaction, and failing. "But I'm going to take a wild stab in the dark and guess that you know about them." I thought back to the video on the DataStream, the mad ramblings of the angry voice. "What do you know about the sunrise?" I asked him.

He looked at me quizzically. "That it isn't my favourite part of the day, I guess." He looked suddenly thoughtful. "How *did* you get in here anyway? Sanctum is invitation only, and I already told you I didn't get any message left by you."

This hadn't occurred to me until now. "Well, *someone* got the message," I said. "I was on the bouncer's guest list. I don't know who the woman who answers your calls passed my message to if it wasn't you, but whoever it was, they happily put me on the..."

"Menu?" he finished. His charm face had fallen again and he looked concerned once more. He kept momentarily forgetting to smoulder. It was unsettling.

"I know who. My boss." He looked irritated. "For future reference, Doctor, nothing that happens in Sanctum goes unnoticed by the boss. If *he* let you in, and knows you were calling for *me*, then we could both be in a hell of a lot more trouble than I thought."

He began to lead me off the dancefloor, away from the bar. "Come, we need to get you out of here, and quietly."

"I'm not going *anywhere* until I've got some kind of answers from you," I protested. "Look, I don't even know you. I don't know anything about you, except that you seem to be some kind of undead professional dance-card with a sideline in nibbling the neck of any lonely human willing to pay handsomely for it. Which in my mind by the way is pretty much prostitution, and also incidentally illegal."

"I *don't* sleep with the clients," he sneered. "I just dance and feed. It's what we do here. You don't need to approve of it. And there's nothing illegal about a consensual act between two adults, even if they are different species." He glanced back at me. "And you *are* leaving. Before *he* spots you. I will call you tomorrow, we will meet, and I'll we will talk then." He was practically dragging me through the crowd now, into one of the darker corners of the club.

"Before *who* spots me?" I asked.

"Yes, Allesandro," a voice in front of us said as we reached the edge of the dancefloor. "Where *are* you rushing off to with this pretty young thing? I'm fairly certain you don't get off shift until two."

Alessandro stopped short like a deer caught in headlights. His hand gripped mine so tightly in a spasm he almost broke my fingers. I didn't know vampires could even be scared, but the one holding me possessively right now was radiating at least a very serious level of controlled unease.

The man who had spoken, who had appeared out of nowhere and blocked our way, was not a man at all. It was another vampire.

Tall and thin, he was dressed in an extremely expensively tailored dove grey suit. Slender lines, tastefully cut to his whip-like body. He loomed over us, looking like a stretched shadow. His hair was short and styled, his face angular, strangely ageless, and slightly amused. His eyes very piercing. If David Bowie had been a vampire, he would be this one.

The presence radiating from this GO was so much stronger than Allesandro's, it almost drowned his out completely like a bad radio signal. This vampire was someone powerful and very old. I could feel it pouring off him. He was a good few inches taller than my dance partner, and he smiled down at the two of us like a wolf.

I didn't like the look in his bright eyes. He looked a little fevered, like the too-intense television evangelists you saw on the Datastream. His face held a permanent wry smirk, the way he leaned over us like a strangely delicate but very poisonous spider.

"Rushing off?" Allesandro said, recovering on the spot. He smirked, like a naughty schoolboy caught in the act, his game face back in place. "Nowhere boss, just out for a little … private time with a client."

Allesandro's boss could not have looked less convinced. The unearthly figure tilted his head quizzically, like a curious cat. His smile had not faded, but it didn't reach his wide eyes. He was staring at me, *into* me. It was hard to meet those eyes, and I'm not easily cowed. When I say it was hard, I mean *physically* hard, in the same way staring directly at the sun hurts your retinas. His look actually felt as though it burned. I wanted away from him on a primal level.

"Your personal recreation will have to wait," he said, still smiling at the two of us.

He gestured to the dance floor with an extravagant sweep of his long thin arm. His fingers splayed like the legs of a white crab.

"Come two am, and your time is your own, Allesandro," he said.

His good-natured smile dialled down by a tiny notch, as his eyes narrowed, almost playfully.

"Until then, you work. For me. You seem to need reminding of that lately."

His eager gaze rolled over the assembled clubgoers.

"There are many fine folk here just dying for a moment of your godlike attention. I suggest you stop hogging the clients and get back to caring and sharing."

He reached past Allesandro in a fluid motion, who only now I noticed had somehow moved so as to place himself between me and the stylishly statuesque master vampire. The older vampire ignored this obvious body language and quite simply took my hand out of that of my companion, claiming me for himself.

His hand was cold. His palm felt unnaturally smooth, as though any lines had been smoothed and worn away. The vampire plucked me from Allesandro's grip with a worrying ease and grace, as though he were cutting in at a formal dance. My vampire watched helplessly as I was pulled past him and into the arms of his boss, the man who had apparently intercepted my message and seen fit to allow me on the guest list.

"Fear not, young man, I will be happy to entertain your young lady until then," the older vampire said, humour evident in his voice.

He practically twinkled. Sweet and chipper on the surface, but the skin crawling up my arm at his touch made me think of him like a sour sugar cube with poison under the sweet dusting.

"I'm sure we can find *something* to talk about, Miss…?"

"Harkness," I replied, unable to do anything else. "Phoebe."

"A pleasure, Phoebe," he said, with almost convincing olde worlde charm. "I am Giovannibatiste Gian Michelle Valeta Cordina de Medica. The owner of this little corner of the underworld, and of others. Please, call me Gio."

He glanced at Allesandro, as though surprised to see him still standing there. Something in his too-bright stare hardened.

"Two am, my friend," he said. "Do what I pay you to do, the time will fly. No rest for the wicked, as they say."

Allesandro smiled and nodded in almost convincing respectful acquiescence. He clearly had no other option. His eyes flicked to mine briefly as he stepped away.

Was he shooting me a warning, or an apology, or a promise he'd come back and rescue me from the master vampire who had just claimed me? I wasn't sure. I didn't know him well enough to read his facial expressions. Hell, I didn't know him at all.

What I did know was that given the choice between him and the vampire I now stood with, I would have leapt on Allesandro's back and let him carry me piggy-back from the club.

He was swallowed by the crowd a moment later, as the tall, suited, and extremely intense vampire Clan-master turned me away from the dancefloor like a ballerina on point. I was left alone with the master vampire.

Giovannibatiste Ridiculously-Complicated-Surname, lord of Sanctum, master and employer of my one vampire contact, and serious creepshow, gestured to a velvet lined booth. They were arranged around the walls here, away from the fury and hubbub of the main floor, like an oldtime American diner; private areas to rest from throwing your body around the place and concentrate on the serious task of getting hammered, I guessed. I would have loved the pre-war retro if I hadn't been in present company.

"Shall we sit and talk?" he suggested genially. "I simply *must* know everything about you."

There was bite beneath his polite words. I clearly didn't have a choice.

I may not have had much personal interaction with vampires or other GOs before tonight, but in my line of work, I had studied them and their ways. I knew something about all the GOs.

The Pale, our human-created mutant killing machine plague, were my personal specialty, but I had also studied, for instance, the pack structures of the Tribals (they were matriarchal and deeply loyal) and the strange abilities of those we called Bonewalkers, modern day necromancers with the ability to reanimate the dead for short periods almost as if they moved the corpses back in time by a short amount.

Some of the more powerful Bonewalkers had the ability to translocate, which essentially meant they could move something – a person, an object, on occasion a whole building – from one place to another. I had spent two years in college trying to figure out how this worked, and had failed. Bonewalker lore was rare.

As for vampires, I knew this much: they existed as a society alongside our own, with its own rules, which had been around easily as long as our own had. It had just been hiding in the shadows before the wars. They operated on a very formal clan structure.

The older vampires were the more powerful, they gathered lessers around them. The 'clan' formed in this way, giving each individual the protection of the whole. Succession and advancement in the clan was largely through duelling or outright violence. It was very rare, however, for any clan member to rise up and attempt a coup of their existing master. The older vampires were old for a reason: they were strong. They held their place of power simply by being the strongest, most likely to rip the insubordinate head off any sons-of-bitches you could imagine.

When you're immortal, staying the MD is a long term career choice.

What all this meant was that Gio was Allesandro's master. He didn't just employ him, he practically *owned* him, along with every other vampire who worked at Sanctum.

I also now knew that Allesandro's note, slipped to me at the lecture, had been an entirely private enterprise. My announcing myself at the club had clearly intrigued his boss, who had lain in wait for my arrival.

Smart move there, Phoebe, I chided myself. God, I would make a *terrible* spy.

I didn't know what was between the two of them, the vampire 'escort' and his master, but it had been pretty chilly. And I sure as hell didn't like being in the middle of it.

The booth to which the oddly ethereal Gio led me contained two other people – one male, one female. I glanced at them as we approached. The woman was a vampire, small and doll-like; her long dark hair like a curtain of ironed silk, a severe blunt fringe making her look like a glamorous, if slightly off the rails, schoolgirl. She was dressed like every other clubber here – sparsely and mainly in leather. She smiled as we approached. The smile turned up the corners of her very red mouth but nothing else on her face moved.

She was nowhere near as old or powerful as Gio, or even Allesandro. I was beginning to get an instant feel for their levels of presence, their vampire auras. I didn't kid myself though, she still could have snapped my neck with one of her dainty hands if she chose to.

The other person lolling in the booth was male, young. He must have been barely eighteen, but had the kind of peaches-and-cream skin and floppy blonde pageboy hair which made him appear even younger. He was human, and looked utterly dazed, blinking his large Bambi eyes at Gio with a kind of hungry hero-worship as we slid into the booth – myself beside the girl vampire, Gio opposite me beside the boy.

"Phoebe, these are friends of mine," Gio said politely. "Jessica here, one of mine, she works here, of course, and this…" he turned to the boy affectionately. "This is one of my absolute *favourite* clients, Oscar."

The vampire leaned in and ran his thumb lightly against the young man's pouty bottom lip playfully. The kid looked delirious, his eyes rolling up in his head at the touch. I wondered if he was either extremely drunk or drugged out of his mind. "Isn't he just adorable?" Gio said indulgently, cupping the boy's face with one hand in a proprietary manner, as though he were showing off a favourite knick knack. The vampire smiled over at me.

"And absolutely *delicious*, I assure you," he added.

I noticed that the boy called Oscar was wearing a leather dog collar. This in itself wasn't really out of keeping for the dress code of the club, but at Gio's words I looked closer. The delicate-looking throat beneath the collar was bruised and puckered, speckled with love bites. There were evident puncture wounds, some fresh, others which looked older.

That explained his barely conscious fugue. He had been fed on, a lot. Almost bled out entirely.

I suddenly had the strong urge to get the hell out of the club, and go home and scrub myself clean in the shower, possibly forever. I kept my smile fixed with an effort, however. I had the impression that Gio was trying to shock me, to get a reaction, and I wasn't going to give him an inch. He was dangerous; I could feel that flowing off him as surely as I could sense his power. His smile was a lie.

"Having a good night?" I managed to ask.

Oscar the cherubic bloodbank just grinned stupidly at me. There was a sheen of sweat on his pale skin, he was feverish. He leaned into Gio like a comfortable lover snuggling affectionately.

"I think you broke your toy, Gio," the vampire called Jessica said, with a cruel smile which turned down one corner of her mouth.

"Hush, Jessica. Now, this here is a friend of Allesandro's," Gio said to her lightly. "The lovely, and very intriguing Phoebe."

He glanced at me with that hot, hard-to-meet stare once more.

"I don't believe I've ever seen you at Sanctum before, my dear. Tell me, where did the two of you meet?"

"I work at the university," I answered, aware that both the vampires were peering at me intently. "Allesandro and I met at a lecture, he left me his number..." I shrugged, not really wanting to say more. "... and well, here I am."

"Couldn't resist his charms, eh?" Jessica drawled, sipping her martini.

So vampires do drink, other than blood I mean. I noted this and filed it away. The more you know.

"I can't say I blame you," Jessica continued. "He certainly has a way with the ladies, that's for sure. Your kind … and mine." She looked distracted, glancing over at the dance floor, obviously searching the crowd for her colleague. I didn't look. She seemed annoyed about something, or wistful, or maybe just a little drunk. The vampire leaned in to me.

"And of course he has a very … deep … bite. Or do you know that already?" she murmured.

"Jessica," Gio said. "Go and work."

He was smiling politely, but there was a clear undertone. His words were close and clipped. I was guessing, for all his affectations of friendly geniality, Gio had a very short fuse.

Jessica finished her drink in a gulp and with a flourish saluted her boss with the empty glass.

"To unexpected windfalls," she said. "A bird in the hand, right, Gio?"

I stood to let her slide past me out of the booth. She glanced from Gio to me.

"Nice knowing you," she said as she departed, not sounding particularly sincere about it.

"Now then," Gio said to me once she had left, leaning over the table and steepling his hands. "You *must* tell me more about yourself, Miss Harkness. What is it you do at this university of yours? To my knowledge, Allesandro has never been particularly academic."

I've never been a good liar. My only real option when the occasion demands is to try and lie by omission, but even this usually results in a red, sweaty face and a stammering stream of completely unbelievable bullcrap spilling out of my mouth. However, any attempt was rendered academic by Gio and his sun-bright burning eyes.

Back in the lecture hall, Allesandro had demonstrated an unusual vampire talent I hadn't been aware of before, carrying on one conversation out loud with another person while at the same time whispering in my ear only, a kind of localised telepathy.

Gio now demonstrated another fun new trick. His presence shot out of him and engulfed me. He rolled my mind under his as though I were a tiny seahorse caught in a large tumbling wave.

There were myths and rumours, of course, that vampires could 'charm' people, control their actions or thoughts, but it was always hard to tell what was real and what was nonsense we had made up ourselves in horror films.

This wasn't mind control, though; this was more like domination.

Gio simply stared at me with his eyes like twin furnaces, his face still set in an amiable white smile, and his mind crushed onto mine from above, hard and cruel, squeezing the truth out of me. My limbs felt suddenly like lead. Neither my arms nor legs were responding to my instinctual urge to duck out of the booth.

"I'm a paratoxicologist at Blue Lab One," I blurted out, as though my tongue were not my own, surprised to hear myself talking. "I study the Genetic Others, mainly the Pale, but your kind as well. It's part of my brief to find a cure, to eradicate the mutants we made."

Gio raised an eyebrow.

"How interesting, Phoebe. Yes, the Pale as you call them, those mindless bundles of anger, hunger and violence, which you and your kind created, certainly are a … pest, are they not?"

He gestured around at the club but didn't once break his gaze from me.

"And yet, of course, if you humans had *not* almost destroyed yourselves and the planet we all share with your tinkering, my kind would never have had reason to … come out … as it were. All this would not be possible. We would still be skulking in the shadows, living off the dregs of humanity's table."

He leaned across the booth. Still holding that paralysing gaze. His control of my free will unbroken.

"Is it not better, in the long run, that our two peoples now co-exist, that there is…" His smile widened, his teeth were even whiter than his skin, and I could just see the tips of his fangs, "… *peace* between us?"

Oscar, the euphoric vampire-addict pulled listlessly at the vampire's lapels.

"I want to go and dance," he murmured, sounding sulky.

Gio ignored him completely. His stare was fixed on me. I was rooted to my chair, the full force of the master vampire's will pushing down on my mind like a splayed hand, holding my thoughts still. I was aware of sweat trickling down between my shoulder blades.

"Do you know how the Pale came about? How this plague on the world was unleashed by you careless humans?" the vampire asked me.

"We engineered them," I answered. Everyone knew this.

"Yes," Gio sounded irritable, "but do you know *how* they were engineered? Do you know what was done? Do you know what the *price* was?"

I stared at him perplexed. He shook his head minutely.

"One day, someone should tell your people the fairy tale which no one knows."

"I like fairy tales," Oscar murmured, reaching up a languorous hand to toy with the vampire's hair.

The gesture seemed outlandish to me, it was like watching someone petting a tiger. Any second now the creature could lash out and tear your arm off. The boy's attempts at affection were curtly ignored by the Master of Sanctum, who shook him off like a bothersome child. Did Oscar even realise that Gio had my mind pinned down like a buzzing fly under a glass?

"Why are you here, Phoebe?" Gio asked me. "Why are you really here, in my domain, tonight?"

"Allesandro invited me," I heard myself answer.

I had tried to bite my tongue to stop myself speaking, but it hadn't obeyed.

"Why did he invite you?" He was pushing harder now. The fire in his eyes was tinged with ice.

Whatever Allesandro had been up to, getting in touch with me, this guy clearly didn't know what it was, and he obviously didn't like his clan subordinates sneaking around behind his back.

"I don't know," I said. "I don't know what he wanted me for."

At least he knew I wasn't lying. I wasn't able to. The building pressure in my head edged into migraine territory as I felt him push harder.

"Really, I don't!" I insisted, my hands gripping the leather of the seating either side of me so hard I was surprised my nails didn't leave puncture wounds.

Jesus, this vampire was powerful. Any second now I would have an aneurism. Where the hell was Lucy? Maybe if she spotted me, she would come over, Gio would surely have to take his fingers out of my mind for a second or two while he played the charming host.

But no one was looking our way. We were hidden in the shadows here, away from the dancers. I had a feeling that if Gio didn't want his staff and guests to notice him, they wouldn't. He could probably have skinned me alive on the table-top and no one would have glanced over.

"Then why did you come at all?" Gio demanded to know of me. "Surely not just to bask in the glory of my staff? Allesandro is indeed pleasant company, but he has never had to resort to handing out business cards to strangers before. *Why* did you come here at his invitation? I can tell you do not like our kind."

His grin was a little lopsided now, as he made a show of leaning in closer.

"I can smell it on you. You're afraid of us. You think we're just another virus gone wrong, like your Pale creatures, those abominations you created. You'd like to cure us all. Make us like *you*. Weak and short lived," he sniggered. "So why on earth would you accept an invitation from a vampire you barely know to come to a place you hate?"

I tried not to say anything in return, I really did, but resisting caused so much pain in my head I felt like I was going to black out.

"I came because my boss at work has been kidnapped, possibly killed by a vampire," I said through gritted teeth.

I hated Gio, I had decided. I hated anyone who could so effortlessly make me feel utterly powerless. I'm not the helpless type. If I had had a stake in my hand, I would have lunged at him in that moment.

"And the vampire who took my boss knows my name, and I'm scared."

Gio tilted his head to the side curiously. His eyes had crinkled. He could see that he was causing me pain and was clearly enjoying it. The sadistic bastard.

"You are scared because you know something?"

Suddenly his voice was inside my head as well as outside. I heard him whisper in my mind.

"You may as well tell me everything, little girl, because believe me, you are in over your head and you are not getting out of here alive tonight, I am going to suck you dry and dance on your corpse."

His threats whispered around my head, echoing off my skull.

"Tell me what I want to know and this will happen quickly. Refuse, and I will make it last for days."

The words rolled straight into my head without bothering to leave his lips or enter my ears. My blood ran cold. I was going to die down here tonight.

"Scared, because I don't know anything!" I cried. "I don't know what's going on, but I think my boss tried to save her own life by selling me out to whoever was torturing her. She had some sensitive information, I don't know what, and she knew someone was after her so she hid it in my workstation. I think they tortured this information out of her, and whoever wants this information now thinks *I* have it, and is coming for me!"

The words poured out of me uninvited. Gio's hand shot across the table and grabbed my arm. His grip was ice. I felt the bones of my forearm grind together.

"And *do* you?" he asked. "Do you have this information?"

I shook my head. It felt as though it were going to fall off my shoulders. I couldn't hear the club music anymore – nothing more than a distant thrum, as though it were a great distance away through deep water. All I could hear was the roar of my own blood in my ears, and cutting through the beat, Gio's voice like a cruel scalpel.

"I did…" I said. "I did have it. I don't anymore. Cabal has it now."

His eyes bored into mine painfully. I tried to look away but his influence in my mind snapped my head back to face him as surely as if he had grabbed me by the chin and wrenched my head around.

"Where…" he growled, through gritted teeth, "… is … it?"

My mouth opened to answer, but before I could speak, a roaring din tore through the club. It was a noise which certainly saved my life, but for a moment I couldn't even interpret what it was.

The noise clearly startled Gio as well, and his eyes flicked away from me, peering around the club in confusion. I felt his hold on my mind falter as he was distracted. It was like a heavy fog was lifted from my head. The music had stopped in the club, I noticed. The clanging siren which filled the air … was a fire alarm?

The second I realised this, that the deafening shrill bell which filled the air was a danger sign, we were suddenly all soaked. Sprinklers had come on all over the club, powerful fire-prevention rain, hidden high in the cathedral-like roof. The throngs of clubbers around us seemed to all realise at once what the noise and the water meant. There was a fire. Perhaps predictably, mass panic erupted.

It's never a good idea to get two or three hundred people into a large underground space, fill them with alcohol and God knows what else, and then suggest to them that they may be imminently burned to death.

No one formed an orderly sensible line for the stairs. Herd mentality took over and within seconds, the club was filled with panicked screams. In the pandemonium, everyone rushed for the stairs at once.

Clearly, this didn't have any useful result other than crushing a mass of bodies into a bottleneck. In the jostling crowds, as people quickly became soaked to the skin from the constant and powerful sprinkler rain, some fell and were trampled. Others, in their panic, fought to get to the fake windows. We were underground, for God's sake. The only way out was back up through the pub above us.

Opposite me in the booth, my captor Gio was on his feet so fast I hadn't seen him stand. He was glaring around the dance floor in fury, his blonde hair already plastered to his wet forehead. His pale suit was darkening in the constant downspray of the sprinklers.

The main lights had come on, filling the club with stark bright light and eradicating every moody shadow and artfully created cove. The pretence of gothic finery was destroyed in the unforgiving strip lighting. The club was revealed for what it was: a sham. The walls didn't even look like real stone; the pillars, just stage dressing.

I blinked in the brightness, shaking my head as my hair, drenched, stuck to my back. I could move.

Across from me, the Helsing-whore Oscar was almost lying back against the booth, his head upturned to the down-pouring mist, a stupid empty grin across his face. He was clearly enjoying the turn of events, too far gone to even sense any possible danger.

"What is happening?" Gio roared into the screaming crowds.

Tables were overturned nearby, as revellers fell, ran and stumbled past, soaked to the skin and fuelled by panic.

"There is *no fire* here!" he bellowed.

He shot a look at me, furious. I was still sitting in the booth stupidly, as I fought to regain control of my limbs.

"You did this! Somehow, this is you!"

"I didn't do anything!" I answered, though if he even heard me over the deafening clang of the constant alarm, I have no idea.

Gio leaned down until his face was inches from mine.

"You..." he hissed. "... are going *nowhere*."

He reached over and grabbed Oscar by the dog collar, dragging him to the edge of the booth.

"Stay with her!" he barked, all composure lost. "See that she doesn't go missing. We're not done here. The only way she's leaving here is in chunks."

The master vampire disappeared into the maelstrom of pushing, shoving panic. I watched as he stalked away, roughly batting people aside out of his path like an intrepid explorer hacking at overgrowth.

Seeing my one chance to make a move and get the hell away, I forced my body to stand. My legs still felt like jelly, as though I had been heavily drugged. *You have to move, Phoebe*, I told myself sternly. You have to get the fuck out of here while you can, or that nasty son of a bitch is going to eat your face – and you will sit like a moron and let him do it.

I felt like I was going to throw up. I staggered as I stood, gripping the edge of the booth with both hands. I had to find Lucy, somewhere in this mess.

Someone grabbed my wrist. I looked up from my shaking feet. It was Oscar. Standing before me like a half-drowned, angelic junkie, he was pouting his cupid bow lips at me, his eyes still unfocused.

"We can't go," he said. "Gio said to wait."

I could have punched him in that stupid mouth. I tried to wriggle free of his grip, but he was surprisingly determined.

"Get the hell off me, Oscar, you don't know what you're doing."

"Gio said to *wait*!" Oscar insisted, his voice almost pleading. "He promised he'd come back. He won't abandon us. He'll be mad if I let you go."

I had almost managed to shake him off, and he must have sensed me slipping out of his grip, as he pulled me over to him and wrapped me in a bear hug, pinning me to him, my arms pinioned at my sides.

"Don't, please," he begged. "He told me to keep you. You have to stay."

"He's going to *kill me*, you stupid brat!" I hissed, trying to throw him off.

People rushed around us, jostling, shouting. In the chaos of the desperate crowd, we were just another struggling couple. No one even noticed us.

"He's nearly killed you too!"

"He wouldn't hurt me," Oscar insisted, his breath hot in my ear, his voice slurred. "He's going to make me one of them. He promised."

"The only thing he's making you is anaemic, you bloody arse!" I growled.

I pushed backwards, throwing us both against the table of the booth. Oscar slipped, clearly winded as I threw my weight against him, but he didn't let go.

"No one will hurt me. My daddy's an important man in this town, no one would dare!"

One of his arms had come up and was around my neck; he had me in a chokehold. I was pinned against Gio's little treat and despite the chaos and the confusion all around us, I suddenly realised to my disgust that he was extremely pleased about the fact. He was practically grinding against my back. The junkie was twisted worse than I'd imagined.

"Oscar…" I gasped, my voice quiet, "listen … it's important…"

I felt him lean in close, his head right behind mine. Sprinkler rain washed down over both of us, dripping off my chin.

"What?" he shouted over the din of the constant alarm.

I couldn't see him, but I could feel his stupid grin. In answer, I flung my head back as hard as I could. There was a crack as the back of my head connected with the boy's face. It hurt me like hell, but I was pretty sure I'd broken the kid's nose.

Throwing him off as he released me with a howl, his hands going up to his busted face, I took a step into the crowd and instantly slipped on the drenched floor. People stepped around and over me, a confusion of legs and feet. I knew I had to get up, and quickly, before someone stomped me to death by accident, or before Gio returned.

Grabbing the nearest body, without bothering to look at them, I hauled myself up. Before I could stand fully, Oscar was behind me again, his hands grabbing my shoulders. He looked furious, his eyes wild, his mouth and chin running with blood as it washed with down-pouring water.

"You stupid bitch…" he began.

He didn't get a chance to finish the sentence, however, as someone came up behind him, lifted him off his feet with a hand around the neck, and threw him to one side as lightly as though he was a rag doll. My captor disappeared into the crowd, taking several other bystanders down with him in a heap, like human skittles.

It was Allesandro. He reached down and offered me a hand.

"Come on," he said.

His hair was plastered to his face, the sprinklers bouncing droplets off his leather biker jacket noisily. His eyes were casting around wildly.

"We have to be quick!" he yelled.

I took his hand and he hauled me to my feet. I went to make for the stairs, following the crowds, but he tugged me away.

"No, not that way, you'll never get out. Follow me," he shouted over the sirens.

I followed, half stumbling, half dragged, going against the flow of bodies, towards the back of the room where Allesandro led me behind the long bar. There was a narrow doorway here. The vampire pulled me through, and along a dark corridor which led to a stock room, piled high on all sides with crates of beers and spirits.

The sprinklers were on in this large room as well, though the fire alarm was less deafening. I noted we were wading through a good three inches of water here. Part of my mind wondered exactly how good the drainage at an underground club was likely to be. Those clubbers who didn't burn to death or get trampled by their fellow revellers may well end up drowning.

"Your boss wants to kill me," I said.

He didn't seem to hear me. Allesandro had let go of my hand and was hauling aside crates at the back of the room.

"What are you doing?" I shouted over the alarm, glancing back the way we had come.

I was convinced that at any second, Gio was going to appear and claim me again. He wasn't going to let me get out of here.

"There's another way out," Allesandro shouted. "This city is so old. All the cellars. You could walk from one side of New Oxford to the other, breaking through walls, without having to come up above ground."

The wall behind the crates was bare plaster. Apparently the decadent gothic finery was all upfront at the club, not in the rather more grubby backstage areas.

"Well yeah … if you happen to have a sledgehammer," I said, still feeling woozy from Gio's stare.

Allesandro punched the wall. Hard.

His movements were fast. It was still unfamiliar to me to see how the GOs moved. They looked human most of the time but when they moved like this, it certainly reminded you that you were in the room with another species entirely.

He hit the wall again, and again, and again, in quick succession. Plaster rained down. On the fourth or fifth punch, the wall gave way with a crunch, and his arm went right through. A hole roughly the size of a car window fell away around him in a rumble of brick and plaster.

"… Or a vampire," I corrected myself.

He had reached into the hole and was busying himself tearing away bricks, widening the gap. He pulled at the plasterwork and masonry, as though it were nothing more than wet sand. When the hole was large enough he turned back to me, a hand outstretched.

"Quickly," he said.

I hesitated. Why the hell was he helping me escape his own clan? His expression was earnest, serious. His wavy hair plastered to his face. His clothing soaked and covered in already wet and grubby plasterwork. Why would I trust a vampire who could well be just about to bury me alive? He could just be buying his way back into his boss' good books by making sure I was kept in a safe hidey hole until things calmed down.

"Your boss was planning to kill me tonight. Why are you helping me?" I asked.

He stared at me as though I were stupid.

"This *really* isn't the time."

"I don't even know you," I said. "I'm only here in the first place because of you, and now look how things are going. That scary son of a bitch is your master. Why would you help me escape?"

He shrugged, his earnest expression subsumed by what I was already coming to think of as his gigolo mask.

"Let us just say that I'm ambitious. Consider yourself an investment," he said. "Now will you *please* come the hell on?"

98

"He'll know," I said, wading towards him. "Your freakshow boss, he'll know you helped me out of here."

Allesandro shook his head, helping me up and practically manhandling me through the hole he had created.

"Leave him to me," he said simply. "I'll think of something. Just *get out of here*, will you?"

I dropped down on the other side of the wall. I found myself in what looked like a very dark and unused cellar. Packing crates surrounded me on all sides. Confused, I looked back through the hole into the storeroom.

"You're not coming with me?"

He shook his head.

"You shouldn't have come here, I should have come to you. You can't go home, it won't be safe."

"Where the hell should I go then?" I asked. Then a horrible realisation hit me. "My friend Lucy, she's still in there, in the fire! I can't leave without her."

He stared at me, his beautiful face utterly astonished.

At first I thought he was taken aback by my brave unwillingness to leave a friend behind, despite any danger to myself. I actually felt heroic, all Linda Hamilton for a moment. But no, he was just amazed at how dim I was apparently being.

"There *is* no fire, Doctor," he said. "*I* set the alarm off. I had to get you away from Gio somehow. It's all I could think of. Your friend is safe. When I left you with him I sought her out. I had her escorted from the club."

He half grinned.

"She was not happy with me for it. She wanted very much to stay, I think."

Allesandro had caused all this chaos, to save me from his scary boss?

"He'll kill you for letting me go," I said. "Come with me, you idiot."

He looked surprised.

"Your concern is touching. Perhaps we will make a Helsing out of you yet? I am rescuing you from my master and you stand here worried about *me*?"

"I don't even know you," I spat, angrily pushing my sodden hair off my forehead. "You brought me here in the first damn place. *Call me when you need me*! That's what your bloody card said. Not call me when you need a near death experience!"

"I didn't tell you to come here," he said, cocking his head to one side. "I think you *are* worried for my safety. How interesting."

I felt like I was losing my mind. I stood dripping wet in the dark cellar.

"And a fucking Helsing? Are you *mentally unstable*?" I practically yelled at him.

"Admit it, I'm the nicest vampire you've ever met."

"I've met two!" I spluttered, holding up two shaky fingers. "The other one raped my brain and told me he was going to dance on my corpse! This has not been a fun evening!"

"Go," he grinned.

How he was finding any of this entertaining was a mystery to me. Allesandro glanced behind, then back at me, less of a grin now.

"He will know you are missing by now. If you stay, he *will* kill you. You'd be no use to me then."

I didn't bother staying to argue. Allesandro was clearly not all there. I made my way through the darkness of the cellar, groping blindly ahead like a blind woman to a set of old wooden stairs I could just make out in the gloom. My soaked clothing was weighing me down as though I had just completed the 'swimming in your pyjamas' badge at school.

"Doctor," Allesandro called when I reached the bottom step.

I glanced back to see him peering through the hole, his arms on either side as he leaned through. His t-shirt was drenched and stuck to his body in a most interesting way, which was rather an inappropriate thing for me to notice given the urgency of the situation. I would later blame this on a surge of adrenaline on my part.

His hair dripped onto his face. I noticed that his knuckles were raw and bleeding where he had punched my escape hole into the wall. And yet I noticed the impossible.

The vampire was, unbelievably, smiling at me.

"What?"

"You look really good tonight."

Before I could swear at him, I saw movement and he turned away. Others had entered the storeroom, and I heard raised voices.

Without thinking, I dragged myself up the stairs, two at a time, abandoning Allesandro as he had told me to. Brave and noble, that's me.

At the top, there was a trapdoor. I prayed to every god I could think of that it wouldn't be locked. It wasn't.

I spilled out into another basement. I hadn't realised how deep underground Sanctum had been. This one was far more modern looking, well maintained and filled with general produce. Cartons of cigarettes, bottles, crates of snack bars.

I half ran along an aisle between the packages. There were stairs ahead of me, lit by a naked florescent strip. Running up them I shouldered the door at the top, and erupted into a brightly lit convenience store.

The cashier almost jumped out of his skin as I burst from the back room, scattering a display of cereal bars across the floor. He was a skinny young man, who had been sitting reading the newspaper, probably whiling away the wee hours of the morning and not expecting a drenched, wide-eyed woman to erupt from his storage room.

He opened his mouth to question me, his face filled with surprise. He pointed at me then the door, but I could hear footsteps in the cellar now behind me, hurrying. I didn't think it was likely to be Allesandro, so I didn't stop to explain or apologise.

I ran the length of the store, my wet shoes squeaking and slipping on the laminated floor tiles, and practically threw myself out of the glass front doors onto the blessed street. I had never been more grateful to be above ground and outside in the cold air.

Disoriented, I looked around wildly.

Further down the road to my left, there were large crowds milling around. Police were there and a fire engine, bathing everything in the dark night with strobing red and blue light. People were still emerging onto the street as the club ejected them into the night, sopping wet.

Looking back, I saw I had emerged from a 24-hour Spar, half the street up from the Eagle and Child. I was back on St Giles, the main strip of the vampire district. I stood shivering in the snow, not knowing what to do next.

Looking down the street, more and more clubbers were pouring out of the tiny pub which stood over Sanctum – their emergence almost an optical illusion, like a rave ending at the TARDIS. My eye suddenly caught sight of a figure, pale against the darkness of the mainly leather-clad crowd. It was Gio.

Like a spectre of death I saw his head turning this way and that, searching the crowds – obviously for me. He clearly had discovered I has escaped from Oscar and had assumed I was coming up and out through the pub. He was lying in wait.

Thank God for Allesandro's way out. But any second now Gio would glance my way, spot me standing here, and it would all be over. His mind would roll along the length of the street and root me to the spot. Game over.

I considered darting back into the Spar, getting back under cover, but there were raised voices from within now. Whoever had followed me through the hole was still in pursuit, and if Allesandro hadn't been able to stop them, I was fairly sure I wouldn't stand a chance. Vampire minions.

Well … shit.

I was having a hard time thinking how things could get worse, when I heard a screech of tyres and a car came tearing down St Giles from the north, the opposite direction of Sanctum's entrance. The bright yellow Ferrari squealed to a halt in front of me, executing a perfect 180 handbrake turn in a cloud of hissing rubber. I stared down stupidly as the passenger door flung itself open.

Inside, looking biblically furious, sat Veronica Cloves, my unwilling Cabal babysitter. She took in my appearance quickly. Drenched, shivering, my hair matted to my skull, blood from Oscar's face tinting the back of my head pink, plaster dust covering my hands and knees.

I don't think it would be possible for someone to look more pissed at me.

"Get … in … the … fucking … car …" she hissed through gritted teeth.

I glanced back towards Sanctum. Gio was standing like a ghost in the crowd, staring at me, his arms loose at his sides. His eyes were like headlamps.

I threw myself into the Ferrari and Cloves immediately floored the accelerator, peeling us away into the night before my door could even close.

16

The city tore by in a blur of streetlamps and lighted shop-fronts. I sat in the hand-stitched leather bucket seats of the extremely expensive car, dripping like a sodden rag and making a small puddle.

Every few seconds, I glanced behind us through the seats. Nobody appeared to be following us. Of course, with the reckless speed at which Servant Cloves was tearing through every traffic light I don't think anything could have kept up with us if it had tried.

The woman drove like a maniac. I didn't know if this was her usual manner, or if she reserved this style especially for when she was whisking inconvenient doctors away from angry vampires, but for the time being I was actually grateful. The more distance she could put between myself and Gio, the better.

I could feel Cloves seething quietly next to me. She hunched over the wheel, her knuckles white, her long nails a deep and garish purple.

"Were you *following* me?" I managed, when I had regained my breath and my heart had stopped slamming against my chest.

I wasn't particularly out of shape. I even jogged on occasion, but I had not had much practice fleeing vampires before, and the adrenalin in my system was starting to make me shake.

"Of course I was following you," she snapped, wrenching the car around a mini roundabout and heading out of the city centre towards the residential Northern Sector. "Good job as well. What the *hell* did you do?"

She shot me a murderous look.

"I didn't do anything!" I snapped back.

"You *set fire* to a vampire club?" she said accusingly. "That's what it looks like! You were supposed to be covertly gathering information! Is this your idea of *subtle*?"

"I never asked to be your spy!" I retorted. "If you wanted some secret agent who could blend into any culture, you should have bloody well used one! I'm a lab drone, remember? The only culture I'm comfortable with comes in a petri dish."

We swung a right so hard I was slammed sideways into the window. With shaky fingers I finally buckled my seatbelt. Safety first, right?

"And there was no fire," I argued. "*And* it wasn't me who set the sodding alarms off, it was the vampire from the lecture. He was trying to help me escape."

Cloves slowed the car a little as we headed uptown, turning onto Aristotle Lane. Other vehicles were still swerving to get out of her way. We cruised along at a comparatively steady eighty.

"Why were you trying to escape? You went there to see this GO in the first place?"

"I did. But that turned out to be a bad idea. He'd expected me to call him at night and arrange a rendezvous. He practically wet himself when I showed up at the club. Couldn't wait to get me out of there."

"Why?"

"His boss, the scary-looking fashion icon in the white suit. I don't know why, but he wanted me to come to the club. He found out Allesandro had contacted me, and when I called the club he made sure I got in, then strong-armed me into a corner and questioned me."

"De Medica?" Cloves eyes narrowed. "We have a pretty big file on this particular GO. What was he after?"

"Me!" I practically yelped. "Not that you seem very interested, but he actually told me he was going to kill me. Right there in the club. If I hadn't got out…"

We turned a right and the buildings around us, all post-wars, became far more affluent than I was used to. We were entering some kind of gated community, it seemed. Wherever we were headed, it wasn't home. This whole area used to be Port Meadow, one of Oxford's more picturesque districts: fields, hills, cute copses of trees. It was high rises now. Very expensive ones.

"He threatened you? Were there any witnesses?" Cloves demanded to know urgently. "We can bring him in on that if so."

I hesitated, aware I was about to sound foolish.

"No, not exactly." I muttered. "He … didn't say it out loud…"

"What are you talking about? He threatened to kill you but he *didn't* threaten to kill you?"

Cloves stared at me again. I really wished she would keep her gimlet eyes on the road. It would be ironic to escape being bled to death by a master vampire, only to die due to reckless driving by my getaway driver and have my body prised out of the grille of an oncoming taxi.

"I don't know how much you know about the GOs' … abilities," I explained. "Although judging from your pretty sketchy intel files, I'm guessing not much. But I discovered a fun fact tonight. Vampires, old shit-scary and bloody powerful ones anyway, can push down your mind with their own. It's not mind control, not exactly. Not hypnotism either, but I couldn't move, and I couldn't lie to him. It was like his bloody eyes were shooting truth serum at me."

Cloves hesitated, glancing from me to the road and back. She looked uneasy.

"Don't be ridiculous."

"Look, he made me answer all his questions, and he spoke inside my head," I insisted. "Whatever it is that got Trevelyan kidnapped, this guy knows about it – or knows *something* anyway, and he thinks *I* know."

I shivered, only partly from the cold.

"And another thing – he's pretty damn pissed about it too. The plan for the evening was to pump me for as much information as I had, and then to … dispose of me."

We pulled onto a private drive of a very tall, extremely well-appointed high rise apartment block. Cloves guided the car into an underground car park, the engine purring as she brought the car under cover, like a fish into dark water.

"Well, we can't touch him on something we have no proof of," she sounded irritated that I hadn't managed to elicit an audible death threat. "The red tape would be hideous. It would be a diplomatic incident. Shame you didn't get him to act violently with witnesses around."

Silly me, what had I been thinking?

I couldn't help but roll my eyes. Cloves turned to face me.

"What did he think you knew about?"

"The files," I answered. "Whatever the hell it was Trevelyan dumped in my workstation. Remind me to thank her for that by the way, if we ever find her alive. I'm thinking a gift basket maybe, or a hand grenade. My life was far too dull before she dragged me into her mess."

I rubbed my eyes. It was hard to see much in the darkness of the underground garage. The Ferrari's headlights cut a path ahead of us as we purred onward between other vehicles.

"I hope you've had a more successful evening than I have, because I'm now pretty bloody interested to know what's in those files that's apparently important enough to murder me over!"

"Still working on that," she said, still seeming less concerned that I had almost been vampire chowder, and more worried that I had caused a public scene.

I could see her Cabal mind working already, figuring out how to spin the incident on the DataStream, to smooth over any GO issues and not damage the tenuous inter-societal balance. My evening of peril was clearly overshadowed in her mind by the ballache of bad PR she was going to have to deal with.

"So what you're telling me is that this was a trap?"

She had finally pulled up in the silent strip-lit car park. We sat there with the engine idling as she worked my story through.

"The vampire who came to the lecture was clearly looking for Trevelyan, this Allesandro of yours. He found you instead, and practically led you by the hand to the club, where his boss could interrogate you. Find out what you know about whatever it is they are so interested in?"

"What? No, it wasn't like that," I spluttered. "He didn't want me at the club at all."

Cloves gave me a look of weary disdain.

"So you say. But perhaps he did. Maybe he got you there, but once his boss found out you neither had the precious files on you nor knew what they contained, your escape was conveniently engineered, in the hope you would then run straight to the files themselves, and they could re-apprehend you later at their leisure."

I didn't know much about my mysterious new vampire friend, other than that he was a remarkably flexible dancer, but I was pretty certain Cloves had this all wrong. I shook my head.

"It's not like that," I said. "There was something between Allesandro and Gio, bad blood maybe. I don't know what Allesandro wanted with me, but Gio was determined to get me away from him and pump me for information."

And later, pump me for blood, I added mentally. This, I reminded myself, is why I don't go out much.

"Harkness, you don't know how they work," Cloves sneered. "I've been doing this an awful lot longer than you have. They play you, Harkness. It's a game to their kind. De Medica is absolute clan *master*; if your precious Allesandro was being insubordinate in any way, he would be dead by now."

She considered this for a moment.

"Really dead, I mean," she clarified. "Decommissioned."

I had to admit, it *would* be out of character for any clan master to allow anyone beneath them to step out of line. Decommissioning, which never officially happened by the way, was the execution of a vampire. The unlucky undead was usually staked, immobilised, and left to face the sunrise.

Decommissioning never officially happened, by which I mean Cabal kept it out of the DataStream when it did. GO business was not our concern officially. No one noticed a pile of dust rolling down the street just after dawn anyway.

If Allesandro wasn't really working with Gio's best interests at heart, surely he would have been offed by his boss by now. Unless, my fevered mind insisted, Gio hadn't *realised* what he was up to until tonight, when my ill-timed phone call had dropped him right in it…

In which case, my enigmatic, mood-swinging undead buddy could be being hideously tortured by his own clan right now.

The thought of him being tortured made me feel queasy. I hoped it wasn't the case. But then if not, then surely Cloves was right and Allesandro was playing me like a flute for Gio.

Which do you prefer, Phoebe? The rebellious-against-his-evil-master yet now very dead or at least dying Allesandro, or the two-faced double-bluffing, treacherous but very alive Allesandro?

I shook my head to clear my thoughts. Jesus, did I even care either way? The man was a stranger to me.

But I did care. He was my only viable link to the vampire world. The only way we were going to find out what happened to my charming supervisor, and why.

"Where are we?" I asked, looking around at the garage.

"My place," Cloves said.

I must have looked shocked, because she became defensive.

"I could hardly take you back to your little flea-pit, could I? They'll be crawling all over it." I could imagine how little someone like Veronica Cloves wanted someone like me in her celebrity home.

"Now get the hell out of my car, Harkness. Your wet arse is warping the leather."

17

I didn't know much about Servant Veronica Cloves of Cabal, other than that she dressed in executive technicolor dominatrix chic, had a loud and garish car, and by all accounts, expensive but crass tastes. As a woman, she was professionally powerful enough to destroy me, and seemed to loathe me for the inconvenience I had lately been to her, thanks mostly to her rather sadistic boss.

If I had any preconceived notions of what her apartment would be like, I was wrong. My own tiny apartment was basically a messy pit, somewhere simply to sleep and eat in between my shifts at the lab. I wasn't much into interior design. But Cloves was in the public eye. I wouldn't have been surprised if her home had zebra-striped chaise-lounges, large ostentatious gilt mirrors and possibly a hideous modern flocked chandelier. All those graceless things which cost money, but proved over and over that money could not truly buy class.

I was surprised then, as the private, key-operated elevator finally opened on the top floor of the expensive high rise and I was practically pushed into her penthouse suite.

It was immense, a vast loft space. The far wall was entirely composed of sloping glass, but the room was rather understatedly decorated in creams and soft whites. Minimalist leather sofas looked rather lost in little islands of tasteful Art Deco furniture. The lighting was soft and carefully placed. To my right stood a tall open fireplace, fake of course, but tastefully rendered in angular white marble.

This room alone was five times the size of my whole flat. My feet sank into the light cream carpet, which was thicker and softer than my duvet. I was aware I was still dripping wetly onto it.

"Nice digs," I said as Cloves slammed the door behind me and busied herself with a complicated looking alarm panel, effectively sealing us in. "So ... this is what a Cabal salary gets you, huh? I am clearly in the wrong line of work."

Cloves ignored me. I crossed the huge room, past the sofas and end tables, skirting a large glass-topped workstation, which held a screen much like my own at the lab – only far more advanced and expensive. It looked nothing more than a smooth sheet of glass opened on the desktop like a music stand. It probably cost more than most of my lab equipment.

Approaching the floor-to-ceiling window, I placed my hands on the glass wall and peered out into the night. New Oxford lay below us, a glittering nightscape in the darkness. We were above most other buildings here. This entire part of the city was built after the Pale Wars.

It had been countryside before, the sweeping green skirt of Port Meadow and Burgess Field, hugging old Oxford, defined by the stately flow of the Thames to the west. But that was then. Our city had expanded itself a lot post-war, before we had finally built the wall and sealed ourselves off from the horror which lay outside. Other high rises surrounded us, sleek towers of glass and chrome, the homes of the powerful, rich and lucky. I was nestled in the elitist real estate of New Oxford.

Beyond this district, I could make out the distant familiar roof-scape of the city I knew. The stubby fat finger of Carfax tower, floodlit at this time of night, looking more like a squat Norman castle than a church. The multi-pointed rocket ship of St Mary the Virgin was just visible from here, reaching against the sky like a crusted stalactite from the bosom of the university. The circular dome of the Radcliffe Camera downtown, and the wide dark unlit sweep of the Botanic Gardens, a patch of inky blackness in the glittering night city.

All of this lay below and before me, along with other, more recent additions to our fair city. In the far distance, near to the great dark high curtain of the wall itself, I could make out the militaristic sentinel which used to be called the Angel of the North, a guardian sculpture which now held court over the upper districts. Far south of here, I could see the Liver Building, rescued from a different city on the brink of collapse to the Pale years ago. It was just visible beyond the river. Smack in the middle of what once had been South Park. Relocated to New Oxford, It now served now as a lesser division of Cabal's serving interests.

I had to admit, it was impressive what the Bonewalkers could achieve when they put their minds to it. Moving little pockets of time and space here and there, as though they were rearranging a jigsaw. It had been the only way to save some of the things which had once meant something to humanity

We had salvaged what we could before the Pale destroyed them. The Pepys building for instance, swept up from Cambridge just before the city-wide fires which had razed that beautiful place to the ground three years ago, and re-deposited in the Oxford University grounds along with most of Magdalene College. It would have been a shame to lose it all to flames. We had gathered what we could. Each walled city of Britannia was now home to refugee pockets of the old world.

Some people feared the Bonewalkers. People will always fear power, and the Bonewalkers were certainly powerful. But without them, we could never have built the wall. And without the wall … well, that way lay rabid screaming death, didn't it?

"It must be nice for you, to be able to stand here and look down on the rest of us," I said to Cloves, without turning around.

"Hands off the glass, Harkness," she responded curtly. "And I don't appreciate that comment. I don't know what issue you have with Cabal, or why you have it. We are Servants of the people of New Oxford."

"All of them?" I asked, half to myself, still staring out at the stunning view. "Or just a select few?"

"You have a real problem with authority, don't you?" she said, crossing to a chair.

She didn't sit in it, but stood with her hand on its tall back. I turned to face her.

"I'm surprised that your attitude has not got you into trouble before now," she sneered.

My eyes widened. I actually found this amusing.

"Trouble? Like this, you mean? You don't consider this trouble enough?"

Her face was a mask of scorn.

"You don't trust your own superiors," she said accusingly. "That much is abundantly clear."

I was too tired and strung out to be careful with my tongue.

"Right now, if I'm totally honest, I don't know *what* to think," I admitted. "My *superiors* have so far worked very hard to cover up the fact my boss has been kidnapped, tortured and, let's face it, probably killed. They have bullied me into putting my own safety on the line because I'm the only person they know who actually *knows* a vampire. And they have me being babysat by you of all people." I blew out my cheeks. "I don't know if I trust you less than the bloody vampires. At least I *know* they are trying to kill me. They seem fairly straightforward."

I wiped my nose.

"Some of them I mean."

"Sit down," Cloves commanded coldly.

I couldn't think of anything else to do at the time, and remaining standing just to be obstinate would have served no purpose other than to make me appear like a stroppy child, so I dropped onto a sofa. My legs were still jellified anyway.

"You think *we* are the bad guys here?" she said. "That maybe we're as bad as every twisted GO out there? That perhaps you can trust your charming Italian more than you can trust me?"

She came around the chair and stood in front of me.

"Well, allow me to illuminate you, Phoebe. If you are having trouble telling who are the good people and who are the bad people, start with this simple equation."

Her eyes were flashing with carefully controlled anger.

"*We* are people. They are *not*. It's really that simple. We are human, and we fight and we strive to keep humanity what it is. What's left of it…"

She pointed out of the window, presumably at vampirekind in general.

"They are *not* human. They are not *people*. They can *look* like people, they can *move* like people. But people do not do *this* to other people."

She reached up and unfastened the elaborately decorative black choker she wore. It wasn't until I saw her take it off that I realised I had never yet seen her not wearing it, even in DataStream shows.

She lowered her hands, holding the glittering beads, and I swallowed hard. Her neck, collarbone and throat was a riot of scar tissue. The woman looked as though she had been savaged by a wild dog. There had clearly been a lot of reconstructive work done, what looked like multiple surgeries, but the flesh was still a mess, with pale, wrinkled scars, one atop the next, making a strata of her skin.

Veronica Cloves stood watching me stare at her wounds. She looked oddly naked and defenceless without the choker on. Her imperfections utterly exposed. She hadn't just been bitten. She had been gnawed on, like an old bone. She stared at me angrily, her eyes practically daring me to look away.

"A vampire did this to me," she said, in a quieter voice. "A long time ago, before I was Cabal. Back when I thought they could integrate, that we were all basically the same underneath. He was charming, much like your sultry Italian friend. He was pretty too ... And I was careless."

She refastened the choker, hiding the hideous scars from view. I didn't know what to say to her. She didn't want my sympathy of course; she had been proving her point.

"They are *not* people," she said. "Not when the lights go out."

She turned away from me. I leaned forward in my chair a little.

"What happened?" I asked. "To the one who did ... *this* ... to you?"

"I killed him," she said simply, looking back. "The Cabal *are* the Servants of humanity. You may not like our methods, but we *will* protect the people of this city. *Whatever it takes* to do so, and that includes putting individuals in danger. For the good of many. We are perfectly willing to risk your safety, yes. Because what you have fallen into here is important. More important than you."

She sneered. "If you can conceive of that."

She stalked away, towards one of the doors which led off this main lounge.

"So what now?" I asked.

"It's three in the morning," she called back. "I strongly suggest you get some sleep. My techs should have finished decrypting Trevelyan's files by morning. We'll take things from there. And for God's sake, take a shower – you look a mess. You can take the guest bedroom."

"We're staying *here*?" I asked incredulously.

If you had told me a day ago that I would be having a slumber party with a high ranking Cabal member, I would have laughed in your face.

"Don't flatter yourself. You're hardly my ideal house guest, but for practicality's sake, it's safest," she said, pausing at the door. "The whole building complex is warded. It's easier to break into Blue Lab than it is to get in here."

She shut the door firmly behind her, leaving me alone in her magnificent penthouse, which I was trying to not think of as her evil mastermind lair. She hadn't even offered me a nightcap. How rude. Warded, eh? So the Cabal had Bonewalkers on payroll? That was unexpected. They were the only ones with enough power to ward a building, which in basic terms involved enclosing it in a bubble of space and time which was impassable for GOs.

Either Cloves was more paranoid than I thought about the perceived GO threat, or she knew more than I did about things.

Face it, Phoebe, I told myself, *everyone knows more about things than you do right now*. I was pretty sure Veronica the Vampire Slayer wasn't telling me everything she knew about our current situation.

I glanced over at her workstation. The idea of firing it up and snooping around in her private files occurred to me, but only fleetingly. No doubt she would have firewalls and encryption in place that made my own look like the old world's Hotmail, with 'password' as my password. Plus, I was too tired to try.

I sat up for a while in the silent room, staring out at the cityscape, curled on a sofa with my knees drawn up. I was wondering if Lucy got home okay.

Allesandro had told me he had got her out, before the alarm had been pulled. But then he could have been lying about that. Why would he have concerned himself with my friend? It would be a surprisingly thoughtful thing to do, and as Cloves and her raggedly chewed neck demonstrated, the GOs were not people. Not really. How had he even known I was there with a friend anyway? I hadn't mentioned it to him when we met on the dance floor.

I checked my phone, which had spent the evening tucked into the extremely tight leather pants I had borrowed from Lucy. There was no signal here. That would be the building wards. Landlines only I guessed. No missed call either. I hadn't really expected there to be.

I briefly considered calling Griff, but it was three am and he would be fast asleep. We were colleagues, not friends – it would have been weird. Lucy, however, I did call surreptitiously from Cloves' landline, but it went straight to voicemail. I left a message asking her to call me when she could.

This pretty much exhausted my social circle, so I gave up and wandered through the penthouse until I found the shower, which was glorious, huge, multi-jet and powerful. Cloves, earnest Servant of the good people, lived like a jewel-encrusted king, and as I scrubbed blood, sweat, plaster dust and sprinkler water out of my hair in her magnificent and heavenly shower, I was momentarily quite glad of it.

18

Waking up in a strange place is an unusual experience for me. Padding sleepily through someone else's home, wearing a black silk nightgown which brushed the floor, looking for coffee, I felt oddly dislocated, like I'd been cast in the wrong movie.

I missed my pjs. The nightgown I had borrowed had a dragon emblazoned on the back of it. Cloves continued to horrify me on many levels.

She was already up and dressed when I entered the lounge, sitting at her workstation in a black and white pinstriped suit. Her hair was its usual immaculate sleek black bob, her war paint ruthlessly applied. I was actually faintly relieved.

I couldn't imagine the acidic Veronica Cloves lounging bleary-eyed over a morning coffee with messy hair and bunny slippers. To see her like that would have made her somehow more human. She didn't strike me as a woman who was ever dishevelled. To be honest, I secretly suspected she slept in a suit. She didn't have shoes on, however, and I couldn't help but notice a small back swirl of a tattoo on her instep. The Mark of Cabal. Every Servant had them, rumour went. I'd never seen one before. They tended to be discreet. I couldn't quite make out what it was from across the room.

"It's about time you were up," she said as I entered, leaning bleary-eyed in the doorframe.

Not much of a greeting. The window-wall behind her was on fire with morning sunlight.

"What time is it?" I asked, hiding a yawn behind my hand.

"Six," she replied. "There's coffee in the kitchen. Drink some, and for God's sake, get dressed. You can borrow something of mine. We have a lot to do and I only have bad news for you."

Good morning to you too, I thought, drifting into the kitchen and thanking the whole host of heavenly minions for the heavenly aroma of vanilla coffee wafting from the percolator.

Everything in the kitchen was chrome and glass. It felt like I was back at the lab. I looked around as I leant on the counter, sipping the hot coffee as though it were the water of life.

There were no personal items anywhere in the kitchen either. Sure, there was the occasional Art Deco ornament here and there, but no framed photographs, no books or magazines. There were no notes stuck to the fridge, no magnets. No items of whimsy at all. It looked as though the apartment had come fully furnished and Cloves had not made a single homely addition to it. She was a busy woman evidently. Perhaps she didn't have time.

Six am, she'd said.

Good God, had I had just three hours sleep? No wonder I felt like death.

There was a DataStream screen built into the kitchen worktop. I passed my hand across it. I had missed the morning news, it seemed. They were re-running part of Cloves' interview from after the lecture.

The anchorwoman, whose unlikely name scrolling across the bottom of my DataStream appeared to be 'Poppy Merriweather', steepled her hands on the spotless desk. Always a sign that we were getting down to serious, beetle-browed journalism. The studio backdrop decorated with the familiar Cabal logo, an Art Deco take on Michelangelo's Vetruvian man. The new symbol for humanity. Emblazoned across it, the logo of Cabal. From Darkness Into Light.

"… and finally tonight, further dips in the ongoing energy crisis gripping all of Britannia caused disruption when the quarterly Cabal R&D release was plagued with technical problems." Merriweather told us this solemnly. Sitting beside her in the studio, looking warm and approachable in her plum suit, was Cloves herself, smiling ruefully.

"Of course, it's frustrating, Poppy, very frustrating," she said sadly. "The issues we are having with power, not only here, but all over Britannia right now, in every one of the Free Cities, are causing these spikes in energy, affecting even our own equipment, our very link to the public we serve." She looked into the camera, her eyes earnest and serious. If there was any doubt as to the sincerity of her servitude, it was there in this soulful gaze. "Cabal have always maintained one simple truth. The tenet of transparency. We are the Servants of the People. The people have a right to know the steps we are taking to ensure their safety, the advances our tireless researchers at Blue Lab are striving towards to ensure that together, we can all build a better tomorrow for humankind, and humankind's supporters, whoever they may be. This is the reason a segment of the public is present at every conference, this is the reason we insist on media coverage."

Yeah right, I thought. As long as it doesn't cover anything you don't want it to.

"You, the public, have a right to know. Too much was done, before the wars, behind closed doors. Too much was kept from the people at large, and we know all too well where that led us. It led us to the brink of our own extinction. To lose much of the workable footage from this evening's illuminating research and development report is an annoyance, yes, but we can at least ensure that the facts are reported."

There followed an enthusiastic discussion between the anchor and Cloves regarding Blue Lab's great leaps and bounds. Cloves was very enthusiastic. Her almost giddy eagerness was infectious.

There was no mention of the vampire gatecrasher, of course.

"As it is, you only have my interpretation for now, until the written paper is released next month of course," Cloves continued. "I can only tell you this. Epsilon has exceeded our expectations. We are still interpreting all the data, but so far, the results have been practically explosive, if you'll excuse my colloquialisms. I'm no scientist, I'm afraid!" She actually gave a little titter, which made my skin crawl right off my body this time and across the floor.

"Thank you, Servant Cloves. I'm afraid that's all we have time for. Please do give our regards to Director Trevelyan," Merriweather said. "I understand she is under the weather at the moment and was unable to give the quarterly in person as usual, although from what footage we have recovered, it seems Doctor..." she glanced almost imperceptibly at her notes, "... Harkness did a fine job standing in at the last moment."

"Oh yes," Veronica Cloves smiled again, straight into the camera. "She's definitely one to keep an eye on."

Miming a gag, I flicked the DataStream off and finished my coffee.

When I returned to the guest bedroom, I noticed that Cloves had laid out clothing on the bed for me. I couldn't really redress in Lucy's borrowed clothes from the night before. They were pretty much ruined.

I had been trying not to think about wearing the Cabal fashionista's hand-me-downs. I had seen how she dressed, like Cruella De Vil on acid. It wasn't my look. But through some sense of good grace, or maybe because she thought there was no way I could pull off her vibe, Cloves had left me tailored black pants and a fairly nondescript long-sleeve black silk top. It was mercifully demure for her, barring the thick gold belt, the clasp of which was a crocodile swallowing its own tail.

Ah well. When in Rome, dress like a Las Vegas gangster's wife, as they say. At least we were roughly the same size. It would do until I could get home and changed into something less … silky.

I scraped my hair back into a loose ponytail, and by the time I had dressed and wandered back into the main room, Cloves was standing by the white marble fireplace waiting for me, looking in her striped suit like an impatient and angular humbug. Above the fireplace there was a large, wall mounted DataStream screen. She looked as though she were going to give a presentation.

"Sit," she instructed, without the merest titter or twinkle of her on-screen alter-ego. "Are you aware of the GO rights movement?"

I eased into a chair, wishing desperately that I'd grabbed another coffee on the way.

"Of course," I replied.

The GOs worked in our city; vampires and Bonewalkers mainly, but some others too. They held jobs, they ran businesses, they even owned property, but technically they were here as our 'guests'. They could contribute to our economy but they couldn't vote and they certainly couldn't hold office. They may have their own separate society but they couldn't get any real foothold in ours.

The GO rights movement were a collection of sympathetic human campaigners, fighting for the ability for GOs everywhere to be recognised as equal citizens. They were largely peaceful, staging protests, holding rallies, distributing GO-friendly literature.

They had picketed Blue Lab at one point last year, waving placards and chanting about the evil and unethical work we presumably did. It was what had led the Cabal to step in and engage in the 'open policy' approach, with the quarterly R&D lectures showing our good-natured findings to the human public at large, so that we could convince them that our work was solely to eradicate the Pale, not to harm any *natural* GO.

The idea had been that if we were upfront and open, we couldn't be accused of anything underhanded. It had kind of worked. The GO rights movement had largely left us alone this past year. They had stopped demonising us as evil mad scientists.

These days they tended to harass the church and they were always at loggerheads with the Mankind Movement, their polar opposites, who basically thought that all GOs needed to be ejected from our walled cities and left to fend for themselves in the wild against the Pale … conveniently overlooking the fact that without GOs, we all would have been dead years ago.

Veronica Cloves clicked a remote control and the DataStream screen lit up, showing a photograph of a young woman. She was twenty-something with long brown hair in dreadlocks, ultra-hip black-rimmed glasses, and a very stern and somewhat earnest expression. I'd never seen her before.

"This is Jennifer Coleman," she advised. "She's *very* active in the GO rights movement. She's been arrested three times for breach of the peace and twice for common assault. She's your standard hummus-eating hippie who thinks that vampires are just nice, misunderstood folk with sensitive skin."

Cloves' disapproval was evident.

"She's basically an enormous pain in everyone's arse. Jennifer Coleman was responsible for staging the three week camp out in the Botanical Gardens last summer, which got all of that news coverage, despite our best efforts. She's also been accused, though nothing was every proven, of tampering with gate deliveries at the wall, ensuring those few luxury supplies which we are still able to get did not reach their intended buyers within the city."

"Let me guess, the intended buyers were Mankind Movement fans?"

I had read about this in the papers earlier this year. Sabotage at the wall always made the headlines. Several large corporations had their expensive summer balls ruined by the lack of produce. I bet Cloves had felt the lack of olives. It was a bit of a first world problem as far as I was concerned.

"Fascinating stuff," I said. "I like the dreadlocks. Very urban guerrilla protester. But *why* am I looking at a photo of her?"

"Because she's missing," Cloves said, tapping the remote control she still held against her chin a couple of times. "Well, most of her is missing. A box of teeth was delivered to Blue Lab at 5am this morning. I've been on the phone to Servant Harrison, who is overseeing things there. He advises tests have been run and they match the public dental records of this woman."

I stared at the photograph.

"Another one?" I said, feeling suddenly sick. "Was there a video? A DataStream note like with Trevelyan?"

Cloves shook her head.

"Not this time, just a packet of teeth. I have no idea *why* they are being sent to Blue Lab, but this woman has clearly been taken by the same person ... or persons ... as our missing Trevelyan. This has all happened this morning. We don't know much else."

Cloves stared at me expectantly.

"But this doesn't make sense," I said. "I mean there's no connection between them. I doubt very much that Vyvienne Trevelyan had *any* interaction with the GO movement, let alone this woman herself. She was *not* a fan of the GOs, trust me."

Cloves clicked off the screen.

"Well, it seems we don't know as much about your old boss as we thought we did, do we?" she pointed out. "Why would she wipe her entire work database before she disappeared? Why hide information on a subordinate's workstation? We have *no idea* what she was mixed up in. Not until the files are decrypted."

I wondered if Trevelyan and this woman, the new victim Jennifer Coleman, were both dead. I was pretty sure in my heart of hearts that they were. Nothing left but their teeth, randomly posted to us at Blue Lab as ... what? Gruesome trophies? A warning? What did the teeth signify? None of it made sense.

"Is this in the media yet?" I asked.

Cloves, the Cabal Spin Doctor extraordinaire, raised her eyebrow disdainfully.

"I'm keeping a lid on what I can, for as long as I can." She looked sour at this. "Which is a full time pain in my arse. This sort of news doesn't stay quiet for long. So far, all that's public knowledge is that Jennifer Coleman, champion of the cuddly vampires, has gone missing. That was

120

on the DataStream this morning. One of her camp has reported it as very 'out of character'. They don't know that the inside of her face is in a box at our lab. And as far as anyone in the general public is concerned, Vyvienne Trevelyan is on a well-earned holiday. The same spiel has been given to all employees at the lab, barring you."

She stared at me sharply.

"If this gets out, that the hippie Helsing activist Coleman has been kidnapped, mutilated and likely killed by a GO, it would be incendiary. The GO rights movement would be in uproar. Conspiracy theories, rioting in the streets, who knows what else? This woman is like some kind of saint to them."

Cloves rubbed the bridge of her nose, pacing the floor.

"The Mankind Movement would leap on it as evidence of the GOs' evil nature. Clashes between the two factions would be inevitable."

She made the word sound apocalyptic.

"Cabal and, by extension, your precious Blue Lab would be caught right in the middle of the whole steaming pile. How would we explain our involvement, why we have two morgue lockers full of teeth?"

She stopped marching up and down in front of the screen to stare me down, pointing the remote control at me to emphasise her words.

"We need to get on top of this *now*," she said. "This isn't just some random serial killer, I'm sure of it. There's a bigger agenda at play here."

"So what do we do?" I asked.

"We?" she blinked at me, her expression incredulous. "Listen, Harkness, I pulled your fat out of the fire last night at the GO club because right now, you are the *only* tenuous link I have to the GOs. But let me make sure you have this straight: we are *not* partners on this. There is no 'we'. *I* am going to HQ to see what we've got on these bloody encrypted files. *You*, Doctor, are going to work. Act normal, do your day job, and when the sun goes down and the vamps are up, call your bloody source."

"Allesandro?" I was taken aback. "You seriously want me to contact him again? You told me last night you didn't trust him and that I shouldn't either."

"That's true, I don't and you shouldn't," she said. "But we *were* right to sniff around him. His boss is clearly involved in this somehow. We need his intel, whatever it is. Arrange another meeting."

She held up her hands to silence me before I could protest.

"Just … be more *subtle* this time."

She folded her arms and glared at me.

"You'll be on your own tonight. I won't be there to watch your back. I have a fundraiser to go to."

"I'm sorry, a fundraiser?" I asked incredulously.

This seemed a little out of left field when I had just been told that the evil tooth-fairy had struck again.

"I have a day job to maintain too," she grimaced. "As Cabal's PR. I have an interview with that bloody Channel Seven reporter at noon, and then this evening I'm representing the Cabal at Marlin Scott's business expo. I can't shirk my other duties just to chase vampires around the city with you."

Marlin Scott was a name I knew. He was a powerful figure in our city, a wealthy entrepreneur and high society blue-blood businessman who had made his sizeable fortune designing the gate technology for the wall. He had worked closely with the Bonewalkers on its construction. Nothing makes you rich more than being the only person able to keep the hordes of mutant death at bay.

Marlin Scott now owned roughly half the industry in New Oxford. He was also, if I remembered correctly, a very vocal Mankind Movement campaigner.

"Will you call me when you decrypt the files?" I asked.

The Cabal Servant looked at me as though I were something she had accidentally stepped in.

"I'll call you if I have any *use* for you," Cloves replied.

Honestly, it truly warmed me to the heart how close we two had become of late.

19

I took a taxi and headed back to my place to change before I headed into the lab. I figured it would be safe enough during daylight when all the GOs were 'sleeping', and I sure as hell wasn't going to turn up to work dressed like Joan Collins. I'd had quite enough of wearing other people's clothes in the last twenty four hours.

My flat was a shambolic mess. For a moment I wondered if Gio and his vampire clan had come round last night and turned the place over, maybe looking for me or the mystery files, but then I remembered it always looked like this. I really had to get around to tidying.

There were no messages on my answer phone, which worried me a little. Not that is was usually full, but Lucy hadn't called me back. Had she got home alright after the club? I reasoned she had probably gone it alone after we got separated, probably onto another club. She was a seasoned Helsing, I had to remind myself. She could probably look after herself.

Probably.

I wasn't reassured. I was such a bad liar, I couldn't even lie to myself.

It was past ten by the time I got to Blue Lab, scanned myself in, descended to BL4 and made my way along our ultraviolet corridor.

I felt inexplicably guilty as I entered the lab proper and saw Griff at his station, same as always in his white lab coat, his glasses reflecting the data which currently surged across his screen. Everything looked normal. I fervently hoped Lucy hadn't mentioned anything to him about our painting the town red.

"Morning boss," he said, looking up as I entered. "I wondered if I was the only one bothering today. Did you get that admin done for Trevelyan yesterday okay? We missed you down here at the coal-face."

"Admin?" I asked, blinking at him blankly for a second before I remembered my excuses for leaving yesterday. "Oh yes … That. Fine."

I frowned as I shrugged out of my coat, glancing at the empty workstation.

"What do you mean the only one bothering? Where's Lucy?"

Griff shrugged, unconcerned, not looking up from his screen.

"Hasn't shown up yet," he said simply. "What with the scary old bulldog, Trevelyan, and you both avoiding the office lately, I half-wondered if the three of you had gone off to form a travelling circus."

He stuck out his bottom lip, making it tremble.

"I sure been awful lonely, Doc," he said in a fake American accent. "But hey, you're in now, and you're going to be glad you bothered."

He was smiling at me like it was Christmas morning. I immediately felt suspicious.

"Why, what is it?"

"I have some *very* interesting results for you."

I was deeply worried about Lucy, but I tried not to let it show.

"What results?" I asked, slipping my lab coat on.

Griff led me excitedly to the rat pens, practically dancing with contained excitement. The pens are located at the rear of BL4, where we keep all our test subjects in a tall bank of individually stacked cages.

"Say good morning … to Brad." Griff grinned with a flourish.

I peered into the numbered cage. A large white rat stared back at me placidly, its tiny eyes like drops of blood.

This was astonishing in itself because all around it, the other twenty-two rats were throwing their little bodies violently around their respective cages, slamming against the walls repeatedly. Their flanks were matted with scabs and crusted blood, muzzles pink with foam.

This was the usual state of the rats in our lab: frenzied, violent, and dangerous. We had made them this way. Each was deliberately infected with DNA samples taken from the Pale.

Cruel yes, I'm sure P.E.T.A wouldn't approve, but how else were we going to develop a successful retardant? The sacrifice of a few for the good of the many, right? And yes, I'm aware I sound like Veronica Cloves.

Angelina had been just like them, furious and rabid, until we had injected her with the Epsilon strain. She had calmed for a couple of hours at least. Right before she exploded in an exciting, artistic, but scientifically redundant manner.

"*This* is Brad?" I stared, open-mouthed.

The calm rodent delicately cleaned its long muzzle with a tiny paw. He was a model of normalcy. I stared at Griff, wide-eyed.

124

"How long has he been like this?"

Griff checked his watch.

"Nineteen hours, thirty minutes," he said proudly. "Angelina lasted four hours before she went critical."

"Is this Epsilon?" I said.

He nodded.

"I ran the numbers again, like you told me to. I checked our existing data against the dailies that we'd gathered overnight. You weren't here to consult, but I had the idea to reduce the potency of the inhibitor. I took a bit of a leap. It's basically a more diluted version of Epsilon, but conversely a larger dose. I've sent the figures to your workstation."

He was leaning down next to me, peering into the cage proudly like God looking at Adam. He smelled faintly of the cinnamon bun he'd had for breakfast, mixed with chemicals. My eyes were glued to the non-homicidal rat, but I could *feel* Griff grinning next to me.

"This is our best result so far."

"Don't jinx us!" I said, swatting him on the arm, but I couldn't help but be astonished.

I wasn't going to jump for joy and declare Brad the first rat to ever be successfully cured of the Pale virus, but this was astonishing work. If we had managed to develop a workable retardant…

"Maintain this dosage," I instructed my assistant. "This is bloody excellent work, Griff. Clearly I need to leave you alone with the rats more often."

"Yeah, thanks for that, boss," he said wryly with a roll of his eyes. "Hey, how about we go wild? A celebratory Starbucks?"

I agreed, if only because it got Griff out of the lab and off on an errand for a while. With Lucy absent, there was something I wanted to do in private.

I know I should have been grinning. This could be the biggest scientific breakthrough since the wars began if it panned out. This was my life's work, for God's sake, my magnum opus.

Yet all I could think about right now was the GO rights protester Jennifer Coleman and Trevelyan. Two women and a pair of pliers wielded by a vampire killer who was surely even less pleasant than the one who had mind-melded me last night.

There was something I wanted to do.

As soon as Griff left the lab, I fired up my workstation. He had indeed sent me the figures for the revised Epsilon formula. I fully intended to look over them just as soon as people stopped being inconveniently kidnapped and tortured around me. But for now I guiltily dismissed the data. Instead, I opened my most secret and invisible sub-sectors and data files.

I wasn't entirely stupid and I still didn't trust Cabal to tell me anything they didn't need to. When I had initially found the files Trevelyan had dumped on my station and transferred them to a data stick for Cloves, I had also made a copy for myself at the same time.

It was still heavily encrypted and there was nothing I could do to unscramble it on my own, but what had caught my eye at the time had been what was *attached* to the encrypted file. Trevelyan's Blue Lab security clearance codes, all of them.

I had been told by Servant Leon Harrison that Trevelyan was head of other, more 'sensitive', departments than just my own little kingdom. Now I wanted to know what other pies she'd had her fingers in.

With a deft flick across the screen, I sent the codes to the printer. My heart was racing, expecting an alarm to go off somewhere in the building or for Griff to reappear at the wrong moment. Stealing higher clearance at Blue Lab is pretty much treason. I wouldn't have been surprised if my monitor had fired a death ray at me.

However, nothing happened other than a security pass sliding innocently off the printer, bearing my boss' name, a rather unflattering photographic likeness and about a thousand megabytes of data squeezed into an elaborate barcode. The printer had even laminated the pass for me, which was so thoughtful I gave it a little pat of approval.

Nervously I pocketed the swipe-pass, shoving it deep down into my lab coat pocket. As an afterthought, I deleted my print history from the workstation. I had no idea how effective this was, but it made me feel slightly better.

I re-hid the encrypted files and read through the clearance codes.

BL4 Toxicology; this was us, obviously. *BL10 M.A*; no idea what that was. *BL26 Archives*; pretty self-explanatory. *BL29 Development*; same again.

So Trevelyan had been busy in, or had at least had access to, four separate departments including our own. We barely knew what the other parts of Blue Lab were working on. Everything was sensitive here, everything classified. Anyone working in any given sector, on any given level, only knew their own work.

After sitting at my workstation for a while, tapping the laminated pass nervously against the table and occasionally glancing over at Brad the rat who was determinedly not exploding, I decided to bite the bullet and stop being a complete pussy.

It was time to take a walk.

I haven't always made the most sensible decisions. Returning to the ground floor atrium, getting into a different access elevator and swiping Vyvienne Trevelyan's extremely personal security pass, I reasoned, was possibly the most stupid so far.

The amount of trouble I could get myself into for breaking protocol like this was mind-bogglingly immense, but I'm a scientist; curiosity is my nature. At random I pressed the button for level 10. MA. It seemed as good a place to start as any.

I was actually surprised when the lift began to smoothly descend. I had half expected that Cabal would have rescinded my boss' clearance the second she had gone AWOL. I pictured metal bars descending with a clang and trapping me guiltily in the elevator until a troop of stone-faced security Ghosts turned up to escort me to Leon Harrison to explain myself. Cloves was a pain in my backside, Harrison actually scared me.

But the lift, evidently satisfied that I was Trevelyan, dropped me down into the darkness gracefully. I guess Cabal hadn't counted on anyone else having access to her clearance.

The doors pinged open ten stories below street level. I took in my surroundings.

There was no plushly carpeted reception area here, no potted plants. It was nothing like the level where I'd had my cosy meeting with the nameless Godfather. Luckily it also wasn't like BL4, my level, with its palm-reader pad and iris scanner security. Here there was just a long concrete corridor, with heavy metal doors set either side. It looked like I had stumbled into the boiler room or some kind of maintenance level.

No one seemed to be around to question me, which was good as I hadn't bothered to think up any reason to be down here. For good measure, I clipped Trevelyan's ID to my coat and made my way forward, my lab shoes making hushed whispers on the bare concrete floor.

The doors were locked and windowless on both sides, I tried them all. They were numbered like cells in functional black stencils. At the far end of the long corridor, once I had passed ten or more doors on either side, the corridor opened into a circular area with bank of workstations. They were all unmanned, but one of the screens was lit.

I glanced around. To my left, beyond the workstations, the corridor continued around a bend and presumably deeper into whatever this complex was. Whoever was meant to currently be on duty here was absent. Maybe they had gone to stretch their legs or take a bathroom break, grab a coffee. Ah well. Their prostate problem was my blessing.

I slid into the chair and ran my hand across the screen to activate it. The system purred awake and silently demanded identification.

I swiped Trevelyan's pass on the side of the glass monitor. Words appeared on the screen.

Trevelyan, Vyvienne. Welcome.

Below the words, an empty box with the dreaded description: *Password.*

Crap.

My fingers hovered over the keys. I had no way of knowing what Trevelyan's password might be. I knew next to nothing about the woman, other than that she made my life unpleasant on a daily basis.

On the off-chance that the universe had a sense of irony, I typed 'password'.

The screen flashed red, and then returned to the login screen.

Incorrect password, attempt 1 of 3.

I hadn't really expected anything else.

Hmm, think this through, Phoebe. This woman had heavily encrypted data and hidden it in my workstation. Whatever her password was, it wasn't going to be something as simple as her first pet cat's name or her favourite movie star.

I checked the code printed along the barcode on her swipe pass. It was fourteen digits long. I typed them in.

Again the screen flashed red.

Incorrect password, attempt 2 of 3.

Shit. This was always a lot simpler in the movies.

I looked around nervously, acutely aware that any second someone could turn up and catch me in the act. Plus, surely Griff would be arriving back in the lab soon with my coffee. I really didn't have any more time to waste down here.

I rather hated Trevelyan for getting me mixed up in all of this in the first place. Why on earth she decided to hide her secret files on *my* workstation, I had no idea. Why make me take the R&D lecture instead of her? She had clearly given *my name* to her torturer, Evil Pliers Guy. Why else would he have mentioned me by name in the DataStream clip?

In a moment of inspiration, my fingers twitched. I typed in the box and hit enter.

Password: Harkness

Password Accepted

To my surprise, I was in. Information rolled across the screen, files and subfolders galore. It was like Pandora's box opening in front of me. I frowned at what I was seeing.

+ Gamma Strain test results, subjects 01-50

+ Delta Strain field test results

+ Gamma Strain results, side effects on subjects 20-40

There were countless others. I clicked open a file at random and scan read the date.

This was *my* work. All the work my team had done at Blue Lab; the failed retardants, the cures we had tried which hadn't worked but which had had other, less *desirable* effects.

The data had been transferred down here and from the detailed schematics I was now seeing rolling through these files, they had used it to make designs for handheld weaponry, modified military vehicles, light aircraft. Everything I had ever retired as not fitting or useless, every strain of virus I had mutated and tampered with before discarding, they were being further developed.

My hand froze on the screen as I realised what I was looking at.

Blue Lab was weaponising my work. In my fight to cure the Pale, I had been helping develop chemical warfare. To use against the Pale? Or against anyone the Cabal saw fit?

The air down on this level was cold. Goosebumps had risen on my arms. So that's was what 'MA' was.

Military Application.

I clicked open the file titled '*Delta Strain test results*' and, with some trepidation, read the reports.

The Delta Strain has been *almost* successful when we tried it on the rats. It had calmed the Pale in large doses, and made them manageable. The problem we had with it was that it had calmed them to the point of coma and then death. What use was a retardant which reduced its subjects to dribbling mindless vegetables, I had thought? Useless. Evidently someone amongst the higher powers disagreed with me.

The files before me detailed the further development of Delta. It had been weaponised as an aerosol. There had been field testing, according to the data, and it had been in Cambridge; crop dusting the city for blanket coverage of the populated areas.

My eyes stared at the words scrolling in front of me.

Pale Eradication level: 74%.

Human Civilian Casualties: 89%.

Protocol Rejected.

Refinement needed, further development required for effective combatant usage. Suggested downgrade to handheld gas canister/grenade dispenser for localised cleansing solution.

The date of the field test was three years ago.

Three years ago, the year that the city of Cambridge had burned to the ground in uncontrolled fires. A terrible tragedy. Fires had been started by the Pale, rampaging through the city, or so we had all been told by the Cabal over the daily DataStream.

My hands were shaking.

They had killed all those people? To stop the Pale from spreading, to *experiment*?

This was friendly fire on a massive scale. No, this was chemical warfare. And we, the rest of the world, had never even known it had happened. They had experimented on a human population at war with the Pale, exposing the mutants and the people alike to the retardant.

I pictured the city, filled with fallen bodies. Humans and Pale lying together, every one of them reduced to drooling mindless creatures, physically and mentally ruined. And then came the fires, of course, to hide the evidence, to cleanse the strain away, to get rid of the bodies.

My mind was reeling.

I clicked open another file. A list scrolled before me:

Gamma strain side effects on subjects 20-40
Subject One: Deceased
Subject Two: Deceased
Subject Three: Deceased
Subject Four: Deceased.

The world rolled along, a roll call of death. These were not rats. These were actual Pale, as far as I could judge. I became blind to that word until, right at the end of the list, something changed.

Subject Twenty: Damaged.
Held for further testing. Room Four.

I clicked on this subject.
Gamma Strain had been useless to us and, apparently, also to the military guys who were poaching my work as well, assuming of course that they had higher ambitions than killing off the Pale one monster at a time.

Room Four, Subject 20.
+ Hostility 100%
+ Sedation 90%
Observation requested: Y/N

My finger hovered over the option for a moment. I had already learned more than I ever wanted to know, but I had come this far...
I selected observation.
A sudden noise behind me, a whirring hydraulic rush, made me jump almost out of my skin. I span, half crouched in surprise. In the long corridor of locked doors behind me, there was now an oblong of light. I had clearly just opened door number four.
Lucky me.
Not wanting to leave the workstation open, I logged off, grabbed Trevelyan's swipe card, and made my way slowly back along the corridor. My mind was still reeling.
Cambridge ... good God, was that really true?

I was not sure what was going to be in Room Four but I was pretty sure that whatever it was, I wasn't going to like it.

The room hadn't opened, not really. The heavy metal door had indeed slid to one side and into a recess. My way into the room, however, was blocked by a thick pane of glass.

The room beyond was small and dark. The floor, walls and ceiling were all bare and tiled, like a wetroom. There was even a small drain in the centre.

Curled in one corner of this strange cell, rocking back and forth like a lunatic in an asylum, there was a thin figure, naked and very emaciated. Its skin was a mottled pale grey. It was tall, male and utterly hairless, it's sinewy arms and legs like bunched coils of wire, its sunken chest and protruding ribs heaving in a fast rhythm, like a dog panting fast. The crouching figure was covered in a sheen of sweat, making it look oiled and feverish, its bald bullet of a head tucked between its knees, with long fingers clasped over the back of its head protectively.

I took a step back from the glass, horrified as realisation dawned as to what I was seeing. The fingers and toes, I now saw, were elongated, far longer than any normal humans. They ended in wicked-looking claws. I couldn't help but gasp and at that small noise, the intake of my breath, the creature's head whipped up immediately.

Its face was monstrous; sunken hollow eyes, black from lid to lid, above a collapsed nose, upturned like the cavity of a skull. It had no lips, its mouth merely a mass of scar tissue from which large, sharp teeth protruded, too many for its face, like a shark grinning.

It was one of the Pale.

They used to look human when we first made them, but that didn't last long. They had mutated further during the years since the collapse of the old civilisation and the wars that followed. None of them had lips now, they chewed them off themselves, making their faces nightmarish death-heads, ghoulish and oddly naked.

It stared at me for a second and we both stood frozen, eyes locked across the small space. Then, with terrifying speed, the Pale leapt up from its crouch, throwing itself across the cell and hurling violently into the plate glass, which shuddered and boomed in a muffled way.

I stumbled backwards instinctively, arms held up defensively to shield myself from the expected attack, and fell on my backside, slamming into the floor against the opposite wall of the corridor. It took me a moment to realise it hadn't gotten me.

The glass hadn't shattered. It must be reinforced, bulletproof even.

The creature thrashed against it frantically, its head slamming again and again against the barrier, teeth gnashing at the smooth surface, leaving bloody trails of spittle smeared across the glass as it tried in vain to get at me. Its arms and legs beat against the wall vehemently and relentlessly, making it wobble each time. The long claws scraping against the surface, it was like a mad dog and it wanted nothing more than to tear into me and rip me apart.

My heart felt like it was going to explode. Shakily, I felt for the wall behind me and slid myself up to my feet.

There was a Pale. Right here in the city. In the fucking lab where I worked every day!

This mutant – the embodiment of rage and hunger, a spectre of living death – growled and keened, furious and desperate, unable to understand why it could not reach me through the transparent barrier. It flung its wiry body against the glass again and again.

I stared at it, frozen in horror, convinced that any second the glass was going to smash.

A few more seconds passed and then there was a loud hiss, a pale mist erupting out of the small drain in its cell behind the monster, diffusing through the room.

The creature struggled a while longer and then began to twitch, as though losing control of its limbs. It shook its head in confusion, losing coordination, and after a few moments, fell backwards into the thin mist. It hit the ground hard, gasping and gnashing its teeth, arms and legs flailing wildly around, fighting the thin air as it fell into convulsions.

The mist poured into the room until eventually the Pale lay immobile on the floor, bucking its hips and gnashing its horrible long teeth. Its skeletal, naked body twitched and jerked painfully, as though being electrocuted.

With monumental effort, it managed to roll onto its stomach and I watched as it dragged itself laboriously back into the corner, where once again it curled up on its side in a foetal position, hacking and spasming against the pervasive, relentless mist.

Gamma Strain at work. A paratoxic nerve gas.

The metal door slid back across the glass with a hiss, cutting off the nightmare vision, and locked itself in a very final and thorough way. Observation complete, I gathered.

I'd seen enough. I felt as though I was going to throw up, my legs barely holding me upright. I stood, propped against the wall in the suddenly quiet corridor, trying to catch my breath.

Movement in the corner of my vision made me jump. My panicked mind was convinced that it was another of the creatures, somehow loose in the corridor, and that any second it would be on me, tearing, ripping me open and burying its snapping jaws in my soft wet insides.

It wasn't one of the Pale, however. It was a regular human person, back at the workstations I had just left. A woman, she had appeared around the bend and was staring at me in surprise.

"Dr Harkness?" she asked, incredulous. "Is that you?"

I stared at her stupidly. For a moment, my mind was completely blank. But then she smiled at me, and my brain kicked into gear.

"Melanie?"

Trevelyan's young assistant, she of the impossibly pert chest, adorable dimples and perfect hair. Part of me wanted to run over to her and hug her fiercely, gibbering insanely about monsters. The other part wanted to run away, to scarper like the trespasser I was. What she was doing down here, I had no idea. She was evidently thinking the same of me, and was peering at me quizzically.

"I've not seen you down here before," she said.

She looked around at the utilitarian corridor we stood in, frowning slightly.

"Grim as hell, isn't it? I hate it down here. I keep thinking I'm going to turn a corner and run into a serial killer. Hey, are you looking for Vyvienne?"

I nodded, tucking a pale strand of hair behind my ear and trying to regain my composure.

"In a manner of speaking," I managed.

"I think she's on sabbatical," Melanie said, friendly enough. "Some Cabal bigwigs have been in her office these last couple of days. I think they're picking up her stuff while she's away."

She looked back towards the workstations, as though checking if anyone could hear,

"To be honest, they give me the creeps, skulking around her offices, breathing down my neck all day. One of them sent me down here to pick up her personal effects."

She rolled her eyes as she walked towards me, her smart heels clicking on the concrete floor, a black box file hugged to her chest.

"Because, you know, I've got nothing better to do with my day than pick up my absent boss' dry-cleaning tickets and cinema stubs. Did the Cabal guys send you down too?"

I nodded again, it seemed the safest route. In a moment of inspiration I brandished Trevelyan's swipe card.

"Can you *believe* she left this down here?" I said, trying my best to sound incredulous. "She doesn't even know it but I'm saving her ass picking it up for her. If they even find out upstairs that she left this thing lying around, that would be..." I paused for dramatic effect, "... *it*."

I raised my eyebrows, trying to look disapproving. Sweat was pouring down my back.

"Oh my God," Melanie looked shocked. "Her *swipe*? That's not like her."

"I know, right? I have to admit though," I added conspiratorially, "I quite like the idea of the boss lady owing me a favour, so please for the love of God, don't mention to anyone I was down here getting this. She asked me to be *discreet*."

She shook her head.

"God, no, of course not. Wow!"

We walked to the elevator together.

"I don't know what's got into her lately," Melanie sighed. "Taking off at a moment's notice like this, leaving things lying around."

She smiled and shook her head ruefully.

"It's a good job she has dogsbodies like you and me, eh Doctor, picking up after her?"

We entered the lift and she hit the button for the atrium. I watched the doors slide closed gratefully. I could not get away from the MA Level and its horrors fast enough.

"Well," I reasoned as we ascended, "between you and me, she's been under a lot of stress what with the quarterly R&D. I just think maybe she needs a little time off."

I glanced at the box file Melanie was carrying.

"So that's all the personal junk she left down there?"

She nodded.

"Hey," I tried to sound as light and casual as possible. "I have to swing by her place anyway to drop off her swipe, why don't you let me take those too? Saves you a job."

Melanie peered at me.

"But I figured the Cabal guys would want to look over it?"

"What, Trevelyan's lunch receipts and handwritten notes?" I said dismissively. "I highly doubt it. Not when everything is backed up on DataStream these days. They probably just don't want personal effects down there cluttering up the labs. It's hardly professional."

The lift doors opened, and we were back on ground level in the brightly lit circular atrium where no violent monsters were trying to eat me. Bliss.

Melanie looked unconvinced.

"I have the Cabal guys sniffing around too," I said. "While our mutual captain is away, I'm reporting in to Veronica Cloves, if you can believe it. I'll run the details past her for you."

Melanie looked impressed, as though I'd mentioned her favourite celebrity.

"Really? *The* Veronica Cloves? Wow. I've seen her on the DataStream. She seems so lovely."

"She's a gem," I said, deadpan.

I held my hand out for the box file.

"Well … if you're sure it's no trouble," Melanie smiled. "To be honest, I have *so much* to do. She's really left me in the lurch running off like this. I'm tempted to tell you to give her a piece of my mind when you see her, but you know … she's still my boss."

She handed me the file and I tried to keep the relief off my face.

"Mine too," I said, in a world-weary show of camaraderie.

I really, *really* needed Melanie to go away now. I was still trembling and I was fairly certain that I was going to throw up on her shoes.

I spotted Griff walking toward us from the main entrance, bundled in his large duffel coat and swamped by an enormous scarf, holding two large Styrofoam cups of coffee. He saw me and Melanie step out of the elevator, and a baffled look crossed his face.

I said goodbye to Melanie, patting her absently on the shoulder, before hurrying past the front desk to Griff who was still frowning at me, his cheeks red from the cold outside.

"You're leaving again?" he said, confused. "But … I thought … Celebration coffees?"

I cradled the box file under one arm, grabbing his elbow with my free hand and spinning him around.

"Change of plan," I said. "I'm going on a field trip and you're coming with me."

I dragged him back towards the entrance.

"But you just *got here* a half an hour ago. I thought … the lab…"

My hand gripping his elbow was knuckle-white.

"I have seen *quite* enough of Blue Lab for today. I need you to drive me. I walked in this morning."

"Drive you where?" he spluttered, trying not to scold himself with a half-caf mochachino as the reinforced metal doors hissed open for us.

"Trevelyan's," I said.

20

Griff was clearly concerned with my behaviour but I forced him into his ancient Kia, and he obediently backed us out of the snowy quad while I opened the box file on my knee.

"You left your coat down in the lab," he pointed out.

"Doesn't matter," I said distractedly.

I was leafing through the contents of the folder. Loose papers, biros, a couple of coffee house loyalty cards jingled around.

"Do you know where Trevelyan lived?" I muttered.

"You mean *lives*?" he corrected me. "No, I've no idea. Why?"

He glanced at me as we entered traffic. It had started to snow again, fitfully, and his windscreen wipers were squeaking across the glass.

"Listen Doc, you really are acting really strangely today, you know."

"Aha!" I cried.

I held aloft what I had been hoping was in the box file: a set of door keys. I was also pleased to find that the dangling fob, when I inspected it, held the address of 24 Hart Street.

"Hart Street," I said. "That's over in Jericho, near the Harcourt Arms. Do you know it? We can be there in ten minutes."

Griff was still peering at me oddly.

"Is this one of those situations where you say, 'Drive, I'll explain on the way'?" he asked hopefully.

"No," I replied, looking out of the snowy window at the buildings of my city sliding by. "It's one of those situations where I say, 'Drive, because I'm your boss, and you have to do what I tell you to'."

He frowned at me over his glasses, so I gave him a smile and patted his knee. Shaking his head, he drove us out of the quad.

Jericho was not far from the St John's entrance to the campus but it still took us twenty minutes, not ten. This was partly because traffic was bad due to the snow. We of Britannia have survived monsters, wars and the apocalypse, but two inches of snow still bring the country to a standstill. Some things never change.

The main reason for our delay, though, was because Griff drove like an old lady.

Hart Street itself, I discovered when we pulled up, was an unprepossessing run of large and well maintained old-fashioned terrace houses. It overlooked a nice enough park, where several children were braving out the snow on swings and slides. It was a quiet neighbourhood.

"I thought she was away on holiday?" Griff asked as we parked and I got out of the car.

"No, she's not on holiday," I said, crossing the street.

I still had my lab shoes on and the snow was icy cold. I climbed the two stone steps up to the front door and tried the key, letting myself in.

"But … if she's *not* gone away, shouldn't we knock?" Griff asked, following me, his hands thrust into his pockets against the cold.

"She's not here Griff, trust me," I said. "That's why *I'm* here. Just come inside will you?"

I had wondered to myself on the drive over whether Trevelyan had been taken from her home. She certainly hadn't been kidnapped from the office. Security was usually pretty tight at Blue Lab (says the woman who had just broken into the Military Applications Level…)

Part of me expected to enter her house and find furniture overturned, crockery smashed, smears of blood on the walls, some sign of a struggle at least. But then I realised that as soon as her teeth had turned up at the lab, gift wrapped for our pleasure, Cabal's Ghost agents would have been swarming all over her home address, looking for leads, clues, anything.

Cabal were the kind of people who covered their tracks, so there were no desk drawers half-tugged open, or wall-mounted paintings laid on the floor with their backs slashed open. Trevelyan's place was pristine. They had probably hoovered and dusted when they had finished turning the place over.

The terraced house was surprisingly roomy inside. It was one of those converted town houses which have the entire first floor knocked through as one huge sitting room, with the kitchen downstairs in the cellar and five or six bedrooms upstairs. I wondered if the decor would give me more of a handle on the kind of person my boss had been.

To be honest, anything which gave me more of a clue as to my boss' non-curricular interests would have been a godsend. I would have been happy to find Black Sabbath posters and black candles everywhere.

I was smack out of luck then.

The entire house was minimalist to a degree which made Veronica Cloves' sky high impersonal penthouse look like a twee homespun craft fair.

I wondered briefly if I was the only person connected to Blue Lab who actually lived somewhere that looked lived in – okay, my place looked *very* lived in, I'll admit – but as Griff followed me from room to room, he seemed to agree that it was all a bit … cold.

"Not that I would dare question your authority on why we're sneaking around an empty house in the middle of the day looking in drawers and cupboards, but whatever it is you're looking for, boss, I'm guessing it's *not* decorating tips?"

I ignored him.

We checked the downstairs kitchen. There was food in the cupboards and the enormous chrome fridge, which at least proved that my supervisor ate and was a regular human, if not pleasant, but nothing of any real interest. There was a lot of bran though. Yep. She was definitely regular.

There were no post-it notes with scribbled shopping lists, no letters, no sign of personal living whatsoever beyond the absolute basic necessity. Who lives like this?

I headed upstairs, hoping to find more. Griff hesitated at the foot of the stairs.

"Look," he called up to me. "Doc, if you don't want to tell me what on earth is going on here then that's your decision, but I think Trevelyan is going to do more than just *fire* you if you go rooting through her bedroom. What *are* you looking for? Her secret loveheart diary? This all feels a tiny bit illegal to me."

I paused at the top of the stairs.

I owed Griff an explanation, I knew that. His bizarre complicity and evident loyalty at even agreeing to drive me over here and basically break into our boss' home (okay, technically we had keys, but only because I'd stolen them) was touching, if a little worrying. But where would I start?

"Hey Griff, Trevelyan isn't going to come back and catch us, don't worry. I think she's dead at the hands of a sadistic vampire who's also the tooth fairy gone wrong. This guy has also now taken another girl and rearranged her smile too, and so I'm moonlighting for the big kahunas we all bow down to and trying to find out why. Oh, and did I already mention that I don't think we're working for the good guys, you and I? Blue Lab is quite literally keeping monsters in the basement."

Yeah, I didn't think so.

I didn't have time to go through the five stages of acceptance with my lab assistant right now. I had just needed a ride here. I was still trying to process the fact that either the Cabal or whoever had sanctioned the Military Applications Division at Blue Lab had signed off on a minor act of genocide.

By *process*, I mean *temporarily ignore*. One thing at a time, Phoebe. One thing at a time.

"I know this all seems weird," I said to Griff, who was frowning up at me, his hand on the banister. "I swear I have a good reason to be here, it's just ... not easy to explain right now. You'll have to trust me. Okay?"

He peered up at me with a worried expression in his big brown puppy dog eyes. I think he suspected his boss had gone off the deep end a little.

"It'll just take a minute. You stay down there. See what's on the DataStream or something," I suggested, forcing a winning smile.

I turned and hurried the rest of the way upstairs before he could reply. I winced inwardly, realising that I had basically just acted like I was trailing a troublesome five year old. I had all but sat him at the kitchen counter with a carton of juice and some cartoons to keep him entertained while mommy was working.

As I made my way across the cream-coloured landing and found my boss' bedroom door, however, I heard the DataStream come on downstairs and Griff beginning to idly flick through channels. Something about crop circles outside the city walls again. There was a lot of that going on lately. It was on the DataStream every other day. No one knew who was making them. Not people obviously. We didn't step outside the walls. I wondered why Cabal would want everyone knowing about them, unless of course they were as clueless as the rest of us? Fishing for information, hoping someone watching would know something about it. Casting their net of enquiry over the DataStream in the hope of catching something wriggling?

I shook my head, shaking off the conspiracy theories. I'm a paranoid by nature, and it's easy to get carried away. Much more likely they were just trying to keep everyone's minds off real issues, such as the current energy crisis, the civil unease over the vampire GO rights movement, and the rumours of Tribals becoming more organised than mere packs. To my mind at least, the crop circle stories was the Cabal equivalent of following a segment on harsh new taxes with a human interest story about a water skiing budgie. Keep the masses entertained, distracted. Keep them happy.

I shook my head to clear it and reluctantly checked out Trevelyan's love nest, leaving Griff to his Stream.

It was a spartan bedroom, like the rest of the house. The bed was neatly made. Wardrobes were built into the walls, a dresser by the window. There were no fluffy toys on the bedspread, no loved mementos of childhood. My boss was a single woman, it wouldn't have surprised me if there had been.

I didn't like being in here, in another woman's bedroom. It made my skin crawl. There's snooping and then there's snooping. I'd happily hack into my supervisor's secret work files but I drew the line at rummaging through her underwear drawers. I wasn't here to discover her bra size, and I was worried in case I accidentally found some fluffy handcuffs or something.

I had already been surprised enough to find that chirpy, smiling Lucy was a closet vampire superfan, I didn't need to know what Trevelyan got up to in her bedroom as well.

After a cursory sweep, I tried the guest bedrooms which similarly came up blank of anything of interest, and I ended up in the last second story room, which I discovered was an office.

I had no real idea what I was looking for, or why I had even come to her house in the first place. It had been opportunistic, I suppose, too tempting not to swipe the box file from the lovely and helpful Melanie and have a rummage.

My supervisor, prior to getting kidnapped and disfigured, had been deeply involved in the dubious MA Division as well as my own. She had my name as her bloody password. There had to be a reason why, and seeing as the only files she still had at Blue Lab were encrypted, I had hoped something might have turned up here too – something I could work with.

A search of the drawers and cupboards of the small upstairs office confirmed my suspicions. Someone had indeed been here before me on a clean-up operation. I knew this because every drawer and cupboard I opened was completely and thoroughly empty. There wasn't even dust. What office contains no paperwork *at all*? Thanks, Cabal.

Atop her desk, I fired up her home workstation, which was nowhere near as sleek and advanced as Veronica Cloves' model, but as I had expected, the same clean sweep had passed through here too. The system was an empty shell. There wasn't even a desktop background. No files at all. Even the recycle bin had been deleted. I hadn't even known that was possible.

I mean, how do you *delete* the *recycle bin*? Where do you drag it into? Itself?

As you can tell, I'm no Matrix-style hacker.

Frustrated, I turned to leave the room and give up this hopeless wild goose chase when something caught my eye.

The decor in this room was as impersonal as the rest of the house but it was obvious that Trevelyan spent more time in this office than any other room. It at least had her framed Blue Lab certificate on the wall, as well as her Doctorate in Applied Technical Engineering plus a few other academic achievements she was either proud of or, more likely, was required to display for reasons of competency.

It wasn't these few framed personal items which I had noticed, though. I had my own certificates framed back at my place. It was a photograph which had caught my eye. Framed, mounted and almost hidden, placed as it was on the wall behind the door. I had almost missed it completely.

Crossing the office, I took the photo down off the wall. It was old, black and white, a formal pose of several people. It looked pre-wars to me.

There were five people in the photograph, all men standing in what was clearly a lab setting. They were holding champagne flutes and wearing white lab coats. The man on the far right was holding the bottle by the neck. They all looked young, mid-twenties to early thirties, and very pleased with themselves. Clearly, this was a commemorative photo. Some kind of graduation? Or the marking of a science team's breakthrough?

The man on the far right, I saw instantly, was clearly related to my boss. He had the same eyes and the same strong jaw. He *must* have been Trevelyan's father.

He had his arm companionably around the shoulders of the next man in the frame, who looked the youngest of them all. He was a thin, gawkish-looking nerd with thick glasses. The photo had caught this guy halfway into a grin, which made him look even goofier than he would probably have appeared. Who was this then? The protégé of Vyvienne's father?

The next man along, in the centre of the photograph, looked faintly familiar to me but I didn't know why. He was a large solidly-built man, also wearing thick-rimmed glasses over heavy lidded eyes, and was sporting a very luxuriant and well-trimmed beard which covered half of his face. He was standing with his arms folded, centre-stage, smiling proudly out of the frame with his champagne glass tucked under his hand. He looked like the most senior of the five present, a proud father-figure with his close knit team around him.

Next along came as something of a surprise to me. I *definitely* knew *this* face. In this old photo, the man was younger, slimmer, and looked far less self-important than every other time I had even seen his face on the DataStream. However, there was no doubting that this was a floppy-haired, smirking version of Marlin Scott, the same super-rich businessman who my new best friend Servant Cloves would be schmoosing at his Mankind Movement fundraiser this evening.

There was no mistaking that hooked nose or clever eyes. Scott was a powerful figure in the industry. I hadn't known he had a background in science but here he was, inexplicably, in the photo. He was an engineer, surely? What on earth was he doing drinking champagne with Trevelyan's old man and the other guys, Nerdboy and Superbeard?

It was the fifth figure, however, which had really caught my attention. It was seeing this man that had made me cross the room and practically tear the picture off the wall.

That man standing next to Marlin Scott. He was young in the picture, grinning like the rest of them, clearly celebrating something and looking as caught up in the moment as everyone else. These five pre-war scientists, with their eyes bright as buttons, smiling out of their black and white world so distant from my own, enjoying a world without the Pale.

The young man on the far right, leaning on Marlin Scott's shoulder and holding the champagne bottle cheekily just out of frame was younger in this photo than I was now. Twenty two maybe, twenty three? He was handsome, if a little thin in the face.

My hands gripped the photo so hard I almost thought the glass would shatter as I stared at him.

I hadn't heard Griff come upstairs, didn't look up when he entered the room or when he stood next to me, looking down curiously at the photo I was gripping.

"Hey, did you find what you were looking for?" he asked, scrutinising the picture. "Who are those guys?"

Beneath the photo, on the card mount, it read '*To my darling daughter Vyvienne, me and the rest of the team, raising glasses to a world without fear – Love, Dad.*'

I swallowed a couple of times before I could answer.

"I don't know all of them," I said, my voice sounding oddly tinny in my own ears, "but *this guy* here? The youngish guy holding the bottle…?"

My finger jabbed the man on the far right of the science team as I looked up at Griff.

"That's my father."

21

I took the photograph with me when I left the house, dragging Griff behind me. I didn't know what to think.

Why the hell was my father in a photograph with Trevelyan's old man and the others? What the hell did it all mean?

I had decided the time had come to take action.

I checked my watch, it was close to 5pm now. The winter days were short and it was already dusk. It would be full nightfall soon.

"Where are we going now?" Griff asked as we climbed back into his car.

"You're going back to work, handsome," I told him, a steely look in my eyes. "But frankly I've had enough of this cloak and dagger crap. I want answers."

I glanced over at him, his face lit by the dashboard in the deepening gloom.

"You can drop me … at the *library*," I said with feeling.

22

The Bodleian Library is not just any old place. Maybe once, it was one of the great libraries of the whole world.

Built around an earlier private library back in the fifteenth century, it expanded and opened to our city's noble scholars later in 1602. It is an ancient and venerable hall of knowledge. Its reading rooms have been home to many a famous mind over the centuries. Five different kings have studied here, forty or so Nobel Prize winners, twenty six of the old civilisation's Prime Ministers, and more writers than you can shake a quill at. Oscar Wilde, CS Lewis, Tolkien…

My interest in the Bod this evening, however, was neither academic nor historical. I wasn't hoping to rifle through its catalogue of millions of printed books and manuscripts in a handy motivational montage which might explain my current conundrum.

I was heading there, to the heart of old Oxford at the centre of the University, because it was here at the Bod where the wealthy Mankind Movement champion, Marlin Scott, was holding his evening fundraiser.

You could hire out rooms at the Library for private or corporate functions. Marlin Scott's shindig was being held in the Divinity School, the University's very first teaching room and its oldest examination hall.

It was a grand setting, which suited Scott. He wasn't, if his public persona was anything to go by, one for understatement. I wanted to know what the geriatric saviour of our city, the man behind the construction of the wall, knew about my father.

"I thought your father was dead, Doc?" Griff said as we drove through the sleet and the gathering gloom.

"He is," I replied. "He died in the wars. He was a field surgeon."

The temperature was dropping and I was beginning to wish I hadn't left my coat back in the lab.

"My mother died when I was born. The wars had already been raging for years, it was just me and dad. I was nine when he died. A skirmish out in Derbyshire, a town almost overrun by the Pale. He was part of an Evac Team, sent in to lift out any civilians still holed up there."

"Something brought his helicopter down right in the middle of the Peak District, out in the wilds. Deep valleys up there, high moors. They disappeared off the radar. A Search and Rescue Team went out after them, of course."

I rubbed my hands together in the cold, trying to coax some warmth into them.

"They found the crash site and the bodies, what was left of them anyway. The Pale had found them. They didn't leave much behind to identify."

"Jesus…" Griff muttered under his breath.

I glanced at him.

"Everyone lost someone in the wars. A whole lot of people just disappeared. I grew up here after he died. Safe behind Marlin Scott and the Bonewalkers' magnificent wall."

I smirked to myself. It sounded like a tribute band.

"And you had no idea that your father had worked with Trevelyan's dad?" Griff pulled up near the Turf Tavern on Holywell, not far from the library.

"None whatsoever," I admitted, shaking my head in disbelief. "I knew he had been a scientist before the Pale, before the wars started, but that was long before I was born."

I glanced down at the photo on my lap in the dark car.

"I've never seen him look as young as he does here."

I re-read the message from Trevelyan's father to his doting daughter again. What the hell had the Development Team been? I had no answers. Trevelyan may have had them but she was gone. There was another source I planned to confront.

Marlin Scott himself.

Griff tried to come with me but I sent him away. He was clearly worried and asked me solemnly if I was in some kind of trouble. I admitted that I thought I was. There wasn't much he could do to help, however, other than keep up the good work with the rats.

I thanked him for driving me around like a chauffeur, and promised solemnly that I would explain to him what the hell this was all about as soon as I could, asking him to check in on Lucy if he was headed her way, and then left the car and disappeared into the snowy night streets of New Oxford.

The Bod is an impressive building, quite monumental and utterly otherworldly in that way so common to my city. Oxford has always seemed fluid in time to me. The strange additions over the years, the salvaged buildings from other parts of Britannia, the sky-scraping glass needles of the new Northern Sector, these all just added to the feeling that this city was half in the present, half in the past, and another half somewhere on the other side of the looking glass.

Yes, I'm aware that's three halves. I did tell you it's an odd place.

The impressive, ancient exterior of the Bod was made to seem ever more eldritch tonight by the falling snow and with enormous spotlights casting a soft bluish glow over the outer walls. Large free-standing pennants bearing the logo of Scott Enterprises (a stylised portcullis if you're interested) flanked the entrance, and there were many expensive-looking cars in the parking lot, with valets rushing here and there while guests poured into the building.

I didn't have an invitation, of course, and I realised I was severely underdressed for such a grand high society gala. There were very official-looking doormen welcoming New Oxford's great and good, and as I reached the steps to the main entrance, one of them gave me a look of alarm.

Come on, I thought, I didn't look *that* bad. Okay, so most of the people around me were either in full tuxedos, evening gowns or a combination of pearls and mink stoles, but I didn't exactly look like a derelict off the street from the south eastern Slade Sector.

I wondered if I looked like some crazy GO rights activist, here to ruin the fun of all the Mankind Movement supporters. Maybe I was hoping to throw a bucket of pig's blood over Mr Scott, for being such an unashamed genetic bigot?

"I'm sorry, miss," the doorman said while not looking remotely sorry, "but this is a private function, invitation only. I'm afraid I can't allow you in."

I stared past him up the steps into the warmly-lit building. There were crowds of people filing though the corridors inside, heading for the Divinity School. I could hear distant band music, upbeat swing drifting out into the dark car park.

"Do you know Veronica Cloves?" I asked him. He looked confused.

"Well, of course, Servant Cloves is one of my favourite DataStream hosts. Everybody knows her, but…"

"She's inside," I said curtly.

"I'm aware of that, miss," he said in his patient yet no-nonsense tones. "However, if you're a fan or a member of the press, I'm afraid you will have to approach her office directly at the Cabal Headquarters at the Liver Building over in the South Park Complex, same as everyone else. There's no one giving autographs here tonight."

He rocked slightly on his heels, fuelled by self-importance.

"As I said, miss, it's a private function."

"I know it is," I said, shooting him my most withering look. "My name is Doctor Phoebe Harkness and I am working closely with Servant Cloves on internal Cabal affairs. I'm not asking for her goddamned autograph. I'm telling you to go and find her, and tell her I'm here."

The doorman raised his eyebrows. He looked slightly uncertain but not entirely convinced.

Frankly, I wouldn't have believed me either. I wasn't even carrying any ID.

"Is there a problem?" said the person standing behind me, sounding bored but impatient to get inside.

The doorman looked past me as I seethed, but something on the doorman's face, the look of abashed surprise, made me reconsider my initial impulse to turn and land a haymaker on whatever silver-spoon blue blood was irritated by my holding him up.

"Mr Scott," the doorman blustered. "I'm so sorry, sir, I hadn't seen you arrive. I was just explaining to this young lady that…"

I span on my heel. Mr Scott?

The figure standing behind me, with an entourage of six or so private bodyguards flanking him from a discreet distance and looking humourlessly stuffed into their tight suits, was not the elderly, hook-nosed industrialist I had been hoping for.

It was a young man in a smart tuxedo. His face was open and smiling, his complexion fresh and rosy-cheeked as though he had just come from a day punting merrily along the Thames. His floppy blonde hair was neatly parted, like a pageboy.

I recognised the neat, expertly placed medical stitch across his otherwise pretty nose.

I should.

It had been my head that had split it.

"Oscar?" I stammered.

The boy blinked at me a few times, clearly struggling to place my face. Then realisation dawned. I watched various emotions cross his face like clouds across the sun in quick succession: shock, horror, embarrassment, guilt, and finally, after a moment's consideration, amusement.

"Oh my Lord," he said, breaking into a grin. "Small world, isn't it?"

He certainly hadn't been this lucid last time I had seen him, but now he was bobbing on his shining heels and looking like a dashed decent chap.

He had in fact been smashed out of his head when we originally met, firstly by being used like a walking wine box by vampires, and then by myself. Literally.

"Mr Scott?" I burbled, staring at the boy shining back at me like a paragon of well-bred innocence. "He called you Mr Scott?"

"Oscar Scott, yes," he held out his hand politely, as though he hadn't tried to wrestle me to the floor the previous evening to stop me escaping his undead sugar daddy. "I don't believe we were properly introduced. You look rather ... different tonight."

I took his hand, not sure what else to do, and fairly certain that head butting him again would not get me inside.

"You too," I said.

He was a far cry from the submissive, dog-collar wearing groupie who had dry humped my back in Sanctum.

"Marlin Scott is my father," he grinned by way of explanation. "I think I did mention something about it last night, but to be honest I was pretty far gone by midnight."

He glanced around us, looking slightly abashed.

"I may have ... overindulged a little."

A little? I thought.

The doorman was looking from Oscar to me politely.

"You know this young lady, sir?" he asked.

"Of course," Oscar shot him a winning, Head Boy grin. "She's here as my guest, Glenn. For goodness' sake, let us in."

To my shock, Oscar Scott, playboy millionaire and erstwhile off-duty Helsing, linked my arm in a gentlemanly fashion and led me inside, dismissing the frantic apologies of the doorman.

Was this really the same boy from the club? He looked as wholesome and good-natured as a choirboy. Did he really not remember what had gone on at Sanctum?

"What the hell are you doing?" I asked under my breath, as he led us with the other guests down the long and highly decorated hallways of the Bod towards the main event in the Divinity School.

"Look, lady…" he hissed back at me. His voice was low and urgent, but he kept up the act of smiling and waving in greeting to several other people as though he were minor royalty. "… If you came here to blackmail me, you'll get nothing but trouble, okay? Don't think just because you happened to spot me out on the town that you can sell your story to the bloody tabloids because none of them will believe a word of it anyway. What are you anyway, some kind of paparazzo? I'm sick of your kind hounding me."

I stopped dead in the hallway and stared at him.

"Do you really not remember what happened last night? I'm not here to blackmail you, you idiot. I didn't even know who you *were* last night. I barely do now if I'm honest. I'm here to see your father on a business matter."

Oscar's manner changed. He seemed to sag with relief.

"Oh thank God," he practically blurted. "I thought … well, never mind. You're not gutter press then. Thank God for that."

He led me on again, positively chummy now, my arm still linked in his as he leant in to whisper.

"I am really sorry but I honestly was so bloody bladdered last night, I don't remember a darn thing. My head was like broken eggshells this morning, I don't mind telling you. Were you feeling delicate too?"

He sniggered like a naughty child.

"Wild night though, with the fire and all? It was like being at a foam party, right? All those sprinklers … I think I remember that."

He looked momentarily confused.

"Hey, did we dance together at some point?"

I blinked incredulously at him.

"Kind of," I said flatly.

So he really didn't remember. I wondered if it was drugs, the blood-letting, or some kind of mind control by the white spidery Gio. It could be a fun combination of all three for all I knew. Whatever the case, my shiny new friend had just bought me a ticket inside and I was going with it.

We entered the Divinity School itself to loud swing band music. The room was resplendent. There were balloon arches in gold and cream dotted about here and there in the massive hall, the official colours of the Mankind Movement.

People drifted around us in elegant, finely-dressed clumps, like a sea of penguins and peacocks. Waiters moved between them, refilling champagne flutes endlessly. Nothing gets cheques written at a fundraiser more than a squiffy audience. If this had been a regular party, I would have called what people were doing 'mingling'.

As it was a corporate event, celebrating big business and unity amongst the elite in their shared distrust of the 'others', most of them were more 'networking'. There were quite a few, however, the richest of New Oxford's rich, who were wealthy enough that they could actually be said to be hob-nobbing.

I'd never seen anyone hob-nob before. In truth, my experience of A-list swanky parties was woefully thin.

I stared upwards as the crowds moved around me, chattering and laughing decorously. The ceiling in the Divinity School is something to behold. I love my city and I knew my history. This place was built in 1488 as a school of Theology, and it certainly was a godlike chamber, a fitting cathedral-like space to ponder the divine. The stonework of the many-vaulted ceilings was amazing.

Oscar noticed me looking and smirked, almost proprietarily, as though his father owned the place.

"Pretty gothic, huh?" he said, referring to the elaborate decorations above us. He was obviously drawn by all things vampire-themed. I bet he had coffin-shaped cufflinks.

"Actually, it's Lierne vaulting," I said absently. "With bosses. It was designed by William Orchard in the 1440s, if I remember correctly. It's in the perpendicular style."

Yes. I'm a geek, I know. My passion for, some might say nerdy obsession over, all things pre-wars extends beyond old pop culture and sometimes to actual history.

Oscar's smirk didn't waver.

"Yeah, it's cool," he said vapidly. "Looks like a big spider web or something, right?"

God deliver me from brainless rich boys.

I accepted a glass of champagne from a passing waiter. Oscar was still holding my arm.

"So, you go to Sanctum a lot then?" he asked lightly. "I mean, you're pretty hot for an older woman, you know. We should definitely hook up sometime."

This brought my roaming gaze down from the ceiling.

"How old are you, Oscar?" I asked, staring at him in disbelief.

"Nineteen, why?"

I gulped my drink down and passed him my empty glass.

"Get me another of these for the love of God," I said.

He flashed me his winning, barely-out-of-puberty smile again and disappeared into the crowd.

Wonderful, in another turn for the worse I was now being hit on by a vain millionaire child with no brains and a thirst for the underworld. I was guessing that with a family as powerful as his, he had never had anyone say no to him before. He probably thought he was genuinely charming. Spoilt little rich boys were not my cup of tea, especially jailbait ones.

I scanned the crowd, looking for Cloves or Marlin Scott, but I couldn't see any faces I recognised. I had moved a little way into the room, aware that I had drawn rather withering stares for my lack of black tie attire, but I was far beyond the point of caring when Oscar reappeared like a bad penny.

"Thought I'd lost you there for a second," he said amiably, passing me a refilled flute.

"So you're Marlin Scott's son?" I asked, clearly unable to shake him.

He nodded, looking disbelieving that I might not know who he was.

"Don't you read the society pages?" he asked me. "I pretty much own them."

"I can never find the time," I said wearily.

I was more impressed that the ancient Marlin Scott was robust enough to have such a young son. In the photo with my father, Scott had already been getting on in years.

"But hang on," I said. "You are aware that your father is a pretty hardcore Mankind Movement bigwig, right? There's a clue here with all the banners and such. And what, you just hang around vampire clubs getting your neck sucked for fun?"

His eyes widened with alarm.

"Keep your voice down!" he said under his breath. "For God's sake! It's not like the old fart knows, is it? Jesus…"

He looked around, as though expecting his father to descend on him out of nowhere.

"I would have thought someone like you would understand," he said to me earnestly.

"Someone like me?" I was confused.

"A fellow Helsing."

Ah … of course. As far as Oscar knew, I was another vampire-loving freak trawling the New Oxford underground in search of a quick, intoxicating nibble. He thought he had stumbled upon a kindred spirit. I didn't have the heart to tell him that Sanctum was hardly my scene. After all, there wasn't much offensive about the boy. Being mean to him on purpose would have been like kicking a puppy.

"I'm pretty discreet going to Sanctum," he said in tones of confidentiality. "I hardly advertise the fact. You have no idea what it's like living in a fishbowl like I do. Everyone deserves something that's just *theirs*, don't they?"

He gave a rueful smile, but there was a lot of bitterness behind it I noticed.

"Don't think it would go down well with the old man, do you?" he sighed.

Talk about your teenage rebellion.

I had only just noticed that Oscar's tuxedo shirt had an old fashioned high collar. It completely covered his neck. I would have bet my life savings that he spent an awful lot of time around dear old Dad wearing a polo neck, hiding his love bites.

"This is too ironic," I said to myself, sipping the champagne, which was glorious by the way. "The son of a vampire-hater is a secret Helsing? Good lord, Oscar! Can't you just get arrested for driving under the influence and snort cocaine like all the other rich kids?"

"There's no buzz like the vampires, you know that, right?" he said, smirking again.

He actually nudged me with his elbow. Who does that?

"Hey, I wasn't kidding before," he drawled, giving me playfully seductive face and turning on the charm. "When this old fart party wraps up, we should head out together and hit the district. It could get wild again."

I thought emphatically not, for *so* many reasons.

"I thought you and Giovannibatiste were pretty close?" I asked. "To be perfectly blunt, I figured you were gay. Now you're asking me out?"

Oscar downed his drink.

"Wow, how old fashioned are you then?" he cackled. "Who doesn't like the best of both worlds anyway?"

"How long have you been going to Sanctum, Oscar?"

The boy shrugged.

"Couple of months, I guess," he said. "I've cruised the district, of course – most of the south St Giles clubs, but out of the blue I get an invite to Sanctum. It's like the best of the best. Then I met Gio. He took a shine to me."

I shivered while Oscar grinned.

"What in the world do you see in that man?" I asked.

Oscar looked genuinely perplexed.

"Power, obviously," he said. "What, you think I should be satisfied with what I have? Daddy is powerful, yeah, he can put as many zeros on a cheque as you like. Wow. The excitement!"

His eyes gleamed with a look I was coming to recognise as the mark of a true Helsing, a full blown vampire-addict.

"But Gio?" he continued. "He's fucking immortal! He has *real* power and he says he's going to make me one of them."

"They don't do that, Oscar," I said flatly. "Ever."

He looked petulant.

"You sound jealous," he said defensively. "You don't understand. I'm different. Gio says he has plans for me. He told me I'm special."

It was like talking to a love-struck thirteen year old girl. I was just waiting for his lower lip to start trembling.

He seemed to notice someone over my shoulder and stiffened.

"Oh Jesus, it's the old man."

Before I could turn around, Oscar gripped my arm, a desperate look in his eye.

"Hey, you said you were here to see him, right? You swear you're not gonna dump me in it?"

I shook him off. Wow, he really was like a little kid. All this vampire business was just fun and sport for him, something to pass the time until the trust fund kicked in and he could get out from under daddy's shadow, I guess.

"Your secret dies with me, Oscar," I promised.

I turned away from him to spy Marlin Scott, making his way through the crowds toward us. He was an elderly man, mostly bald. His hook-nosed face was like a mummified and liver-spotted vulture, and he walked with a cane, but he had the well preserved air about him of someone who could afford the very best hip replacements. He had the sour facial expression so common to those who lived at the top and only had people to look down on.

I barely took him in, however; I was far too busy grinning sheepishly at the woman who walked toward us beside him. Veronica Cloves, resplendent in her black choker and a long black evening gown, which wrapped her like cling film and seemed studded all over with tiny jewels like the night sky. She was gripping her champagne in a hand covered with an elbow length evening glove, and wearing a frankly hideous fascinator which looked to me like a raven fighting a tarantula.

The reason for my sudden, sheepish smile is that the look on her face at seeing me here with Scott the Younger was priceless. She had the fury of a gorgon in her wide eyes.

"Veronica!" I said brightly as they approached.

Oscar muttered a respectful hello to his elderly father by my side. The old man barely glanced at the boy.

"How wonderful to see you again so soon," I beamed.

Old Man Scott was eyeing us both with interest, looking grumpily confused. He had probably thought I was a waitress or some other serving-class attendant working the room.

"Ah, Doctor!"

Cloves had gained control of her face with impressive speed and restraint. Her game face was on. But then this was what she did for a living. She smiled sweetly at me, taking me by the forearms and dragging me into one of those hideous 'mwah-mwah' air kisses.

"How wonderful of you to be able to come at such short notice," she gushed.

Cloves turned to Scott with a warm smile.

"Marlin dah-ling, this is a very very dear friend and colleague of mine," she said smoothly. "Dr Harkness works over at Blue Lab. She is absolutely one of our best and brightest. I do hope you don't mind my imposition inviting her tonight."

"Actually, she's here with me," Oscar interjected proudly, but everyone else ignored him.

I shook Marlin's offered hand. It was dry and leathery like the rest of him.

"It's so nice to meet you, Mr Scott," I said, trying my best for professional and winsome. "I'm a huge fan of your…" I cast around for something complimentary to say. "… wall," I finished lamely.

I'm not good at small talk. It's likely that I will never achieve the level of professional hob-nobber.

The old fossil cracked half of a grim smile. It fell off his face gracelessly as soon as it had come, as though it were costing him money.

"Most people are, Doctor. I only wish it could keep all of the monsters on the outside."

He looked me up and down, clearly disapproving of my work clothes and lack of exciting headgear.

"I was not aware that Blue Lab folk cared about our cause here," he said. "My understanding is that you people are trying to cure the monsters, not destroy them."

His tone was withering. I could see how Oscar found him so lovable. He had probably grown up under that disapproving glare his whole life. Poor kid. I felt absurdly sorry for him.

"Actually, Mr Scott," I said, "I do believe we have a mutual friend in common. Phillip Harkness? He was my father. Didn't you used to work with him, before the wars?"

Scott stared at me hard, as though I had just slapped him. It was the first time he has seemed anything other than a grumbly old man. From the look that crossed his face, I might as well have thrown my glass of champagne over him.

"That was a long time ago," he said, composing his features again. "Different world back then. I'm not the fool I was. None of us are anymore."

He turned to Oscar, glaring at him witheringly.

"Fetch me a drink, boy," he barked.

Cloves had gripped my arm.

"Actually, Marlin," she said sweetly, "I'm so sorry but if I could just borrow the good Doctor a moment. I need to powder my nose. Couldn't possibly go on my own. You know how it is with us girls. Doctor Harkness, would you mind?"

Her smile was a happy ray of sunshine beaming down on us all, but her fingers were digging into my elbow so hard they were going to leave bruises. I may as well have had my arm trapped in a vice.

Before I could speak, she practically dragged me away, leading me through the crowds. The Scotts, older and younger alike, watched us go. Marlin was frowning after me suspiciously, Oscar looking a little abandoned, obviously unhappy at being left with the patriarch.

When she had me in a corner, behind an enormous and elaborate ice sculpture shaped like a swan, and was sure that no one was watching us, the benign smile dropped from her face and the Veronica Cloves I was more used to resurfaced.

"What the fuck are you doing here?!" she gnashed at me, dropping my arm. "I nearly had a heart attack! Are you trying to get me fired?"

"I need to talk to you," I replied, ignoring her fury. "And to him."

I pointed back at the distant figure of Marlin Scott.

"Scott is a very important contributor to the safety and prosperity of our city!" Cloves hissed at me. "What business you think you could have with him is beyond me!"

She raised a warning finger to my face.

"You have already caused an incident between humans and the GOs last night. Harrison was on my ass for the chaos at the club today. I have had a very stressful afternoon making nice with the Channel Seven reporters and dispelling the rumours about the missing activist girl, to the point that my face is aching from smiling and telling the people of New Oxford that they have nothing to be concerned with."

She took a breath, and leaned in even closer.

"I have picked up Trevelyan's files, which have finally been decrypted. I haven't even had a moment to look over them yet. I want to see for myself what's on them before I turn them over to Harrison. Call me curious. I will not have you showing up here and upsetting the running of a Mankind Movement fundraiser just because you don't agree with the cause. You're supposed to be pumping your vampire."

I raised my eyebrows.

"For information," she hissed. "What use are you to me here?"

"You think I came here to make trouble for you?!" I spluttered. "Good God, the world does not revolve around Veronica Cloves, you know."

High level Cabal Servant or not, I had had enough today. Cloves thought her day had been tough being a talking head on the DataStream? Try my day: facing genetic mutants and government cover-ups of mass peacetime genocide.

I wondered briefly if she knew anything about the MA division. I doubted it. She was PR. Organisations like the Cabal succeeded by keeping their arms very much uncrossed.

"The Cabal walk the political tightrope, Harkness, and it takes a hell of a lot of balance," Cloves said, walking me over to the large and generously laden buffet table.

I glanced at the food as she made a show of selecting a few *hors d'oeuvres*. There was lobster, more cold meats than I could count, and a debauched abundance of rare and imported foodstuffs, all hard to come by in our new world. Trade routes were not what they once were. I felt guilty even looking at it knowing that within our city, people were crammed together in the lower district slums, practically starving.

"I may well be here making sure the rich and powerful of the Mankind Movement know that they have our trust and support," Cloves said to me, "but you can be pretty sure that at the next GO Rights march, there will be another representative of the Cabal making sure they know we are right behind them all the way. We work all the angles, Harkness. We keep the peace. It's what keeps civilisation moving along. You, on the other hand, seem to make things anything but peaceful!"

"Listen, I'm here because I found something," I said, "and I think it's important."

I'd had the framed photograph under my arm the whole time; now I thrust it, quite violently, at the Cabal Servant.

"What's this supposed to be?" she demanded, still angry.

"This," I pointed to the glass, "is Vyvienne Trevelyan's father. This is *my* father, and this guy is the rich old fart you have been licking the boots of all night. There's a connection, I just don't know what."

Cloves stared at the photo for a moment.

"Where did you get this?" she asked.

"That's … irrelevant," I replied, sounding childish.

My list of crimes, now including trespass in a private home, breaking lab protocol, DataStream espionage, and petty theft, didn't need airing right now.

"I don't know who the other two men are, but I was hoping Scott would remember them. That's why I'm here."

Cloves was still staring at the photo.

"I don't know who the chubby fellow with the beard is, but this one…"

Her gloved finger brushed over the young, gawky looking man I had been unable to identify.

"I've seen his file at Cabal HQ this morning. I recognise the face."

"This morning? Are you sure?"

Cloves stared up at me, looking baffled.

"Yes, when the news came in about the GO rights activist, Jennifer Coleman, the hippy whose teeth we had delivered today. Obviously, we checked her file. Known associates, any links we could exploit, that kind of thing. We have a lot of data to draw on at the Liver. This is Riley Coleman."

She frowned down at the photograph again before looking back up at me.

"Harkness, this little ninety pound lab rat is Jennifer Coleman's father."

I stared back at her in disbelief.

So Coleman was linked to me and Trevelyan after all.

I opened my mouth to reply but at that moment, the lights in the grand Divinity School went out.

The spacious echoing hall was pitched into sudden darkness.

23

I was utterly disoriented.

Before I could react to the lights going out, a deafening boom tore through the hall and there was a flash, as bright as a nuclear flare.

People screamed all around me. There were musical tinkles as champagne flutes dropped or were knocked from startled hands. Plates clattered on the floor.

I blinked and nearly fell, sure that a bomb had just gone off. Someone slammed into the ice sculpture next to us in the darkness and it fell, shattering into countless pieces on the floor like a spray of glass. The swan's transparent, icy head must have slid across the floor. I jumped a little when it butted the toe of my shoe.

There was another flash, bright as the sun. It burned my eyes.

I tottered against Cloves, trying to blink away the lurid red after images.

Above the screams, I heard the high staccato of gunfire. Dim red emergency lighting flickered on and I saw the room was filling with smoke. We were being shoved as people stumbled in panic in the sudden darkness. Diners crashed blindly into the buffet table, knocking its contents to the floor in a slurry avalanche.

"What the fuck is happening?" I heard Cloves shout, a faceless shadow next to me, but her voice was distant.

My ears were filled with a high-pitched whine. I had been almost completely deafened by the blast.

Looking up, I saw one of the high windows shatter as something like a hand grenade sailed into the blood-hued hall and landed among the guests. It didn't explode, but began to pour out more white smoke, spinning like a top.

"We're under attack," I yelled, but nobody heard me.

There hadn't been a bomb. It had been a noise blast, designed to disorientate. The flashes were light grenades, meant to blind and incapacitate. And the smoke bombs, well, they smoked.

There were crashes from the bandstand as people fell into the music pit in their efforts to escape. More gunfire. The flash of the muzzles spread throughout the dark old hall like fireworks in a night sky.

Men entered the hall, a dozen of them, moving through the crowds. They were demonic black silhouettes in the low crimson light. Holding semi-automatics, they fired them into the air. People everywhere dived to the ground, frantic with the sudden gunfire. Shouting and chaos surrounded the silent invaders. They stalked through the mist like soldiers, their faces hidden behind gas masks. The torches strapped to the muzzles of their guns swept the room in wide arcs, searching.

Who were they? Terrorists? GO rights protesters gone militant in reaction to the disappearance of Jennifer Coleman?

I looked around but Cloves had disappeared into the crowd. I made to follow, tripping over fallen people in the darkness. An old woman in an elaborate chiffon ball gown had fallen to the floor. Men and women stepped and tripped over her as she held her thin arms up in self-defence, her many rings glittering in the burst of gunfire.

From what I'd seen, these mercenaries were not shooting people, at least not yet. They were firing into the air, into the unique and ancient famous ceiling of the Divinity School. The stone dust and the white smoke from the grenades were indistinguishable from one another.

Fucking Philistines, I thought, then immediately felt guilty for being more concerned about the historic building than the people inside it. I eased my conscience by crouching and helping the old countess or whatever the hell she was to her feet. She was panicking and broke away from me, swept off into the crowds. People were trying to get out of the main doors, but the mercenaries had blocked them, keeping everyone penned in while they swept their torch beams around in the confusion.

Something in the smoke bombs was making me hack and cough. It burned my eyes and lungs. Was it pepper spray? Tear gas? I lost my balance and stumbled to my knees.

In a small rational corner of my mind, I made a solemn vow to never, ever attend another social gathering. Clubs, fundraisers, even children's birthday parties. They were all well and truly off my list.

Someone grabbed my wrist and pulled me to my feet.

For a second I fought, blinded by tears and still deaf, thinking it was one of the gas-mask wearing invaders, but then my watery eyes cleared and I saw it was Oscar, his mouth covered with a silk handkerchief from his tux, his wide eyes streaming with tears from the gas.

He dragged me clear of the panicking crowd and behind one of the elaborately carved pillars where there was a smaller exit from the hall.

I half ran, half fell after him, my hand wrapped in his, stumbling through the door. It was almost pitch black out in the corridor. I was guessing the entire power supply to the building had been cut. The only illumination came from ghostly emergency lights set at intervals along the walls, red and flashing. Despite the gloom, it was relatively free of the smoke out here.

A few other resourceful party-goers had made it out this way. A balding old man was on his hands and knees on the carpet, retching spittle. A young woman in a long green gown was being enthusiastically sick into a tall potted plant.

"Saw you in the flash," Oscar managed between heaving gut-wrenching coughs. "What's happening? Bloody hell!"

"No idea," I gasped. "Where are your bloody bodyguards?"

My throat was raw as I heaved air into my lungs in ragged gasps. I was still rubbing the stinging tears out of my eyes as Oscar dragged us away, down the corridor and away from the Divinity School. We could still hear the chaos in the room behind us, more gunfire and shouting.

"With Dad, I guess," Oscar gulped.

He glanced over his shoulder briefly, past me and at the closed door behind us.

"Fuck him," he said with feeling. "Let's get the hell out of here."

I didn't argue with Oscar's daddy issues. I had no idea where Cloves had gone and I had lost the photograph somewhere inside. I just wanted fresh air – preferably without bullets.

We stumbled along the corridor, feeling our way in the flickering red light. Turning a corner, we saw a green emergency exit sign was ahead of us. We stared longingly at it for a moment like a twin pair of Gatsbys and then we ran.

We threw ourselves against the heavy push-bar fire door. It gave, spilling us out onto the snow outside and into icy, fresh and blessedly breathable air.

I looked around, dragging my sleeve against my eyes to try and clear my vision. There were steps here, leading down to the pavement. We stumbled down them in the snow. We were still on campus here, I realised, off the city streets. There were dark university buildings all around us. No pedestrians, no visible help.

I noticed a large black van waiting at the foot of the steps.

Shouting came from behind us. I risked a look and saw two of the men in gas masks running down the corridor toward us as the fire door swung shut. We had been spotted.

Shit.

"Doctor Harkness?" Oscar brought my attention forward again, sounding panicked.

We ran down the stairs onto the pavement. The large unmarked van across the street had its engine idling, the low growl of a panther. I saw the side door slide open with a whooshing clatter. There were more gas mask men within. Two of the mercenaries stepped out of the vehicle, like black-clad executioners.

"Oh bollocks," I said quietly.

Oscar let go of my hand. The cold night air bit at my face as I watched one of the men raise his gun. I had just enough time to register the fact that I was about to be shot before they pulled the trigger.

Twin coils, like fishing wire whooshed across the narrow campus path with a whistling trill. The metal spikes at the ends buried themselves in Oscar's tuxedo jacket and flickered with electricity, a rattling crackle emitting from them like popcorn kernels exploding. Oscar jittered and danced next to me, then bonelessly dropped to a crumpled heap on the pavement.

The doors behind us burst open and two of the men ran down the stairs towards his fallen body to scoop him up. They ignored me completely. I looked wildly down the dark street.

Here on campus there was still no traffic, no witnesses, no one to help. I decided I really had to invest in a gun or at least a baseball bat. As I lacked either, I settled for staggering un-heroically away, tottering sideways from Oscar's fallen body.

But then I saw the figure by the van reloading his gun. Another of the gas masks pointed to me.

I was next.

I would have joined Oscar in an electrocuted dogpile right there on the stairs, but as the man turned to face me, a motorbike suddenly roared around the corner. It tore up the street, mounting the snowy steps, and slid to a juddering halt between me and my attackers. The rider turned to me, his arm outstretched urgently.

It was Allesandro.

He wasn't wearing a helmet, but then I suppose health and safety were less of a concern when you are practically immortal. His white face was bright in the darkness.

"Get on!" he yelled.

I didn't question him. I stumbled forward, still light-headed from the gas, and threw myself at the bike, practically jumping on it like a circus performer leaping onto a horse.

Without so much as a backwards look at my assailants, Allesandro gunned the throttle and skidded in the snow, almost throwing me off the bike before I had found my grip. Making an effort, he wrenched it upright and we leapt away, juddering down the steps so hard that I almost bit my tongue off.

I clung onto the vampire for dear life as we screamed away down the quiet campus street. Too shocked to speak, I risked a look back over my shoulder, the wind whipping my loose hair around and making it hard to see.

My legs dangled either side of my ride. I'd never actually been on a motorbike before and wasn't sure what to do with them. I was overwhelmingly glad I hadn't dressed for the occasion. It would have been impossible to stay on this thing in a billowing gown.

I shook the hair out of my eyes and immediately saw Oscar. I had left the poor boy behind. I could see him being roughly folded into the van.

I was clinging to Allesandro so hard it would probably leave bruises.

"Who are they?" I bellowed, still looking back.

The gas masks had all climbed into the van now, and I watched in horror as it moved off, gaining speed.

"Fuck! They're chasing us!"

"Are you hurt?" Allesandro shouted to me.

"They got Oscar. Did they kill him?" I yelled. "And what are you doing here?"

I saw him check his mirrors. The van was gaining on us, roaring up behind like a juggernaut of death. He leaned the bike into a turn and left the tarmac of the street, mounting the pavement and cutting across a deserted quad lawn. The wheels sent up a spray of mushy snow and mud behind us.

"They are the Black Sacrament," Allesandro yelled back to me. "And you're welcome by the way."

They were still following us but not across the grass. They had skirted the corner of the quad and were making for the road parallel, obviously aiming to cut us off at the corner.

"Hold on tight," he said. "I can get us to the main road."

I knew what he meant.

If he could get us off the campus and out into the city streets, we could probably lose them. His bike could cut through the busy, city centre traffic, but the van would be stuck. These lanes were empty roads. They were gaining on us.

I knew I should be worried about Oscar, even if he *was* the vampire bride of the evil son of a bitch who wanted me dead, and I should even probably spare a thought for Cloves too. I had no idea what had happened to her in the confusion.

I seemed to be in the habit lately of leaving people behind with the bad guys. First Lucy, now Cloves and the rich Helsing kid. But right now, my only thoughts were to run and to get the hell away from these people, if they even *were* people.

"How the hell did you know I was at the library?" I shouted, as Allesandro beat the van to the corner by seconds, and peeled the bike back onto the road.

We span around a bend, roaring past the Applied Sciences building and down the narrow lane. Ahead, I could see the gatehouse where the campus proper let out onto the street. In the old world, the university buildings had largely mingled with the city general. But this was all private now, no through traffic. Right now, it was one of the changes to our civilisation I could do without.

"Why are you helping me?" I yelled.

Allesandro still didn't reply because at that moment, something white and large dropped onto him, seemingly out of thin air. Perhaps it dropped out of a tree or from a high lamppost, I had no idea, but it crashed into us in a flurry of motion. I realised that it was a figure in a pale suit, leaping down on us from out of nowhere.

I lost my grip, knocked aside by the impact, and suddenly the bike was out from under me. The world turned upside down, and then the ground came up to meet me like an old friend. An angry old friend.

Thrown from Allesandro's bike into a thin snowdrift on the grassy verge of the lane, I hit the ground like a dropped rock and rolled along fitfully, bouncing on the grass and snow, my world turning over and over as I was pummelled by the impact. I must have dislocated my shoulder as there was an audible crack and a sharp shooting agony pulsed through me, as though someone had stuck me with a hot sword. My head also bounced across the ground a few times, knocking me almost senseless.

When I finally skidded to a halt, I was face down in the snow. My arms and legs felt like they were on fire, and I could taste blood in my mouth. I couldn't breathe. The air had been thoroughly knocked out of my lungs.

From the corner of my eye, with the world still spinning, I could see Allesandro's motorbike on its side in the road, its wheels still spinning furiously. Wherever he was, I didn't see my vampire.

I tried to move but the pain was so great, it made my vision disappear down a long tunnel of watery agony, so I lay still, gasping and hoping to hell I hadn't broken my spinal cord.

I heard footsteps crunching in the snow then rough hands grabbed me, more than one pair, and I was dragged across the snowy grass like a rag doll, limp and helpless. Every movement sent jolts of pain through me. I felt as though I'd broken a rib or three.

Someone picked me up and threw me over their shoulder in a careless fireman's lift. The world was upside down again, my hair in my face. I tried to call out for Allesandro, for anyone, but I couldn't make a sound, other than a soft, painful moan.

My captor threw me roughly down on a hard metal surface. I heard a rolling shutter and then I was in darkness.

They had put me in the van. Oh fuck.

I felt and heard the vehicle pull away quickly, knocking me off balance. The windows were blacked out and I was laid on an uncomfortable lump, which I realised must be Oscar. I shook my head gingerly, trying to come to my senses.

Slowly, in the darkness before me, I focused on a large pale shape, the same shape which had dropped onto Allesandro's speeding bike and knocked me off it. As I blinked blearily, it slowly resolved into a man, tall and pale, in a creamy suit. He was sitting on his haunches in the back of the van, looming over me like a demonic goblin.

It was Gio. His eyes were like molten lava, gleaming in the darkness above his gentle, evil smile.

"Hello again, Phoebe," he said softly in the darkness. "I think you and I have some unfinished business."

I was shaking uncontrollably. Part of me was wishing I would just pass out. But I didn't, of course.

I was wide awake when he leaned over in the darkness of the van, grabbing a fist full of my hair with his long white fingers, and sank his teeth viciously into my throat.

I remember screaming as I passed out.

24

I awoke feeling as though I had the worst hangover known to man. I was disoriented, bleary and sick. My head insisted that I'd spent the previous few hours on a rollercoaster while downing mojitos, tequila and gin, before following the entire thing with a bucket of greasy fried chicken topped with slimy bacon.

My body, on the other hand, was telling me the complete opposite of what I knew I should expect. As I swam up slowly from the deep, murky waters of unconsciousness, I was braced to feel bruised, battered, and broken-boned; all of the usual little aches and niggles one might expect after being thrown from a speeding motorbike and then gored by a vampire.

On the contrary, though. The grogginess and sickly feeling in my head aside, I felt physically fine. Not even bruised.

I risked opening my eyes but this didn't immediately do any good as wherever I was, it was pitch black. There was not the smallest sliver of light. It was also very quiet.

I wondered briefly if I was dead, but it was only a fleeting consideration. If this was some kind of afterlife, it was incredibly dull so far. Plus, I doubted very much that anyone had ever shuffled off the mortal coil and then awoken in heaven or hell to find themselves tied to a chair.

From wriggling my arms and legs, I knew it didn't feel like rope. I was guessing duct tape. I licked my lips. So I wasn't gagged then. This meant that either my kidnappers expected me to remain unconscious or that wherever I was, screaming for help wasn't worrying enough for them to do anything about it, so probably wasn't worth the effort.

I shook my head a few times, testing my overwhelming mental yuckiness. My head didn't quite fall off, but it was close. I figured the light-headedness probably came from having Gio drink me like a thick milkshake until I passed out.

Something brushed against my face as I moved, rough cloth? Ah. There was a bag over my head then. That would explain the darkness. It didn't, however, explain why I felt so hale and hearty. Why the hell wasn't I bleeding internally?

"She's awake, go get Gio," said a woman's voice somewhere in front of me, startling me and making me jump.

"You're sure she's awake?" growled another voice, male and unfamiliar.

"Just bring him down, will you?"

The woman sounded impatient. I heard footsteps, then a creaky door opening and closing.

A hand grabbed the bag on my head and whipped it off. I blinked, disoriented, breathing hard through my nostrils, staring around at my surroundings.

I'd seen this room before but I couldn't quite place it. I was in a small circular chamber with rough stone walls, old grey flagstones, no windows, and one ancient-looking wooden door, banded with black iron. Oh goody, I was in Rapunzel's tower.

There would be windows in a tower, though, surely? I must be underground then. A cellar? The room did look old. My mind tactfully tried to avoid the word 'dungeon'.

Suddenly, I realised why I recognised this place. It was on the DataStream video.

The one which had arrived with my supervisor's teeth.

I coughed. The air down here was musty and there was an odd smell. Something animalistic, like the fetid bottom of a lion's cage.

A slender female vampire stood in front of me, smiling down in an unsettlingly friendly manner. I didn't recognise her at first. This was largely because other than the very pale skin, she didn't look very … I hesitate to use the word … vampy.

She was wearing simple grey slacks and a chunky black pullover. Her hair was tied back from her face in a high ponytail. The vampire wasn't wearing any makeup, not that she really needed any. Most of the vampires have flawless complexions naturally, as though they have been lightly dusted with icing sugar. In fact, the way she was dressed made her look less like a wicked vampire kidnapper and more like a wholesome soccer mom – albeit a very anaemic one.

"Good to see you again, sweetie," she smiled.

I recognised her voice more than her face. That soft, lazy drawl … it was Jessica. This was the vampire who had been sitting with Gio and Oscar in the club, the one who hadn't been particularly keen on me dancing with Allesandro.

"Where am I?" I stammered. "People will be looking for me, you know."

I had no idea if this was true or not, but I thought I'd better say it.

"Doesn't really matter where," Jessica said, unconcerned.

She walked away from me and I looked around more. The old stone block walls were damp and crumbly. There was something behind me, the back legs of my chair were butting against it when I moved, but I couldn't see properly. My movements were more than somewhat restricted by being tied to the chair in question.

Bizarrely, I noticed, someone had moved furniture into the room; a battered-looking old leather sofa, and incongruously, a table on which stood a coffee maker and a few mugs. There was a newspaper too. I guess kidnappers can't just stand over their hostages menacingly twenty four seven, even if they are vampires.

I watched Jessica pour herself a coffee casually, reaching up to tuck a lock of stray hair behind her ear. She was humming distractedly to herself.

"What's with the outfit?" I asked, trying to get her attention. "You look a little less like a bondage queen than the last time I saw you."

She glanced up at me, her eyes narrowing.

"It's an improvement," I said.

"Oh please," Jessica rolled her eyes at me. "Do you honestly think that's how we all are? That we swan around the place in tank tops and leather pants all the time? That we have closets filled with antique lace shirts and that we love nothing more than to slap on more makeup than a gothic drag queen?"

She folded her arms and cocked her head to the side, her ponytail bouncing in a preppy, defiantly cheerful manner. She blew delicately on her coffee.

"I'm more than three hundred years old, honey. I'm over the moody vamp look. To be perfectly honest, the only people who expect that crap from us are you, predictable humans. Got to look the part while we're working, don't we? All the precious little Helsings would be pretty darn

172

disappointed if they came to worship us at the club and found me swanning around in my country casuals, or dear old Gio in a pair of comfy loafers and an argyle sweater."

She tittered to herself, clearly amused.

I had to agree with her logic. So the dark and moody vampire vibe *was* an act after all. It made sense, I guess. Give the people what they expect. This was still an odd sight, however, like unexpectedly walking in on Audrey Hepburn and finding her slobbing around in a shell suit eating pizza from the box.

"I hate all that childish shit," Jessica said, sipping her drink. "But hey, work's work, right? We all have our part to play. I guess I'd be pretty disappointed if I went to a fifties-style diner and the servers weren't all on rollerskates and chewing gum..."

She flung herself onto the sofa.

"And yet you stick with the traditional vampire den motif," I said, glancing around the room. "Very homely. Where are the coffins?"

Jessica smirked at me.

"Eww, as if I *live* here. No sweetie, this is just where we bring the offerings."

That didn't sound good.

Before I could question the vampire, the door opened and another woman entered the room. She was tall, statuesque, with a shock of long, white blonde hair trailing down her back. She was a vampire too, and again surprisingly un-gothic. She was wearing a coral twinset and kitten heel shoes. She looked more like a perky estate agent than anything.

"Does Gio know the last one is up and awake?" the blonde vampire asked Jessica after looking me over. "He's going to want to know. You know how he gets if he's not kept informed, the dandy old queen."

"I sent Amano to wake him," Jessica replied.

She looked me over to me too, waving an introductory hand.

"Phoebe Harkness, this is Helena. You might have seen her at Sanctum. Helena is one of our highest earners. All the men literally fall at her feet," she smirked. "If you ask me, I think it's due to the red getup. I'm sure I read about it in some magazine or other. It's a subconscious thing with men. Wear red on a first date and a guy will spend more money on you, or something like that."

"Hush, Jessica," Helena smiled, raising her eyebrows at me. "It's not the PVC, it's raw talent, that's what it is. Don't listen to her, she's so sarcastic. You don't live as long as I have without learning how to charm the wallet off a mark."

I realised I recognised this one too. When I'd seen her back in the club, her hair had been in dreadlocks down her back and she had squeezed into a bright red jumpsuit so tight, it had looked spray-painted on. She had been smoking with an affected elongated holder and holding court over a gaggle of love-struck clubbers like a red queen.

She looked altogether respectable now though. I could almost have believed I was at a church coffee morning with these two. You know, if I hadn't been tied to a chair and all.

"Are you going to kill me?" I asked simply.

I was impressed at how steady I made my voice, considering I didn't feel very steady. I was bloody terrified.

The two women exchanged glances.

"Not *us* sweetie," Jessica said. "Gio might."

She sounded speculative, as though we were discussing the weather, toying absently with a broach on her lapel.

"To tell you the truth, he's still pretty pissed at you for making a mess of the club. He really doesn't like to be made a fool of."

"He might not though, you never know," Helena said with a rather patronising and encouraging smile, which made me want to hit her very hard. "He doesn't *need* to after all. He only needs the teeth technically. But you never can tell with Gio, he has his tempers. It doesn't really take much. The others didn't end up walking out of here."

"What do you mean, he needs the teeth?" I asked. "What the hell did you mean by offering? And can I just say, while we're all sitting around chatting like this, is it absolutely necessary to have me tied to a chair like we're in some crappy noir thriller?"

They both looked at me thoughtfully.

"I'm human, you two are vampires," I explained in as friendly a voice as I could manage. "I'm fairly certain you're faster and stronger than me. If I was going to try and make a run for it, I don't think I'd get very far, do you?"

They exchanged glances again.

"It's just … look, I've had a really awful night. I would love a coffee."

Jessica shrugged, seemingly uncaring either way. Helena crossed over to me and, in a few swift moves, tore off the duct tape from my wrists, behind my back and round my ankles. She wasn't gentle about it, or maybe I was just a wuss, because I yelped a little. I couldn't help it. Everyone has arm hair, even if it is very fine, and it bloody hurts.

"Look, honey, just so we're clear," Helena said to me good-naturedly. "If you do decide to do anything stupid, I will have to rip your head off your shoulders. And I really *will* do it. I don't want to, to be honest. It's messy and dry cleaning is expensive. So just play nice, okay?"

I rubbed my wrists angrily as she stepped away.

"I don't recall you Black Sabbath guys playing *nice* when you tazered that boy and then ran me off the road and threw me in a van."

Jessica had stood and was pouring me a coffee by the counter. I hadn't actually seen her get up from the sofa. These two might look like the cast of *Desperate Housewives* while out of their uber-gothic Halloween costumes, but I had to remind myself that they were still vampires. They moved faster than I could follow when they wanted to.

"It's Black *Sacrament* dear," Jessica said. "And don't blame *us* for your kidnapping, we weren't even there. Those were Gio's boys. They're can be a little heavy handed. Personally, I think they've played a tad too many video games. Gio wasn't leaving things to chance though. Not after you gave him the slip at the club. He's pissed enough as it is that your loverboy Allesandro got away."

Of course, Allesandro had gone flying off the bike at the same time as I had. So he had got away? How? And where the hell was he now?

"It would have been a lot simpler if you'd just stayed put at the fundraiser," Helena said, as though I had been deliberately difficult just the vex them. "We weren't even there for you. Not yet anyway. But I guess two birds, one stone, right?"

I remembered the sight of Oscar, crumpling on the snowy steps as a few thousand volts ran through his idiotic body. God knows why, but I couldn't help feel sorry for the kid. He was just a dumb Helsing, playing a dangerous game because he was bored. I wouldn't wish this on him. I wondered if they had him somewhere else in the building.

"You were there for Oscar."

Helena made a face.

"God, no! That little crack head? He's a pain in the arse," she said. "Do you know he actually tried to chat me up at the club one time? He thought he could charm me. Unbelievable! He was pretty out of his skull at the time, I admit, but he does seem to be labouring under the delusion that he's an irresistible catch."

She shook her head.

"No, we had to *settle* for Oscar. If it was him we wanted, we could have taken him any time at the club. No theatrics needed, no dramatic rat-a-tat-boom and all that crap."

"But then…?" I was confused.

The door opened and my least favourite person in the world strode in.

Gio wasn't wearing his customary pale suit, probably because I had bled all over it back in the van. He was wearing jeans and a black cotton jumper. It was like dress-down day at the vampire office. He smiled at me as though we were the best friends in the entire world, his too-bright eyes flashing happily on his thin pale face.

"We were *there* to collect the *old man*, my precious girl," he trilled. "Dear old Marlin Scott. One has to seize the opportune moment when one can."

He closed the door gently behind him and stalked across the room, his shadow thrown up against the wall. I saw from his glance that he noticed I was no longer tied to the chair and he shot a rueful look at the two female vampires.

It was a strange sight, like seeing one of your teachers outside of school in their own clothes. A bit comical, but his towering presence rolled into the room before him, an almost physical thing, a wave of power. I shrank back in my seat involuntarily as he made his way across the chamber to me. Once bitten, twice shy. That's me.

"It was *easy* to take Vyvienne Trevelyan," he explained. "She lived alone, she's not very high profile, and she drove the exact same way to work every day – so predictable."

He shook his head, evidently amused by the quirks of humans.

"We had to pick her up ahead of schedule, of course. She wasn't a *completely* unintelligent woman and she knew she was being watched, being followed."

He reached me and hunkered down in a squat, rocking on his heels as he brought himself to my eye level. He looked like a little league coach about to give his team a pep talk.

"When we saw she was spooked, we moved in and took her, right off the street, just like that," he clicked his long white fingers in front of my face, making me flinch. "Trouble was, we also needed her information. I'm sure you agree that I can be *very* persuasive when it comes to getting people to tell me what I want to know, so you can imagine my irritation when she told me she had destroyed all her files – destroyed everything *we* needed access to."

A tiny frown creased his brow.

"Troublesome bitch," Jessica growled from the sofa.

"Access to what?" I asked, still trying to lean back out of his reach.

"Not your concern," Gio said. "We did eventually convince her to share the fact that she had another copy. We even got her to tell us where it was, in your very own workstation, safe down in Blue Lab where none of us wicked, wicked Genetic Others could get our nasty mitts on it."

"Did you *convince* her with a pair of pliers?" I asked, forcing myself to meet his stare.

Jessica snorted a harsh laugh.

"Not me, my dear," Gio replied, his eyes narrowing.

He didn't like my defiance. Not one bit. For all his friendly airs, he wanted me scared, cowed by him. The friendly smile returned quickly, though.

"That work was done by another. Our dear friend the Bonewalker needs the teeth, you see. We need to supply the goods so it can do what must be done. All that hoodoo-voodoo nonsense is the Bonewalkers' area you see. They're good with the dead. I simply haven't the time."

He spread his hands plaintively. "I have an entertainment industry to run after all."

Gio and his crew were working with a Bonewalker? This was unheard of.

"And Jennifer Coleman?" I asked. "Are you behind that too?"

His head was on one side like a curious cat. I hadn't forgotten the feeling of his teeth tearing into my throat. Looking at him was like staring down a panther, who had decided to be playful but might tire of it at any moment. He was searching for a reaction. I gave him none.

"She just *loved* vampires," Gio said. "She thought, as all her activist friends do, that we should all just fall into line and pay taxes and mow our lawns, like the rest of your little world."

His smile fell instantly.

"We didn't have to pull her off the street." He snarled. "We just invited her here. Of course, it wasn't *quite* the meeting of inter-species minds she had been expecting, but … the end justifies the means."

"She put up a bit of a fight that one," Helena grinned, raising her coffee cup to Gio. "I liked her. While she lasted, I mean."

"*Marlin Scott*, however, now that's a trickier fish to catch," Gio said, nodding knowingly at me. "How exactly does one get one's hands on one of the city's most powerful men? A man who is famously anti-GO, hugely paranoid and lives in a high security, private estate surrounded by security twenty-four hours a day? He's almost impossible to gain access to, even for us."

"But thanks to Oscar…" Jessica piped up.

"Ah yes," Gio smiled benevolently. "Dear, sweet, stupid and delicious Oscar, my little baby bird. I was so happy when we saw him in the district. Imagine our good fortune, a Helsing right within the old man's camp. All we had to do was invite him to Sanctum, ply him, spoil him, make him feel welcome. Give him what he wanted." Gio looked nostalgic. "I do truly find myself fond of the child. His blood is sweeter than most."

My skin was crawling. Gio was deeply unhinged, that much was clear.

"He certainly gave us what we wanted, information on his father's movements," the vampire told me. "I don't know if you know this, Doctor, but Marlin Scott is not a well man. He hardly ever leaves his estate these days, barely ever attends any society functions anymore. He's like a ghost. When Oscar let it slip that his dear old daddy would be attending his annual fundraiser in person … well, we had to seize the moment, didn't we? To strike, as they say, while the iron is hot."

"Harder to get to him than the others, though," Jessica said. "Big public event, lots of security, hence the 'terrorists'."

She actually made quotation marks in the air with her fingers. Gio just nodded.

"The DataStream news is frantic with it already this morning," he smiled. "You've been out cold all day. It's all over the news. The attempted sabotage of the Mankind Movement by suspected GO rights militants. Let them take the blame. We left enough evidence at the scene to incriminate them."

He shrugged. "We can't afford to have the full fury of the Cabal rain down on us before our work is done. We of the Black Sacrament are only five, you see. Even if your people are weak, they outnumber us enough to make a difference so I didn't use any vampires at the library. All my men at the fundraiser last night were human. You would be amazed what services money can buy, and I am not a poor man."

"What did you want with Marlin Scott?" I asked. If he was going to kill me, I wanted answers first.

"What the hell are you people trying to achieve? And what does *any* of this have to do with my father?"

Gio held up a finger. He looked impressed.

"Ah, clever girl. You're a natural detective it seems."

He actually sounded pleased.

"What we wanted with him was his *teeth*," he hissed, his mood darkening   a   little. "But the best laid plans of mice and vampires … you can imagine the irony, when I had gone to so much trouble – causing a scene, frightening all those poor, innocent people who were just out to have a good time and show their support for the abolition of my kind – when we cornered old man Scott in the chaos, only to discover…"

"… The old fuck didn't have any," Jessica interjected.

Gio frowned over at her, irritated at having his monologue interrupted. He's eyes flicked back to mine.

"*False teeth*," he muttered, spitting the words disgustedly as though they were rude. "You humans. Honestly. Seventy or eighty years and you all start falling to pieces. Marlin Scott had not had his own teeth in his wrinkled head for many a year."

His face had darkened. I'm a big enough girl to admit that look scared me.

"Lucky we had a plan B," Helena said soothingly to Gio.

She seemed to sense his temper was rising and was trying to buck him up. I wondered at their strange relationships. He simply nodded, blinking away the fury.

"Yes, of course. Dear little Oscar. I would have liked to have used the original. The Bonewalker tells me it's stronger that way, for the sacrament it will perform for us. Otherwise, of course, I would have used the boy weeks ago, but we work with what we have. Oscar the blood junkie is to come in useful after all. The same bloodline, you see? The same DNA, the same family."

He couldn't help but see the disgust on my face.

"You still think we are the bad guys here, don't you, Doctor? That *we* are the monsters under the bed? You haven't got a clue. You sit there judging us, when you know nothing."

He wasn't remotely smiling now. Helena made a soothing, shushing noise at him but he ignored her.

"What we want is *revenge*; for what was taken from us to be returned. And what we want is for you humans to be held accountable for destroying this world we all used to enjoy. If you want to know who the villains are, look to your own."

"The sun will rise," Jessica said, her drawl making the words sound odd, "and the Pale will become once again what they were always *meant* to be."

"I don't know what you're talking about!" I said. "You all seem to think I should, but I'm fucking clueless here!"

"You don't have to know anything, my dear," Gio told me. "All I need from you are the files I should have gotten from Trevelyan and then, once everything is in place, your teeth. The files are no good to me whatsoever encrypted. I want to know if your flunkies at the Cabal have managed to open them for us yet."

His eyes flashed at me and I felt his power suddenly rush out and engulf me, as it had back in Sanctum. He was trying to roll me under his mind again.

"Who has the files?" he demanded inside my head.

But I was astonished to find that this time around I *could* resist.

I hadn't stood a chance last time we met. In the club he had rolled me over like a puppy and I had wagged my tail, but now, although I could feel his will crushing down on me, I found myself pushing back against it.

"Fuck … you!" I managed through gritted teeth, struggling against his willpower.

I pushed all thoughts of Veronica Cloves and the Cabal deep down in my head. I didn't know how I was managing to withstand his mental assault so well but I reasoned that if he couldn't get the information out of me, it could buy me some time before the overenthusiastic dentist arrived.

Gio looked momentarily shocked. I felt him redouble his efforts, glaring at me. His presence hit me again like a wall. Pain shot through my head but my body felt strong and I pushed him away with my own mind.

"Answer me, damn you!"

He was becoming annoyed. Behind him, Jessica watched with detached interest, seemingly impressed, but it was Helena who came forward and put her hand on his shoulder.

"Gio, honey, you bled her remember? You won't be able to."

Realisation dawned on Gio's face.

"I can still crack her," he insisted. "It's been long enough for her to build her blood back up."

"Evidently not," she said, her tone still calm and relaxing. "Here, let me."

Gio stood, evidently irritated. He shook her hand off her shoulder and let the blonde vampire take his place in front of me. She smiled down at me encouragingly.

"Look at me, please."

I stared determinedly at her chin. I had no idea why the fact Gio had drank from me meant I was immune to his persuasion, even if it was only temporary. I had no idea how these things worked. But I sure as hell wasn't going to look into this woman's hypnotic, friendly eyes.

"Come on now, don't be silly about it," Helena purred softly, as though she were trying to coax a nervous child.

She bobbed in front of me, trying to catch my eye. I stared down in avoidance, focusing on the pink and coral broach which she had daintily pinned to her jacket lapel.

She slapped me suddenly, across the cheek and very hard. The motion was as swift and unexpected as a viper strike. The pain and shock was so sharp that my head whipped to the side and I found myself staring furiously at her. She was still smiling, and in that second she had me in her eyes.

I immediately felt her mind cover mine like a smothering blanket.

Shit. I am comprehensively terrible at vampires. This much I have concluded.

There was no resisting her as I had done with Gio. I could see him stalking around in my peripheral vision irritably. I had wounded his pride by resisting him. The others had said he was moody, after all. Psychotically volatile, I would have said, but hey, *tomayto tomarto*, right?

Helena's eyes were like diamond, drilling into my head.

"Now then," she said softly. "Are the files decrypted yet?"

"Yes," I answered, against my will.

"Wonderful," she said encouragingly. "See, that wasn't so bad, was it? Now … who has the files right now?"

"Veronica Cloves," I heard myself say. The side of my face stung as though I'd just been lashed by a whip. Helena wanted more. "She's a Cabal Servant. She's just finished decrypting them."

"And where is she now, honey?" Helena asked me lightly, probing gently like a high-school counsellor.

I tried to fight back but my mind was like a dandelion in a hurricane. She blew it apart and pulled the truth out through my lips.

"I don't know. She was at the fundraiser, but she didn't have the files with her, at least I don't think so. They're probably at the Liver, Cabal HQ."

"Why don't we just use the old man?" Jessica said. "Make him bring Cloves in, hand over the files that way."

Gio shook his head. He was stalking the room, his arms folded.

"He's too far gone," he said. "It's becoming less and less convincing. I don't want to risk it and have Cabal come down on us, not when we're so close. Better to get them ourselves."

"We cannot storm Cabal HQ," Jessica pointed out.

"She'd back them up at home." Helena reasoned, glancing at Jessica and Gio for a split second before staring back at me. "Where does she live, Doctor?"

I gave her the address, selling Cloves up the river against my will.

"But you won't get in. The building's warded."

"*We* can't, you stupid girl," Gio said behind her, "but my hired chaps can. They're as human as you are."

"Thank you," Helena said to me, sounding truly grateful, as though I had been playing nice and not just had my brain picked through entirely against my will.

"Go to Hell," I managed to say.

Her sweet smile didn't falter. She walked away and I blinked rapidly as she released my mind. Sweat was beading on my forehead, cool against my hot skin.

Damn it. Now they don't need me anymore. If I was no further use for information, then…

As if on cue, the door behind the trio of vampires opened again and another figure entered, flanked by two male vampires I hadn't seen before. The other members of the Black Sacrament, I assumed. But I wasn't interested in them. It was the apparition standing between them that held my eyes.

My blood ran cold. I wouldn't have believed that I could find anyone other than Gio the scariest thing in a room, but the person who entered was terrifying.

Almost seven feet tall and cloaked from head to toe in a long black hooded robe, it looked like the mad monk Rasputin. Looming into the room larger than life, its face, like with all of its kind, was hidden entirely behind a white porcelain mask with blank, expressionless features.

Whenever I had seen these GOs on the DataStream or in history vids, they had always reminded me of the old Japanese stage demons, like actors clad in Noh masks, their expressions frozen. Through the eyeholes of the terribly blank face, I could see its eyes. They were inky black from lid to lid, like pools of tar. Shark's eyes.

It glided into the chamber, its feet – if it even had feet – invisible beneath the long robes. Its hands were tucked into its voluminous sleeves like a Gregorian friar. Moving slowly, like a ghost or a deep-sea creature drifting along the current, it was utterly silent.

It was a Bonewalker.

I had never seen one in real life before. We didn't know a whole lot about them, unlike the other GOs.

A vampire was a vampire at the end of the day, and those who called themselves Tribals fit pretty closely with our werewolf mythology. But the jury was out on what the hell Bonewalkers actually were. Some suggested they were a kind of ghost, a spirit made flesh. Others, including some very vocal Mankind Movement supports, insisted they were demons walking the earth. I was wondering, in the light of recent events, if they were the truth behind the myth of the Tooth Fairy.

They rarely spoke. They came and went as they pleased, and seemingly on their own whims, deciding their own allegiances.

Cabal had dealings with Bonewalkers. They had used their powers to move a lot of Britannia's furniture around. No one knew what the price had been or what the Bonewalkers had wanted in return. A lot of people, myself included, agreed that Cabal had balls just for engaging with the otherworldly entities. But our government were not the only ones who had made contracts with them.

Marlin Scott himself had managed to commission the services of a Bonewalker somehow, in the course of making his fortune. Their unique talents, bending and reordering space amongst them, had enabled him to develop the technology for the wall in the first place.

Again, no one could say for sure what they had asked in return for their contribution to his work, if anything. Some of the more hysterical tabloids had suggested Marlin has sold his soul for wealth and fortune. It was ironic really that he was now such a staunch opposer of all GOs in his old age, when the bell was quite literally tolling. Maybe the Bonewalker would be paying him a visit again someday soon.

The Bonewalker drifted further into the room, its black eyes silently taking in the three vampires and then me as it towered over us all. I felt very vulnerable in my chair.

It tilted its head slowly and questioningly at Gio, who looked uncharacteristically demure in its presence.

"We have what we need from this one," the vampire said, gesturing to me. "She is the last offering. What of the boy? Has our dentist upstairs done his work?"

The Bonewalker parted its hands. It had been carrying a small black package in its sleeves. It held this out toward Gio silently. Its hands were long and thin, with elongated fingers.

The vampire smiled down at the package as though it were a Christmas present.

"Good. Excellent. We will deliver those, like the others. And then," he smiled coldly at me, "we will take the last of our ingredients."

I stared at the ghoulish apparition of the Bonewalker, dominating the room like a silent grim reaper, and at the small box it carried. I knew instantly what was in the box.

Teeth. Oscar's teeth.

Did this mean he was dead? I had no idea. But I knew I was next.

Gio crossed the room toward me, dwarfed by the Bonewalker which had turned its empty, masked face toward me and was regarding me with cool, inscrutable indifference.

"Sadly, *you* will never know how the story ends, my dear Phoebe," he said, baring his teeth at me.

He dragged me to my feet roughly and turned me around. For the first time, I saw what lay behind me in the centre of this subterranean room, a deep stone well flush with the floor. My chair had been right on the brink of it. A dark abyss. The animal smell I had noticed was wafting up from it.

Just when I was wondering what could make this happy gathering even more fun – vampires, a Bonewalker, a creepy dungeon, a less than gentle dentist waiting to meet me. Ah yes, of course, a big black well of despair. That's the ticket.

"I need your teeth," Gio growled, "but we have a little time to play yet. It doesn't matter to me what state the rest of you is in."

His breath was hot on my neck. I stared down into the pit, my eyes wide.

"I don't like being made a fool of twice. I think it's time for you to find out what happened to your friends."

Before I could react, he pushed me lightly in the back. For one horrible, timeless moment, I teetered on the lip of the stone pit. From the corner of my eye, I could see the Bonewalker watching me. Its pale mask was stone, its black eyes glittering. Helena and Jessica were behind it, both leaning against the sofa looking thoroughly unconcerned, as though this were the most normal thing in the world. Jessica was still sipping her steaming coffee.

And then I fell – arms flailing, into the darkness below with an unheroic shriek.

25

The pit wasn't as deep as I'd imagined. I fell for maybe a couple of seconds before I hit the floor painfully in the darkness, jarring my knees badly as I fell, sprawling on my front and grazing the skin off my hands.

I managed to land partially on my side, preventing my head from smacking against the floor but winding myself terribly in the process. I lay gasping for a few seconds. The ground beneath my hands was wet. It was two or three inches deep in rank water or sewage, I couldn't tell which.

I rolled painfully onto my back and stared up at the circle of light above me. At least I hadn't broken anything. Gio was silhouetted against the well's mouth, and he gave a little wave.

"Enjoy your family time," he called down to me. "We'll be back to pick up the teeth shortly."

I couldn't have replied if I'd wanted to; the air had been knocked out of my lungs. I forced myself to get to my knees despite the screaming pain.

So much for feeling hale and hearty.

I was guessing my miraculous healing after the bike accident had something to do with Gio feeding from me. Had it mended me? With the first moment's leisure I'd had since waking up, my aching hand went to my neck. I'd expected a ragged wound, but there was nothing I could feel there other than two small lumps, tender to the touch. Vampire bites, nothing more. If I hadn't just been thrown down a pit of death, I'd be feeling fit and ready to take on the world.

The stench down here was terrible. In the darkness, strange shapes surrounded me, lumps on the wet floor. Piles of garbage?

Before I could investigate, I heard a commotion above. Raised voices. Were the vampires arguing amongst themselves?

And then I heard a phone ringing. The everyday sound seemed ridiculous in this setting. The tinny sound of Gary Numan's 'Cars' floated down to me – just the opening bars, over and over. It was my ringtone.

I make no apologies. Retro pre-war classics are not to be sneered at.

The bastards had my phone up there, probably taken when I'd been grabbed, and now someone was calling me.

No one *ever* called me.

"Boss," a male voice said, up in the room. "We have a situation upstairs."

I was guessing another member of the Sacrament.

"What are you talking about?" Gio's voice demanded, over the electro pop. "Will someone turn that damn thing off?!"

I heard the clatter of heels across the flagstones – Jessica I guessed – and the ringing phone stopped.

"There are people outside, upstairs in the street," the new male vampire was saying, sounding worried. "A lot of them. I think … I think they're Cabal."

A flurry of expletives filled the room above me. I struggled unsteadily to my feet in the muck. They all started talking at once.

"How?" Gio demanded silencing the others. "No one could know we are here!"

"Gio, we need to deal with this, now," Helena's voice was calm and reasonable as always. "They've no reason to come down here. But if the Cabal are snooping around—"

"I'll fucking deal with them," Gio snapped. "Get upstairs, all of you. They can't possibly know we have the boy and the woman here. There's no way they could. We weren't followed. I'll get rid of them."

I heard them all leave. The door slammed.

Leaving me alone in the dark pit.

I was panicking more than a little. But if what they said was true, if Cabal were here (wherever *here* was) and snooping around Gio's secret den…

A tiny glimmer of hope ignited in my chest.

They would want to come in, look around. The Cabal had the right to do that everywhere, all as part of the common interest legislature. And if the vampires of the Black Sacrament resisted or refused, there would be trouble. You didn't refuse Cabal.

Had the cavalry really arrived? Tracked me here somehow? I had no idea how anyone could. Then, up there in the room I had fallen from, my phone started to ring again.

Of course, my mobile, I thought. GPS.

Vampires, for all their insistence that they had moved with the times, apparently were not that up on basic tech.

It would be Cloves behind it no doubt, tracking my whereabouts like a true government snoop. For once I was grateful for her stalking me. She must have had my phone tapped. I wondered if she was here in person or if she had just sent a fleet of Cabal ghosts, hopefully armed to the teeth.

As I stared up, a black shape suddenly leaned over the lip of the pit. It was the Bonewalker. It hadn't left with the others. Was it staying behind to guard me? Or just to creep me the hell out?

The sight of the GO staring down at me like an empty-eyed corpse startled me, its face as unsympathetic as a store mannequin. I stepped backwards, losing my footing in the pit, and fell over one of the large misshapen lumps. I lay sprawled in the muck again, spitting out rancid water and cursing the creepy shit above me with every foul word I could think of.

"I suppose you think that's funny, do you?" I yelled up furiously. My voice was cracking with fear. "Well screw you, you big silent bed sheet-wearing fuck!"

My hand grabbed at the lumpy mass to steady myself, and I froze. I had grabbed a forearm. Shakily, I felt along the length of the cold wet limb, my eyes straining to see in the darkness.

I had just fallen over a body.

A wispy nodule atop what I guessed was the torso bobbed at my grasping fingers and, at my fumbling, the head of the corpse wobbled on its neck and fell with a crack to face me.

I screamed.

It was a good scream. I didn't know I could scream like that. People did in old black and white horror movies, but I had always thought it was a little over the top. Apparently as I now discovered, when occasion demanded, it was pretty bloody fitting.

It was difficult to make out in the darkness, but I was staring at the ravaged, bloody-mouthed face of a young woman. Her blank, staring eyes were wide, already covered with a filmy cataract of death; her face leered at me like a monster from a haunted house, the lips and chin coated in a thick crusty beard of dried blood. I dropped the dead arm and scooted backward in the muck on my rear. Goosebumps were fluttering up my arms.

Her head had long matted dreadlocks, glued together with filth and blood. She was even still wearing her ultra-hip glasses, though they were askew on her face in a way that would have been comical if she hadn't been so extremely dead and extremely close to me.

There was no mistaking the identity of this body. I had seen her face on the DataStream only yesterday morning at Cloves' apartment. This rotting, disfigured corpse was Jennifer Coleman, the GO activist. Her teeth may well be sitting in a box at Blue Lab, but the rest of her was inches from me in a stinking charnel pit, merrily decomposing.

I covered my mouth to cut off my scream, my hand shaking uncontrollably. I almost bit my fingers off. Far above me, I was dimly aware of loud noises in the building above; shouts and crashes above the basement. Was a there a struggle going on up there? What the hell was happening? Were the Cabal storming the building?

I risked a look upwards. In the basement room at the top of the well, all was calm. The Bonewalker still stared down at me, utterly unmoved by my macabre discovery. I wondered if the body here was its handiwork.

I had shuffled back so far into the darkness that my back hit another soft object. I jumped away from it with a yelp. My nerves were utterly gone. I turned, wide-eyed.

This second lump was a body as well; face down in the water, its arms and legs splayed at odd angles and its ample frame bunched up. It looked as though it had been either unconscious or dead when it was thrown in the pit. From the smell, I'd say it was definitely dead now.

I couldn't see its face, but I saw that one of its legs was missing a shoe. Oh dear God.

Swallowing the urge to cry uncontrollably and vomit at the same time, which would have been neither brave nor useful, I forced myself to inch back toward the bloated, waterlogged corpse instead.

Through some tremendous overriding of natural instinct, I kicked at the shoulder a few times with the toe of my shoe, each time uttering a small 'ew ew ew' noise of revulsion. Ultimately, I made the body roll over in the shallow water so it lay face up.

I slowly lowered my still trembling hand from my mouth.

"Oh Vyvienne," I breathed, staring at the ruined face in the darkness.

I couldn't tear my eyes away from that the wide, empty stare or the sunken, toothless mouth, bloody as though it had been painted with too much glossy lipstick.

I had found Trevelyan at last. What was left of her.

"I'm so sorry."

Most people have wished their manager dead at least once during a particularly frustrating day at the office. I was no different, but this was not an end I would have wished on my worst enemy. She had never been much of a looker in my opinion, but having the inside of your face removed and then floating face down in sewage for a couple of days was never going to make much of an improvement.

I don't think I'll ever forget that face. Thank God for the darkness.

I was shaking all over. Gio and his Black Sacrament buddies had taken these women, torn out their teeth and thrown them away like garbage down this godforsaken pit.

We were nothing to them. We weren't people. We were offerings, just lumps of meat to be harvested. And now they had Oscar and me too. I didn't want to end up like this.

I wouldn't even be in this mess if Trevelyan hadn't gotten me involved. Obviously she had known something about our fathers' past which I did not. I only knew my father had been a biologist. It's partly the reason I went into science myself; to honour his memory. But by the time I was born, our world had changed. He was drafted into the wars as an Army Medic. He was an old man when he died, leaving me clueless. I wish I'd spent more time hacking her system, although all that had been left was the Military Application details. I was guessing whatever was going on was to do with a different department she had been involved in. What had they been? Archives and Development?

I had lost the photo I had stolen from her house somewhere in the chaos at the library, but I remembered what it had said underneath.

Me and the Development Team

What the hell did you know that I didn't, Trevelyan?

I fought between the twin urges to cry over her body with horror at her death, and kicking it repeatedly in frustration.

Above us, the Bonewalker still stared down impassively, and beyond the door I heard more shouting and what sounded like muffled gunfire.

My eyes roamed around the pit. They were becoming adjusted to the darkness down here.

It was a small space no more than twenty feet across, an oubliette at the bottom of the well shaft. There was no way in or out that I could see. The crumbly walls were too slick with slime and water to consider climbing. And besides, I doubted the Bonewalker would just let me haul myself out at the top. Although it might. Who knew what their kind were actually thinking?

Against my instincys, I forced myself to look at the corpses of the two women. For God's sake Phoebe, they're just dead bodies. You're a Doctor, it's not like you haven't seen dead people before. Get a grip.

And that's when my roaming eye saw that one of the late Jennifer Coleman's legs had been gnawed on. It was a ragged, bloody stump. Interesting fact about vampires: they don't eat human flesh. They will drink you dry if you let them and sometimes, I had most recently discovered, even if you didn't. However, they weren't, as far as I knew, much into the habit of ripping off chunks of flesh to eat.

Beyond Coleman's body, I noticed another dark shape, a lump hunched against the wall. As I noticed it, I saw that it wasn't another body, not a dead one anyway.

It was something crouched, very still in the darkness-now that I had seen it, I realised that its chest was moving quickly. It lurked in the shadows, watching me with interest. Quickly I realised, it was the source of the animal smell.

I moved backwards, very, *very* slowly, barely making a ripple in the fetid sludge. Its head twitched and I froze, watching as it cocked its head to one side as though it were sniffing blindly for me.

I gave it a moment and then moved slowly away again, my heart thudding in my chest. I tried to manoeuvre so that the remains of Jennifer Coleman were between me and the thing, but it also moved forward, slowly, stealthily. It was stalking me in the darkness. It came toward me enough that the dim light which fell from the well shaft above threw some faint illumination on its shape.

It had bald, skull-like features, as though the bones were protruding against its tightly drawn, mottled grey skin. It was naked as a babe with scrawny, sinew covered arms and legs, and an emaciated sunken chest.

Slowly, it slithered on all fours in my direction. Its lower face was all long sharp teeth, grinning like a demon in the darkness. Its eyes were dark pits.

A Pale.

Gio and his buddies were keeping one of the Pale in this pit as a pet. Vampires, Bonewalkers, and now this?

"Oh, come *on!*" I complained aloud to the universe. "*Seriously?*"

This was the second Pale I had seen in as many days. The first had been behind toughened glass and sedated with nerve gas, and it had still scared the hell out of me. You can imagine how I felt at the bottom of a dark well full of corpses, with one of them circling me in the gloom, eyeing me hungrily.

Fuck. I was going to die. There were no two ways about it. The Pale killed. It was what they did – what they were made to do.

If I'd been holding a machine gun, I might have stood a slim chance against one of them in a confined space. As it was, armed with nothing but harsh language and the freshest meat this man-made ghoul had seen all day, I was well and truly shafted. No down-the-well pun intended.

I wondered briefly if it would be disrespectful of me to try and wrench off the rest of Jennifer Coleman's leg and at least use that like a club. It wouldn't stop the nightmarish bastard from tearing me to pieces, but I could at least go down fighting. I might even land a few good blows before it took me down. I could die kicking my murderer in the head with someone else's foot.

The Pale growled deeply at me. It hadn't attacked me yet. Was it sated, only just fed? Or just taking it's time? I had nowhere to run after all.

I had time to wonder whether Trevelyan and Coleman had been dead already when their bodies were discarded down here, or if Gio's crew had let their Bonewalker friend harvest their teeth and then just thrown the women down here, still alive. A little entertainment for the monster.

I hoped they were dead beforehand. Gio hadn't bothered taking my teeth, whatever the hell they were needed for. He had Oscar's to play with for now. He had wanted me down here beforehand, with this thing, for fun.

If I ever got out of here, I swore I would kill that vampire myself.

The Pale opened its mouth slightly, a long rattling hiss escaping its throat. I could see its breath clouding. It was cold down here. I braced and gritted my teeth as I saw the beast lower into a deeper crouch. It was getting ready to pounce, to throw itself at me. I had seconds to act.

Above me, the noise was getting worse. The vampires of the Black Sacrament had clearly not cooperated with the authorities. I heard something slam repeatedly, twice, three times. Someone was throwing themselves against the door up there, trying to shoulder it open.

I glanced upwards. The Bonewalker had turned away, no longer looking down but away from the well, at the door to the basement.

"Help me!" I shouted at the top of my lungs, hoping to hell that it was the Cabal guys at the door.

There was definitely a skirmish of some kind going on up there. Had they forced their way in?

"Hey, I'm down here!"

The sound of my voice seemed to startle the Pale. Did it regard my bellowing as a show of aggression? A warning? Whatever it thought, it didn't like it. It roared at me – an inhuman, low shriek.

Above me came the sound of splintering wood, and then a familiar voice.

"Doctor!"

Was that Allesandro?

I couldn't see the Bonewalker above me anymore. My whole attention was on the Pale, mainly because it had just made its move, throwing itself toward me through the darkness, jaws open, claws outstretched. Jesus, it was fast.

I threw myself to the floor, splashing into the water so that the abomination sailed above me. I slammed against Jennifer Coleman's body and instinctively grabbed at it, pulling it into a macabre bear hug and rolling it over so that I was beneath it, the water almost closing over me. I felt the Pale land atop the corpse, heavy and urgent. It began to rip and tear into what it thought was its prey, as I rolled out from under the poor woman above me.

I would feel bad later. The way I saw it, she was already dead. She wouldn't mind. I, on the other hand, wanted to stay alive as long as possible, even if that was only the next few seconds.

I crawled away through the muck on my stomach.

"Phoebe!"

The voice called out to me from above. It was definitely Allesandro. I heard struggling, was he fighting the Bonewalker? *Could* you even fight them?

I didn't have much time to ponder this because the Pale, hunched over what was left of Coleman's body that now resembled shredded pork, flicked its head my way, realising that I had escaped its attack.

There was nowhere left to run, no hiding. I wouldn't get a second reprieve. It stood, its furious gimlet black eyes, like sparkling lumps of coal, were trained on me as gore dripped from its jaws.

There was a thump from above. The Pale and I both looked up at the same time to see the surreal sight of the Bonewalker and Allesandro tumbling down the well shaft towards us. Allesandro had his arms wrapped firmly around the Bonewalker.

He must have thrown himself at it, diving for it in a rugby tackle and driving both of them stumbling over the lip of the pit. He looked, as he descended, as though he were wrestling an outlandish oversized bat, as the Bonewalker's black robes whipped about them.

They landed directly on top of the Pale, crushing it into the water in a confusion of limbs and struggling movement in the darkness. Water erupted, blinding me.

I had half pulled myself to my feet when out of the flailing pile of bodies, the evidently unharmed Pale disentangled itself and threw itself at me.

It hit me hard, slamming me into the floor, its solid, bristling weight above me. Its jaws snapped inches from my face, once, twice, as I thrashed to keep out of its range. And then it sank them into my collarbone.

The agony was immediate and unbearable. I felt it tear through meat, sinew and muscle until its sharp teeth scraped against my bone. I heard a scream, distant and horrifying. I didn't immediately realise that it was coming from me. I felt its long claws puncture the skin of my upper arms where it was holding me fast. Each nail was like a slim knife, sliding into my flesh.

Then something landed on top of the Pale, yanking it away. Allesandro had just dragged me from the jaws of living death. I felt each blade-like claw tear out of me.

The vampire looked wild. His face was grazed and bloody, his hair drenched and plastered to his head. He had the Pale in a headlock, the creature roaring furiously and snapping at his arm. His teeth were grinding, fangs fully extended. He didn't look much like a human there in the darkness. Pulling backwards, the two of them rolled away from me in a confused tangle.

My hands went to my throat, choking and coughing, and came away shiny with blood I was losing a lot. The pain was almost too much to bear and I knew I was going to black out soon. I couldn't afford to do that.

I rolled onto my knees and crawled away from the vampire and the Pale, who were rolling around in the water, each trying to get the upper hand. Allesandro was strong but he had only taken the creature by surprise. It was adjusting now.

That was what they did. They adapted, they reacted. It was what made them such efficient killers. It was already gaining the upper hand. The Pale would kill him, there was no doubt about that.

Next to me, rising into a standing position, was the Bonewalker. Its robes were drenched but its expressionless mask was still in place. It seemed to survey the chaos around it with interest. It noticed me and though its dead black eye-holes seemed to pin me to the spot, it made no move toward me.

"Allesandro!" I shouted. The effort tore through my body. The Pale had cut me badly. Part of my rational science brain was telling me it was all over – there was no point struggling now. Even if the Pale didn't kill me, I was as good as gone now.

It had bitten me, tore me up good. In a matter of hours or maybe less, the virus, the genetically engineered code of the Pale, would spread through my system, infecting me. I would become one of them, or else my body would reject the virus and collapse on a cellular level. Either way, to put it in proper clinical scientific terminology, I was well and truly fucked.

But I was damned if I was going to sit here and die quietly. I wasn't going to let the one person who had come to try and help me get ripped apart.

As I watched, the Pale slashed at Allesandro, tearing through his sodden shirt and opening deep red parallel wounds across his stomach.

The move would have disembowelled a human. Vampires were physically denser than us, but it still looked like it hurt.

The vampire went down, his head slamming against the flagstones under the water. The abomination stood, reached down and grabbed Allesandro's head in its claws – it slammed the vampire's skull against the floor three times. Allesandro went limp in its arms. Throwing its head back with a triumphant howl, the creature gathered my now unconscious saviour up in its arms and threw him like a light rag doll towards us.

The vampire landed at my feet in a twisted heap, raising a slurry of water over my knees. I stared down. His lips were bloody but I heard him moan faintly, his eyelids fluttering. He wasn't dead.

I leaned down and put my hands under his armpits, heaving him upwards to his knees. He was larger than me and soaking wet so he felt as heavy as lead – a dead weight in my arms. Or an undead weight, I suppose. The blood loss was making me feel lightheaded and a little giddy.

I hoisted him up, wrapping one arm around his waist and holding him to me protectively, though the effort of doing so made my vision blur and threaten to fade altogether. I shook my head, trying to clear it, trying to ignore the searing pain now coursing through my body and spreading outward from my wounds like a fever.

The infection of the Pale was taking hold.

With my free arm, I reached up and gripped a handful of the Bonewalker's robes, twisting the fabric around my hand tightly.

I looked up to see the GO looking down at me. Its mask regarded me solemnly, as though it had only just noticed the blood-soaked human woman kneeling next to it, cradling the half-conscious vampire lying sprawling at its feet. It seemed to regard us both with faint interest, as though observing lesser creatures in a detached manner.

"Get us out of here!" I shouted up at it.

It stared back at me blankly, its black eyes beyond the mask like dark mirrors.

"I know you can! If we stay here, we all die," I spat. "You will too, you know. You might not be human but you're physical. You have a body and that fucking thing is going to tear it apart as surely as it will mine and his."

The Bonewalker looked over to the Pale, as though noticing it properly for the first time. The grey skinned monster was flexing its claws, looking at the three of us, sizing us up. Its weight shifted from foot to foot. It was preparing to jump for us. We had seconds before it was on top of us again.

"You will die down here too," I insisted. "Move us! You know how. That what you do! You move things around. Take us out of here, or die down here with us. Do it!"

There was nothing I could feel under my fistful of robe that seemed like a normal body. But I held on tight, making it drag me and my vampire with it.

"Now!" I screamed.

The Pale leapt. I saw it leave the ground in a spray of water and sailing through the air towards us, a blind knot of aggression, fury and intent to kill. The Bonewalker's hands were suddenly in view, long and white in the darkness. It made a small gesture in mid-air, like elegant tai-chi.

As the Pale descended onto us, I closed my eyes instinctively and braced for the attack, but then the world shifted. My stomach lurched, like when a rollercoaster drops you, and my ears popped.

There was suddenly silence around me. Cold kisses on my face and shoulders, soft and chill.

My eyes shot open. It was snowing. The flakes fell onto my face, onto the vampire before me, and onto the wet black robes of the Bonewalker.

We were outside. The pit, the Pale, the dead bodies and the slurry were all gone. The Bonewalker was standing in an inch of snow on a deserted side street, myself and Allesandro in a tangle by its feet, exactly as we had been a second ago.

I let go of the robe in shock and the GO moved slowly away from me, still staring down inscrutably through its mask. I couldn't guess what it was thinking. It was utterly alien. It didn't feel particularly hostile. I wondered why on earth it was working for Gio. Why did any of the Bonewalkers work for others, when they were so powerful?

I looked around frantically. The street we were on was no more than a large alleyway emptying out from the backs of shops with cold cobbles underfoot. I stared down at the cobbles incredulously, watching the snow turn red slowly, drop by drop. I didn't immediately realise that it was my blood tinting the scene. I was bleeding from the throat, where the Pale had bitten me.

Infected me.

"W—where?" I tried to ask.

At the end of the alleyway, I could see out into the street beyond. There was a lot of action out there. Several police cars were pulled up, and a few dark tinted unmarked vehicles that I guessed were Cabal. They were arranged haphazardly in the street, parked in a rough semicircle around what I saw was a church. I recognised the stubby square tower. It was Carfax, which meant we were on the corner of St Aldate's on Cornmarket Street.

Suddenly, there came the muzzle flash of gunfire within the church. Was that where we had been? Beneath Carfax? Gio's private torture room, right here in the heart of the city? Good transport links, excellent Wi-Fi and an en-suite monster pit in the basement.

The Bonewalker, for reasons I couldn't understand, had done exactly what I had asked. It had moved us from the pit beneath the cellars under Carfax to street level, just a little way from the action.

I watched the Bonewalker take in the scene at the end of the alleyway; the chaos of the firefight within the church, its dark windows occasionally blossoming with muzzle flashes, the straggling crowds of rubberneckers it was attracting. It seemed to reach a decision.

Turning to look down at Allesandro and myself one last time, it took another step away from us and simply vanished. It faded away almost instantly, like a shadow blown apart. The last thing to go was the mask, which floated in mid-air alone for a millisecond before disappearing altogether.

We were alone in the snow. Allesandro coughed, his head resting in my lap as I knelt sprawled in the shadows.

"We're alive?" he asked weakly.

I couldn't speak, so I nodded down at him. My body was racked with agony from my infected wounds and it seemed to be getting worse by the second.

"Thank you for coming for me," I managed. "… I got bit."

He forced himself into a sitting position, his eyes widening with alarm.

"The creature?"

I nodded again.

"'Fraid so … Hurts…"

My voice was coming in a croak. I was finding it hard to form coherent sentences in my head now. I knew what this meant. The virus was spreading, much faster than I had thought.

I could feel something building deep inside me, a latent rage, and I knew it was growing. It would get bigger and bigger until it ate me whole and nothing else was left. My mind falling apart as it took over. It wouldn't stop until I became one of them. One of the Pale.

Allesandro rolled off me and to my amazement, he managed to stand, bracing himself against the brick wall of the alleyway. His clothes dripped with the filth from the well. His hairline was bloody, but he didn't seem to notice.

"You can stop it," he insisted. "The infection, you can stop it."

I stared up at him.

"There's no cure," I said. "I'm sorry … if you wasted your evening."

I felt drunk, not all there. It seemed such a shame to me that he had gone to all this trouble for nothing. My beautiful would-be rescuer.

"This makes three times you've tried to save me now … Is it a hobby for you? Didn't work out so well … in the end."

I could hear my words slurring.

The vampire reached down and lifted me roughly by my elbows, dragging me upright. I howled in agony, but he ignored my cries.

"Third time's the charm," he grinned, though it didn't reach his eyes. "Epsilon. I was at your lecture Doctor, I know your work. You must try."

I shook my head, sending spasms of pain shooting down my neck.

"Not a cure, just … a … retardant," I said. "Plus … Boom."

I tried to convey a rat exploding, but I didn't feel coherent enough to do so. I knew I was dead. I had gotten him out alive, or undead – whatever he was. In one piece anyway, more or less. That would have to be enough for me.

"Saved your life," I croaked. "We don't have to keep taking turns you know. They have a boy, Oscar, save *him* … try to, anyway."

I gripped the sodden front of his shirt.

"Promise me."

Allesandro, who seemed to be already healing from his wounds thanks to his nifty undead constitution, caught me under my arms as my legs went from under me completely. My head lolled on his shoulder as he took my weight.

"Save him yourself," he insisted.

He lifted me up and threw me over his shoulder in a fireman's lift. I tried not to throw up as he started to walk down the alleyway, carrying me with him.

"Your serum, it's at your laboratory, right?"

He didn't wait for me to answer. I wasn't sure I could have if I wanted to. I was losing all reasoning. My speech had gone and the anger was building in me, slowly but relentless as a forest fire. Not all of the wetness on my cheeks was blood. I was crying. I didn't want to turn into one of them. I didn't want to disappear and become the thing that went bump in the night.

"My bike is this way," the vampire said, heaving me away from the pandemonium still raging inside Carfax tower as the police and Cabal battled Gio and his men within.

I wondered how Allesandro had found me, how he had gotten down to the basement. But I couldn't have asked him if I'd tried. I was already beginning to think sharp red thoughts, like how good it would feel to bite into his shoulder, to tear at the skin just to feel it rip. I forced the thoughts away, but the hunger was rising.

26

I didn't really remember the ride across the city. Only glimpses, sensations. Streetlamps blurred by, the bike roaring under me. New Oxford slid by in a drunken blur-I passed out more than once, the icy wind whipping around my hair. I felt hot, burning all over with the fever of the Pale.

I awoke to feel myself being carried in his arms across the snowy silent quad, the buildings of the university rearing up dizzily around me, hallucinatory. I felt weightless in his arms, my arms and legs like lead, my head lolling.

And then we were somehow inside, in the blinding antiseptic glare of the entrance corridor.

Mattie, our night security guard, rose from his chair as we approached, a look of shock and horror on his round face. Allesandro said something to him, I didn't catch what. The vampire waved his hand in front of the man's face and the guard dropped out of sight behind the counter – unconscious, I think. I have no idea how he did that.

Another blur and we were in the elevator, descending into the ground. Allesandro was crouched over me, pinning my arms to my sides. I was sat on the floor of the lift, thrashing against him furiously. I don't remember why; I only remember the anger, the furious bloodlust. I wanted to hurt him, to eat him.

He was stronger than me though, for the time being anyway, and held me pinned like a spitting cat. He was talking to me, trying to calm me I think, but I couldn't understand his words anymore. I could hear nothing but my own blood roaring in my ears.

He dragged me out of the elevator and I passed out again, drifting in and out of consciousness. In my brief bouts of downtime, I dreamed of teeth and claws and redness, all primitive lusts and hungers. And part of me liked it.

I came to with my a bar of light sliding across my bleary eyes. I felt my hand roughly slapped against a panel, held tightly by Allesandro and forced into place. He was getting us through the lower security – the iris scanner, the palm pad. He was using me to get in.

The small rational part of me which still existed wanted to warn him about the corridor, the long ultraviolet walk between here and the lab. It was impossible. We couldn't make it.

But the next thing I knew, I was being carried again and on every side of me was blinding blue light, stinging my ever more sensitive eyes. We moved forward haltingly, step by step, shuffling. When I managed to focus enough to look up at the vampire as he carried me along, I saw that his skin was blistering badly. Smoke was rising from the neck of his shirt, from his sleeves, everywhere. He was roasting as though we had stepped into a nuclear reactor, his beautiful face blackening and cracking.

But he didn't stop. He moved onwards still and didn't drop me, gripping me to him so that I could feel the heat and pain radiating from him like a furnace.

The last thing I recall is the lab itself.

I was on the floor, lying in a pool of blood. Allesandro was on his hands and knees next to me, shaking in agony, almost unrecognisable. His clothes had burned to cinders and were glowing with dancing ash. If before he had looked like a renaissance angel, now he had clearly been cast burning from heaven and had landed, scorched and in tatters, deep in the pit. He had fallen.

Someone was shouting, incoherently, and then there were hands on me. Griff's face was above, staring down, filled with shock. I heard him shout to someone else and from the corner of my eye, Lucy, dear sweet Lucy was there, holding a syringe while Allesandro barked orders at the two of them, even as his own body convulsed in shock.

I closed my eyes.

Lucy was alive. This was strangely important to me. A tiny part of me let go, stopped struggling. I couldn't think anymore. I just wanted to rest, and then to wake and feed … and feed … and feed.

27

I woke up on a mortuary slab, which is never a good start. I was disoriented, and groggy. But instantly I felt, I was me.

I wasn't a monster.

The terrible knowing void of hunger was gone. I tried to move but my head rolled weakly to the side. I was in pain, a *lot* of pain. I was dying.

"She's stable, I think," I heard Griff say, somewhere beyond my vision.

His voice sounded tinny and far away, as though through a bad telephone connection in a storm.

"The retardant's holding. Her vitals have evened out but she's lost too much blood. These wounds…"

He sounded desperate.

"I can help."

It was Allesandro's voice – rough and ragged-sounding, his accent thick – and suddenly there was an arm in my view. It was bare and white, still badly blistered here and there but already healing. There was a fresh, messy wound across the wrist, already dripping blood.

"Drink," I heard him say thickly, and he lowered his arm onto my face.

He seemed weak, almost about to stumble. I thought I saw someone behind him, helping him to stand as though he was drunk. Griff?

Instinctively, I tried to turn my face away but his other hand caught me. His grasp was soft but firm, cradling my head.

"It's okay. It won't make you like me, I promise. It will heal you. Drink, or you will die."

He held my face firmly against his arm until I opened my lips and closed them around his wrist. I could taste the salt of his skin on my lips as his blood flowed into my mouth. I drank. I fought the urge to retch as my throat filled with the metallic taste of pennies and blood.

I drank and drank until I passed out again.

28

I woke again.

I didn't know how much time had passed but the lights were low in the lab, as though everyone had gone home for the night. Only the rat cages and the soft private lamps over each workstation were illuminated. That didn't mean much in Blue Lab. It could have been one in the morning or three in the afternoon for all I knew. That was one of the pitfalls of working four levels underground. On the plus side, I seemed, however, to be alone, not a monster, and not dying.

I sat up carefully. I was still on the mortuary slab at the back of the lab. It was the closest approximation we had to anything resembling a hospital bed. The lab was very quiet around me. After my semi-fugue and the chaos of the trip here, it was odd to be surrounded by silence.

I found I was dressed in a white lab coat, and nothing else. Luckily, it was quite big and covered everything from neck to knee. My hands went tentatively to my throat where the Pale had torn into me under Carfax, afraid of what I might find there.

There was no wound, no ragged tear. I checked my arms. No puncture wounds where the claws had slashed into me, just small red crescents like old bruises. I felt … fine. Importantly, I didn't feel like a homicidal bloodthirsty creature which was a definite plus. I was still human … I thought. I seemed to have my mind back.

I slid slowly off the gurney, testing carefully to check my legs could hold my own weight. I was a little lightheaded, but not as though I had just almost died a few times over. It was more like I'd had a sugar rush from one too many M&Ms.

Vampire blood, I thought. It's the new hair of the dog.

Griff appeared out of nowhere, popping his head around the corner of the cubicle space. He must have heard me moving around. So I wasn't completely alone after all.

His hair looked a little wild and he had dark circles under his eyes. I pulled my lab coat tighter around me self-consciously, acutely aware that I was naked underneath. And yes, I was also aware how ridiculous my prudishness was considering I had recently been thrashing around on the floor in my own blood, foaming at the mouth.

My assistant stared at me. I stared back. I couldn't think of a single thing to say.

"Doctor Grace," I said, my voice sounding small in the quiet lab.

"Welcome back Doctor Harkness," he replied hoarsely.

We stared at each other some more, both of us deeply uncomfortable.

"Epsilon?" I asked eventually, when the silence had become deafening.

I watched his Adam's apple work a few times before he answered. He was staring at me like he'd never seen me before. His eyes looked red.

"My revised version, yeah," he said eventually.

He looked scared like he was about to get a scalding from the teacher.

"Brad's still alive and well," he added reassuringly, obviously wondering if I might be concerned about imminently exploding.

A reasonable concern, I'm sure you'll agree.

"We're not cleared for human testing of course but..."

He looked helpless. He ran his hands through his shaggy hair.

"There wasn't much choice, Doc. You were ... turning. I was ... we were losing you."

I nodded slowly. I knew exactly how close I had come to being lost. If the vampire hadn't gotten me here in time, tearing through the city like the proverbial bat out of hell...

"Allesandro? Is he..."

"The vampire's fine," Griff replied, a little curtly I thought, but I didn't have the energy to wonder about this right now. "Resting. He was pretty burned up. I've been watching him while he's sleeping."

He hesitated, looking embarrassed as he realised how odd that sounded.

"Observing his condition, I mean," he stammered. "He's healing faster than anything I've ever seen. I mean, you can literally see his skin reforming. Two hours ago he was covered in third degree burns-and now? Bad sunburn. His rate of regeneration is astonishing."

Griff was a scientist at the end of the day. It didn't matter how much weird the world threw at us, we will always want to study it. We can't help ourselves. We're the ones who run toward erupting volcanoes, measuring tools in hand, while everyone else runs the other way.

I was leaning against the gurney, my legs crossed at the ankle, still hugging the lab coat closed.

"Erm … where are my clothes, Griff?"

"Oh," Griff's face reddened. "That wasn't me! That was Lucy. They were ruined, Doc. Blood, some kind of rank sewage, and burned up in places where the GO had carried you in. She had to pretty much cut you out of them. We put them through the incinerator."

Of course, Lucy. I hadn't hallucinated about her then.

"Where is she?" I asked.

"She went home to get you a change of clothes. She's swinging by mine too, for you know, the dead guy. He was in as bad a state as you almost. Not infected, of course. I don't think the vampires are susceptible but still, he was a mess. We burned all his stuff too but then he set most of his clothes on fire talking a stroll down the security corridor."

"He's *called* Allesandro," I said, walking towards Griff, slightly unsteady still. "Not the dead guy, not the GO – Allesandro. Where is he?"

Griff gestured over my shoulder.

We have three morgue cubicles in the lab; big, oversized silver lockers. We've never needed to cold store anything larger than a dog before. I saw that one of the drawers was now closed.

"It's the daytime boss," Griff told me. "He had to sleep, or whatever it is they do when the sun's up. I think it speeds up their healing too."

I took a moment to register the fact that there was a butt-naked vampire asleep in the dark corpse drawer behind me. It didn't faze me as much as you would expect. The last few days had been all kinds of strange. I was kind of getting used to it.

It was odd to realise it was the daytime. It had been dark when Allesandro brought me in. I must have been out a long time while Griff administered the Epsilon serum and let it take hold, working through my system, undoing the work of the virus.

I took a moment to consider the magnitude of what we had done.

"We are in so much trouble," I muttered. "We have a GO in the lab. The lab designed to keep GOs out. This breaks every possible level of protocol…"

I suddenly remembered something from my fugue; the security guard hitting the floor upstairs at the main entrance.

"Jesus! Mattie!" I yelped.

"It's okay!" Griff said, his hands raised reassuringly. "It's okay. Your crispy vampire just put him under or something, Jedi mind tricks. I've been up to check on him once you two were both, you know, stable. He was reading his newspaper. He doesn't even remember anything. As far as he knows, I think he thought he fell asleep in his chair for ten minutes, that's all."

Griff looked concerned, glancing at the drawer behind me.

"I didn't know the GOs could do that to people," he said in a low voice.

"Oh, they have all *kinds* of fun skills we know nothing about. Trust me," I said, "I've been sampling their less fun party tricks."

"Anyway, he's been off shift for a while now," Griff told me. "It's nearly five o'clock."

I shuffled over to a seat at the nearest workstation and collapsed into it. My mind was still reeling. I put my head in my hands, rubbing my eye sockets with my palms.

"Doc, you know at some point you're going to have to tell me what the hell is going on," Griff said, turning to lean against a desk.

I looked up at him. His face was earnest, serious and worried.

"It's one thing pretending there's nothing wrong while you don't show up for work and then take me casing our boss' house. It's quite another when an undead on-fire GO bursts into the lab carrying your body and telling us that you are turning into one of the Pale."

He shook his head, as though he still didn't quite believe what had happened.

"Lucy claims she knows the vampire guy, from some club or other you two went to? Since when do you go to vamp clubs? Am I the only person out of the loop here?"

I sighed, and rubbed my eyes again.

"Could you get me a coffee, Griff?" I said. "We're not leaving the lab until the sun goes down and I can talk to the deeply sunburned vampire taking a nap in the fridge over there. I need some answers myself and I'm not letting him out of my sight until I get them, so I might as well tell you everything while we wait."

He looked at me expectantly.

"Seriously, Griff," I said, smiling weakly. "Coffee. It may take a while."

I told Griff everything, from start to finish. From Allesandro turning up at the lecture to the alley outside Carfax and all the insanity between. Cabal, the Black Sacrament, the Bonewalker, the bodies, the Pale. My list of horrors seemed endless as I poured it out to him. In retrospect, I reflected, it had been a pretty rough couple of days.

The only part I left out of my story was my clandestine trip down to the MA level and what I had found down there. I'm not quite sure why but I figured he would have enough to deal with digesting our immediate problems without discovering that certain divisions of our employer, our very government, were responsible for mass civilian executions in the name of war. Something told me this was very, very dangerous information to have.

I had tried to keep Griff and Lucy out of this. To keep them safe, I supposed. I supposed that was irrelevant now.

 To his merit, my assistant barely interrupted me, except with the occasional outburst of shocked expletives. He seemed genuinely surprised by my thumbnail sketch of Veronica Cloves. That figured. All anyone ever saw was her earnest, trustworthy, reassuring face on the DataStreams. As the spokeswoman of the Cabal to the media at large, she was practically lovable.

I thought of Lucy, our ditzy chipper lab assistant by day, leather-clad vampire-worshipper by night; Cloves, hardly the beatific charmer once she was off screen; Oscar, the nicely turned-out rich boy with the world at his feet, slumming it undercover as a submissive blood junkie.

And then there was Allesandro, smooth-moves gigolo by trade, seemingly selfless action hero by choice. Even the other vampires I had met, Jessica and Helena, were hardly what they seemed, their gothic image just a false front to pander to our expectations.

Somehow, I found it more disturbing that they had been holding me in a dungeon looking like they had just stepped out of Harvey Nicholls. You expect to be tortured by leather wearing, chain-clad monsters. It was more disturbing when the violence came from someone dressed like a schoolteacher and sipping a macchiato.

Finally, I thought of Gio; the self-styled lord of Sanctum lovingly welcoming his darling Helsings, the mortal children, into his domain each night while secretly hating them all.

Honestly, I wondered if *anyone* in this town was what they seemed.

Did Griff have a double life too? Right now it wouldn't have shocked me to discover that when he wasn't running maths through the system or tinkering with his vintage car, he was moonlighting as a high-wire, fire-eating trapeze artist.

But I doubted it. Griff was the most honest, dependable person I'd ever met. We had worked together for nearly four years. He had never questioned me once. He was loyal to a fault. Now he sat, holding his untouched coffee with both hands. It had gone cold while I had been talking. His face was pale.

"She's really dead then?" he asked. "Trevelyan? And that other woman, the one who's been all over the news yesterday, Coleman, right? This vampire group calling themselves the Black Sacrament, they killed them both … for their teeth?"

I confirmed this with a nod.

"They have Oscar Scott's too," I said. "I don't know if they've killed him yet. I hope not."

"From what you've said, he sounds like a prick," Griff muttered, looking unimpressed.

"Oh, he is," I nodded in happy agreement. "But that doesn't mean he deserves to die, just for being stupid. If people were killed for that, there would be less of a housing crisis in the merry walled cities of good old Britannia. They wanted mine too – my teeth. This Bonewalker they have, they're using it for some kind of magic sacrifice or offering; I don't know, whatever the hell you want to call it. They can do things we can't imagine, the Bonewalkers. I just don't know what it is the Sacrament are trying to achieve."

I had told Griff about the DataStream clip which had arrived at the lab with Trevelyan's teeth; the angry ranting of the guy with the pliers. I was pretty sure by now this was Gio. The portentous warnings that the 'sun would rise'. It hardly sounded like a vampire-centric threat.

I had expected anger from Griff, or at least resentment that I had hidden all of this from him until now. Naturally, I was surprised when, instead, he put down his cup and slid his hands across the desk, taking hold of mine reassuringly.

I looked up at him, confused.

"Don't worry Doc," he said with a small grim smile. "We'll figure this out; you, me and Lucy. We're a team, right? It's what we do. It's what friends do."

I stared at him in blank shock for a moment. His hands squeezed mine. I felt very tired.

So far I had enemies, dubious acquaintances and questionable allies. I hadn't considered adding friends into the equation. I suppose part of my overall problem is that I never had.

I squeezed his hand back silently.

The doors to the blue security corridor suddenly swished open and Lucy came in, rolling a small pink travel suitcase behind her on wheels. I noticed it had a black Hello Kitty stenciled on the side. Of course it did.

She saw me sitting at the table and let out a small yelp. Before I could say anything, she dropped the case and ran across the lab, flinging her arms around me and gripping me in an unexpected hug.

While she squeezed the life out of me and I fought to politely disentangle myself from her, Griff went to fetch the suitcase.

"Oh my God, don't you *ever* do that to us again!" Lucy babbled. "You scared the *shit* out of us! We thought you were dead, and then I thought you must have gotten into trouble at the club the other night and I felt *awful* because after the fire, when we all got thrown out, I couldn't find you and I went on to Bat-tastic because they have half price jello-shots on weekdays and I met this really cute guy, but he ended up being a douche, then I went to my sisters and I was so drunk, *seriously* drunk that she made me stay over and I slept right through and missed work and I didn't even *call* you to see if you got home okay and I lost my phone in the club, then when you came in tonight with that vampire guy from the club and you were both bust up I could have *died*!"

"Lucy!" I said, prising her off me. "Slow down."

She hugged me again for a second then let go, blinking at me with wet eyes.

"I'm sorry, Doc," she said. "I'm such a moron. I shouldn't have left you at the club. Your vampire guy escorted me out. He said he was going back in for you, but then you didn't come out and neither did he, so I figured you two had … you know…"

Her eyes flicked from Griff to me. She raised her eyebrows knowingly at me in what I supposed she thought was a discreet manner.

"… *Gone off* somewhere together? So I ditched you."

"It's okay," I insisted, releasing her from her soul-destroying guilt. "I've been worried about *you*."

I glanced over at the suitcase that Griff had wheeled over to us.

"Please, God, Lucy, tell me there are clothes in there."

Lucy nodded enthusiastically.

"For you and … him," she said, giving me a knowing smirk. "God, I nearly *died* when he burst in here carrying you. What a shock! You should have heard Griff squeal!"

"I didn't *squeal*!" Griff blustered angrily.

"I thought he was going to wet himself," Lucy said, grinning. "Your vampire guy is standing there, smoking and flickering like a roman candle. He was actually *on fire!*"

She fluttered her hands excitedly

"God, it was like something out of a horror movie. He's still pretty hot though, if you'll excuse the pun. So yummy, just carrying you in like that, all draped in his arms, shirt burned right off. I'm so jealous!"

Jealous of me foaming at the mouth and almost dying, because I got to be manhandled by a barbequing vampire? I chose to ignore this and took the suitcase from Griff's hands.

"Oh yes, clearly he has smouldering down to a T," I agreed. "That's ultraviolet light for you."

I took the case into the semi-privacy of the small booth where we had found Angelina the rat's disastrous end. I tried not to think about that as I pulled out the clothes Lucy had brought. Mercifully, there was nothing too outlandish. I settled on black pants and a white wool sweater, with black ankle boots.

I couldn't help thinking about poor, little Angelina.

The same strain of retardant which had caused our beloved lab rat to combust now flowed through my veins, damping, if not completely eradicating, the Pale virus. I sincerely hoped that both Brad the rat and I would last. I glanced over at his cage, and he stared back at me placidly.

We're in this together now, buddy, I thought. You and me against the world.

Griff's final tweaks to Epsilon had stabilised it but the base formula was my own work, so I knew full well what Epsilon was. It wasn't a one shot cure. If the serum held (which was in no way guaranteed), then this was something I was going to have to dose myself with regularly for the foreseeable future, at least every twenty four hours, until we could improve it and maybe make it a permanent inhibitor.

Yay, the remainder of my future on medication. I sighed. It still sounded better than the alternative to me.

I should turn myself in, I realised, report myself to the Cabal and let them know I was carrying the infection, even if it was currently under control. I knew that was what I should do.

I would be considered a Level Two threat and almost certainly quarantined. But is that all they would do? Keep me locked up until they knew the extent of my 'cure'?

From what I had learned of their methods downstairs in the MA division, I didn't trust that. Knowing that part of my company was developing weapons for the Cabal, I wouldn't have expected anything less than medical testing, possible dissection, and then the disposal of my body in a clean incinerator.

I was an unknown quantity now. Cabal wasn't fond of those.

Griff had relayed my story to Lucy by the time I had dressed and freshened up as much as is possible in the lab toilets. I had pinned my hair up off my face but avoiding looking at myself in the mirror, trying to convince myself it wasn't because I was afraid I might see a stranger there.

I had been infected and cured of a bio-militant mutated virus, bitten by one vampire, and I'd drunk from another. All three of these things had had remarkable effects on my physical wellbeing. Was I still a regular human? I sure as hell hoped so.

Just when I thought I couldn't feel any more uncomfortable, I came out of the bathrooms and found myself immediately confronted with a half-naked vampire.

Thankfully, I had been in the bathroom when Allesandro had first awoken so by the time I came out of the ladies room, he was only *half* naked. As I re-entered the lab, he was finishing buttoning up a pair of

Griff's borrowed jeans. Lucy had just handed him a lab coat, her face an odd shade of pink. She looked a little quivery. He didn't seem to notice as he took the lab coat from her graciously.

He noticed me though, and slid his arms into the sleeves as he turned. He looked relieved to see me and strode over to where I stood, the open lab coat flapping around him like a cape. I stared wide-eyed, shocked to see him up and about but also surprised to see there was not a scratch on him.

His blisters were healed, his skin was flawless, his hair its usual wavy mop. The only notable difference was that instead of his customary white skin, he looked remarkably tanned all over. He was positively glowing with health, like a lifeguard in Barbados. I couldn't help but notice his coffee coloured chest and stomach, dark against the white lab coat slung carelessly over his shoulders.

He could have passed for human now. The burns he had received had literally tanned him. My vampire looked less like a crispy mess and more like a lifeguard.

I really had to stop referring to him as 'my vampire', I told myself sternly.

"You're … awake," I made myself say, forcing my roving eyes up to his face and away from what I couldn't help but notice, with scientific detachment of course, were perfectly sculpted obliques. "And dressed – after a fashion."

My voice squeaked a little with embarrassment as Allesandro looked down at me, a tiny smile on his golden face. He was clearly enjoying my attention.

"You too," he said. "More's the pity."

He flicked a thumb over his shoulder without looking away.

"Your companions were kind enough to find me clothing, but I cannot fasten the skinny human's shirt, I'm afraid. We are differently built it seems."

I glanced behind Allesandro to see Griff standing with his arms crossed, looking quite sulky, while Lucy teetered on a chair, her fist crammed in her mouth as she gestured rather rude things at me excitedly. She was practically miming 'hubba hubba' like a cartoon character.

I pointedly ignored her.

"For God's sake, button the lab coat at least," I said. "It's … distracting."

I stepped forward and buttoned the coat up for him. He stood still and let me do so, looking down at me curiously as I slid the buttons together one by one. The sleeves were too short for him, I noticed, and I glimpsed on his darkly tanned wrist a thin white scar, still healing.

"Thank you," I said quietly, as I fastened his top button.

My fingers lingered on the pin. I swallowed hard.

"Thank you for saving me, for the blood. You didn't have to do that."

"You too," he answered. "You could have left me in the pit to die."

His hands closed over mine. They were cold. I looked up at him.

"You came to rescue me. I wasn't going to leave you there."

His blue eyes flickered over me as though he were taking me in, checking I was healed, no longer mutating into the Pale. He seemed so invested in me. I couldn't explain it.

"And besides," I said briskly, pulling my hands out of his and patting his chest in a rather matey way, trying to diffuse the tension quickly. "I needed you to give me a ride here, didn't I?"

He smiled lopsidedly. It wasn't his deliberate Sanctum charmer trademark smile. It seemed like his very own.

"I am very glad you are not dead, Doctor," he said.

"Yeah, me too," I replied. "Although after what we've been through, I think you can probably call me Phoebe."

"Phoebe then," he said softly.

It was almost a whisper. I was painfully, agonisingly aware that Griff and Lucy were both watching us intently and I felt my face reddening like a plum.

"Allesandro," I said firmly, focusing on the matter in hand. "You and I? We need to talk."

29

The four of us sat together around my workstation. Griff had fetched fresh coffee for us all. It must be after sundown, since Allesandro was up and about.

The ruckus at Carfax Tower had been in the early hours of the morning. Surely it was over with now and, if so, either Veronica Cloves and the rest of Cabal or else Gio and his murderous troupe would be out looking for me. Blue Lab was the safest bolthole to be in, I knew. Even Allesandro couldn't have got past the iris and palm scanner without me so we were safe from other GOs, but Cloves could certainly come down here and it was surely an obvious place to look. I didn't know how much time we had.

"It's time you explained to me what the hell is going on," I said to Allesandro. "My life has been one very unpleasant rollercoaster since you slipped your telephone number in my pocket, and I want to know why. Who are the Black Sacrament? What's with the teeth? Why have you double-crossed your admittedly charmless and clearly unhinged clan master? What is on these files everyone is so interested in, and what the hell does this have to do with my dad?"

The vampire looked sidelong at Griff and Lucy, both of whom were watching him intently.

"Your people here, they can be trusted? You are sure?"

"Dude," Griff said irritably, "you're wearing my jeans. What more do you want?"

"They're tight," the vampire complained.

"They are, aren't they?" murmured Lucy distantly, eyes glazed.

"They're my team," I said to Allesandro. "My *friends*. They just saved my ass. They broke every rule we have down here to stop me from dying, and they didn't sell you down the river, when they had all night to do so. You're damn right I trust them. It's everyone else I have a problem with."

Allesandro considered this a moment, and then nodded.

"Very well." He leaned forward. "The Black Sacrament, the ones who have been causing all your problems, are a breakaway group within the vampire community. It's important, to me at least, that you understand that they do not represent the motivations or the interest of the community at large."

He sneered, his fists balling on the workstation.

"They don't even represent the interests of my clan at large. Gio is a fanatic. The others – Jessica, Helena, and the two male meatheads – they follow him out of loyalty; they believe in his cause. Or perhaps they are just used to following orders."

He shrugged, leaning back in the chair.

"I am not one of them. I love my clan brothers and sisters, but they have been led astray by this poisonous sect. They are living in the past, in Gio's obsession."

"What do they want?" I asked.

"The Black Sacrament, Gio and the others, believe that you humans are responsible for ruining what was the old world. Back when we lived in secret, when you thought of us only as myths. Life was better, in their opinion. They do not want to integrate. They do not want to fit in, here in this new world of ours. They don't want to play nicely with others. But that is not all they are angry about. Most of all they want their master back."

"Their master?" Griff asked. "I thought Gio chap *was* the clan master?"

The vampire nodded.

"He is, *now*. He wasn't always." His eyes flicked back to mine. "We are a long lived people, Phoebe. You call us immortal, but you humans know so very little about us really. Gio has been clan master since the wars began. Since our true clan master, a very old and very powerful vampire named Tassoni Bonaccorso was lost to us."

"He was killed when the wars began?" I asked. "You say Gio took over when the wars started, so your clan's original master died before then? When the Pale virus mutated and the world went to hell, I mean?"

Allesandro's eyes were very direct.

"Tassoni didn't die just when the world went to hell …Tassoni *is* the reason the world went to hell."

Allesandro pushed his coffee aside with a sneer. I glanced at Griff and Lucy. They were watching the vampire with looks of suspicion and awe respectively, but were both clearly enthralled by what he was saying.

"Mankind, your people, created the Pale. Everyone knows this. They were intended as a weapon, a defence system – the ultimate super soldier, yes?"

Griff nodded from behind his coffee cup.

"An army of near perfect killers, combat perfect, their DNA tweaked and engineered to make them faster, stronger, quicker to heal, harder to damage."

"A noble cause for your human scientists," the vampire said. "Such an army would be unstoppable, the ultimate deterrent to terrorism and to war. Imagine their dream; a nation protected by near invincible peacekeepers, the whole world saved."

"This isn't anything we don't already know," Griff interrupted, lowering his mug. "We know our own history well enough, thank you."

Allesandro shot him an angry glance.

"Do you?" he challenged. "I'm not sure."

He looked at all of us in turn. There was fire in his eyes now, a deep buried anger I hadn't seen there before.

"Do you not wonder where the technology *came from*, this sudden leap in bio-medical engineering that appeared out of nowhere in the old civilisation. How do you think the Pale were made in the first place?"

He looked around at our faces, his blue eyes now just thoughtful, almost sad.

"Do you really believe they are the product of tampered human cells? Reconditioned human DNA? Impossible. The government of the old world, before the wars, started a quest for a perfect solider, yes, but then they stumbled upon a most wondrous find. Something that would shift the balance of their research."

He leaned forward.

"They found a vampire," he said. "This was long before we had come out of the shadows to drag you back from the brink of your own extinction. This was before the wars, before mankind even knew of our existence. Your human scientists, the government and military of the old civilisation, they found and captured a live vampire."

"Tassoni Bonaccorso," I said, suddenly finding my throat very dry.

The vampire nodded at me.

"The humans took our clan leader. The strongest and most powerful of us. They buried him in a secret laboratory, far from the world of prying eyes. What a *find*. Another species, long thought to be myth. I'm sure they were quite excited by it; better than the missing link, better than the Holy Grail."

His face soured.

"So they experimented on him. They discovered that he was stronger than a human, faster, could regenerate wounds at a phenomenal rate. We believe he suffered greatly at their hands in the name of science; filled with drugs, sampled, dissected, harvested. They didn't care. It's not like he was human, is it? Just a strange animal to be studied and dissected."

His mouth turned downwards in disgust. I couldn't help but think of the Pale in the cell on the MA Level of Blue Lab.

I thought of the test results, all those subjects, all of them dead. But I hadn't felt as bad as I did when I'd discovered the deaths in Cambridge, because they were people. Actual human deaths.

I found I couldn't meet Allesandro's gaze as he continued.

"Tassoni was a powerful being. Old and strong in ways you cannot imagine. How your humans kept him captive and under control, I can only guess. Our clan has spent the last thirty years gathering together the information we have, but even the Black Sacrament don't have all the facts. So much history, ours as well as yours, was lost in the wars. We're never found where they held him."

"They used Tassoni's DNA to create the Pale, didn't they?" I said flatly, feeling numb. "The Pale are made from vampires?"

"Not *just* vampires," Allesandro responded. "We have weaknesses of our own you know, specific to our kind, which you humans do not; our inactivity during daylight, our reaction to sunlight, the aversion of certain precious metals."

He smiled humourlessly.

"Your people of old were ambitious, Doctor. The scientists, the military, the government – those who dreamed of building their super soldiers, they wanted the best of both worlds. They spliced the DNA of my kind from their 'subject' Tassoni with human DNA, trying to counter the negatives."

He spread his hands with a flourish.

"A hybrid creature was born; albino, human in appearance, pale. But these things were merely cosmetic. The superior being had been created. The mission had been accomplished. The new race was born, a race to serve and protect mankind in its infinite wisdom. The Pale had arrived in the world; the bastard child of your people and mine."

"But the Pale went … wrong," Lucy said. "The virus, their genetic makeup, the alterations, they ended up mutating at an exponential rate – the rational thought of the new super soldiers broke down."

Griff nodded.

"By the time the new creatures began to devolve, there was no pulling the plug on them," he said. "It was too late to abandon the project by then; there were already tens of thousands of the Pale produced, all test-tube grown and hyper-matured through adolescence to be stationed all through the free world. When the genetic decay came, it was swift and unstoppable, and those who were attacked became infected. The virus transmits biologically, as Doctor Harkness recently demonstrated."

Allesandro shook his head at Griff.

"But *this* is the important truth. *This* is where the misconception is," he said. "The Pale did *not* 'go wrong'. They rebelled against and attacked humans because they were *instructed* to."

We all stared at the vampire in confusion.

"Instructed to?" I echoed.

"As I have said, your people know little about mine," he explained patiently. "Do you know what happens when a vampire 'makes' a human? When their DNA is mixed outside of a lab, I mean?"

Lucy actually put her hand up as though she was in school.

"That person becomes a vampire too," she said. "Well, I think the vampire has to bite you and drink your blood, and then you have to drink the vampire's blood as well. The same one, I mean. Then you … become a vampire yourself?"

Allesandro was staring at her, and her voice had lost all its enthusiasm by the end of the sentence.

"No," he responded simply, leaving Lucy more than a little deflated. "Vampires are not made from amended humans. We are not an infection. We are a separate species of being altogether, as different to you as Bonewalkers are. When a vampire deliberately makes a human through genetic bonding, the result is what we call a ghoul."

He looked back to me as I leaned forward, intrigued.

"What's a ghoul?" I asked.

"A ghoul is a pathetic creature; half dead, basic animal instincts, servile, obedient. They are the perfect, if extremely unattractive, slave. They do not think for themselves. They obey only their master, and they are endlessly hungry. They can be useful to us. We can control their actions, their movements, like puppets."

He laced his fingers together on the table top.

"The Pale, all of them, came from a mixture of human DNA and the DNA of *one* vampire, one *master* vampire. Tassoni. And he was understandably angry at humanity. The Pale were, and are, his ghouls."

"Christ," Lucy said, looking horrified. "But if a vampire can control any ghoul it makes—"

Allesandro smiled ironically.

"Of course *these* ghouls, thanks to human scientific intervention, were strong and bold and clever. They were filled with killing aggression on a scale unheard of. You unwittingly created your own perfect murderers. We can control ghouls remotely, using our minds. You must know by now, Phoebe, that my kind has advanced psychic potential. We can speak directly into your minds. We call this the whisper. We can force truth from your lips. We call this persuasion. And we can command those who we have created. We call this will."

Out of the corner of my eye, I could see Griff look from Allesandro to me and back again. Eventually, my vampire broke our gaze.

"From inside his prison, his personal hell, Tassoni bided his time. He watched through the eyes of his creations and chose his moment carefully. When the ghouls – the human-engineered hybrids – were globally positioned, he awoke them with his will, and with them he tore your civilisation to shreds."

This revelation settled over all of us in the quiet lab.

"They created his own sleeper agents for him," I breathed. "The humans did this. They used him for themselves but they were building his army, not theirs."

"But he was stopped," Allesandro said, holding up a finger. "As the wars raged, as mankind fought to retain their world and Tassoni's Pale sought to tear it apart in vengeance, the very people who had stolen his

DNA and who had tampered with his genetics to make this race of monsters, they pulled the plug on him. Someone shut him down."

He shook his head, the sad look in his eye again. I wondered what it was like to lose your clan master. Did Allesandro feel the same way I did when my father never came home?

"We don't know when they realised the connection, but some bright spark, maybe one of the scientists who made this mess in the first place, one of them killed him. They cut the head off the hydra."

"But the Pale didn't die," Griff said, frowning. "They're still out there."

"The ghouls do not die if their master dies," Allesandro explained, "but they do lose their focus, their purpose. In a regular ghoul, made by a vampire in the old world, they become pathetic, aimless creatures. They usually starve to death eventually, mindless and inactive with no instruction from their master. But *these* ghouls…

"This new breed were deliberately spliced with the most aggressive instincts, genetically enhanced and engineered to be so much more than either of their parent species. They lost their purpose, their organisation and their direction. But with no higher mind to guide them, they became what they are now: feral, animal, lost things in the darkness. But they are still filled with the anger they were made for, still fuelled by the hunger they cannot sate."

The lab was silent for a moment. It was like the air around us was heavy with what we were being told.

"That's when the tide turned, isn't it? That's when we started winning the war. Slowly. It was when the vampires, the Tribals, the Bonewalkers, all the others – one by one, you came out into the world to help us and announced your existence to help combat this common enemy who was threatening to wipe out the world."

The vampire nodded.

"A world without humans would be no good to us." A tiny smile played across his lips. "We have to have a food source after all. I'm sure most of the other GO races thought along similar lines. We have a symbiotic relationship, your kind and mine. We needed each other to survive. We would starve in a world of ghouls and no humans, and you would all die if we didn't help you survive."

"And the rest is history," Griff said quietly.

He took off his glasses and slowly rubbed his eyes.

"I understand," I said slowly, still trying to digest this information, "why your vampire clan would want vengeance. Why Gio wants revenge … it was humans that were the scary monsters in the night, not the GOs. It was us who kidnapped and tortured your leader, us who were responsible for creating the ultimate tool Tassoni could use as revenge for our mistreatment and, well you know, accidentally ending the world…"

I cleared my throat as Allesandro smiled grimly at me.

"But this still doesn't explain what Gio and his mini-cult is doing now. Why *us*? Why the teeth and the Bonewalker mojo? How is this getting revenge on humanity? Tassoni is dead, you just told us as much."

My vampire looked tired then. I realised that he was old.

Unlike me who had been born into this world and had never known any other, he must have lived back in the old civilisation. The world I was obsessed with. He had witnessed its death, its loss, the end of everything he knew. Unlike the rest of humanity, he knew the awful truth of how and why it had happened.

"Gio and the Black Sacrament have never given up on Tassoni," Allesandro explained. "They have spent the last thirty years, since the walled cities were built and since our kinds have begun to reform some kind of civilisation from the ashes of the old world, searching for a way to bring him back."

"From the dead?" Griff asked incredulously. "That's impossible!"

Allesandro peered at him questioningly.

"Last night, myself and your good Doctor were teleported from a hole deep underground to a distant street on the surface. Bonewalkers deal in magic. They are practically made of it. We don't know what they are truly capable of. *Nothing* is impossible."

He noticed our expressions and bristled.

"I know '*magic*' may be a dirty word to you scientists," he said. "But it is a very *real* force in our shared earth, whether you like it or not. Call it by another name if you wish; unexplained phenomena, existential will. Magic is just science which has not yet been explained by you people."

"So the Black Sacrament are trying to resurrect Tassoni," I said in wonder. "They want to bring him back to life … so he can finish what he started."

Allesandro nodded grimly.

"So he can take control of the Pale again. Right now, they have become nothing but mindless animals, scattered throughout the countryside, aimless. He will mobilise them, focus them into purpose again. They will attack the walled cities of Britannia, and everywhere else; not as thoughtless feral animals but as the unstoppable fighting force they were designed to be."

Allesandro leaned back in his chair.

"The Black Sacrament wants to finish the apocalypse, to bring things to the bitter end. For all of us."

The message on the DataStream made more sense now.

Gio's voice was now such an angry grumbling roar, so thick and distorted, we could barely understand his words. I had misheard what he had been saying all along. He had not said *the sun* will rise. He had said *Tassoni* will rise.

I stood, feeling too twitchy to stay seated.

How could no one know this? How could our public not be aware that we had committed such crimes against another species, incurring their wrath and bringing destruction down on our heads with our own hubris?

I paced around the floor, all of their eyes watching me. At the end of the day, I was a scientist. I had to make sense of this.

"So, why the teeth?" I said. "What does Gio and the rest of the doomsday group want teeth for? When they had me under Carfax, Gio told me that they'd wanted Marlin Scott's but that as he didn't have any, they had settled for Oscar's. Same bloodline, same family."

"I don't know how the Bonewalkers work," Allesandro shook his head helplessly. "There are many in our clan who disapprove of Gio having any dealings with their kind. But it is said they have many talents, other than twisting space and matter. They speak with the dead, I'm told. They can *control* the dead. Perhaps, with the right ingredients, they can *bring them back*."

"It's pretty clear to me that this Black Sacrament think you're one of the ingredients, Doc," Griff said. "You told us that the torture video that was delivered with Trevelyan's teeth was aimed at you. They said *your* name."

I waved his comment away with my hand. I was trying to think.

"They said my *surname*," I said. "I don't think they were speaking to me, I think it was aimed at my *father*. Trevelyan knew something about our respective parents, about the link between us all. I don't know if she'd always known or if it was something secret she had stumbled on, being head of so many highly classified departments. It was something to do with her *own* father, long before the wars. She wouldn't have been able to resist looking into it more, who could?"

I hugged myself by the elbows, my voice quiet.

"When they came at her face with the pliers, I imagine she told them everything she knew. I know I probably would have."

I couldn't help seeing Trevelyan's corpse in my mind's eye, dumped at the bottom of the pit under Carfax. She had been all alone in the darkness until Jennifer Coleman came to join her – and who knows, maybe even Oscar by now.

I swallowed hard. I tried to turn my thoughts to more useful and less nightmare-worthy things.

"Trevelyan has my name as one of her passwords. I wonder if she has her father's name as another, or maybe Marlin Scott's?" We need to know what was on those encrypted files. Trevelyan had been snooping; she *knew* she'd found something dangerous. She knew the bad guys were coming for her. It's why she hid them. I need to speak to … to Cloves."

My speech trailed off. I stopped abruptly, frozen in mid step, my eyes staring wide.

Oh … Mother … Of … Fuck.

"What is it?" Allesandro began to rise, seeing my horrified expression. "Phoebe? Is the serum…"

"Cloves!" I yelled at them, almost making Lucy fall off her stool in shock. "Oh, bollocks! Cloves!"

"What about her?" Griff asked, baffled.

"We have to find her! She's in danger! When the vampires rolled me under back in Carfax…"

Allesandro looked quizzical.

"Rolled you under what?" he asked

I rolled my hand in the air frantically, searching for the word he had used.

"Persuasion," I said. "When they forced information out of me, that blonde one Helena, she scrabbled around in my brain. They said they were waiting for the files to be decrypted, letting the Cabal do the work for them, and then they were going to seize them. Jesus, I told her about Cloves."

I cursed Helena, the softly spoken vampire whose smile had been friendly, so sweet and reassuring, who'd been ever so nice to me. Except for the slap, of course, which hadn't moved her smile an inch – not to mention the fact that she had stood and watched with faint interest and absolutely no concern for my predicament as Gio had shoved me into the pit with the Pale.

"I told the blonde bitch that Cloves had the files," I said. "I gave them her bloody address! If they didn't go down in the standoff at Carfax…"

I stared straight at Allesandro, panicking.

"I get the feeling that when the Bonewalker left us in the alley and disappeared, it went back for them. I think it went to pull them out of there the same way. If I'm right, Allesandro, they could have found her by now. She could be dead, or worse."

"I thought you couldn't *stand* her," Lucy said.

"That's not the point," I snapped. "I don't want her blood on my hands. If she's attacked by Gio, it will be my fault."

I stared around wildly, trying to think.

"I don't even know how to get in touch with her," I said. "It's not like she gave me a pager. We didn't even have each other's numbers. Crap!"

"Phoebe," Allesandro was standing in front of me, "please calm down. I think I can help."

"Unless you have some super-magical vampire skill to whisper into her head from all the way across the city and through four stories of subterranean bedrock, I doubt it."

I paused, considering this for a moment.

"You *don't* have that skill by any chance, do you?" I asked.

"Not quite."

He crossed the lab to the small desktop where those parts of his clothing which had not been scorched or burned had been carefully placed. His boots, a rather twisted and burnt belt, and a few other less flammable peripherals. He brought something back for me, holding it out like a gift.

"But I do have this," he offered.

He was holding a very scorched and partially-melted mobile phone. The glass surface had cracked in the exciting heat blast as he had strolled down our security corridor. It looked warped, as though it had spent a few minutes in a microwave, but the screen still lit up as he unlocked it.

It must be a Nokia, I reasoned.

I took it from him. The phone displayed twenty three missed calls, all within the last few hours. The name by each: Cloves.

"You have her *number*?" I spluttered, staring up at him. "How?"

Before he could answer, the phone vibrated in my hand. I almost dropped it in surprise. The incoming call read Cloves. She had really, *really* been trying to get hold of him recently. Twenty fourth time is the charm, I thought.

As Griff and Lucy watched me closely, I answered, holding the phone to my ear. I wasn't sure what to say.

"Hello...?" I said haltingly. "Erm ... Allesandro's phone. Phoebe speaking."

Through the terrible, half-melted earphone, I heard Veronica Cloves sigh deeply, a rattling exhalation which sounded half relief and half jaw clenching anger.

"Harkness? I have been calling this number all day. That had better fucking be you on the phone!" She snapped down the line. "I don't know where the hell you are, but—"

"Listen," I cut her off. "I'll explain everything but you're not safe. Your apartment—"

"No *shit*, Sherlock," Cloves spat angrily at me. "I have had a very entertaining few hours fleeing my own home and evading some pretty fucked up people! I know they want the files. I know *someone* told them I had them."

She said this very pointedly and I have to admit, I felt guilty.

"Lucky for you, I'm slightly more competent than you are. I have the files on me. I think I've lost the motherfuckers who have been trailing me all damn day and I've spent the last God knows how long trying to get hold of your bloody vampire, who *swore* to me he would bring you to me when he got you back from those gun-toting arseholes. The lying little bastard..."

I leaned my ear away from the headset a little. Her volume was rising.

"Doesn't he know how to answer a phone? What has he been doing for the last half a sodding day anyway?"

"Sleeping, for most of it," I said slowly. "That's what they do. Where are you?"

"Right now?" she bit back her fury long enough to tell me. "I'm at some shithole greasy spoon on the Slade, near the east gate of the wall. I'm in hiding, trying to shake these assholes. I don't care where you are, Harkness, or what you're doing. Get *here*. *Now!*"

"Give me the address," I sighed.

I repeated it to Griff, who jotted it down on his hand. Griff is the kind of man who always has a pen.

"Stay put," I said. "We're on our way over."

"The files," Cloves said. "I told you, they're decrypted. I read them while I've been holed up in this shithole – you're going to want to see what's in them."

I didn't need her to convince me of that.

30

The Slade was in the south east sector of walled New Oxford. Well out of Veronica Cloves' comfort zone, I imagined.

It had probably been a respectable neighbourhood once, long before the wars, but these days it was something of a ghetto. Like all the walled cities of Britannia, we had a housing crisis; too many people trying to live in a space that simply couldn't expand anymore. The rich moved to the north of the city, to live in the sky in spears of glass and steel where there used to be meadows. The poor and the desperate had ended up here, like sewage running downhill.

If you lived in the city, you knew better than to wander south of the Churchill Hospital after dark. There had been a golf course there once but it was gone now, fenced in. Now it was home to most of New Oxford's Tribals – those who didn't own the Botanical Gardens, that is. To the east of the Tribals' turf, everything from the hospital to the woods were shantytowns. Once there had been leafy streets and choice, middle-class real estate but three decades can bring a lot of changes. The slum spread from the Slade – long ago an innocent enough B-road, now an invisible no-go barrier – to the wall itself beyond the woods.

Don't let me fool you into thinking 'the woods' are anything picturesque. When the wall went up, Marlin Scott's great gift to mankind and the Bonewalkers' magical and unfathomable handiwork, it cut through the three woodland areas which had existed in the old world, beyond the circle of the old city's bypass. Brasenose, Magdalen and Monks Wood, all three forests had been suddenly inside the city.

You might wonder, with the Slade slums brimming over with the poor and disenfranchised, why the woods had survived. Why they hadn't simply been cut down, the land razed all the way to the wall itself for housing, when tiny lean-to shacks jostled for space in the now narrow streets, practically built on top of one another.

The reason was simple, really. The woods had already been claimed by Gos, and not the kind you want to tangle with either. There are more types of GO that you can shake a stick at, and trust me, if you ever come to New Oxford, stay out of the woods, steer clear of the south east slums at the Slade, and don't wander south of the Churchill hospital.

Veronica Cloves had, of course, ignored this advice in her efforts to shake Gio's goons. Probably in the steely certainly that there was nobody – no desperate gun-toting gang member, no drug-crazed head case, rogue blood-lusting vampire or wandering hungry tribal – who was scarier or more pissed off than she was.

And so now, we headed there too, venturing into the south east sector. I clung to the back of Allesandro's bike as we raced to the corner of Old Road, Windmill and the Slade. We were just on the borders of the poor, overcrowded sector, north of the aptly-named Boundary Brook.

Griff and Lucy had insisted on coming with us at first but I had refused as I needed them back in the lab. Griff was now busy duplicating fresh batches of the revised Epsilon, the retardant which was keeping Brad the rat in the land of the cohesive and reasonable – and now, me too.

I'd decided it was a very good idea to lay a stock of Epsilon aside. A lot of it. I didn't want to miss a dose and devolve, especially not into what I now knew was a half-human, half-vampire ghoul. If Tassoni the alpha and omega of every Pale did indeed rise, I would rather be fighting *against* him and his crusade to end humanity for good, than fighting *for* him. I planned to stay human.

Lucy had been given the task of cleaning the lab, and by that I don't mean hoovering up and dusting with Pledge. I meant deep clean. We had to remove all traces of Allesandro's presence there. More than merely our careers were on the line if it was discovered a GO had breached Blue Lab with such ease.

My own hide was at risk as well if they figured out he had gone there to save me from my very own mutant zombie plague. If that fact got out, I would be lucky to find myself locked in one of the cells on the MA levels and observed for the rest of my days.

Besides, I had reasoned. Four of us wouldn't all fit on the bike. It would look ridiculous.

Griff has suggested we could take his car. Allesandro had laughed, rather unkindly I thought. At least he had the good grace to look guilty for laughing afterwards.

Getting *out* of Blue Lab without suspicion had been easy enough. We had shut down the ultraviolet corridor of course, at least until Allesandro and I were at the far end of it. Any problems I might have had getting the vampire out through the atrium were solved by the fact that he looked remarkably human.

You just didn't get vampires with deep golden tans – never. They were whiter than the palest human, all of them. Still wearing his closely-buttoned lab coat and hurrying out by my side, his head down, Allesandro didn't draw anything but the most cursory of glances from anyone we passed. As far as anyone could tell, he was just a perfectly normal, perfectly human, rather unusually beautiful doctor.

As we passed reception, Miranda, the day shift receptionist had called after me.

"Oh, Doctor Harkness! I had no idea you were in. A lady has called several times for you today, a Ms Cloves?"

I saw her giving Allesandro a none-too-subtle once over, her curiosity clearly piqued as we marched by.

"I would have put her through to the lab, only when I came on shift to relieve Mattie this morning, he told me it was just your team down there. I didn't know you had checked in today."

"Thanks Miranda."

I had not stopped walking, gripping Doctor Sun-Kissed-Vampire by the elbow and pretty much dragging him towards the main doors, and freedom.

"I got her message. I've been pulling kind of an all-nighter down there. Haven't even been out for coffee yet, just drinking the swill down there, need a Starbucks. Bye!"

We had pushed through the whooshing heavy doors into the cold evening air before she could answer.

Allesandro had no idea how the gunfight between the vampires and the Cabal ghosts had gone after we left for Blue Lab, no more than I did. We'd had rather more pressing matters on our minds at the time.

Now, as the bike purred along the edge of the slum sector, making its slow and careful way down the Slade, I realised I would very much like to know how that had panned out.

Had Gio and the rest been captured? Were they in police custody right now? Or had they gotten away? And, if so, how? Was I right about the Bonewalker? Was it working for Gio, had it gone back and poofed them out of there to safely?

The fact that Cloves had been chased from her apartment suggested they were still at large and very active, currently out there combing the city for her and the now unscrambled files she carried, and no doubt also looking for me too.

I wondered if the media had descended on Carfax yet; if in the aftermath of last night's events the police had found the bodies, Trevelyan's and Coleman's. Had they found the Pale? Was Oscar still alive?

I hoped Cloves would have some answers for me. I hadn't liked the ones Allesandro had given me so far. You don't really think you can get worse than 'serial killer', but I had discovered when you got to 'apocalypse-inciting vampire cult raising the dead', you know you were wrong.

Lesson one of dealing with Gos: things can *always* get worse. I was consciously not dwelling on the fact that Allesandro and Cloves had swapped numbers at some point. The vampire hadn't elaborated and despite an oddly possessive grumble in the back of my mind, it was really none of my business how, why or when the two had become bosom buddies.

"What was the name of this place?" I asked Allesandro, to take my mind off it as we cruised down the street.

The main strand of the Slade was a hubbub of tiny shops, cut price laundrettes, grimy bars and pretty unwholesome-looking shops. It was only just close to 7pm but everywhere there were metal roller shutters, every one of them covered in gang-tag graffiti, the people of the district presenting a closed and armoured face to the world outside.

Metal grills fortified many of the tiny shops. There were few people on the littered streets. Some tough-looking youths lounging listlessly on corners, their faces lost behind hooded sweatshirts. An old derelict woman aimlessly pushing a shopping cart along the broken flagstones of the pavement. It seemed to be piled high with bin bags.

"Sal's Chicken Kitchen," the vampire replied, scanning the seedy-looking establishments to the left and right as the bike purred along like a panther.

I felt very conspicuous. We were the only vehicle on the road. And it was being driven by a bare-chested vampire in a flapping white lab coat.

Undercover – clearly not my forte.

231

"There," I took my hand from around his waist and pointed.

A filthy-windowed diner slid by on the right, with the name spelled out in tired stencilling. It looked as worn down as the rest of the neighbourhood. We could see a few shadowy figures inside, the windows obscured with steamy condensation that ran down the glass.

As we pulled up in front, the door opened with a jangle and Veronica Cloves appeared, looking harassed and deeply unhappy. She was wearing a long black trench coat, like a Russian spy, wrapped tightly against the night. Underneath it, I saw, she was still dressed in her sparkling jet gown from the fundraiser the night before.

Fantastic, I thought, very low key. I'm sure she was blending in fine here with the local residents. At least she had lost the fascinator.

She hurried over as I jumped down off the bike, giving Allesandro a startled double take.

"Well, fuck *me*," she muttered unhappily. "I've been chased all over the goddamn city today by assholes in black vans, trying to get hold of you two, and here you seem to have had a spa day. Nice tan."

"Long story," I said.

She shook her head dismissively.

"Not interested. Follow me," she said. "I don't want to be out on the street. Those goons are still cruising around."

She led us down the side of the grimy diner, into a cluttered and litter strewn alleyway. We huddled under a fire escape behind a large stinking dumpster, startling a very displeased and feral-looking cat, which leapt away with a hiss.

"You were a pain in my arse before," Cloves spat. "But telling a psychotic vampire where I lived?"

"I know, I'm sorry," I replied. I genuinely was. "In my defence, they made me. It's hard to say no to them when they want you to cooperate. How did they get to you? I thought your building was warded?"

I remembered her telling me as much. The Cabal had dealings with a Bonewalker. The Liver Building was warded strongly also. Blue Lab couldn't afford warding. We were run by Cabal but only partially funded by them, hence our own defences: the ultraviolet corridor, the morning check-ins.

"It is. However, that's only good against Gos," she responded. "Your charmless friends have a squad of hired humans on the books."

She looked like she had a bad taste in her mouth, shaking her head in disbelief.

"*Humans* working for *vampires* … What next?"

"You managed to get out, though, with the files?"

She nodded. "After the fun and games at the fundraiser, and once your new pal here had found me and strong-armed me into locating you and tipping the police to Carfax, I picked them up and took them home. Those arseholes were waiting for me. I didn't even get into the parking lot. They must have torn my place apart looking for the files."

She looked furious. I could tell the thought of grubby-booted guns for hire traipsing all over her ridiculously expensive and immaculate penthouse was causing her almost physical pain.

"You went back to the fundraiser to get Cloves help?" I asked Allesandro. "After we came off the bike, I mean?"

"I knew she would be able to track you," Allesandro shrugged, his face shadowy in the alleyway. "It's what her people do. She was my best chance to find where Gio was talking you."

Cloves glowered at him. "You promised to bring her straight to me." She looked as though she was about to slap him. Instead she turned to me. "You wonder why I advise you not to trust them?" she said. "My arse is on the line if I lose sight of you. Harrison put you under me in this ridiculous little shenanigan. You're my responsibility, so when tall, gold and pulse-less here turns up, right in the middle of my post-riot media spin, what choice did I have? I even dispatched a fleet of Cabal Ghost agents to follow him to you. God knows how much shit that's gotten me in."

"We couldn't go anywhere after we escaped," I said, carefully editing the truth. "We had to lie low for a while. I was injured, and Allesandro, well, the sun was coming up, so we holed up for the day."

Cloves looked me over sceptically. "You don't look injured," she accused menacingly. "In fact you look pretty bright-eyed and bushy-tailed for a kidnap victim. Manage to get eight hours beauty sleep, did you?"

I didn't want to mention drinking Allesandro's blood. The memory of it was quite intimate, primal almost. I doubted Cloves would approve, I wasn't really sure I approved myself.

"Never mind me, what happened when you got back to your place?" I changed the subject, deliberately not looking at Allesandro, though I could feel his eyes on me in the dark alleyway.

Cloves' face twisted into a grimace of irritation.

"They saw me coming. The bastards were lying in wait for me," she explained. "I figured out they were bad news, that my location had been compromised, so I got the hell out of there, but they're relentless. I've been dodging them but everywhere I tried to go, they were there. I managed to lose them near the Boundary Brook. Had to abandon my goddamn car though. It's hardly an inconspicuous ride."

She looked livid at this.

"I've been lying low in the slums since then; in the fucking slums! Trying to get hold of your sorry arse."

"Why didn't you call for backup?" I asked. "Surely Leon Harrison would send some ghosts to pick you up, bring you back safely to HQ?"

Cloves stared at me, hands on her hips.

"Harkness, do you have *any* idea how it would sound if I called in to my superior and told him that not only had my brief to use you to discreetly gather information gone horribly, *horribly* wrong, but that I had also *lost* you, had no idea where you were, and had – without Cabal sanction – dispatched a ghost squad to aid the police and a random GO in what turned into a shooting match in the middle of one of New Oxford's venerable churches?"

She sighed.

"I have my reputation as a Servant to consider. I don't think the higher powers would be best pleased with me declaring war on a pack of GOs when we are supposed to be, above all, *diplomats*."

"What happened at Carfax?" I asked. "Allesandro and I got out and … got the hell away from there. I have no idea what went down after that."

Cloves snorted.

"You've clearly not seen the DataStream today then," she said. "It's headline news. We've managed to spin it so that officially the police were involved with a gang war incident, unrelated to any of the events at the fundraiser, which is the main story on everyone's lips right now anyway. I've kept the Cabal out of the picture as much as I can. All the media knows is that there was police involvement, and that arrests were made. The good people of New Oxford can sleep soundly in their beds. Nothing on their minds but crop circles."

"Is that true?" I asked hopefully. "Arrests?"

Cloves gave me a look of withering scorn.

"Of course it's not true, you idiot," she snapped. "Our men had your kidnappers cornered in there, like rats in a hole, but then they just vanished into thin air."

She peered at Allesandro suspiciously.

"Can you actually do that," she demanded, "turn into mist or whatever? We lost them. The church was empty."

Allesandro shook his head.

"No. We can't do that," he glanced over at me. "Not on our own anyway."

I saw what he was thinking.

"These guys are working with a Bonewalker," I said to Cloves. "We kind of forced it to get us out of there. It had disappeared afterwards. My guess is that it went back for its pals. That's how they got away. It's how they were able to send people for you. God knows where they are now."

"Well, there's a police warrant out on Di Medica right now," Cloves said. "I doubt he'll head back to the club. He's probably out there looking for you again, while his goon squad chase my arse around."

"Cloves, you said you had the files," I interrupted, trying to get her to focus. "What's in them?"

She looked at Allesandro suspiciously.

"How much do you know?" She asked him directly.

"He knows everything," I answered for him, "and now so do I. Unlike you and everybody else, he's the one person so far who *hasn't* kept things from me. I know about the Pale, Cloves, what they really are, where they came from. I know about Tassoni…"

I watched her reaction and stepped towards her.

"And I think you do too."

Cloves was tight lipped.

"Well, you *have* done your homework, haven't you?" She said. "Yes, Subject One, the father of the cursed race we created, was spliced from humans and a vampire. That's hardly public knowledge. Let's keep it that way."

She looked to Allesandro, her eyes narrowed.

"How do *you* know about Subject One?"

"He was my clan master before the Pale."

"Well that certainly makes you super trustworthy then," she snorted sarcastically.

"I'm not part of Gio's Sacrament," the vampire growled back. "He and the others, they took those people and want those files because they believe they can bring Tassoni back from the dead. They want to reignite the apocalypse, bringing the Pale down on humanity in one final fell swoop."

"Sacrament?" Cloves looked at me, eyebrows raised. "Back from the dead? I'm lost. How about you share what you know with the rest of the class?"

I flicked a thumb at Allesandro.

"*He'll* fill you in," I said, "while I look at what was on these files."

Cloves gave the vampire a look of undisguised distaste.

"I don't trust him," she spat. "He's one of their kind."

The vampire loomed over her.

"I don't trust you either," he said. "You're a shady government spook. It's practically your job to lie to people."

"Only the general public, dead man walking," she sneered. "I might spin the truth, but only the unpalatable parts."

"Which is pretty much everything these days," he countered.

"Children!" I snapped, glaring at them. "We don't have time for this."

They both peered at me sulkily, openly hostile.

"*You*," I said to Cloves, "practically threw me at *him* for information. He gave it to me, mission accomplished. And *you*," I stared at the vampire, "you didn't have any problem going to *her* to help find me. So for God's sake, play nice and give me the damn files."

I had had enough. Enough attempts on my life, enough dead bodies, enough with monsters trying to eat my face. I wanted to go home to my tiny messy flat and drink hot chocolate and not worry about *any* of this. Instead I was hiding in an alleyway in the most dangerous part of town with two very unlikely companions, not to mention the fact that I was infected with a mutagen virus which could at any moment turn me into a ravening monster.

Cloves stared me down for a moment and then sighed heavily. She reached into her Russian spy trench coat and withdrew a DataScreen, handheld and portable, which she dropped into my open palm.

"You're not going to like what's on there, Harkness," she said ominously. "Trevelyan didn't. It's a scientific log. Most of the entries were damaged beyond repair. There are gaps, but there's enough that was salvageable."

I leaned against the wall behind the dumpster, loading the data and watching the screen flicker into life before me. Its light reflected coldly on my face as Allesandro and Cloves stepped away, giving me space. The vampire began to fill in Servant Cloves on Gio's vendetta, but I wasn't listening. The file menu appeared.

Archive data file 011. Classified. Authorised personnel only.

I flicked a finger over the password, which had been thoughtfully hacked by Cloves' techs, and the files opened for me.

31

Project Sentinel Program Notes:

The date is September twenty-fourth. I am dictating these field notes for scientific record, to the secure server cloud at Norfolk military base, location 452. We have been instructed to detail progress to be fully disclosed to Her Majesty's Counter-Terror Unit at Scotland Yard, to Internal Military Defence at M15, and to select Eyes Only authorised personnel in Level One military and parliamentary ministers.

If you have accessed this information and are not the intended recipient, you are both committing treason and an act of information terrorism. You will be held accountable and detained.

Right. That's out of the way then.

I am the project leader for the Bio-Engineering facility, presiding over Project Sentinel. For the record, I should name myself and the team. I am Doctor Alistair Rutheridge. Other than myself, the Bioengineering Team working here at the classified Norfolk base consist of Dr Richard Trevelyan, bio-engineer Riley Coleman, Professor Marlin Scott, and biologist and gene-mapping expert Doctor Phillip Harkness.

Each of the team has been vetted thoroughly, each is the top of his respective field, and each of us have signed the Official Secrets Act, plus at least eight other military documents which bind us to secrecy. Our work here at the base is classified to an unprecedented level. We have signed our lives over to the project.

Trevelyan suffers the most from the isolation here. He has a wife and baby daughter, down in Mayfair I believe. He misses them terribly. We are allowed to write but everything is checked, double checked and triple checked before it is allowed to leave the base. We cannot really say much other than that we are fine and well, and working hard to make the world a better place.

Harkness works hard, but I know he misses his fiancée too. Five years here, until the Sentinel Project is complete. It's a long haul.

Scott is a genius. He is bad tempered and aloof, the eldest of our team, but his breakthrough work on the embryonic stages of the Sentinels has been astonishing.

Coleman, I cannot help but think of as a child. We plucked him from Oxford. He's still a student technically but he has some inspired theories, and his experimental approach is bringing the project along awfully well.

So far, the Sentinels are still embryonic. Fifty of them are held in deep storage in our underground facility. The man-sized test tubes lining the walls down there are a magnificent sight to behold.

They are still cryostasis adolescents. We find the gene-manipulation takes hold more effectively during the mutable stages of physical growth. Our rejection rate of new tissue is down to 38% now, and the bonding of the major macromolecules – the DNA, the RNA, and the enhanced and revised proteins – are taking well.

On a side note, one unusual result of the engineering has shown in several extreme mutations on a cellular level. In samples taken from the embryonic Sentinels, we have observed triple-stranded helices containing three long biopolymers of nucleotides, not the usual two. Coleman believes he can stabilise this.

Log 899:

Coleman's hunch was correct. We have introduced recombinant DNA, constructed by Drs Harkness and Trevelyan. After transforming these into basic organic plasmids and utilising a viral vector, we have reduced rejection rate of manipulated cells to 2%. This is truly a phenomenal breakthrough. We can now purify the DNA for true manipulation, restriction digests and polymerase chain reaction. We have begun profiling.

Log 902:

Batch One of the Sentinels will be activated tomorrow morning. The team are insisting on celebrating the birthday of the Sentinels. I don't approve.

Scott refers to the fifty as our 'wondrous children' while Harkness terms them the Nephylim. Coleman simply calls them the Pale Soldiers.

We will have to work on cosmetics once motor functions and other primal instincts have been successfully programmed. The Sentinels will be the world's new peacekeeping force but mankind at large will only accept them if they do not seem threatening. We are developing them to protect us, after all.

Their albino appearance, a form of severe achromatosis, does give them an unsettling otherworldly appearance, I must admit. Of course, such a congenital disorder – the absence of pigment in the skin, hair and eyes – is common throughout all vertebrates. Recessive gene alleles result in defective tyrosinase, the copper rich enzyme which produces melanin. It is curious that this affects every one of the fifty Sentinels. They all share the same human DNA gene pool, however. Our very own chromosomes were used to bioengineer them – all five of us.

I suppose in a way Scott is therefore correct. We are all their fathers, the five members of the Development Team. Our mixed DNA provides the building blocks for us to engineer the Sentinels. But the other samples, those DNA slices we are given to play with from Subject One, I wish I knew more about them. Their complexity is fascinating.

Harkness tells me he believes that the mysterious Subject One is actually right here in the Norfolk base with us on one of the deeper, secured levels.

This may well be the case.

None of us know where the bio-samples come from; the other half of our DNA recipe.

Log 927:

It has been three weeks since the activation, or birth, of the Batch One Sentinels. Of the fifty originals, seven remain functional, the others are retired.

Seven are still alive, the rest are dead.

Trevelyan says we should have anticipated the violence levels. We have engineered them to this level of aggression ourselves, after all. But in our foolishness, we had thought there would be more control. They slaughtered one another – immediately after we woke them from stasis.

It was particularly brutal in the holding pen. We extracted seven who were merely unconscious. Better to do that than have to start afresh again with our DNA in Petri dishes and lose all our work so far. The military torched the dead ones. It still smells of burning fat down on this level. We have been promised relocation to a deeper subsection, but who knows when that will happen.

Harkness, Scott and Coleman work on extracting what useful material we can from the surviving Sentinels, while Trevelyan and I work on tweaking the primal chromosomal restraint levels to be inserted into batch two. The seven survivors of batch one will then be torched.

Log 934:

More samples from Subject One arrived today. We are still marvelling at the cellular structure it comprises. Coleman is convinced we are the British Area 51 and that the military have a captured alien down there somewhere beneath our feet. Where else could this DNA come from, he argues.

Log 1135:

Batch Eight. Our magnum opus at last. It has been two years since Batch One, and finally we have living, breathing, and above all else, compliant Sentinels.

Scott has now taken to calling them Übermensch, after Nietzsche's theoretical supermen. I admit they are a dazzling and vital breed: stronger than humans, faster, denser, molecularly speaking, far more complex. Superior in almost every way, except of course that they are far more compliant than any human has ever been. I should hope so too. We made them to obey us.

Log 1256:

They have been active for seven months. So far from testing they have astounding levels of physical strength, endurance, and regenerative tissue capabilities. We cannot make them speak. All are mute but they fully understand and comply with our orders.

The one flaw we cannot seem to fix is the alopecia. Hair loss occurs shortly after full maturity on a full body scale. Again, with the albino condition, this does make for a startling appearance, but our government and military masters seem more than pleased with the results.

Harkness was granted shore leave last month. The only one of us to leave the base since the project began. He was heavily guarded, of course, for security's sake. Imagine our surprise when he returned with the ring on his finger. He has married his girl, the young rascal. Good times are ahead, he says. Scott firmly believes our good work here will make us all rich beyond our wildest dreams.

Coleman and myself I feel are more idealistic than the others. We seem to want only to be remembered for bringing a tool of peace to our troubled world. Imagine an end to all war. A golden age of mankind is approaching, where our civilisation can finally flourish in perpetual peace. We will never again fear the uprising of a nuclear armed nation, never hear of a London bus exploding or a gas attack in Tokyo, because everywhere our Sentinels will be there. Our guardian angels, they are the strongest of us, the fiercest.

The ultimate deterrent.

Log 1384:

The military bosses came to oversee the handover today. Batch Eight is ready to be passed into higher hands than ours. They have been perfected, ready for mass production.

Bio-labs have already been prepared nationwide in Britain, with similar facilities worldwide in our allied countries. A proud moment for any father, I suppose, watching your children go forth into the world to multiply. This will be our legacy, Trevelyan told us. Our DNA, the five of us with help from the mysterious yet miraculous Subject One, cloned and living on forever to serve the people of the world.

I feel Harkness has spent too much time interacting with the Sentinels. It is in all our natures to be fascinated with what we have achieved here, of course, but he seems at times unsettled by them. They are placid enough, unless instructed otherwise, but he says he does not like their silence, and the way they watch us. It's though they are all speaking to each other without words, he says.

We have wondered if some extreme instinctual bond has formed between them, a kind of latent, low-level telepathy resulting of their shared genetic heritage. But these are not tests for us to consider any longer. We have made a huge leap forwards, and soon everyone in it will know about them. I think it's best for us to get back out there and live our lives, our children watching over us.

Log 1389:

This will be my final entry. Our team has been disbanded and there is little more for me to log or record other than my findings on our final night at the Norfolk base. Even now I am unsure what to make of it.

I record it here in the hope that whoever these reports are eventually filed with will make more sense of it. I assume those working in other levels of the base are required to make similar logs. I hope the records of whoever presides over Level Thirteen will shed more light on my discovery.

It was Coleman who came to us with the pass code. All through our long project here, it has been a constant source of speculation as to the origin of the samples from Subject One. Their DNA structure was so complex and so unlike our own models, our human contribution to the engineering of the Sentinels, or the Pales as we have all seemed to settle on calling our silent white super soldiers.

Coleman would not say where he had obtained the access codes to Level Thirteen. We all knew he had strokes of computing genius in him, but we did not know that in his hunger to know more, he had been steadily hacking every firewall and security code in the base. It was all under the radar, of course, covering his tracks.

I realise that by naming him here I am exposing him to dire consequences. It was, I suppose, treason, this breaking of high level military security, but if he is to be damned by his transgression then I must take the fall with him – for I admit that, despite my reservations, I was overcome with curiosity myself.

Please understand: we had to know what we had been working with these last five years. We are scientists, each of us.

Harkness, Trevelyan and Scott wanted nothing to do with our proposed breach. Let the record state that they cautioned us against it, even tried to talk us out of it. They would not accompany us. It is, in fact, testament to the strong fraternal bond which has by necessity grown between us over this five year project that they did not report us.

The base is sparsely manned now, being taken apart piece by piece. Most of the military personnel have already moved out. The Sentinels have been shipped out for cloning worldwide. Soon the world will be full of them.

We made our cautious way, Coleman and I, using the security elevator and the hacked codes my colleague had obtained.

What I found on Level Thirteen has raised more questions for me than it answered. There is a single laboratory on this deep level and one holding pen with the highest level security. We could not gain access to the pen itself but there was a viewing gallery, looking down to the pen itself.

What I saw is still hard to describe. It seemed a corpse, a single withered husk of a man laid out on the medical slab. The vast array of tubes and electrodes connected to its carcass made it difficult to discern much specifically, and from almost every angle the view was blocked by the many machines which surrounded it – their purposes I can only guess.

It reminded me of an old anatomy lesson from when I was studying medicine in my youth, and corpses were opened for our observation. The figure's legs were gone, removed mid-thigh, one of its arms the same. Its chest was held open, peeled back in the manner of a post mortem, the skirts of flesh pinned back like butterfly wings. Wires and tubes fed into the cavity. It had no jaw, and one eye had been removed clinically.

It dawned on me slowly, and must have to Coleman too, that this was Subject One. The thing which had so generously supplied our missing link, the genetic data which added to our own, and had made the Sentinels possible.

Was it even human? I could not say. But I almost dropped on the spot when I saw, even from this distance, its remaining bloodshot eye move slowly in its socket, roaming the room until it settled finally on us.

The thing was alive. Even in this lamentable condition, they were keeping this wasted abomination alive. Is this how they had supplied us with our samples? How it was still living, I had no idea. It was nightmarish to behold and in the piercing stare with which it fixed me and Coleman, I swear I detected such agony, such fierce and un-relenting pain, that it took my breath away.

Beneath that pain, though, I saw anger; a fury which seemed to somehow roll across the holding pens and break over us like a wave. How long had this thing been down here, this mystery medical breakthrough which had made our world-saving work possible? Surely not the entire five years while we worked blithely above? Perhaps longer, much longer, before our Development Team was selected and put to work here. In that stare was something terrible, and neither of us could remain a moment longer.

We did not speak of what we had seen to Trevelyan, Scott or Harkness. We told them the lab had been empty. There had been nothing down there.

Perhaps it is better to think that. I do not wish to tarnish our good work. Surely whatever individual sacrifices are made, the greater good outweighs them in the long stretch of history.

This was last night and we leave tomorrow, after we are debriefed. I do not know if the man, if it was a man, remains down there or if it will be moved as well.

On a final, perhaps unscientific note, I must add the unsettling dream I had, here on our final night. I dreamed I was once again in the lab on the thirteenth subfloor but there was a man there this time, standing in the holding pen. Not a monster, only somehow not a man either. Something else.

In my dream he spoke to me and told me that we had changed the world together, he and I, and that his children would tear down his enemies.

Dreams are such odd things. I know, of course, that this was nothing more than an anxiety dream brought on by the stress of our macabre discovery. It was in other ways ludicrous. Only in the madness of a dream would my addled mind replace a burned out mutilated corpse with a stern man's bright, fierce countenance, and then give him of all things an Italian accent.

I will sign off now. In a way I will miss these logs. Trevelyan made all of us pose for a photograph today, our final day together. He says he is going to frame it for his daughter even though she will never know of our work here. None of our families will, even when the Sentinels go public, but he is still proud. We all are. Harkness had obtained champagne. We had a jolly time.

I will still be glad to see the back of the Norfolk base, however. It will be good to get back out into the shining future we have made possible and to live again.

On behalf of the Sentinel Development Team, this is Doctor Alistair Rutheridge signing off.

32

My hands were numb, holding the datapad there in the darkness of the alley. The words on the page dictated long ago, before the wars had started, before Tassoni had turned the Pale on mankind, blurred before my eyes.

I looked up to find Cloves and Allesandro both watching me silently. They were almost lost in the darkness. Cloves' expression was hard to read. I knew she had already read these files herself. She had made the links. She understood.

"This is why they want us," I said, forcing my voice to sound as normal as I could. "Whatever the Bonewalker is planning to do, whatever 'magic' the Black Sacrament are hoping will bring Tassoni back, they need the original DNA."

I looked up at them both.

"They need the Development Team, the ones who made the Pale. My father, Trevelyan's, Coleman's, the others; they all gave their own genes to the project and mixed it with Tassoni's."

"The original message which came with Trevelyan's teeth makes a little more sense, that's for sure," Cloves said darkly. "There will be payment, an eye for an eye, and a tooth for a tooth. Five sinners, five will pay."

"They need us, somehow, to bring him back," I said mostly to myself, still clutching the datapad. "They couldn't get Coleman. He killed himself years ago. Trevelyan, he's also dead from cancer. My own father died in the wars. So they took their children instead: Vyvienne Trevelyan, Jennifer Coleman, and me. The only member of the Development Team we know is still living is Marlin Scott. They tried for him, of course, but found him toothless. Now they have his son, Oscar."

"And the sins of the fathers…" Allesandro said softly.

Cloves had obviously filled him in while I was reading the files.

I was still in shock. How could my father have never mentioned this to me? I was born after the collapse of the old world, the wars already raging. My mother dead, he was the only family I'd ever had. In the new world order he had found a new role in our society as a field medic. I had never known that the armies of the Pale against which he fought were partly his own creation, that they all on some level shared his DNA.

Shared *my* DNA…

A hideous memory resurfaced. Gio hadn't been kidding when he had thrown me into the pit with the feral Pale under Carfax and instructed me to enjoy some family time. He knew so much. Who was involved, who to harvest. He didn't have access to these files. What information was on them that they didn't already know?

I wondered if this was this the reason the Epsilon serum had bonded with me successfully, because the genetic virus the Pale carried was partly me anyway. The same genetic footprint?

"What about Rutherford?" I asked suddenly. "What the hell happened to him?"

Cloves and the vampire looked blank.

"He was the other guy in the photograph I took from Vyvienne Trevelyan's house, the Development Team line up," I said. "It must have been the photo they talk about in these logs. We identified everyone else but the large guy with the beard must be Rutherford – the one who dictated these logs. Do the Black Sacrament already *have* his teeth? Did he die years ago? Did he even survive the war? We don't even know if he had children. He and Coleman were the only ones who saw Tassoni at this production base of theirs and Coleman ended up offing himself, probably out of guilt at unleashing the Pale on the world. Did Rutherford do the same?"

"I've already run a remote trace on him in the archives from the workstation in my car," Cloves said, shaking her head irritably. "There's no intelligence on him after the wars. You have to remember, Harkness, when the world went to shit we had something of a mini Dark Ages. There wasn't a whole lot of careful census taking going on. We lost a large portion of the population before we regained the upper hand and started to repel the Pale. A lot of people were never found; a lot of people died unburied."

"We only gained the upper hand because *someone* realised Tassoni was still controlling the Pale," I insisted. "*Someone* found him, what was left of him anyway. Wherever the military were holding him, they found him and finished him off. If it was Rutherford, he might still be alive."

They were both looking at me questioningly.

"Well, it's obvious to me that the Black Sacrament have already found him, or some direct descendant anyway. On the DataStream clip, it said five would pay – the five members of the Development Team, obviously – and when Gio had me under Carfax after they had taken Oscar's teeth, he referred to me as the *last* offering."

Cloves phone suddenly rang, startling us all. She stared at the incoming number, looking worried, which was an unusual expression to see on her face.

"It's Harrison," she said, seeing Allesandro's questioning look. "My boss."

We watched as she took the call, turning her back to us for a modicum of privacy. From what we could make out, she was being quite forcibly questioned about a fracas reported at her home address. Then there was some heated discussion about alleged Cabal involvement at the Carfax shootout the night before.

Cloves sounded contrite. It was unsettling to hear her sounding apologetic. I realised even hard-assed government power mongers have their own bosses; harder-assed have even more powerful ones.

She hung up, staring at me and Allesandro.

"Well, fuck us all," she said after a moment.

"What now?" I asked.

Cloves looked furiously at me.

"That was my boss, Servant Harrison. You've met him, of course. He's at Blue Lab right now. With the minister!"

"Who's the minister?" I asked confused.

"Oh, you've met him too," she said, "in our friendly little meeting, when we'd received the teeth of Trevelyan? Ministers are higher in the Cabal than even the highest Servants. They are only called in to oversee things when enough shit has hit the fan that it stops spinning altogether. Such as when a senior member of Blue Lab is kidnapped and her teeth gift wrapped to us, for instance."

"The big fat guy?" I realised.

I had guessed he was the most senior of the three in the uncomfortable meeting we'd had. He had been the creepiest too; that overweight, sickly looking man, who slurred his words lazily like a bullfrog perched behind his desk..

"Yes, the big fat guy," Cloves said through gritted teeth. "He's at Blue Lab with Harrison because Blue Lab security footage flagged up a level one incident last night, and it landed on Harrison's desk an hour ago."

Her eyes flicked from Allesandro to me.

"Apparently, a GO strolled into the atrium, carrying an unconscious woman, disabled a security guard and broke into one of the labs."

My face froze.

"Does any of this sound *familiar* to you?" Cloves said.

Allesandro made to speak but she held up a quivering finger in front of him.

"Just … don't," she said, using every vestige of self-control. "I don't even want to know. It's *not* my problem anymore. This is way above me if the Minister is aware of it. Harrison wants me at the lab, ten minutes ago, with the goddamn files we've been run all over for. He wants you two as well. I think you can figure out why."

My stomach sank. Of course we wouldn't have gotten away with it. How ridiculous I had been to think that we had somehow managed to sneak Allesandro in and out of Blue Lab without anyone seeing.

We had cleaned the lab, we had Mattie the security guard covered. But this was Blue Lab. Everything was monitored. It was what the Cabal did best. And now there was security footage, no doubt being added to my own manila file somewhere in the Liver Building.

"We have to go in," she said, sounding defeated. "I've probably lost my job over this. The incident at Carfax, the fundraiser, being compromised at my home address…"

She shook her head in disbelief. I was expecting her to follow this up with something customary, like 'I wish I'd never met you Harkness', but to my surprise, she looked at me with something almost close to pity.

"But you … is there a rule you *haven't* broken? A GO inside the lab for God's sake? This is bigger than me now. You understand that, don't you? I can't *protect* you, not from this."

I did understand. I still held the file in my hands. At least we could give the Cabal all the information we had. I had never asked for any of this private eye crap anyway. Maybe they could finish what we'd started and stop the Black Sacrament without me.

I was probably going to spend the rest of my life in quarantine, or worse. I could run, but where? We live in a walled city run by these people. It's not like I could flee to the countryside.

My number had been well and truly called. I looked at Allesandro. I had no idea what they would do to him. I found myself caring about that more than I liked to admit.

I nodded to Cloves, her mouth set in a thin line, and handed the datapad back to her. Then we did the only thing we could.

We went to face the music.

33

Harrison sent a car to pick us driven by one of Cabal's ghosts. As we climbed into the car, Allesandro told us he would follow on his bike. Cloves snorted with derision, clearly still utterly distrustful of the vampire.

"Of course you will, and that's the last anyone ever saw of the mysterious vampire with the perma-tan," she said waspishly.

He ignored her. As I climbed in next to her I looked back at him.

"You don't have to come," I said. "You could disappear."

He shook his head and gave me his lopsided smile again.

"I'm not about to let you out of my sight again, Doctor," he said, leaning down to the window. "You're my investment, remember?"

He closed the car door for me, still smiling through the open window.

"You've said that before," I said, frowning up at him out of the window. "What *are* you talking about?"

"He wants to be *clan master*, you idiot," Cloves piped up. "Isn't it obvious? If the Black Sacrament are stopped and the charming vampire extremists are removed from his clan, there's a spot open for the top job."

I stared at the vampire, my eyes wide. I hadn't considered his angle on all this.

"Seriously? This is why you saved me? All that deeply touching concern for my wellbeing, just so you can become lord of Sanctum?"

He shrugged.

"I was originally aiming for Trevelyan," he admitted. "The Sacrament knew she was getting antsy. As we now know, she'd been digging around in archives and found out the truth. When I attended the lecture, I was hoping to meet her."

He must have noticed the look on my face. He tilted his head to one side.

"If it's any consolation, finding you there instead was a very pleasant turn of events."

"It's not," I replied coldly. "And what if they'd got to me after Trevelyan? If they'd gotten my teeth next?"

He considered this.

"Well, there was always Oscar," he reasoned. "Any one of you would do. He would have been harder to keep out of their hands, though, considering Gio already had his claws in the boy, using him to get to his father."

Cloves smirked.

"Looks like *you* were the *easy* option, Harkness," she said.

My face felt hot. I stared up at the vampire who was looking down at me, frowning slightly, as though he didn't understand why I was angry or upset.

"I'm nobody's gambling chip, Allesandro, least of all yours," I said coldly. "Don't follow us."

I rolled up the window with a push of a button before he could reply, and the Cabal ghost drove us away down the slum street.

"How naïve can you possibly be?" Cloves said, with genuine wonder. "What on earth did you *think* he was so interested in? I told you, you can't *trust* their kind. They have their own interests before ours."

"Cloves," I muttered, staring angrily out of the window. "Shut the fuck up, will you?"

34

By the time we pulled into the white dusted quad before the entrance to Blue Lab One, it was nearing eleven. Most of the staff would be gone by now. Only the die-hards worked through the night.

There were only two other vehicles in the car park. A black van and a fine looking Bentley, which I was guessing was either Harrison's or the Minister's. I was dimly aware that whatever trouble I was in with them for bringing a GO into the lab, a more pressing issue was that it had almost been half a day since Griff had given me my dose of Epsilon. I was going to need a shot soon.

The doors to the atrium opened with their customary whoosh and we were escorted inside by the ghost. Mattie was at his post behind the large, brightly-lit reception desk and standing with him, waiting for us, were Servant Leon Harrison, five Cabal ghost agents, and the large and ominous figure of the Minister.

I hadn't seen him stood up before. The fat, grey-complexioned man was taller than I'd expected. He stared at Cloves and I as we walked towards them, his eyes looking as bored and utterly disinterested as they had last time we met. I figured he was most likely pissed off at having to come down here so late and getting his hands dirty for once.

"Servant Cloves," Harrison said, disapproval plain on his face, "you should know that there will be a full investigation on your handling of this case. Your brief was to quietly and unobtrusively gather intelligence. Instead, we find ourselves with a diplomatic incident in the vampire district due to your mole here setting fire to the GO's place of work, a rather inexpert handling of the attack at the Bodleian Library and the kidnap of a very high profile member of a very important and influential family."

He was glaring at her. She looked contrite but didn't give him an inch. I was impressed.

"In addition to this, a gangland shootout occurred at one of our city's finest historic churches where, I might add, several media sources saw Cabal agents whom you had sent on an anonymous tipoff. Thankfully, our presence and involvement there cannot be proved and remains speculation only – and then there was an incident reported by the superintendent of your building, a break-in at the home of a Cabal Servant."

He shook his head, looking thoroughly disgusted.

"I am officially relieving you of further duties temporarily pending full investigation and debriefing."

Cloves nodded respectfully.

"Understood, Servant Harrison," she said. "Despite the somewhat unorthodox methods, I have, with the assistance of the Doctor here and her exploitation of her GO source, uncovered intelligence of the highest importance; a breakaway cult within the GO community, calling themselves the Black Sacrament. Requesting permission to file my report immediately, sir."

Harrison looked over at me, his expression still unpleasantly disapproving.

"The Doctor's GO source?" he said, looking at me most distastefully. "Yes, both myself and the Minister are very interested to hear about that, especially given the GO's recent admittance to a high security, closed access lab right here in this building."

I opened my mouth to reply, but from behind Harrison the Minister cut in, his voice the usual gravelly rumble.

"Do they have the files Trevelyan discovered or not?"

Harrison held out his hand and Trevelyan dropped the datapad into it. The Minister came over and took it from him, barely looking at any of us.

He waddled around and disappeared behind the desk, practically shoving Mattie out of the way with his large bulk, and hooked the datapad to the reception workstation. The files appeared, and the minister began reading through them quickly, his odd unfocussed eyes sliding listlessly over the pages.

We all watched him curiously. This was not normal behaviour for a Minister. Why he was so interested in the files was a mystery to me. I figured that must surely be Harrison's domain.

After a moment, the Minister paused and looked almost pleased, his rotund face twisting into a humourless smile.

"Excellent," he said, his voice slurring lazily. "We have what we need."

"What we need, Minister?" Harrison asked, polite but clearly confused.

"You can come in now," the Minister said, muttering to himself, barely intelligible.

Behind us, the outer doors to the quad opened and I turned to see figures entering from the dark night outside.

It was Gio, Helena and Jessica. The Black Sacrament had just strolled straight into Blue Lab.

They were flanked by six others, the same combat-ready humans who had stormed the fundraiser and later chased Cloves all over town. Gio was smiling, as though delighted to see us all again. He raised his arms in greeting, as though to hug us all.

The men were all armed with machine guns.

"What the fuck?" I heard Cloves say quietly.

"Excellent, excellent," Gio said, looking very pleased with himself. "We only need the girl."

He spoke in a breezy offhand way as they stalked toward us down the entrance corridor, one bony finger pointed directly at me. Before any of us could react, the men had raised their weapons and gunfire rattled through the atrium, deafening and startling. To my immediate left, Servant Leon Harrison's head exploded, obliterating his incredulous expression.

I'd never seen someone get shot in the head before, not outside of the movies anyway. I would have expected him to go down gracefully, maybe with a neat pound-coin sized hole in his forehead. Instead, his head flew apart like a watermelon. I watched with numb shock as his body was lifted off the ground with the force of the impact, thrown back against the desk with a thud. To me, it seemed to happen in slow motion. His headless body hit the ground sprawling, a red mist of blood coating his expensive white shirt.

More shots were being fired around me and the six ghost agents fell. The highly trained Cabal security staff were mown down in a hail of bullets. I saw them fall back, as if landed with invisible punches. It was so swift only one of them had managed to get his hand on the butt of his gun before they were killed.

Echoing around the large atrium, the noise of the gunfire was deafening, a brief staccato burst which slammed against my ears. Directly behind me, dear old Mattie, a look of disbelief on his face, took three slugs to the chest and disappeared behind the reception desk as if he had fallen through a secret trapdoor.

Amidst the deafening rain of bullets, I heard Cloves yell and spun to see her flying backwards, hitting her head hard as she fell against the desk. She landed in a crumpled heap face down on the white floor then lay, completely still.

The whole massacre had lasted no more than five seconds.

Suddenly, I was standing alone, hunched with my hands raised like a shield in front of my face – an instinctual defence which would have done little good against their bullets if they had wanted me dead. Bodies surrounded me everywhere, harsh smears of crimson in the otherwise clean white lines of the atrium.

Gio's goons fanned out, professional and silent, guns still raised and trained on me.

"Well," Gio said lightly after a moment, as the musical tinkle of spent shells clattering on the tiles had fallen into silence. "*That* was satisfying, wasn't it?"

Jessica and Helena flanked him on either side. Jessica looked rather irritated. I noticed there were a few ragged holes in her sweater. The Sacrament vampires hadn't managed to escape the fight at Carfax completely undamaged then; they looked like bullet holes.

I had no idea if you could put a vampire down with regular bullets. After watching Allesandro regenerate from body wide third degree burns in a mere matter of hours, I doubted it.

Gio was surveying the scene like a chirpy master of ceremonies, as though he were here to give the light hearted company speech at the Blue lab Christmas party. He seemed to be enjoying the carnage.

"You are a slippery little pup, Doctor Harkness." He shook his head good naturedly, as though I were a cheeky child. "Twice now you've given me the slip. Twice I've had to chase you around after you made me look a fool. You escape my club, you escape my little pet Pale … and yet everywhere I turn, there you are, like a bad penny."

His smile was warm, but I had learned that his bright shining eyes were very cold indeed.

"It must be fate," he purred. "Don't you think?"

"Maybe you're just not very competent, Gio," I said, forcing my voice to sound steady.

Helena's eyes widened in surprise behind Gio as his face twisted, the smile falling away. He glared at me with utter loathing.

"You can *act* as brave as you wish, you pathetic human creature, but I can *smell* the fear on you. Sweat and shit. And you are *right* to be afraid."

The exterior doors of Blue Lab opened and two vampires entered, both male and dressed in the same combat ready getup as the human mercenaries. The final two members of the Black Sacrament.

They were almost identical, possibly twins. Between them they were dragging the unconscious body of Oscar. His arms were draped over their shoulders as they held him up, his shoes scraping behind him on the floor. He would have looked like a drunken student being carried home by his friends, had the front of his now filthy tuxedo not been spattered with blood. He looked as though he had thrown up on himself at some point.

I couldn't see his face; his head was lolling between his own shoulder blades too much. In a way, I was glad I couldn't. I knew they had already taken the boy's teeth.

Behind the vampires and their captive, the Bonewalker itself glided like an angel of death, looming over them, tall and black-robed. Its white mask caught the bright strip lighting, so that it seemed to glow.

"Is he alive?" I demanded desperately of Gio.

"For now," the vampire replied, still glaring at me angrily. "After your goddamned phone led your Cabal friends right to us at Carfax, we had to get out fast. We haven't quite had time to finish things off."

He forced his face back into the bright, friendly expression he seemed to favour. I had come to the conclusion that in his extremist mindset, this vampire was what we would medically term batshit-crazy.

"Besides, I thought it would be more touching for the three last offerings to go together. Right here, at the end of all things. We didn't keep Trevelyan alive, or that Coleman girl. They were so loud," he complained fussily. "Such a handful, you understand, but our Bonewalker friend here is the worker of miracles and he tells me the fresher the better."

Jessica had walked over with interest to where the Cabal agents lay sprawled, quite dead in a messy heap. She squatted and delicately rolled a finger over the blood on the floor, tasting it experimentally, as though she were dabbing up sherbet.

"I'm starving," she said. "When can we finish these ones off?"

"Right now of course," Gio said to her happily.

"The last three?" I questioned.

I had been trying to subtly move backwards but the reception desk was at my back. My heel caught on something and when I glanced down, I saw that I had nudged Veronica Cloves' leg. Her body was very still on the floor. The sight of it made me want to heave. I had seen more than enough death in the last forty eight hours.

I looked over at the Minister, who was still standing at the workstation, looking uninterested and solemn. He hadn't spoken once since he had summoned Gio and the Black Sacrament into Blue Lab. He hadn't even looked up or moved during the shooting. He just stood there like a dumb statue, while bullets flew around him, utterly unconcerned.

"Minister," I implored. "I don't understand what's happening here. Why are you working with the vampires? You're Cabal, for God's sake! You just got two of your own Servants killed, not to mention your agents."

"Good lord," Helena called to Gio, looking mildly astonished. "The girl really is quite dense, isn't she?"

Gio laughed and bizarrely, so did the Minister. They snickered in perfect harmony.

"Of course you don't understand," the Minister grumbled. "You have never held a single conversation with the Cabal Minister."

The fat man looked up at me, his face grey and empty of feeling, chilling as I had always found it like the dead, glassy face of a fish. I glanced at Gio. With every word the Minister had said, the vampire's lips had moved silently, mimicking the words.

Gio grinned, showing long, sharp fangs behind his lips, and on the other side of the desk, the Minister copied him.

"You've been speaking to *me*," the Minister rumbled in his gravelly voice. "Our dear Minister has, for some time now, been my very own ghoul."

Gio's words were coming from the Minister's body. I stared, disbelieving. The fat man's lustreless appearance, his glazed, sleepy eyes, his death rattle of a voice … He was a ghoul. Gio had been controlling him. It's how he had got us here tonight, with the decrypted files and me, the last offering.

"It's good to have eyes and ears in a place of power," Gio said, this time from his own mouth. "We apprehended the good Minister several weeks ago. He had noticed, you see, that Trevelyan had been digging around in the archives here at Blue Lab and that she had discovered something she shouldn't have; something that *he* wished dearly would remain buried."

"How would a Cabal Minister notice what someone like Trevelyan was doing?" I asked.

I didn't understand. He was a powerful figure, she should have been completely beneath his notice.

"Oh, our dear minister has kept an eye on her, and you, of course, since you first came to work here at Blue Lab. How could he *not* take an interest when he realised that your supervisor, the *daughter* of one of the Development Team who doomed this world, had dug up a past which threatened both herself *and* him? He called her to a meeting, somewhere anonymous, somewhere discreet, down in the Slade sector, over by the boundaries of the woods."

Gio walked towards me, slowly, his hands causally thrust into his pocket as he spoke.

"We were watching her. We had been for some time. We had to be sure she had extracted the files we needed before we apprehended her. So imagine our delight when we followed her to her secret rendezvous to find that she had been summoned by a Minister himself."

I watched as Gio moved up to the reception desk, standing beside his ghoul and gently patting him on the shoulder as he continued his story.

"He didn't threaten Trevelyan, of course. The Minister here was a good man, or he believed himself to be. Trying to build order out of the chaos, trying to make amends for the destruction of the world. He tried to dissuade her, to warn her about the dangers of digging up the past."

The vampire gave the minister a look of utter disgust.

"He thought he could convince her to let the ghosts lie, you see. Everything had changed after the wars. To rise to such heights as he had, to reinvent himself and then to risk having everything torn down by the snooping of a curious lab supervisor who had happened upon her own family name in some classified archives."

He looked back to me.

"Trevelyan didn't listen to him. As you probably know, she was a stubborn and opinionated woman. High ranking Cabal or not, when she figured out *who* he was, she only looked harder. They parted badly. Trevelyan left and the Minister, alone without his usual entourage in the darkest sector of our fair city, far from his golden towers in the Liver, was *ours* for the taking. I made him my ghoul and for all intents and purposes, I have lived and breathed through him since."

I looked back to the Minister, the empty puppet Gio had been using.

"But how did *he* know what was in the files?" I questioned. "Why was he even *watching* Trevelyan and me? I've never even met the man."

"No, but your father knew him well, Doctor," Gio explained. "Don't you understand yet? My, you are rather slow. The Minister, saviour of mankind and leader of the city in the ongoing struggle against the Pale menace, is, or at least once *was*, Alistair Rutheridge, the original leader of the Development Team."

35

Of course.

I knew I had recognised the face of the large bearded man in the photograph on the wall in Trevelyan's office, that I'd seen his face somewhere else. Shave off the beard, add a couple of hundred pounds and thirty years, and it was the Minister.

Gio called an elevator and at the insistence of his armed thugs, we all took a ride down into the pit, my mind still reeling.

I was alone in the small, horribly confined space, stuck with the vampire clan master, the ghoul Minister, and the smiling blonde sociopath Helena. Jessica had taken another elevator with Oscar and his handlers. The Bonewalker, presumably, was making its own way down into the depths of Blue Lab, leaving the armed mercenaries to guard the atrium above.

"It doesn't make sense," I said, staring at the corpulent, somnambulistic bulk of Minister Rutheridge. "There's no record of him. Cloves told me. When she decrypted the files, she searched all of Cabal's databases. There's no record of Alistair Rutheridge after the wars at all."

"As good a time as any to disappear, don't you think?" Gio smiled at me.

He was leaning nonchalantly on the other side of the elevator, his arms folded casually, watching me like a hungry cat. I was pretty sure he could smell my fear.

"In the chaos of the apocalypse, any number of people disappeared. When we vampires and the rest of the GOs came to pull your fat out of the fire, and the world was being rebuilt anew, it would have been easy enough to reinvent yourself if you chose to. To hide your shameful past and become someone new."

He leaned forward and picked an imaginary piece of lint from the Minister's lapel. The shell of a man didn't respond.

"The poor human. He must have been wracked with guilt," Helena said in her soft dreamy voice, "knowing what he had done, what he had unleashed on the world. He was always an ambitious man and that didn't change after the wars."

Her eyes wandered over his crumpled, pinstriped suit before focusing on me.

"When the Cabal was formed, he entered its ranks. He's been climbing steadily ever since. He had a new name, new identity, a new mission to right the wrongs of old. You humans are so sentimental. It's almost as though he thought it was possible to make amends, to wash the blood off a ruined planet."

"So now we had the Minister," Gio said as Helena returned her gaze to the ghoul, "and we had our first ingredient for the Bonewalker. The teeth of the first sinner. Our goal was made so much easier now that I could walk and talk through the meat puppet of Rutheridge himself, giving orders, digging deep."

He sighed, looking me square in the eye.

"But you people, you are so troublesome, aren't you? Before I could access the files, Trevelyan gets cold feet and breaks cover. She deleted *everything* from the system, hid the files and ran."

"We caught her, of course," Helena smiled, "which is where you came in, sweetie."

The door of the elevator pinged open. We were faced with a long, dimly lit corridor. We were deeper than I'd been before. We were on the Development Level.

The Minister's hands suddenly shot out and grabbed me, pinning my arms to my sides as he walked me out of the lift. I tried to wriggle free, but the ghoul was freakishly strong. Gio smirked at me.

"Walk, Doctor," the Minster growled at me. "And don't try anything or I'll have him break your arms."

We made our way down the long, featureless corridor. It was emergency lighting only down here, red bulbs at intervals along the corridor, turning the very air into a murky crimson wash.

"We were furious, you see," Gio said from behind as his ghoul shuffled me along, still captive. "Trevelyan had hidden the files with you, deeply encrypted. The Black Sacrament do not have access to the level of technology your Cabal enjoy. We needed to decrypt the files, but we could not risk raising suspicion. If a Minister was looking into the matter on a personal level, it would seem odd to all. Questions would be asked.

I'm sure you've noticed, but he hardly looks fresh any more, our dear Doctor Rutheridge. We couldn't have people looking too closely at him."

Gio was ahead of us now, leading the way through the crimson corridors, his voice sickly sweet as it carried over his shoulder to me.

"So instead we used him to call in Servant Harrison and his lackey Cloves. Neither suspected they were being issued orders to investigate the matter by anyone other than the real Minister. Why would they? Certainly he is a little grim looking and somewhat stoic, but neither had met him in person before. They could not have guessed he was my ventriloquist's dummy."

We reached a door in the corridor and passed through into a deeper subsection of the Development Level.

"We set Cabal the task of decrypting the files," Helena said, walking beside me. "It was only out of curiosity that we suggested you become involved. Why not kill two birds with one stone, we figured; get you chasing our little traitor in the midst."

She sounded so pleased, her awe of Gio so genuine, I was surprised she wasn't skipping with happiness down the corridor.

"Gio has eyes everywhere, sweetie. He *knew* Allesandro was not a true believer, that he had approached you at the lecture. We knew he was trying to bring our great work down around our ears. How perfect to use him to lure *you* to the club? We already had Rutheridge and Trevelyan, it would be insulting not to collect offering number three along the way?"

We had reached a large sealed door: black, metal and windowless. I heard footsteps behind us and knew that Jessica was following, bringing Oscar with her.

I couldn't think of any way out of this. I was alone with every enemy I had.

"Why have the teeth delivered here though, to Blue Lab?" I asked, as the Minister, his invisible strings pulled by Gio, began to tap in the access code to open the door.

"Initially, just as with Trevelyan, we needed a starting point," Gio explained. "Some horrific crime to act as a rallying point to muster the righteous fury of Cabal into action. We knew Harrison would perhaps have been less likely to start a city-wide search for someone who was probably dead, while Cloves would be too busy with the far more important business of using her techs to decode the files for us. We needed to engage you."

Gio shrugged absently, leaning against the wall as he watched his puppet opening the door, one arm still clamped around me.

"After the first lot, we thought we might as well have Coleman's sent too, and then young Oscar's. Keep the great and good Servant Harrison busy, thinking there was a personal message in them."

He gave a mock sympathetic look to the Minister.

"Perhaps I was too cruel, making him be the one to wield the pliers each time, to be the one to hurt the children of his former team." He saw my horrified look. "Oh yes Doctor, he is still in there … somewhere. But he has no control anymore."

The vampire leaned into the grey Minister's face. It had been the Minister's voice on the DataStream video then; it was him torturing Trevelyan. Or rather Gio, speaking through his ghoul's vocal chords.

"I wanted him to *feel* what he had done. His precious project had tortured our leader, our beloved Tassoni, for *five long years*. And when our master took his righteous revenge and led the Pale armies against his torturers, what did this man do? He returned to the holding pen where our master's ruined body still lay, and he killed him. He denied him his vengeance, and then buried the truth."

Gio's eyes flashing furiously as he turned on me.

"Why should he get to rebuild a new life? Why should the children of his guilty associates flourish in the new world? How is that justice? No, how *delicious* to make him tear into the children of his dear old companions, to force him to bloody himself to the elbow in their corpses, to pull the teeth from their mouths. He suffered as he went about the work I set him," he grinned at the slack-faced ghoul, "and somewhere in there he suffers still."

The door before us whooshed open.

"And now you will *all* suffer for your sins," he finished.

We had been led, I saw, to a large circular chamber which I assumed had once been a development lab. I had been expecting horrors down here. God knows I knew there were monsters on other levels. I had seen them myself. But whatever equipment and machinery had once filled this room had long since been cleared away.

The metallic floor, grimy and dusty with disuse, was covered in a complicated sigil, some kind of multi-layered pentagram. It filled the floor of the round, high-ceilinged chamber, spray-painted floor in black and red. It was intricate and elaborate.

There were five points to the vast star. At three of their peaks, there was a pile of teeth, like upended popcorn boxes; miniature cairns of glistening molars, bicuspids, canines, incisors, macabre little pyramids. I knew whose they were: Vyvienne Trevelyan, Jennifer Coleman, and Oscar Scott.

And waiting for us in the very centre of the vast pentagram was the Bonewalker.

The Rutheridge ghoul released me and at Gio's silent instruction, walked off to take his place at one of the two empty points.

The other was for me.

Behind me, Jessica and the two male vampires hauled the still unconscious Oscar into the room. They dragged him over and dumped him unceremoniously at the point of this dark compass which held his teeth. His body fell to the floor in a heap.

Jessica walked back to Gio and Helena, brushing her hands together briskly, as though she had just been taking out the trash.

"I don't see why we brought the boy," she grumbled, her glossy ponytail swishing as she walked. "His teeth are already here, we didn't need the rest of the meat."

"Because Tassoni will be hungry when he gets here," Gio said reverently.

I couldn't think of any way to escape.

I was deep underground in the hands of my enemies. Everyone else here – the other offerings – was either already dead, like my boss and the activist girl, worse than dead, like poor Minister Rutheridge, or else out for the count.

"The files," I said to Gio.

One of the twin male vampires, a tall dark haired and sour looking creature, had positioned himself behind me. God knows why, it's not as though I could make a dash for it.

"The files?" Gio repeated politely, cocking his head at me.

"I've read them," I said. "What's on them that you need so much? You already knew what happened and where the Pale came from, who was responsible for them. You have your bloody sacrifices or whatever this billowing lich-lord calls them."

"Tassoni," Gio revealed simply. "The ritual of the Black Sacrament, which our friend the Bonewalker has promised to perform for us, can hardly be performed without his body."

I stared at Gio incredulously.

"You don't know where it is? Thirty years of searching, uncovering the facts one by one, but you haven't been able to find where the old world's military scientists hid your precious clan master's corpse?"

The vampire stared back at me, his pale face tinted red by the generator lights above.

"Even when you turned Rutheridge into your ghoul," I said, "you couldn't get the location out of him. Sure, he worked at this lab for five years, but even he didn't know where he was other than somewhere in Norfolk."

I couldn't help but laugh at the all-powerful clan master.

"Norfolk is a big place," Jessica piped up, "like looking for a needle in a haystack."

"Or to be more specific," Helena chimed in, "a secret, very well-hidden government base in a vast swathe of countryside practically overrun these days with the Pale. Too dangerous for even us five hardy souls to make a daytrip of, you see."

Gio raised his hands to silence the two.

"The decrypted files give the *location* of the base," he said. "It's encoded into the final log entry. Norfolk military base, location 452. A simple designation. Thanks to your Cabal friend's tireless work unlocking the files for me, it took me but moments working through the Minister in the atrium just now to locate the exact coordinates which the files give."

Realisation dawned.

"And that's where the long tall freak-show comes in," I said, looking over at the Bonewalker, which regarded all of us in its blank yet somehow deeply threatening way.

"You can't get to the body. You'd be torn apart by the Pale if you tried an excursion from New Oxford to Norfolk. So you're making it bring the body to you. You're bringing Tassoni's corpse *here*."

Gio smirked at me, and walked over to the Bonewalker. The gaunt, evil bedsheet-wearing bastard leaned down as the vampire muttered GPS coordinates into what may or may not have been its ear.

The Bonewalker straightened up. It stood thoughtfully for a moment and then vanished, fading from our view in layered stages, just as it had when it had abandoned me and Allesandro outside Carfax. The last thing I saw was its expressionless mask, hanging ghost-like in the air. Then it was gone.

"If you bring Tassoni back, it will be the end of everything," I snapped at the vampires. "Is everyone except me fucking high here?"

"That's the *idea* sweetheart," Helena said. "The world is gone already. Surely you can see that? The fire has gone out and all of us, we're just huddling pathetically around the embers."

"Tassoni will rise with *your* death," Gio declared, the fervent light of the true believer in his eyes. "You *deserve* to die. You cannot argue that. You're practically a *sister* to the ghouls, just as my dear stupid delicious Oscar is their *brother*, while this man – my personal ghoul, the great and mighty Cabal Minister – has the blood of millions on his hands."

He prowled towards me, circling me like a predator on the savannah.

"*Our* only crime was to have our clan leader – strong, proud, powerful – ripped away from us by your kind and tortured for years so that you could make monsters which would kill us all."

He practically spat on the floor.

"And *still* you think we are bad guys."

"We'd all rather be dead than have to mainline into your pathetic new world order," Jessica sneered. "Do you honestly think that after living for hundreds of years, any of us want to whore ourselves out at clubs for the entertainment of you people? You are our food!"

I thought of Allesandro. He certainly seemed to want to integrate. He seemed to *like* our new world. I thought of the people I cared about: bumbling Griff and excitable Lucy, carving out little lives for themselves, even in a world rather more savage than it once had been. There was still light and warmth. It wasn't all cold ashes in the fire. The vampires were wrong.

"I still don't understand why the Bonewalker is helping you," I said. "What's in it for that thing?"

Gio rolled his eyes.

"Nothing's in it for the blasted thing. I *won* the damn Bonewalker," he said, exasperated. "Two years ago, in an online auction."

I stared at him, my mouth dropped.

Okay … *What*?

"You really know *so little* about the entities you purport to study, don't you, Doctor?" Gio said with wonder. "There's a *very* lucrative slave market in our alternate society. Bonewalkers are not demons, nor are they are entities from another plane of existence. They are Djinn. Surely you've heard of them? The 'grant three wishes kind'. Well, that's not specifically how they work, but Bonewalkers are slaves, property. They change hands, from master to master, until they have earned their freedom."

He saw the look of surprise on my face and laughed.

"Did you *really* think the charmless Marlin Scott managed to convince a troop of Bonewalkers to help fortify the cities of the world? No, of course not. He *bought* them, heart and soul. The Cabal uses Bonewalkers to cast wards on certain buildings they own: the Liver here in Oxford, the Shard over in York. They *own* the Bonewalkers. Your masters have slaves just like the rest of us. The Bonewalkers' talents in manipulating space are unparalleled but once they are bound to a master, they obey his whims."

"There's a downside, though," I said. "There has to be. No creature could evolve to give that much power to someone else without taking some for itself."

Jessica cackled.

"It depends on your long-term view," she smirked. "Once a Bonewalker has earned its freedom, once the bond of contract is released through whatever mute internal code of honour guides them, they come for their former masters and take them away."

"No one knows where," Gio said. "Neither the freed Bonewalker nor the one who sold their soul by buying them is ever seen again."

He was stood where the Bonewalker had been, staring at the empty space.

"That's not an issue for us, of course. We don't plan on living long once Tassoni is back. No one will. He will use the Pale to end humanity and we will follow you into the darkness. Better that than this. Better vengeance than submission. Perhaps in the end, there will be nothing but

Bonewalkers left in this world, wandering silently like ghosts. Perhaps then … they will take off their masks."

I made a mental note. If I got out of this alive, I was going to start two new branches of important para-research. Firstly, how to identify a bloody ghoul on sight. Secondly, actually find some cold, hard facts on the Bonewalkers.

There was a shudder, a vibration in the air, and the subject of our speculation reappeared in the exact centre of the pentagram. At the Bonewalker's feet lay a shrouded body. Its wrapping looked filmy and plastic as though it had been vacuum-sealed, like a chrysalis filled with meat – raw and bloody.

The remains of Tassoni, freshly imported from Sub Level Thirteen of the long-defunct Norfolk military base.

The remains looked small, sad, and very dead. But as they appeared like a silent magic trick in the middle of the chamber, a change came in the atmosphere; a deep pressure, a discomfort before the storm. The presence of the other vampires, even powerful Gio, was nothing in comparison to this.

Waves of energy seemed to roll invisibly from the mummified corpse at the Bonewalker's feet. The air became electric with anger, suffering, and a deep and persistent low level rage.

If vampires could haunt their own corpses, this guy was a serious poltergeist.

I glanced over at the slack-jawed Minister, the former Doctor Rutheridge, who had unwittingly created the Pale so long ago with my father and the others. He had known on some level all those years ago, when he had stolen onto Level Thirteen and seen the corpse, that this was evil.

He had gone back to the base later; it must have been him. He had killed Tassoni, tried to finish things, and now here he was faced with the vampire again. I wondered if there was any small spark of consciousness remaining in the ghoul, anything of my father's old boss that hadn't already been driven mad at the torture of Trevelyan, Coleman and Oscar, which was aware of what was now happening before it.

The Black Sacrament gathered reverently around the body of their clan master. Gio looked as though he were ready to weep. He looked up at the Bonewalker.

"We have provided what you need," he said to it. "The offerings are here. The oldest magic is yours to command and you are mine to command. Bring him back to us!"

Across the chamber, one of the unnamed male vampire twins pulled Oscar effortlessly to his feet. The one standing directly behind me placed his arm around my neck. I saw the flash of a blade, which he now held to my throat.

They were going to kill us – me and Oscar. We were the last offerings. The sins repaid.

I wouldn't even live to see the big finale, the destruction of the world. It was like walking out just before the end of a movie.

I thought of Servant Harrison, Mattie and Cloves, dead and sprawled in the atrium upstairs. I wondered where my vampire was now. Somewhere in the city, planning his next takeover bid?

"Master Tassoni," Gio said, stepping back from the corpse as the Bonewalker removed its hands from its long sleeves and raised its arms. "We bring these offerings. You whose teeth have torn into mankind for five hundred years, you who were taken, defiled and disgraced by the human cattle, your fangs torn out by them. We bring you theirs and urge you to return. Follow the path opened by the Bonewalker."

"Live for us," Jessica intoned, staring lovingly at the bones.

The vampire at my neck pushed the blade hard against my skin.

"Kill for us," Helena said, gripping Gio's hand tightly. "We of the Black Sacrament would gladly die for you."

"Good to know," a voice said behind me.

The vampires whirled, surprised. I flicked my eyes to the left, toward the door where we had entered the old Development Lab.

Standing in the doorway, both holding the same guns Gio's hired killers had carried, were Griff and Allesandro. I stared at them for a moment. Their being here was so unreal I thought it was a fevered hallucination brought on by my imminent death.

Allesandro fired. The vampire holding me was hit square in the head, inches from my own. I heard the bullets fly by, inches from the back of my head, and I swear I felt the heat of the blast. My captor was thrown off his feet as though he had been hit by a car. I went down with him, pulled by his weight as we collapsed in a tangle of limbs.

He might not be dead but a gunshot wound to the head was at least going to disorient the undead bastard. I thrashed and kicked, throwing his flailing arms off me as I rolled away from him. Above me, I heard more frantic reports of gunfire and then a furious animal scream of rage from Gio, like nothing I'd ever heard before.

Scrambling to my feet, I saw that Jessica was down, as was the vampire who had been holding Oscar. Gio had moved across the room with inhuman speed, a blur of motion, and Allesandro emptied the rest of his magazine into his master, bringing him crashing to a heap at his feet.

"Get out!" he yelled to me.

I didn't need any more encouragement.

Griff was still firing into the room, seemingly at random. The noise amplified and echoed in the acoustics of the chamber, the bright muzzle flashes filling the red room in strobes of lightening. I was on my feet and running toward him, towards the door.

He looked so surreal. Had he ever even fired a gun before? His face was a grimace as he tried to keep the jumping gun under control. Helena ran for Griff, her blonde hair flying out behind her, her face a scream of pure rage. Whether by accident or design, his arc of bullets rose up and crossed her face, taking out her eyes and sending her flying backwards. She landed on her back within the pentagram, staring blindly upwards. She twitched for a moment then lay still.

The bullets must have embedded in her brain, I thought. Heal that, you smiling bitch.

"How?" Gio roared from his heap at Allesandro's feet, staring in horror at his fallen comrade.

The front of his clothes were torn and tattered from gunfire, the white skin visible underneath glazed with blood, but I knew he would already be healing.

"How did you get in here, you little fucking traitor? The guards!"

Allesandro brought the butt of the gun down onto Gio's face with all his force, sending the older vampire back to the floor.

"Those? They were only human," he said.

As I reached Griff, he held something out to me. It was a handful of long, thick test tubes, sealed with syringes like darts on the end, and filled with milky fluid.

"Brought you your meds," he grinned.

There were three of them. I grabbed the syringes from him. My face must have been pure confusion.

"Rejected strains," he yelled over the gunfire. "Highly exothermic reaction."

He was shooting at the vampire who had held me at knifepoint again. He had started to get to his feet, the left hand side of his face a bloody pulp.

I saw from the corner of my vision that across the chamber Gio had reached up from the floor and grabbed Allesandro's leg. With a mighty heave, he threw the vampire off balance and leapt on top of him as he fell, like a furious lion. Allesandro went down under him in a flurry of blows.

In the midst of the chaos I saw the Bonewalker, still standing sedately in the centre of the chamber, its arms outstretched, as indifferent to the hail of bullets around it as it had been to the Pale in the pit.

The vampire twin with the blade, moving faster than Griff or I could react, was suddenly in front of me, leaping up from a crouch. He still held the knife. I could see bone fragments jutting out through the torn muscles where Allesandro's bullets had shaved off his face. At least you could tell him apart from his brother now, I thought.

As he reared up for me, I raised one of the dart syringes and drove it like a stake down into his good eye. The vampire grabbed for me and fell in agony to his knees. I watched the milky fluid disappear from the glass chamber into its body as the pressurised seal of the dart flushed the serum into its skull.

He opened his mouth to scream, suddenly spasming, and I jerked out of his grip, jumping back and dragging Griff with me just in time.

The vampire seemed to swell like an over-inflated tyre for a moment, its skin bloating and purpling as it let forth a horrific gargle. Another beat and then it exploded like a water balloon, showering us in bits of wet vampire like red rain. It was more impressive than a rat – faster too.

Jessica, who was back on her feet, stared in disbelief at Helena's blind, fallen body and the dripping remains of the twin. Her eyes found us as I dragged Griff towards the doorway.

"The bullets won't stop them," I yelled, as Griff's gun suddenly clicked on empty. "All it does is slow them down, we have to go!"

"You're going nowhere," a voice said roughly behind Griff as he was dragged off his feet.

The other vampire twin, the one who had been holding Oscar, had come around behind us. He lifted Griff effortlessly off the floor from behind, looking like he were performing the Heimlich manoeuvre, and then buried his face in Griff's throat and bit, tearing into him. Griff gagged and dropped his gun, his limbs flailing and kicking uselessly.

I threw myself at the two of them, wrapping my arms around Griff. The vampire seemed to think I was trying to pull my assistant free and I heard a rough dark laugh escape him, amused by my futility. He stopped laughing, however, when he realised I was just trying to get a decent angle on him.

I slammed the second syringe into his thigh as hard as I could.

Shocked, the vampire jerked away from me, twirling Griff through the air like a ballroom dancer. His face came up from my assistant's torn neck, suddenly horrified. I scrabbled backwards, trying to put some distance between us before he exploded.

An exemplary exothermic reaction, I would later think. At the time, all I did was shield my face from butchered vampire chunks flying through the air and watch Griff as he was thrown by the blast across the room. He skittered along the floor and came to rest against the wall, winded and grabbing for his neck, drenched from head to foot in vampire juice – but most importantly, alive.

Allesandro's hand gripped my arm from out of nowhere and hauled me to my feet. I hadn't even realised he was close to me.

"Move," he said. "We have to go!"

"But Griff!"

I tried to shake him off. I looked back to see Oscar also, still a crumpled heap. I couldn't leave them here.

"They don't want Griff, they want *you*! They can't complete the ritual without you."

Allesandro thrust me towards the door, following close behind.

I heard Gio screaming obscenities behind us. Allesandro has left him bloody on the floor, but Gio was older and stronger, and would not stay down for long.

We ran.

The corridor which I had been marched down earlier now seemed nightmarishly long as we raced back down it, heading towards the elevator.

"How ... how are you here?" I managed, still winded from the exploding knife-happy goon and struggling to keep up with the vampire. "And Griff? What the fuck? I told you not to follow us!"

"I know," he glanced down at me. "I didn't listen."

He hauled me through the doorway and into the long corridor beyond it. The red lights flicked by us as we ran, as though the air was misted with blood.

"I made a bit of a mess upstairs," he said. "I didn't know where you were, so I went to your lab. Lucy let me in. Even deactivated the ultraviolet corridor for me. Your team had no idea what had happened upstairs but I could follow your scent. Your boy wanted to come too. We took a couple of guns from the humans in the lobby."

"You killed them?" I asked. "Gio's Hired guns?"

"They were only human, it wasn't difficult. It's the ones behind us that are the problem."

The elevator was in sight. I glanced back over my shoulder.

They were after us. Jessica, like a Greek fury, was tearing along the corridor, her face contorted with rage. We had ruined their resurrection. Their great leader lay decomposing at the feet of the Bonewalker. I had the very certain notion that if Jessica got hold of me, she would tear my head clean off, carry it back to the chamber, and shake my teeth out onto the floor like loose change.

When I looked forward again, my brain could hardly register what I saw. The elevator door was open and Lucy, who loved vampires but was too squeamish to clean up exploding rats, was standing inside, her foot holding the door for us. She looked terrified.

Allesandro practically lifted me up and ran with me the last few yards. We threw ourselves into the lift and Lucy swiped for the doors to close.

They slid shut with agonising slowness as Jessica raced for us, covering the corridor with inhuman speed. I almost thought we made it but as the last sliver of space closed, white fingers thrust into the gap and began to force the protesting doors back open.

Allesandro pushed Lucy and me behind him, crushing us up against the wall of the lift, using himself as a barrier between us and the furious vampire tearing the doors open like tinfoil. Jessica's face appeared. She looked feral, her fangs bared, her eyes wide and alarming.

"You fucking traitor!" she screamed at Allesandro. "You bring shame on the clan, on all of us! You filthy human-loving Judas! Give me the bitch!"

She was trying to force herself into the lift with us. Lucy screamed behind me. I didn't blame her. Jessica was like a foaming snapping dog, any pretence to humanity lost in her anger and desperation to reach me.

"You're a worm, Allesandro! A traitor to your own kind! You're worse than the humans you bow to!"

His hand reached back to mine, grabbing the final dart syringe from between my fingers. I had forgotten I even had it. Bringing it up swiftly, he grabbed the top of Jessica's dark hair in one hand and with the other, he rammed the dart into her wide, gnashing mouth.

"Jessica," he said, "shut the fuck up."

It lodged in her throat. She gagged in surprise, pulling herself away, falling backwards onto the floor of the corridor outside. As the doors finally slid shut, I glimpsed Gio appear round the corner. He looked as beat up from his tussle with Allesandro as my vampire did, but was staggering along the corridor towards us, blind fury on his face.

The doors closed and we heard a muffled, wet thump, as though someone had thrown a bucket of pasta against the other side of the doors.

That would be Jessica and her explosive temper. I heard Gio scream with fury, and then the lift was ascending.

"I've called Cabal," Lucy stammered, "and the police, and the fire brigade. I wasn't sure who else to call. Where's Griff? What's happening?"

"How did you all even get down here?" I asked breathlessly.

Bits of vampire were dripping in my hair. I was way past caring.

"Gio opened all levels," Allesandro said. "Was that the *Minister* stood down there?"

I looked up at him, noticing for the first time how damaged he was. Gio had done a class one vampiric number on his face. One eye was swollen shut and already blackening.

"Yes," I said, getting my breath back, "only he's not really, he's just a ghoul. It was Gio playing puppet master from the get go. Oh, and he used to be Rutheridge. That makes a full house. Five sinners, right? Told you they already had him somehow."

In the crazed adrenalin of the moment, I grinned up at him. In return, the vampire brushed some lumpy gunk from my shoulder in what might have been an affectionate manner had it not been so gross. Something fell from my shoulder to the floor with a plop.

"Wait," I looked to Lucy. "Gio opened *all* levels?"

She nodded, still looking shell shocked. I jabbed the button for Level 10.

"You can't hide from them," Allesandro said. "They'll follow your scent."

"I'm not hiding," I said.

The elevator let us out on the Military Applications floor. I left Lucy inside, making her promise to go straight up to the atrium and get the hell out of the building. The police would be here any minute, Cabal, backup. She nodded frantically and continued upwards.

Allesandro refused to go with her. He followed me along the cell block corridor, with its heavy metal doors on either side.

"Still protecting your investment?" I asked.

I fired up a workstation in the semi-circular area where I had discovered some of Cabal's dark secrets the last time I ventured down here.

"Still saving your sorry arse," he said, but he was smiling. "What are you doing? They'll be coming for you."

I logged on to the workstation as Trevelyan and accessed the file I wanted. I knew we only had seconds before Gio reached us. I searched for the door number I was looking for. Each cell faced another. The cell opposite the one which interested me was empty. Perfect. I unlocked it, hearing it whoosh open behind us.

Then I told Allesandro what to do.

When the lift pinged open several seconds later, Gio stepped from it looking like a demon from Hell. His clothes were ripped and shredded from his fight with Allesandro. His face was torn and bruised, his hair was sticking up all over like a scarecrow, but his eyes were bright and shining. I felt his presence roar down the long corridor to where I stood alone at the workstations.

I was caught like a rabbit in headlights.

He bared his fangs at me in a snarl, his white hands clenching and unclenching at his sides. He was breathing heavily.

"Found you," he growled. "Did you really think you could get away from me *again*, you difficult little bitch?"

I didn't move. The only way off this level was through him, back through the elevator and out of the pit.

"You killed my people," he spat. "Helena, Jessica … they had been with me for longer than your pathetic human mind can conceive. Amano and Christopher, they were brothers. I brought them into the clan myself. You just can't stop, can you? You can't stop killing my kind!"

"Says the psychopath trying to start the apocalypse," I replied.

I hadn't moved away from the workstation, I stood with my back to it, facing the vampire along the corridor.

He started towards me slowly, limping. He was in no hurry. He could see I had nowhere to run.

"I want vengeance," he hissed. "Justice! I want your kind to pay the price for what you did, for bringing this world to its knees!"

He advanced, passing doors, coming ever closer to me. I felt his mind begin to push into mine.

"I will drag you back down there, Doctor, and we will *finish* this!"

His voice was inside my mind as he passed in front of door number four.

"Gio," I said. "It *is* finished. Stop living in the past. In fact, do me a favour, stop living altogether."

My hand found the screen behind me and I hit the button I had set up in anticipation. No observation this time. This time I wanted interaction.

The metal door to Gio's left whooshed open, startling him. With a frown he turned his head to peer into the room. No plate glass barrier this time, you fucker.

My hands found the screen behind me again and door three, set in the opposite wall, also opened. From this empty cell, Allesandro erupted like a demonic jack in the box. He blindsided Gio, crashing into his shoulder at full force. Taken by surprise, Gio lost his footing and flew headlong into cell four landing sprawling on the tiles as Allesandro scrambled backwards.

I whirled at the workstation, my fingers flying over the keys. The safety glass barrier slid swiftly closed, sealing Gio in. I heard him roar with anger as he got to his feet within the cell.

I raced back along the corridor to where Allesandro waited and, standing side by side, we peered within. Gio threw himself against the glass, which shuddered, but did not break. His eyes were wild, he was practically foaming at the mouth.

"Open this now! Open this fucking door!"

He screamed angrily, so loud that his voice seemed to tear. He threw his fists against the glass in furious blows though the sound was muffled.

"Do you really think you can keep me here? That I won't get out? I will tear you both apart! There is nowhere you can run that I won't find you!" he bellowed.

"We're not going anywhere," I said grimly, shaking.

Allesandro and I stood in the corridor staring into the cell, I was aware we were both liberally splattered with dripping vampire chunks.

In his desperate fury, Gio hadn't noticed the figure huddled behind him in the corner of the small room, which now began to stir, slowly unfolding from its crouch. It growled, deep and low in the darkness of the cell.

Gio heard the growl. He stopped attacking the glass and turned to see the Pale standing slowly behind him. Its smooth grey skin damp with fever, it regarded him curiously with its black on black eyes, its head tilted enquiringly on one side. Its mouth was a deathly grin, as though it saw the joke that Gio didn't.

The vampire looked back to us. The fury previously frozen on his face had been replaced with shock and fear.

"You were a terrible clan master, Gio," Allesandro said. "Tassoni would have been *ashamed* of you."

He leaned close to the glass.

"I will be better."

"You don't have much luck with my family, do you?" I said to the trapped vampire. "My father ruined your world and I've been a difficult bitch. Well, now you get to meet my half-brother."

I managed a humourless smile. My voice was thick in my throat.

"Enjoy your family time."

Gio opened his mouth to speak, his eyes wide and bloodshot, but the Pale leapt.

We stood and watched, Allesandro and I, like visitors at an aquarium. It wasn't pleasant. It took a long time. Gio was strong and he fought back but the Pale was stronger than his kind or mine. We made them that way, after all.

Eventually, after what seemed like an eternity, it was quiet and still in the cell. We couldn't really see much anymore anyway. The glass was too smeared.

The heavy metal door finally slid shut with a definite and very ultimate thud. Observation over.

"What now?" Allesandro said quietly.

I looked up at him. His face was battered and bruised. Underneath, it was still lightly tanned, though it was fading already.

"Now?" I said wearily. "Now I want a dose of serum, before I start wanting to do to you what that thing just did to Gio."

I turned away from the door, staggering slightly on watery legs.

"And then I want a fucking hot chocolate."

We walked towards the elevator wearily. Allesandro leaned a little on me for support. I put my arm around him, to hold him up. I hadn't realised how badly Gio had damaged him.

He pushed the button for the elevator.

"I can think of some other things you could do to me," he suggested lightly.

I looked at him sidelong.

"Don't push it, clan master," I muttered darkly after a moment. "It's been a long week so far."

Epilogue

It's been a month now since the events at Blue Lab. The aftermath of Gio's little massacre and his failed attempt to end the world was messy to say the least. The clean-up was horrible, the administration horrendous, the lies told to the media … *huge*.

Griff healed. It's taken him a month and he's still in physiotherapy. There was a lot of muscle and nerve damage from the bite. Personally, I think he now has a phobia of bear hugs but on the plus side, Lucy brought him coffee every day in the hospital.

Those two have been spending an awful lot of time together in the month since the events at Blue Lab. I can't help but speculate that hearing how he raced to our rescue and took down a vampire cult with a submachine gun has made him seem somewhat more attractive to Lucy.

I'm still taking the serum – the *revised* Epsilon that is, not the version which makes you explode. So far I haven't degenerated into a bloodthirsty monster consumed with rage.

Well, perhaps occasionally, but we all have our bad days.

Brad the rat, you'll be pleased to hear, is also still going strong. We have a bond of brotherhood, him and me.

With Servant Harrison dead, Veronica Cloves has been temporarily drafted in as the Servant Administrator of Blue Lab One. She didn't die in the atrium.

I don't know why I was surprised by that. I doubt whether a direct hit from a nuclear missile could kill that woman. When the bullets had rained down in Gio's attack, she had taken a slug to the leg. Missed the artery, luckily for her, but she had cracked her head badly on the desk when she fell. It was lucky we all thought she was dead at the time or Gio would have had her put down there and then.

In my opinion, she played possum. That woman was built to spin the truth. Playing dead to save your own skin, while not being the most noble of acts, is at least smart, and Cloves was always good at self-preservation.

I can't say she's best pleased about taking on Harrison's role and being in charge of the lab. For me, the thought of reporting to her on a regular basis fills me with a cold dread. It almost makes me miss Trevelyan.

But if I'm honest, there was a small part of me that was actually relieved when she made it through. I'd kind of gotten used to her charmless presence and horrific dress sense.

The Minister, previously known as Alistair Rutheridge, was never found. Officially, he is missing, presumed dead. The Cabal are still working on the admin to find a replacement. No one except Cloves, me, Allesandro and my team know he was a ghoul.

I wonder if he's still out there somewhere in my city, in the warren of the Slade perhaps or wandering the woods, a shadow of his former self.

The Bonewalker disappeared too. My thinking is that with Gio's death, it was freed from its indentured contract and went wherever Bonewalkers go. It took Tassoni's body with it as well, it seems. I don't know why. Something tells me we haven't seen the last the blank-faced Djinn.

All we found in the chamber down in the Development Levels were Helena's body and Oscar Scott.

Alive. Just...

Oscar made headline news, of course. The city's golden boy, freed from the breakaway terrorist group who had captured him to ransom against his father's wealth. Cloves' media spin on the whole thing was impressive. She managed to keep both vampires and Blue Lab out of the Oscar Scott rescue story.

Officially, he was the third victim of a lone serial killer, rescued by New Oxford's brave police force during the showdown at Carfax. Trevelyan and Coleman were the killer's first victims. They have been buried now. Flower tributes for them both are still being placed outside the church, even a month later.

As for Oscar himself, he's had extensive dental reconstruction work done now, not to mention the cosmetic surgery on the facial scars. Last I saw, he was back living the high life and doing the media circuit. He likes the attention. The boy keeps calling to ask me out. I've changed my number twice but he has resources. I'll shake him off eventually.

As for me? Well...

What do you do when your world is turned upside down? When you discover your father had a direct hand in the genocide of much of the world's human population? Well, what *can* I do? I'll work through it on my own. Finding out that you're indirectly related to a breed of monstrous mutant killers is not the sort of thing you can hug out in a therapy circle.

I've gone back to work. I took some time off but frankly, after everything that happened, I was bored. We have another R&D presentation coming up next quarter. I have to present the latest findings of Blue Lab to the general public. And instead of having Trevelyan breathing down my neck and making my life hell, I have Cloves breathing down my neck and making my life hell. In awful clothes.

Given my new 'condition', let's just say I'm now a whole lot more invested in finding a permanent cure. I still scan as human when I check in every morning, which I'm taking as a good sign. I've decided to be positive.

Cloves has decided, in her infinite wisdom, to keep my unofficial promotion to what she terms as 'Official Cabal Interspecies Ambassador' open.

By Interspecies Ambassador, she means snoop. I'm still Cabal's best if most reluctant link to the GO community, after all. I have a feeling she'll find some new rock for me to turn over sooner rather than later. I'm not looking forward to find what might come crawling out from under the next one.

And as for my reluctant link himself? Well, he's king of all he surveys now; clan master and Duke of Sanctum, amongst other holdings. He got what he wanted. Well, not everything, I'm sure.

I'm still pissed at him for seeing me as a meal ticket to his power and glory. But he saved my ass at least four times, one of those even successfully, and so far I've only saved his once – and I hate owing people.

I haven't seen him much. He keeps inviting me to come back to Sanctum. Last I saw, he'd lost his tan and was back to his smouldering pale look, but he looked happier than I'd seen him before. A model vampire citizen, I suppose. I haven't taken up the invite yet.

My life at the moment is quite complicated enough, thanks, dealing with my secret knowledge of what happened in Cambridge and deciding what to do about that. Besides, I know he'll just be after something. It pains me to say it, but Cloves is probably right. Vampires don't think like we do. They always have an angle.

When I got into the lab this morning, however, there was a delivery for me. I still don't like opening anything delivered to the lab. I'm always worried it's going to be teeth. It wasn't though.

It was a box of premium grade Peruvian cocoa. Almost impossible to get these days. It looked pretty damn expensive and for a horrible moment I thought it might be a wooing gift from the ever-determined Oscar. But there was a card inside the package, a little crumpled.

It was a business card from Sanctum, the exact same one he'd slipped in my jacket back when we first met at the lecture, and on the reverse, still in very un-gothic biro, a telephone number and the words *When you need me – A.*

Gio may have been right. We may have destroyed the old world, but we're building something new here. It's a brave new world, and I intend to live long enough to be part of it.

Setting aside the gift I slid into my chair and fired up my workstation. There was an email from Cloves.

Harkness,
See attached. Am putting you on this, stat. Second in a row and I need to keep this out of the Datastream. My office asap. Everything else on hold.

Succinct and friendly as always, I thought with a frown. I clicked on the attachment. A classified Cabal file. 'Second violent murder in Portmeadow – victim unknown/ corpse unidentifiable, cause of death, violent assault/animal mauling.'

My frown deepened. With a rising sense of foreboding I noticed there was a photo attachment. Hesitantly I clicked.

It was messy. This wasn't a person; this was shredded pork. I swallowed hard. What the hell did this have to do with me?

Cloves handwritten notes scrawled under the crime scene photo explained everything in a single word.

'Tribals.'

I scooted my chair backwards, closing the gruesome picture file down It seems Cloves intended to keep my role as paranormal Cabal snoop active. I pictured the screaming headlines if this went public. 'Maniac Werewolf killer on loose in New Oxford!' No wonder Cabal was keeping this out of the DataStream. It was one thing people being killed in New Oxford, but people being killed in Portmeadow New Oxford? That was Rich folk territory. Cloves clearly needed a link to the GO world here, and I'm her only choice.

I grabbed my security pass and headed for the doors. If Cloves wants me to peek under every paranormal rock in the city that's fine, I decided, but we're going to discuss a pay rise.